Wrath
The Devil Duke

USA Today Bestseller
CHRISTI CALDWELL

Wrath
The Devil Duke

Copyright © 2024 by Christi Caldwell

All rights reserved. No part of this book may be reproduced in any form by any electronic or mechanical means—except in the case of brief quotations embodied in critical articles or reviews—without written permission.

The characters and events portrayed in this book are fictitious. Any similarity to real persons, living or dead, is purely coincidental and not intended by the author.

This Book is licensed for your personal enjoyment only. This Book may not be re-sold or given away to other people. If you would like to share this book with another person, please purchase an additional copy for each recipient. If you're reading this book and did not purchase it or borrow it, or it was not purchased for your use only, then please return it and purchase your own copy. Thank you for respecting the hard work of the author.

For more information about the author:
www.christicaldwellauthor.com
christicaldwellauthor@gmail.com
Twitter: @ChristiCaldwell
Or on Facebook at: Christi Caldwell Author

For first glimpse at covers, excerpts, and free bonus material, be sure to sign up for my monthly newsletter!

Printed in the USA.

Cover Design and Interior Format

Other Titles by Christi Caldwell

ALL THE DUKE'S SINS
Along Came a Lady
Desperately Seeking a Duchess

ALL THE DUKE'S SIN'S PREQUEL SERIES
It Had to Be the Duke
One for My Baron

SCANDALOUS AFFAIRS
A Groom of Her Own
Taming of the Beast
My Fair Marchioness
It Happened One Winter
Loved and Found

HEART OF A DUKE
In Need of a Duke—Prequel Novella
For Love of the Duke
More than a Duke
The Love of a Rogue
Loved by a Duke
To Love a Lord
The Heart of a Scoundrel
To Wed His Christmas Lady
To Trust a Rogue
The Lure of a Rake
To Woo a Widow
To Redeem a Rake
One Winter with a Baron

To Enchant a Wicked Duke
Beguiled by a Baron
To Tempt a Scoundrel
To Hold a Lady's Secret
To Catch a Viscount
Defying the Duke
To Marry Her Marquess
The Devil and the Debutante
Devil by Daylight
My Heart Forever

THE HEART OF A SCANDAL
In Need of a Knight—Prequel Novella
Schooling the Duke
A Lady's Guide to a Gentleman's Heart
A Matchmaker for a Marquess
His Duchess for a Day
Five Days with a Duke

LORDS OF HONOR
Seduced by a Lady's Heart
Captivated by a Lady's Charm
Rescued by a Lady's Love
Tempted by a Lady's Smile
Courting Poppy Tidemore

MCQUOIDS OF MAYFAIR
The Duke Alone
The Heiress at Sea

SCANDALOUS SEASONS
Forever Betrothed, Never the Bride
Never Courted, Suddenly Wed
Always Proper, Suddenly Scandalous
Always a Rogue, Forever Her Love
A Marquess for Christmas
Once a Wallflower, at Last His Love
Endlessly Courted, Finally Loved

Once a Rake, Suddenly a Suitor
Once Upon a Betrothal

SINFUL BRIDES
The Rogue's Wager
The Scoundrel's Honor
The Lady's Guard
The Heiress's Deception

THE WICKED WALLFLOWERS
The Hellion
The Vixen
The Governess
The Bluestocking
The Spitfire

THE THEODOSIA SWORD
Only For His Lady
Only For Her Honor
Only For Their Love

DANBY
A Season of Hope
Winning a Lady's Heart

THE BRETHREN
The Spy Who Seduced Her
The Lady Who Loved Him
The Rogue Who Rescued Her
The Minx Who Met Her Match
The Spinster Who Saved a Scoundrel

LOST LORDS OF LONDON
In Bed with the Earl
In the Dark with the Duke
Undressed with the Marquess

SEVEN DEADLY SINS
Wrath: The Devil Duke

BRETHREN OF THE LORDS
My Lady of Deception
Her Duke of Secrets

THE READ FAMILY SAGA
A Winter Wish

MEMOIR: NON-FICTION
Uninterrupted Joy

DEDICATION

To: Scarlett
From the beginning of **'Wrath-The Devil Duke'** to some 400 pages later, you were with me. Each chapter, you cheered me on. And, when I got hit with some hard moments and couldn't get all my words in for the day, you reminded me to be kind to myself.

Thank you for always making me laugh.
Thank you for your unwavering support.
Thank you for always lifting me up.
But what I'm most grateful for is your friendship.

Wrath: The Devil Duke is for you.

LETTER TO READERS

WRATH—THE DEVIL DUKE IS THE first book in my brand-new series—*Seven Deadly Sins*.

I always say my books are special to me. I love each one. After all, when a story isn't fun to write, it is *agonizing*. The words just don't come, and well, you can't force words that aren't there.

That said, some titles and series are extra special: where each chapter is thrilling and all you want to do is live in the pages. And when you're *not* in the story, all you are doing is thinking about it and counting the moments until you can return.

For me, that is what *Wrath (and the Seven Deadly Sins* series) has been.

There is complexity and depth to the characters and plot that sucked me in.

If you've been reading my work over the years, you know, there are times I write: Dark (*Sinful Brides and the Brethren of the Lords*). Romantic. *(Heart of a Duke)*. Sexy (*Scandalous Affairs*). Sweet (*The Duke Alone*) Romps (*Wantons of Waverton*).

As you can expect by the title, *Wrath* brings readers a dark, angsty, and emotional story. It is also one of my sexiest books and series, to date.

I truly hope you, my readers, enjoy this next journey I'm about to take you on!

As always, I remain grateful to you for your support.

Thank you so very much for reading!

Huge hugs,

Christi Caldwell

CHAPTER 1

London, England
Lucifer's Lair
1831

NOTHING MADE EDWARD DE VESY, Lord Malden, the future Duke of Craven, harder or got him off faster than savage, merciless revenge against the foolish ones who dared wrong him.

However, the red-haired whore enthusiastically bobbing up and down on said cock certainly didn't come a far second—at the moment, anyway.

From upon the gilded throne where Malden sat, overlooking his sinful kingdom Lucifer's Lair, he moved a lazy stare back and forth, alternating from the real-life sinful Sodom and Gomora he'd built, to the titian Cyprian servicing him.

Each sight—his hellfire club and the beauty subservient on her knees—proved equally salacious. Both fired his blood.

Fucking in any form, always had.

The rapacious lust for revenge had proven to be an unexpectedly powerful predilection. A good swiving lasted but a fleeting moment. Revenge? Sweet, sensuous revenge, now *that* saw a man satisfied and kept him that way until they lowered his cold, dead body into the dirt.

Cyra drew Malden so deep his ballocks touched her chin. She played with his sac and his flesh tightened painfully. A hiss slipped from between his teeth. He squeezed his eyes tight and fought the urge to empty himself into her throat.

Fighting that baser urge to come quick and hard, Malden slid his fingers through her tight curls and urged Cyra to a slower pace. Not unlike a slow, deliberate, drawn-out avengement, restraint made the climax sweeter for Malden, too.

He managed to breathe easier, and this time fixed his heavy gaze out at his empire. All the while Cyra attempted to ring an orgasm from him, he took in the sight of what he'd created.

The room, purposely designed in the form of a hexagram, featured a different perversion at each Latin-labeled point.

Malden surveyed the fortunes being tossed away at his gaming tables, the Cyprians sprawled with their legs on either side of a patron and fucking him while they wagered, the married couples being led throughout the room and guided on to the Ludere Suites—Orgy Suites.

Because, of course. Men were not made for one woman. Lust fueled a fascination that, after enough fucking, eventually slaked those needs. And when they did? Those men…and women… came to Malden's Hellfire Club—sometimes the bored couples came together.

His hips moved reflexively, arching toward Cyra's scarlet mouth that hung vacuously open to accommodate Malden's length and girth.

From around his cock, the Cyprian moaned and murmured her appreciation.

Absently, he reached down to test her wetness.

Whimpering, Cyra parted her knees wider.

Her sodden channel dripped with a like lust.

Cyra gasped and moved her hips, attempting to steal some relief.

"Slow," he murmured.

She whimpered.

More benevolent than she deserved, Malden continued stroking her. She moved her hips wildly back and forth; her desperate search for satiation made her efforts on his behalf, sloppy.

Some were incapable of restraint. Sadly, Cyra proved among that disappointing number. Those women were the ones who bored him most. Of course, she'd stay on in her role as every man had a different predilection and she'd serve those fellows well.

But with Cyra's efforts now proving tedious, Malden surveyed the vulgar scene unfolding on the center stage—the latest—and most—depraved for Malden's most debased patrons—Auction Virginis.

For the latest addition of debaucheries provided at Lucifer's Lair, every night, seven *innocent* ladies, each draped in a matching filmy white peignoir and elaborate feathered mask affixed to conceal her identity, lined up behind a gilded rope. They stood as gentlemen each approached and evaluated them the same way they did their horseflesh.

The virgin's expressions were all the same: gazes downcast. Heads bent subserviently. Hands clasped before them, as if in fervent prayer; each woman praying for salvation.

It'd proven a magnificent addition to his club. Malden's profits tripled and his memberships doubled.

It turned out the respected lords of London were more debauched than most men knew, and all mamas feared.

Auction Virginis was also nothing more than a cruelly scandalous show.

After all, gentlemen might lust for the libidinous idea of it all, but ultimately, they—for the most part—had enough restraint to not debauch a virgin.

Not that noble fathers cared for their useless daughters. They didn't. Powerful peers didn't possess puling emotions for any of their kin, not even the sons and heirs who continued their lines.

What they did, however, care about was expanding their power, wealth, and influence—all feats best achieved through the sale of their daughters.

Yes, ultimately, all virginal ladies were auctioned off. The ton merely dressed those transactions up as respectable ventures. They called it the Marriage Mart but they may as well have named it the Virgin Auction. For, in the end, it was all the same. Ladies for sale, and always to the highest bidder with the deepest pockets.

Malden's gaze locked on a lone woman moving through his club. She walked with timid steps, stealing furtive glances at the lascivious tableaus as she went.

He narrowed his eyes. Malden knew firsthand the peril that came from allowing an innocent lady into the midst of his club.

She'd donned a flimsy black disguise that left parts of her face exposed. Between enormous eyes revealed by an entirely insufficient mask and the amazing height her dark eyebrows climbed, she stood out as clearly as a whore in church.

It was how he knew she didn't belong; both by her face and how she moved. He knew the identity of each and every person who stepped foot inside his palace. Malden himself met each potential patron and either personally approved or declined membership.

Langley, one of his guards, kept a safe distance, but also a determined gaze on the impudent intruder who'd invaded Lucifer's Lair.

Just then, Cyra's teeth grazed the plum tip of his rod, reminding Malden she was still there.

As attuned as he'd been to the woman who'd infiltrated Lucifer's Lair, he'd forgotten all about the Cyprian framed between his legs.

"That is enough," he said coolly. "We're done here."

He'd far more pressing matters to attend than wringing his cock dry on her mediocre attempts.

Nodding wobbly, the Cyprian stood.

Cyra forgotten, Malden stood and stuffed his shaft back in his trousers. All the while, he kept his gaze directed outward on the interloper.

His uninvited *guest* stopped in her tracks and stared at a gaming table where three lords and ladies in various stages of dishabille played a game of strip poker. If possible, the lady's eyes grew rounder.

Malden stepped on a nearby circular call button the same color as the dark mahogany flooring and pressed it.

There came a short rap on the door.

His head guard, Gruffton, the only man Malden took from his former establishment, Forbidden Pleasures, stepped inside.

"You called, my lord."

Cyra took the cue and hastened from the room.

Gruffton stepped out of the way to allow her to pass.

Only after she'd gone did Malden freely speak.

He redirected his singular focus to the one who'd infiltrated his kingdom. "There's a problem," he gritted out when Gruffton finally reached the window. "More specifically, a 'her'."

Malden jabbed a finger at the still motionless figure. The clever mirror which magnified the floors and patrons below displayed the crimson fire that touched the lady's elfin-shaped chin and an inch or so of her unconcealed cheeks.

"I'm aware, my lord," Gruffton assured. "I have Langley following her. He's already alerted the other men stationed below and the guards in the private suites."

Had the older man not learned firsthand that innocent ladies were as dangerous as Eve?

His annoyance high, Malden grunted.

"I figured it'd be more helpful to get her identity and find out what business brought her instead of sending her away," Gruffton added.

The old guard's logic made sense. Annoyance filled Malden that he'd not been of the same thought. Sloppiness had been letting the mystery woman in Lucifer's Lair. Letting her leave, would have been even sloppier.

He and Gruffton continued to watch her.

"Want me to lead the questioning?" Gruffton asked, his stare still trained on the cloaked woman.

"Oh, no. I shall see to this one," he murmured with an unholy glee.

There'd be an inquisition of the virtuous lady who'd inserted herself into a place of sin and vice, and no one but Malden would be the one to do it.

Malden's lust stirred again. Not because of her innocence. Even *he* wasn't a deviant enough to lust for a virgin. This time for altogether different reasons; the delicious appeal of interrogating a clearly virtuous lady who'd risked reputation and ruin by stepping foot inside Malden's establishment.

Through his previous proprietorship of Forbidden Pleasures and his current one of Lucifer's Lair, he'd perpetually beggared men and acquired a healthy number of enemies. *Someone* had sent her, and Malden had absolutely no doubt who was behind the lady's presence.

DuMond. Argyll. Latimer.

Hatred singed his veins.

Credit for this infiltration went to his former friends who'd become his blood rivals in a war of dominance for power in England's casino arena—and for power over society.

They were behind it. Nay, maybe not Argyll or Latimer. The latter two didn't possess the same thirst for power as DuMond. Those two followed DuMond like pathetic sheep—just as Malden once did.

What those men hadn't anticipated, however, was from the ashes of Malden's weaknesses had grown a man of power; a force to be reckoned with.

How thrilling it would be when they discovered the man they now played games with was nothing like the man they'd known. They'd killed him as effectively as if they'd plunged a blade in his body and their betrayal was the last favor they'd ever done him.

At last, the still-blushing lady gave her head a slight shake, as if to clear the haze of desire cast by the naughty tableau she'd witnessed.

He and Gruffton tensed. Their heads moved in like motions as they each followed her every step.

Again, the lady paused. Then, like she was a lone partner in some nearly motionless waltz, she did a circle in her spot, until she finally stopped, frozen upon the star at the center of the crimson hexagon embroidered into that portion of the gold carpeting.

Malden narrowed his eyes. *What are you up to, little minx?*

The lady's gaze remained transfixed on a spot directly adjacent her.

He followed her stare, directly over to the Virginis Auction which had commenced.

Neil, the guard responsible for overseeing the safety of those lady participants and ensuring overzealous patrons didn't cross a line, collected the first woman. He caught the subservient beauty by the black satin rope fastened about her hands and led her onward to the gold hexagon that marked the spot for each woman to stand when they were auctioned off.

Neil called out. And then the auction began. Old lords with a foot closer to their grave than living, young dandies, notorious rakes, all vied for the lady's favors. They lifted a paddle containing their club number. Over and over.

Normally, Malden's sole focus would be on the rising cash value that each raised paddle indicated.

This time, however, he remained locked on the still-motionless lady who took that vulgar scene in. Her body partially angled enough toward him revealed another one of those telling, pathetic blushes.

Even with the distance between them, Malden caught the telltale rise and fall of her back and shoulders.

She is aroused, then.

Not that he was surprised. The only reason virgins didn't embrace society's depravities was because the world kept them deliberately blind, deaf, and dumb to all the perverse pleasures that awaited them if they but looked.

For the world knew, once they did have their eyes opened, there'd be no turning back, and those virtuous ladies would quite happily and eagerly spread their legs for anyone who could satisfy their itch.

"Maybe she's just here to enjoy the club?" Gruffton ventured.

"No," Malden murmured. If that'd been the case and she'd only come here to throw herself wholly into the depravity to be enjoyed, she'd have donned the mask and had the full experience.

Suddenly, the lady began moving purposefully toward the stage.

"Bring her to me," Malden whispered.

Gruffton was already gone before the final command had left Malden's lips.

He burned his gaze into the lady's slender, narrow back as she gingerly made her way to a place she had no place going to.

He dropped his brows. Nay, nothing good had brought her here. Certainly not curiosity.

Before this night was through, he'd have answers and find out on whose behalf she'd come. And he was going to enjoy exacting that information from her.

CHAPTER 2

Miss Edith Caldecott walked through Lucifer's Lair, London's newest, most debauched betting hall, owned and operated by London's most debauched gentleman, Edward de Vesy, the Marquess of Malden.

In the months she'd spent devising a plan to avenge her late sister's murder, Edith understood she'd be forced to enter places no respectable lady ought.

She wasn't completely naïve as to what went on in men's only establishments. She'd overheard her elder brother and his best friend indiscreetly talking about trips to White's and Boodle's and Brooks's.

As such, she'd expected lively conversation, men sipping spirits and exchanging bawdy jokes. And of course, gambling would be featured—that, *and* ribald laughter.

Those vices were all featured at this particular hell, but that was where the similarities ended.

Nothing could have prepared her for Lucifer's Lair.

Through the heavy haze of cheroot smoke hovering in the air, Edith skimmed her eyes around the room.

Sin, skin, and vice oozed from every corner. Try as she might, Edith could not stop herself from gawking at the display of opulence. Every last furnishing, from the gleaming, ornate gilded chandeliers to the long gaming tables, and lush carpets, glittered with gold rivaling the mythical kingdom of El Dorado.

Those tables also featured masked patrons who, with one hand, tossed coins down and placed their bets, and with their other, fondled a scantily clad woman beside them—or, on them.

Everyone appeared to not only be immensely enjoying themselves, they appeared almost euphoric, part of a heightened plane of joy that mortal humans could never hope to achieve.

A blush scorched Edith's cheeks.

I'm going to have to burn my eyes to purge this scene from my memory.

Edith gave her head a shake. *Focus.*

The longer she remained inside Lucifer's Lair, the greater the risk of discovery became. That should be Edith's greatest worry. After all, fear of ruin was certainly the proper concern every innocent lady in the entire kingdom carried.

Edith didn't know a normal amount of fear. In fact, Edith didn't know *any* fear. She found herself curiously and welcomingly immune to it.

That hadn't always been the case.

There'd been a time when she'd felt all the emotions that made a person human: Amusement. Hope. Dread. Happiness. Serenity.

She stared blankly ahead. Around her, the debauched sights and raucous sounds faded to a distant hum.

Edith still knew those emotions, but more like a muted version of what had once been keen and vibrant and all-powerful. Now, it was more like she was a voyeur viewing the world and seeing it through a filmy curtain.

She closed her eyes.

Not here. Not now.

Alas, she never had power enough to stop the interruptions in real life. Not when past moments whispered forward and demanded a lead spot upon the stage of Edith's actual existence.

"Edith, you are going to find yourself in trouble again."

"I will not."

Her eldest sister, Evie, squeezed her shoulder. "That's what you always say."

Edith and Evie's laughter melded and twined as it always did; as all the Caldecott laughter did.

Suddenly, Evie grew serious. "And then when you are discovered up to mischief, you always cry so very badly, and I hate your sadness so."

Then came the soft, quiet weeping her sister aptly predicted, because Evie knew Edith so very well—better than anyone had or ever would.

The mournful wails came louder, an eerie echo. Edith ached to free herself from the hold of past memories.

Her lashes twitched.

That crying, *this* crying, was no echo. It was no memory—at least not one that belonged to Edith or her sisters. Nor did it bear the lower, deeper quality of her grief. There was a shrillness to this weeping. A strident note, as if it didn't come from deep within the soul of the person shedding tears, but rather from someone who faked grief.

Edith managed to force her eyes open.

It'd been just a memory.

Edith blinked slowly and finally cleared herself of the hated, dazed state she often found herself trapped within.

The noisy blubbering, however, persisted.

Confused, Edith looked about. Her gaze landed on the source of that *suffering*.

A young woman, in what resembled a lacy, see-through version of a wedding dress, stood at the front of an altar. Her hands had been fastened tightly about her delicate wrists. A mask concealed the lady's entire face. Even from seven paces away, Edith saw the way that poor woman's body trembled. Her palpable grief stood in stark contrast to the revelry of the hedonists around them.

Edith's stomach churned.

Her sole reason for being in this club momentarily forgotten, Edith looked perplexedly about. A man, some six feet tall, and his body so muscular it strained his elegant, black evening attire, stood beside the poor woman. He rapidly shouted amounts. Patrons seated in three cordoned-off rows, each holding a numbered racket, periodically shot a hand up.

What *was* this? The event they took part in put her in mind of a horse auction Edith had attended with her brother when he'd been looking for a new stallion.

Why would—?

Edith's body jerked.

An auction *did* take place here, but it wasn't a mount on the auction block but a *woman*.

And here, after her sister had been murdered, Edith believed nothing could shake her.

Fury on behalf of the poor women all lined up to be sold this night filled Edith and she fought a battle with herself.

I'm here for Evie…

She kept reminding the part of herself that wished to intervene on those poor creatures' behalf. The hungering for revenge warred with a sense of right.

This isn't your business. Do you really think you can stop what is happening?

Edith couldn't. Hadn't she learned long ago she didn't possess the power to right wrongs? Why, that was the very reason for her even stepping foot in this horrid place. Unjust as it may be, women were powerless in a world owned, ruled, and dictated by men of influence. Edith couldn't save anyone. She hadn't been able to save her sister against one shadowy villain. She certainly couldn't take on an entire room of them.

Armed with that reminder, Edith took a step away from something horrible that had nothing to do with her or her family or her late sister.

You certainly can't stop it if you don't do anything, the voice in Edith's head tauntingly reminded her as she walked away from the auction.

Her steps slowed, and she halted once more.

Edith hovered there; on a precipice between avenging her sister's death and helping a stranger whom she didn't know, but who also happened to be a woman in desperate need of help.

What if there'd been someone aware of Evie's murderers' intentions and they had done something to intervene?

On a more selfish note, there was also no surer way for Edith to earn a face-to-face meeting with the club's owner.

Edith bolted for the stage. She wove in between lords and ladies and the barely clad women serving flutes of champagne.

She collided with one of the servers and upended the poor woman's tray.

People grabbed for Edith, but she eluded their grasping hands.

She remained fixed on the auction; the barker and bidders hadn't registered her approach.

Shouts went up as she knocked against patrons and sent drinks flying. In Edith's wake, she left a spray of champagne, shattered glass, and shouting.

Her breath coming fast both from her exertions and the attention she'd drawn, Edith neared the front where velvet roping had been set up quartering off the auction site.

Not breaking stride, Edith hiked her skirts up about her ankles and jumped the barrier.

She landed on her feet and belatedly attracted the attention of the bidders.

A hulking guard reached for her, but Edith launched herself atop the altar, positioning herself between the bound woman and the barker.

She grabbed the lady's tied hands and gave her right one a squeeze to compel her into movement.

The golden-haired woman remained rooted to the stage.

Edith recognized all too well that familiar state of shock.

"Come with me," Edith said frantically. "I can help you." Her breath came in frantic spurts, and she struggled to get air into her lungs. "We can—"

The captive wrenched free of Edith's grip. "What do you think you are doing, simpleton?" the woman hissed.

"I'm rescuing you," Edith continued hauling the woman to safety.

"Rescue?" Through the eye slits of her mask, the 'captive's' eyes glittered with fury. "Do you think I came here to be rescued?" she asked in nasty tones that brought Edith up short.

"I…you don't need help?" she whispered in abject confusion.

"The only help I need is for you to remove yourself from this stage and allow me to return to the pleasure I came for, you dumb chit."

"But…but…"

What the woman had said slammed into Edith like the weight of a thousand bricks being dropped upon her chest.

This wasn't an *actual* auction where women were being bought and sold. Rather, Edith had borne witness to a staged act where ladies pretended to be innocents and eagerly took part in a debauched game of pretend, Edith couldn't have ever imagined was played.

Suddenly, Edith registered the thick, noticeable quiet that had descended over the previously cacophonic club. Had an embroidering needle dropped it would have sounded like a shot in the silence.

With no small amount of horror and dread, Edith looked about.

Every last stare of every last patron remained set, fixed, and locked on Edith. Frowns of varying depths filled the faces of lords and ladies, furious at having had their night's pleasures interrupted.

Her stomach dropped. She tried to swallow around a lump of dread, but the reflexive movement proved impossible.

This couldn't be worse. This—

Someone grabbed Edith's arm, ringing a gasp from her. She found herself hauled against some man's broad chest.

She made to scream the place down, but her captor slapped a big, powerful hand over her mouth.

He leaned down to bridge the gap lent by their disparate heights. The warm sough of his brandy-laced breath brushed her cheek.

"Not a word, wench," he whispered harshly against her ear.

Edith trembled. Trapped in his unforgiving, punishing hold, his face a mystery, she felt like the cornered fox she'd hunted with her brother.

Never again. She squeezed her eyes more tightly shut so flecks danced across her vision. Never again would she partake in a hunt.

Then, the heat of the gentleman's breath drew fainter, indicating he'd moved.

"My wonderful sinners," the man called out to the still painfully quiet onlookers.

Edith's body rumbled under the boom of his commandingly deep baritone.

"You have been the appointed witnesses and participants of the newest performance offered for your viewing pleasure—a sister coming to the rescue of her virgin sister."

A palpable energy hummed throughout the room.

"You can be assured," he called in a smooth, oratorical voice better suited to a scholar than the sinner he in fact was. "This is the manner of proclivity you can expect to see more of…"

The imposing stranger dangled that pause so temptingly, Edith found herself briefly lulled into a serene calm and sucked into his enigmatic pull.

"That is if you hunger to join in an even greater display of depravity."

There was a beat of silence. Vociferous cheers erupted throughout the club; a rumble shook the floors as patrons stomped their feet in thunderous approval.

With one hand still fastened over her mouth, Edith's captor raised his other one; a hush instantly fell over the hall, and he may as well have been Marcus Antony, silencing the Romans.

"Now, if you will excuse me, I must drag this innocent miss and punish her with my mighty rod."

Edith's head began to spin.

Another round of eager cries of encouragement split the room.

She instantly renewed her struggles to be free of his hold. Her attempts went unnoticed as the patrons of his hellish place bought fully into his farce.

God rot him, she'd sooner let him haul her off for whatever punishment he intended to exact. Edith sank her teeth into the flesh of his palm.

The metallic tinge of blood—his blood—filled her mouth.

For how powerful as her bite had been, Edith may as well have been an inconsequential gnat. Her captor didn't so much as flinch at the damage she'd done to his hand or break his determined stride.

All the while she flailed and twisted to be free of his punishing hold, he continued dragging her on. Edith's dread redoubled and she choked on the acrid sting of bile as she fought to keep the contents of her stomach down.

Maybe she shouldn't. Maybe if she vomited in his hand, she'd startle him into releasing her.

With the indifference he showed your strongest bite, he's more likely to suffocate you on your own spew.

Ultimately, the decision was made for her—or more accurately, taken from her.

They approached a doorway, heavily guarded on both sides by four men. Of equally tall stature and stockiness, that sentry stationed on either side of the doorway may as well have been quadruplets.

One of those guards didn't so much as remove his stare fixed on the wall; from where he stood, he reached and opened the door so the menacing beast dragging her could continue without breaking his swift stride.

The still faceless man hauled Edith inside.

He kicked his foot back behind him and the heavy panel slammed shut with a thunderous *thwack*.

Then, Edith found herself free.

She stumbled and tripped over herself to put safe steps between herself and the twisted stranger.

"I'd like to speak to the Mar…" Her voice trailed off. *The Marquess of Malden?*

Even though Edith's father held a respectable viscountcy, the Caldecotts' had never held the manner of prestige and power to make them acceptable company for this man's family who'd possessed titles and holdings dating back to William the Conqueror.

Over many years, she'd seen this gentleman a handful of times at ton functions. They'd barely crossed paths, and she'd only spied him from across the room of a respectable affair they'd both attended. One ridiculous time, she'd thought he was looking at her, but he hadn't been. On the contrary, Edith would recognize his loose golden curls, sharp, chiseled cheeks, and obdurate jawline *anywhere*.

"Lord *Malden?*" she said dumbly; surprise brought his name creeping up into a question.

He flashed a cold, mocking smile and dropped an even more derisory bow. "At your service," he purred.

Edith scoured his strikingly beautiful face for some sign of the measured, pleasant-mannered gentleman who'd politely danced that night with other ladies who hadn't been Edith. Maybe, she'd just imagined him to be a proper, respectable lord.

His dark, punishing gaze drilled through her. Despite her best efforts, she couldn't quell the shiver that wracked her frame.

Had this man's eyes always bore such a heavy darkness? Before now, she'd never been close enough to see. What drove him to a level of coldness that not so much as a speck of light shone through?

If she were a different woman, she'd be curious enough to find out.

Edith had neither the time, energy, nor inclination to wonder about some coldhearted lord. She'd but one purpose, one role left to fill in this life.

On the other hand, Lord Malden's purpose in life appeared to be winning at the Game of Silence she'd played with her sisters to determine who could stay quiet the longest.

She knew why he stood motionless with his arms folded and stoic as the dead of night—to intimidate Edith, to make her fear him.

He was destined to be disappointed. He'd not succeed in bullying her.

"Very well, Lord Malden, you win, I'll go first. I confess, your club doesn't look as I'd expected it would."

He only met her pronouncement with a glacial silence.

Edith resisted the urge to squirm under that unbreakable, unforgiving glare. He *was* good at this.

Edith, dredging forth all the casualness she could muster, lifted her hand. Her reticule dangled and twisted at her wrist. "This is where you should ask *what* I thought it might look like."

"Do you think I give two fucks what you think, sweetheart?"

Edith gave thanks for the cover made by her partial mask and the heavy shadow in his offices that concealed her blush.

She forced her biggest, most winning smile. "Based on that rather candid question, I should think your question doesn't require an answer."

He met her with more of that silence, meant to scare no doubt.

Unfortunately for the duke, after the death of her eldest sister, and months of wailing family members, quiet eventually settled into the Caldecott household and became something Edith was all too familiar, and comfortable, with.

"El Dorado," Edith murmured.

The marquess's lashes narrowed imperceptibly.

When he still offered no response, Edith loosened the clasp of her taffeta cloak, and drew her hood partially in place to allow some protection from the chill this man cast over the room.

"Do not make yourself comfortable," Lord Malden said in steely tones. "You are not staying."

"Oh, certainly not." Edith grimaced. "That is the last thing I'd want to do," she murmured distractedly.

She anticipated questions about what brought her to his club. She should have known better. He offered only more of that frigid nothingness.

Edith contemplated his office.

Unlike the nearly blinding gold gleam of the gaming floors and winding halls he'd led her along a short while ago, the duke's office looked like…just *that*, any respectable, prim, and proper nobleman's tastefully decorated office.

His long, wide, and curiously curved Genovese desk, with a checkered marquetry painted into the side panels, appeared better suited to his Mayfair townhouse in Grosvenor Square than his Curzon Street casino.

Edith's gaze alighted on his desk chair.

She cocked her head. Curiously unlike the comfortable, leather seating sported in most gentlemen's offices, the Marquess of Malden had chosen a severe, ancient, and uncomfortable-looking wainscot armchair for his proverbial throne.

A stiff seat for a man ruthlessly emotionless and sinister as sin.

Edith's skin tingled and she looked over to find his gaze fixed on her.

She looked away first, her eyes landing upon the window which ran the length of Lord Malden's office and overlooked the gaming hell floors.

A faint breath stirred the nape of her neck. Edith gasped and whipped about—too late.

The marquess grabbed her tightly by the forearm and not for the first time since she'd set out on her quest, a sickening dread rooted around her belly.

"Step away now," he growled, even as he all but dragged her away from the viewing glass.

Lest she be pulled to the floor, Edith tripped over herself to keep up.

The marquess released her so quickly she stumbled several steps and then righted herself.

"Who sent you?" he whispered, while she retreated.

A shout would have been less menacing.

"Wh-who?" At that mortifyingly weak tremble in her voice, Edith made herself speak again. "Who?"

"What are you, a goddamn owl?"

Edith laughed. It was the first free, unchecked one to have slipped out since her sister's illness and eventual death.

"I understand," she said between her mirth. "Because I said 'who' twice."

He stared blankly at her; his blue eyes which, to this point, had proven unfathomable reflected an adorable and unexpected glimmer of confusion. It softened him. It made her wonder—

Slowly, with sleek steps the king of the jungle would have envied, the marquess started for her again.

"I'll ask once more who sent you here," he whispered. "If you don't answer me, I promise you'll regret it mightily."

Rage twisted Lord Malden's features and contorted the beautiful, chiseled masterpiece that was his face into one befitting a pitiless beast.

This time, she didn't fight for braveness.

Her pulse pounding, Edith dashed away from the marquess.

She darted her panicked gaze to the door.

Lord Malden tracked her focus.

With an ugly chuckle, he stepped between Edith and that panel. Having stolen her only escape, he resumed his advance.

With every retreating step she took, Lord Malden's grin grew, revealing gleaming rows of perfect pearl-white teeth.

Edith shivered. Never before had she known it was possible for a smile wide as his to possess absolute *nothingness*.

Her back collided with the wall.

Trapped.

The marquess stopped a half pace away. Even with a slight bridge in space between them, he soared nearly a foot over Edith, so she needed to tip her neck back to meet his stare.

She eyed him warily.

Up close she detected the specks of gold in his blue irises. Like a real-life Midas who'd struck an arrangement with Dionysus, even Lord Malden's eyes were gold.

In one fluid motion, the marquess unsheathed a dagger from his boot.

Edith gasped and recoiled into herself.

The marquess placed the tip of his knife against her trembling lips.

Only when that cold steel no longer touched her skin did Edith breathe easier.

Her reprieve proved short-lived.

With a maddening languidness, Lord Malden glided his blade lower.

Edith bit the inside of her cheek hard enough to make her taste blood for a second time that night—only, this time, that salty tinge belonged to her.

"Tsk, tsk," he remarked in a playful air, completely shattered by the steely edge that robbed it of any hint of levity. "I warned you, wench, not to make me ask a third time."

Whimpering, Edith drew more deeply into herself.

"Which begs the question…" He moved closer so his lips brushed her ear. "How shall I punish your disobedience?"

She should be horrified enough to beg for mercy, leave, and never look back.

Only, for as terror-inducing Lord Malden was to her, he'd also demonstrated an unbreakable wrath, capable of taking down any and every man who stepped in his path—including Sir Markley.

And she needed that very invincibility to take down Evie's killer.

"We have gotten off to an awkward start, my lord."

"Is that what we call your breaking and entering into my club and interrupting the evening's entertainments?" he asked on a low, lethal purr that sent gooseflesh rising on her arms.

But she'd faced—and continued to look in the eyes of a murderer—and as such this man couldn't scare her.

Before her courage deserted her, Edith took a breath. "Lord Malden, I have come to enlist your help."

CHAPTER 3

FOR A VERY LONG MOMENT, Malden thought he'd been wrong in his initial suspicions. His former business partners hadn't sent this woman to infiltrate his club, but rather, madness brought her to his doorstep.

What else could account for the stupid smile on her small, round lips?

She continued staring at him with enormous and also stupidly friendly, chocolate-brown eyes.

But then, a peculiar creature like this one would be the ideal lady for his former partners to send.

"I asked you a question," he layered steel within that purr. "And instead of answering, you put to me a request for help?" Malden brought his blade up quick.

The lady's throat moved wildly, in a small display of her fear.

He slashed the clasps of her cloak, so it fell in a puddle about her feet.

His visitor gasped and whipped her gaze downward. The moment she looked up, outrage in her eyes, Malden sliced the satin ribbon on first one side of her mask and then the next, until the satin scrap fluttered to the floor between them.

When she stood, fully exposed to him, Malden flicked a gaze up and down her painfully slender form.

In a display of virgin-like modesty, she brought her arms up to shield herself from his view.

"Drop your arms so I can see all of you," he ordered.

She only curled deeper into herself, denying Malden's demand.

He brought the tip of his dagger against an intriguing birthmark he'd failed to notice before, and he found himself peculiarly fascinated by that blemish.

"I told you to lower your arms," he repeated grimly and succeeded in securing her compliance. "Good girl. You *are* capable of obedience." He contemplated her in a new light.

"Yes, well, having a blade against my face will do that," she spat bitterly.

Malden, as perverse as he'd always been, found himself reveling in her bruised pride. "Aww, poor poppet," he crooned. "You are scared."

She compressed her lips into a firm, flat line, and said nothing.

With his view now unfettered, Malden returned to his evaluation of his nighttime visitor. All the while, she remained motionless.

Possessed of a slightly pointy oval chin, and high, narrow cheekbones, there was a gauntness to the lady's nearly pale, and very ordinary, features.

The dark sapphire day dress she wore sported a painfully modest neckline and even worse, over accentuated her narrow waist and even narrower hips. The only favor that slenderness did her physique was to make her bell-shaped breasts appear ampler than they likely were.

In fact, but for the lone tear-shaped birthmark on the graceful line of her neck, her features weren't apt to leave an impression upon a person. Largely nondescript—the stoic wench was a person to be forgotten and never again recalled.

He curled his lip in a sneer. No, she wasn't anyone he'd keep company with. The women he made his lovers were exquisite beauties, not polite ladies with dull hair to match their dull eyes.

This time, instead of flinching under his scrutiny, the fair-skinned to the point of sickly-looking lady lifted that point of her chin in a bold challenge. "I see your reputation of being boorish and menacing also extends to young ladies."

At her unexpected intrepidness, Malden's body instantly stirred.

"Young *ladies* do not visit my club," he whispered.

"*This* one has."

Malden dropped his eyebrows. "What a tart-mouthed shrew you are."

"Why?" she shot back. "Because I pointed out a fact?"

"You are no lady," he murmured.

She wrinkled her nose. "I most certainly *am*."

Another wave of lust bolted through him. Despite himself, despite knowing everything about her being here represented great peril, Malden found himself sheathing his weapon and staring at her with a new and sudden interest.

Now, he saw her prim dress in a new light. Malden imagined laying her down on his bed, strapping her to each of its four posters, and truly using that knife on her—only to cut away piece after piece of fabric: of her dress. Her chemise. Her petticoats. Until she lay shivering and begging for a different kind of mercy.

His nostrils flared as he breathed in deep, sucking her apple blossom scent through his nostrils. All of a sudden, he hungered for that sweet fruit.

His former friends and partners, knowing Malden's preference for the feisty, spirited bed partner, had certainly sent her. No harm in sampling the chit before he sent her packing.

Malden would give this chit nothing in return. He'd leave her hungry, panting, and begging him for surrender. He could slake his lust, which still remained unquenched from Cyra's earlier failure to get him off.

He leaned in to take her lips.

Like she was the lady she insisted she was and not some well-skilled tart who'd come to seduce him for some reason or another, the lady blanched.

It is a ploy. This virginal innocent who quavered and quaked in fear one instant, and the next met his gaze more boldly than any man would dare do.

Women possessed the same wiles and ways as the first woman to sin, Eve. Ultimately, they offered nothing but a man's falling and failing, and, aside from their bodies, provided nothing of value.

Fuck her and when you have her begging and crying for release, then have your answers.

Why shouldn't he?

Malden caught Edith's chin between a thumb and forefinger and examined her with a new interest.

"I know you want to scare me," she repeated, in a clear attempt to convince herself.

"You have no idea what I want," he purred. If she did, she'd have fled long ago.

"It shan't work, Lord Malden."

"Oh?" he drawled. "Do tell, my dear."

"Well, by your own admission, you *want* to frighten me."

He flashed a wolfish smile. "And I'm succeeding."

"You are succeeding *some*," she reluctantly conceded. "*Some*."

God, she was a tigress.

Gripping her by the hip, Malden dragged her close and pressed his cock against her soft belly so she could feel his length.

She gasped.

"What are you *doing*, Lord Malden?" she whispered, with enough horror in her low contralto to give him pause.

A virginal blush filled the wench's cheeks.

"Isn't it clear?" he purred.

Her cheeks turned as red as the brightest sunset.

"The only thing that is *clear*, my lord, is that you are *no* gentleman."

"Ah, so those full lips are capable of some truths." Malden released his hold on her.

"I am no liar." She stared incredulously at him. "Furthermore, any respectable man would chafe at having his honor called into question," she whispered. "They fight duels to defend themselves against such charges."

"Are you here to duel me?" he mocked. "Is that the reason you infiltrated my clubs?"

She wrinkled her nose. "No—"

"God, not even the most innocent debutante is as naïve as you—"

"I'm not a debutante," she cut him off.

"Clearly."

The lady furrowed her brow. "Given your boorish and surly demeanor, I did not take you as a gentleman given to jests," the young woman said as though she'd not even heard him.

But maybe she heard and didn't hear what she wished because it made her less afraid.

He sneered. "One more time, I am no gentleman."

Once, he had been. Once, he'd been the dutiful son, the loyal friend, the most respected gentleman throughout London.

"But you were," she said, almost beseechingly. Did she do so to remind herself or Malden? "You were a well-respected, honorable, good, *decent* man."

And what did that get me?

"You presume to have ever known me?" he mocked. "We've never crossed paths."

Her cheeks blazed even brighter. "No, that is true."

"Even in the days I was a stupid pup, I wouldn't have ever partnered with you." He could say that with absolute certainty because they actually *had* attended several of the same affairs, and he'd never written his name on her card.

She didn't so much as flinch. "I recall, my lord."

Another lady would have been reduced to pitiful tears at Malden's slight.

If he were a different man, her gumption in the face of being so callously insulted would have earned his respect. But then, if he were that gentleman she even now recalled, neither would such cruel words have ever passed his lips.

Fortunately, that weak man was dead, and from his ashes sprang a strong, powerful figure no one would dare to cross.

Malden stuck his nose near hears. "If I have to ask you one more time, I'll bend you over my knee and spank you and only stop when you are begging for more."

"Whyever would I beg for a spanking?" Horror filled her whisper.

"Oh, if you were that innocent, I should take great pleasure in showing you."

Tired of this exchange which had already gone far too long, Malden gripped her by the shoulders and pressed her back firmly against the wall. "Who?"

Fear sparked her eyes. Her bosom heaved.

Good, the chit should be terrified. No man entered into Malden's kingdom without his explicit approval and lived to tell the story.

"I will have that information, even if I have to shake it out of you." He did just that. "Who?" he thundered.

"M-Me," she cried. "I came of my own volition…and need."

"Lies," he hissed and released her so quick she collapsed at his feet.

"They are not lies," she rasped, looking up from the floor.

Malden scoured her face for answers and truths, but the shadows of his darkened office played off her features, effectively preventing his study.

With a sharp curse, Malden grabbed a candle from a nearby sconce and brought it nearer her face.

She held her palms up as if to shield her identity.

"Let. Me. See. You. Now," he seethed.

The woman let her arms drop.

Tears ravaged her cheeks.

He brought his light closer and those pathetic drops glimmered in the glow of the flame.

The lady flinched away. "I hate you," she whispered.

Malden smiled coolly. "That is perfect, wench." Aside from terror, respect, and power, he wanted nothing less from a person. "Now, you've learned to never cross me, and never be so foolish as to enter my empire on someone else's behalf."

"What is wrong with you th-that you c-cannot believe me?" The lady sat up on her knees and lifted her palms as if in supplication. "I I sp speak the truth, *n-no* one has sent me."

Without taking his gaze from the pathetic creature at his feet, Malden returned the long, tapered candle to its gold sconce.

"As tempting as you are on your knees, with your mouth at my cock, wench," he said frostily, "I do not tolerate those who seek to deceive me." He scraped another stare over her supine form. "How very sad for you," he murmured.

He turned on his heel and headed across the room.

"Wh-what are you doing?"

He ignored her and continued over to the whips hung neatly upon the place just beyond his desk. Malden eyed them a moment, and then made his selection: a favorite birch switch. Rod in hand, he turned and faced her.

Her panic-filled eyes flew from Malden to the instrument he now held.

"What a-are you d-doing?" she whispered, dread making her query barely audible.

But that pleading, he could identify in a rowdy concert hall.

"Why, as I'd vowed, I'm giving you *one* of my mighty rods."

She scrambled so quickly, she toppled backward onto her arse.

Malden gave her a cursory once over. To think moments ago he'd almost admired the chit's strength.

With his spare hand, he reached for her. The lady brought her leg up quick, nearly catching him square between the legs.

He grabbed her delicate ankle to keep that strike from landing.

"You little hellfire," he said, a hard smile in his voice.

The minx brought her other leg up in another attempt to kick him. Chuckling, Malden snatched the lady's other ankle and held her immobile.

His appreciation—and lust—again stirred.

Fury flooded her cheeks with fiery color. Hate blazed from her eyes.

Malden again contemplated her, this time in the way in which she lay, disarmed, and in repose at his feet. In her struggles, her skirts had climbed about her thighs.

He lingered his focus on that white, creamy expanse of her leg. Gaunt and painfully thin, as he'd taken her, Malden noted with a masculine interest and surprise that her lower limbs were well-muscled, as if from riding, and *other* pursuits.

His mind went to thoughts of this feisty creature in his bed, under him, her athletic legs wrapped firmly about his waist as she met each drive of his hips, in an unbridled and matched lust.

Malden's momentary lapse cost him.

The hellcat renewed her struggles. She sliced her legs frantically up and down and wrenched them back and forth. She managed to shake free of Malden and got herself to her feet with an impressive agility.

The little harridan darted across the room until she had the full length of Malden's office between them.

More than a little amused, he allowed her that false sense of triumph. There was no place for her to go, nowhere to run.

She glanced frantically about. Left and then right. At the door. The mirrored viewing window.

Malden called her attention his way. "You're trapped, wench," he took delight in informing her.

"You are mad," she whispered.

"Oh, I assure you, I am the epitome of sane. You, on the other hand, breaking into my club and refusing to divulge answers to the questions I seek, puts *your* sanity in question."

Malden gripped his favorite birch rod, and started for her.

"I am Miss Caldecott," she cried. "No one has sent me here. I've come of my own volition."

Miss Caldecott. *Caldecott.* Hers was a familiar name of a family Malden and his dying father had no dealings with. The duke maintained a tight circle composed of people with the most power, bluest blood, greatest wealth, and the oldest titles to match the Craven dukedom. In short—the Caldecotts had never possessed enough influence to be worthy of a connection to Malden's family.

The young lady erroneously interpreted his silence as encouragement to continue.

"I am here to ask for your assistance with a personal matter, my lord."

His assistance? He eyed her dubiously. "*You* expect *me* to help *you*?"

She nodded quickly.

Malden tossed his head back and roared with laughter.

When he'd gotten his dark humor in check, he found Miss Caldecott watching him with serious—and sad—drab brown eyes.

Oh, this was rich. In sending a damsel in distress, some rival out there had thought to appeal to the man Malden used to be. Whoever had enlisted her aid had certainly done their work. They'd selected a young, respectable lady, not of any real status or stature but with enough social connections that one would not doubt her intentions.

Malden flexed his jaw.

He narrowed his threatening gaze upon her. "Do I strike you as one who goes about helping anyone, other than myself?"

Miss Caldecott shook her head. "No," she murmured. "You strike me as a man capable of taking down anyone and everyone in your path."

"*You* have an enemy?"

"Not me, per se. Rather, my family."

"I'm listening. You have four minutes," he said silkily.

"And then?" Her voice trembled slightly.

Malden curled his lips ever so slightly into a menacing glare. "Then, I decide your fate."

CHAPTER 4

I DECIDE YOUR FATE.

With Lord Malden's ruthless spirit and pitiless soul, Edith rather suspected this king of the underworld could both decide anyone's fate and then destroy them if he wished. She also suspected he might very well do so not for just those who'd wronged him or posed a threat, but just for the thrill of doing so.

"The clock is ticking." That taunting warning shook her free.

"May we sit?" she murmured, gesturing to his desk.

"Of course," he said so quickly, hope suffused her breast. Perhaps the honorable man he'd been rumored to be lived in him, still.

"Shall I also ring for tea, Miss Caldecott?"

Tea.

She froze. After her sister's sudden death, Edith developed an aversion for the brew she felt confident had killed her sister.

"Miss Caldecott?"

The marquess's impatient voice snatched Edith back from that dark place of fear and darkened memories.

"Uh, no," she said. Edith could pretend to drink the offering. "Thank you for—"

"God, you are a simpleton," he said with false cheer. "Do you truly think we are sitting down to partake in refreshments?"

"What I believe is you shouldn't offer something unless you intend to give it. It's all very confusing."

"Do you know what I know to be fact?" he asked tersely and didn't so much as allow Edith a breath to breathe. "You have now wasted over one minute of your time."

Her gaze flew to the gilded clock with figures frozen in a naughty tableau, and she saw the time.

No sooner had Edith seated herself on the stiff-backed mahogany chair at the foot of his desk, did Lord Malden claim his place on the king-like chair directly opposite her.

The marquess steepled his fingers.

His message couldn't be clearer. This whole world was his empire. They were all just living in it.

"What is your name?" he asked.

"I've already told you; my name is Miss—"

He laughed, a cold, harsh sound. "You would invade the most wicked hell in all of London or Paris, watch orgies—"

"I didn't watch orgies," she said on a furious whisper.

But you wanted to, that sinful voice in her head whispered.

"Not because you didn't want to," he jeered.

In addition to the world, Lord Malden even owned Edith's thoughts. Unnerved as she'd never been, she had to force herself to meet his glacial gaze.

"And this is what you'd draw the proverbial line at?" he drawled sardonically. "Sharing your given name."

"It doesn't matter—"

"No, it doesn't. But I want it and I get anything and everything I want." He paused and gave her a meaningful look. "And that includes…"

Her breath hitched and her feet twitched with the urge to take flight.

"Your name," he finished. "Give it to me."

"Edith," she said quietly. "My name is Edith." How very awful and wrong it felt sharing her name with a man so undeserving of that intimacy.

He gave her a cool, frosty once-over.

"Edith." His lips curled up in a hard, jeering grin, stripped of all warmth and infused with only ice. "A marm's name to go with your marm looks."

She supposed that harsh assessment would upset most young ladies. Edith, however, had always been practical enough to know she'd not been born a grand beauty, and accepted her features as passable, at best.

When he failed to get a rise out of her, he arched a frosty, blond eyebrow.

Eventually, all bullies backed down. Lord Malden proved no exception.

He stared implacably at Edith.

At last, he'd stop this cat and mouse game he played with her. He'd grant her the chance to speak her piece.

That was the very reason she'd risked reputation, life, and limb to be here. She'd planned everything she would say. Only to find herself stuck on the part she'd not considered retelling—the obvious part—about Evie. No matter how many times she'd thought of it—which was every day, reliving it proved as painful as the first day it had happened.

Please, do not die. I need you, Evie… Please. Please. Please…

The whisper of her own voice from years ago spread across the chambers of her mind. Her gaze began to tunnel; all periphery vision faded first, and that curtain of blackness swept slowly out.

Do not get lost, Edith. Not this time. Not now.

And somehow, for the first time ever, she managed to wrest herself back from past memories of sorrowful days.

Edith drew a deep breath.

"Someone killed my sister," she said quietly. "Her name is… was…is—" She'd never know the accurate way to refer to Evie. For she'd always be, in the here, now, and ever after, Edith's sister. "She was poisoned."

In further testament to his ruthlessness, Lord Malden did not so much as flinch at the mention of an innocent young lady's death.

"Why would anyone kill a debutante who hadn't even had her Come Out?"

He knew that. Of course, he would. There'd been a time the Marquess of Malden had been London's most respectable, most sought-after bachelor. He'd have been abreast of all the *ton's* happenings.

How things had changed. But then, life did things to a person that left them forever altered. Edith knew that all too well.

"She wasn't the intended recipient," Edith murmured.

"Who was?"

"I suspect my brother."

Lord Malden sharpened his gaze on her. "He has enemies then?"

Affronted, Edith drew back. "He most certainly does not. He is not like—" She stopped herself short of completing the thought.

A harsh grin cocked the marquess's lips up. "He is not like me?" he purred.

"No, he is not. He is good and kind and loyal and respectable and decent and loving."

Cruel eyes mocked her. "And yet, you do not go to that good, kind, loyal, respectable, decent, loving brother for aid, but rather *me*?"

"That is precisely the reason I've come to you. Darkness must be met with darkness."

"Don't you mean strength must be met with strength?" he jeered.

"I suspect we are both right," she murmured.

Edith smoothed her palms along the front of her skirts before she registered that distracted gesture. She made herself stop.

"Furthermore, all people, regardless of whether they are good or bad, man or woman, have people out there who wish them ill will, my lord. I should think one who comports himself as you do would know that."

A muscle ticked at the corner of his right eye.

"I do," he said. "I did not, however, expect an innocent young lady would."

Her gaze drifted to a point over his head and collided with a long, rectangular rendering in a gilded frame of Artemis, adorned in white and gold filmy robes that revealed her most intimate parts. The Greek goddess of the hunt lay twisted and twined in the arms of the enormous, bearded, Norse god of hunting, Ullr. That powerful pair were engaged in the throes of making love.

Feeling a blush heat her cheeks, she averted her gaze and looked back at Lord Malden.

The marquess watched Edith with scornful eyes.

"I'm not any young lady, my lord," she finally said, when she found the words to speak. "One can hardly be innocent and untouched by life after one's beloved sister has been killed."

"This again," he muttered.

She bit the inside of her cheek hard to keep from snapping and spitting like a cat at him. Insulting the man would do her no good.

"Have there been additional attempts on your brother's life?" he asked.

Edith worried at her lower lip. She knew precisely what opinion he'd draw were he to have her actual answer.

"After Evie died," she hedged, "Hutchinson began traveling. He spends but a short amount of the year in London."

"That isn't an answer," he said bluntly. "I'm certain a lady with her nose deep in some kind of mock investigation—"

"It is not a mock investigation," she gritted out.

"Would have surely heard or known something about whether the gentleman had suffered any close calls, if not abroad, while in England."

God, he was as astute as he was cruel.

"I am not aware of any attempts," she admitted and then added on a rush. "But it does not mean—"

"That you have a fruitful imagination and are given to outlandish ideas?"

"My brother is safe," she finished over his interruption.

She'd not let him get a rise out of her with his insults and mockery. That was what he wished, but she'd far more of a backbone than he'd ever known.

He assessed her with that cynical stare. "Let me get this right," he drawled. "Your sister suddenly fell ill."

"With no accounting for it."

"No one else in your household exhibited any symptoms?"

"At the time of Evie's illness, my brother had a megrim, which he never suffers from." Of course, in the months after when she'd reminded Hutchinson about that headache, he'd had no recollection.

"What about after her death?" he continued his interrogation. "Did any other Caldecott—more specifically, your brother—exhibit signs he'd been poisoned?"

"No," she said.

Her previously only fledgling hope began to die like a tulip that grew too soon in the winter months.

"Who is the suspected nefarious villain?" he asked, so bored and sardonic she wanted to slap him across the face.

"Our cousin—"

"Never tell me, a distant relation set to inherit on the unlikely chance your father and brother perish? I'm trusting there are no additional brothers or heirs in line before him, otherwise, he'd have an entire killing spree to see to."

Edith felt hope slipping and desperation beat like a drum in her chest. "I'm not some silly lady with an inventive imagination. I'm not!" she exclaimed.

He gave her a smug look.

This was slipping away. She couldn't have gotten this far only to walk away without his help.

"I understand how this sounds, my lord," she said, more calmly. "Believe me, I do. My sister is the one who came to me with her suspicions and—"

"How old is your sister? Obviously, the one who is still alive."

Edith's breath hitched. Was his life such a miserable one that being cruel made him feel better about his existence? "How can you be so hateful?"

The marquess smirked. "I assure you, it comes quite easily."

Edith lifted her chin. "If only you were capable of ruthless actions and not mere words, my lord."

Lord Malden's entire body snapped erect. His muscles strained his shirt. The hard wall of his chest jutted out. A spine-chilling glint iced his eyes over.

"Do not ever," he whispered, "ever, question my strength or power over anyone. Or I can promise, you will regret it. Am I clear, Miss Caldecott?"

Her courage instantly flagged. Edith managed a nod.

"Say it," he ordered, his voice as ragged and gravelly as shattered rock.

"You are c-clear," she said, through a mouth sapped of all moisture.

He glanced past her to where the clock he'd indicated earlier stood.

Edith scampered to her feet. "What are you doing?"

Her hopes of avenging her sister and protecting her brother hinged on this man.

"I've given you eight minutes," he said, bored sounding. "Far more than I allow anyone. Take your concerns to your parents, like a good girl."

He came out from around his desk.

Panic rooted around Edith's chest.

"My parents believe I'm being fantastical," she said, with a calm she didn't feel.

"Listen to them," he said flatly and sailed past her.

It was all slipping away. All of it…

"I will do anything," she implored.

That managed to halt the marquess. With an excruciating slowness, he faced Edith.

"Aside from your body, you have nothing to entice me." He scraped a derisive stare over her person. "And you barely have that."

He sought to scare her and nearly proved successful in his efforts. After losing her sister, nothing and no one, however, could hurt Edith.

"Ah, but I do tempt you *some*." Edith lifted an eyebrow. "Therefore, you cannot truly say I don't have anything to tempt you."

Lord Malden eyed her like she was the cream to his cat. "Are you offering me your body?" he asked silkily.

Edith swallowed convulsively.

I went too far.

The marquess gripped her at the waist, and with a sensual laziness, he drew her closer. He ran his searching hands down the small of her back and lower in an unexpectedly smoothing, soothing rhythm that lulled her senses into a peculiar calm.

Ever so gently, Lord Malden filled his palms with her buttocks. *Oh, God. This is wrong. Draw back. Kick him. Wrestle him.*

So why then could she not bring herself to a rightful indignant horror? Why did his unexpectedly tender caress hold her trapped, feeling a sense of harmony?

"I've never schooled a virgin," he said, contemplatively, a man speaking to himself through the decision of whether to bestow his attentions on said virgin or save his time in favor of the experienced women he no doubt regularly had in his bed.

Edith managed to find her voice. "I'm not looking to be schooled." She promptly wished she hadn't said a word.

Lord Malden's feral grin, so pearly white, put her in mind of the wolf Red Riding Hood had tangled with.

As if he'd read Edith's silent capitulation, the marquess placed his lips close to her ear and drew the lobe into his mouth. He suckled for a moment.

Edith's lashes fluttered shut.

A shameful heat stirred between her legs.

What is wrong with me?

"Tsk, tsk," he continued in his silky seductive baritone that added to Edith's growing dazedness. "You know I do not tolerate those who don't answer my questions."

Had he asked a question? She couldn't recall. She barely remembered her name.

The marquess gripped her buttocks more tightly, and she gasped at the force of his hold.

"Are you offering to spread those delectably shapely legs of yours and take me inside your virginal sheathe?" he teased against the sensitive shell of her ear.

His words were vulgar. Utterly horrid and uncouth. But even worse, they proved shamefully titillating.

Her heart hammered with what *should* be dread. Only these curious flutters in Edith's belly, *they* didn't feel like fear. And that in and of itself at last managed to rouse a suitable terror.

The marquess curled his lips at the corners. "*Afraid*, little dove?" he purred.

"N-No," she murmured, only her voice quavered, doing Edith no favors.

"And yet," he drew her close, "you tremble."

Under her skirts, she pressed her also quivering knees together.

The jeering glint in his gold-flecked eyes said more clearly than words he'd felt that slight movement.

"Yes. I am afraid…*of you*," she lied. That admission was far safer than Lord Malden discovering the *actual* reason: his touch moved her in ways that terrified her.

Disappointment replaced the earlier unidentifiable glint in his eyes. He released her.

"Get out," he said sharply. "Before I change my mind and give you a different rod for daring to set foot inside my empire."

No!

"Go," he thundered.

Hurrying to do his bidding, Edith jumped and raced to collect her cloak and mask. Desperation consumed her. There had to be something she could say, *something* she could do.

Except what could Edith possibly have that might persuade this pitiless man to help her? He'd already demonstrated a lack of male interest in body—which had he wished, she was desperate enough to barter.

As an innocent young lady, she was useless to one such as—

Edith stopped at the doorway.

Her mind raced. Innocent young ladies. Of course!

Everyone knew about the enmity between Lord Malden and his former best friends and partners, Mr. Rex DuMond, the Marquess of Rutherford, and the Duke of Argyll. It'd been reported there'd been a falling out after Lord Rutherford married Lady Faith Rutherford, formerly Lady Faith Brookfield. It in turn spawned a rivalry of the ages between Lord Malden and the families involved.

She could profess her friendship with Lady Faith's younger sister, Lady Violet, and offer to bring the marquess anything Edith heard, anything discussed by those families.

Of course, there was no friendship. Not between Edith and the Brookfield girls. Yes, their families often received invitations to similar affairs, but beyond that, the Caldecotts and Brookfields moved in entirely different social circles.

Lord Malden, however, needn't know that.

This is folly. He'll learn of your lies and when he does, he'll punish you mightily...

She shivered.

Edith would do nearly anything to avenge her sister, but hurting another young lady was decidedly not one of them.

This required a lie of the biggest order to a punisher of people, and would earn Edith the most powerful, dangerous enemy for life; one who'd exact cruel and vicious revenge against her.

"What are you still doing here, Miss Caldecott?"

She closed her eyes.

What choice do I have?

None. Edith had no other choice.

Armed with that reminder and filled with a renewed sense of hope, Edith faced Lord Malden.

He stood exactly where she'd left him, his gaze hard, his arms folded.

"There is something I can offer that you may find of value, my lord," she said solemnly.

The marquess gave her another one of those derisory once-overs. "I've already told you. You don't possess the charms to tempt a man of my tastes and appetites, *Edith*."

Never had she heard her name fashioned into the ugliest of insults.

"No. I am well aware of that," she murmured. She took a step nearer him. "What I'm proposing is something *different*."

Lord Malden inclined his head ever so slightly; that nearly indiscernible movement indicated he'd heard and was faintly interested. "Go on."

"I am dear friends, *best* friends," she thought to correct, "with someone whose family I have grounds to believe you might be feuding with."

The keen glint in his eyes sparkled. "I'm listening."

"Lady Violet Brookfield." Edith distinctly dropped each syllable.

The air crackled with an invisible but nevertheless terrific charge.

Had she not been studying the marquess so intently, Edith would have missed the way his features tensed, and his eyes filled with a primordial bloodlust.

But Edith *did* watch him that closely and so, she knew—she had him.

Lord Malden swiftly regained his composure. His face became an unfathomable mask and the feral grin he donned found its way back to his lips.

"You'd betray a friend?" He sounded amused by the prospect.

"Desperate people will do desperate things," she said, adroitly evading answering him. The fewer lies to trip herself up on the better.

The marquess didn't speak for a long while but she knew the wheels of his mind were cranking and churning. She knew she'd held forth a cherished gift he'd covet above all others—ears and eyes inside the Brookfields' and DuMonds' households.

Knowing her opponent was but a breath away from capitulating, Edith sighed. "You are not interested in my offer, then. Very well."

She made a show of drawing on her nearly useless without its fastening cloak. As she did, she locked eyes with his. "I told you, my lord, one way or another, I *will* avenge my sister. I sought you out because I suspected you were the most ruthless, admirable opponent."

In the same derisory fashion he'd used during their exchange, Edith looked *him* over. "But there are others whom I can turn to. Good evening, my lord."

Curtsying, Edith made to leave. She managed to open the door no more than three inches. The marquess slammed a palm against the oak panel and forcefully pushed it back into place.

"Who?" he demanded in a gruesome whisper.

Fear traversed her spine. "I don't know what—" Her words ended on a breathless squeak.

Lord Malden grabbed her firmly and yet also, with an unexpected gentleness—and pushed her back against the door.

"Do not play games," he seethed. "You will not win. Who?"

At the power of his barely suppressed bestial rage, Edith trembled. There was certainly a danger of going too far in this match she'd entered with the marquess. Grounded in that reminder, her throat moved up and down, and she gave him the name he sought.

"The Duke of Argyll," she said quietly.

Lord Malden said nothing for a moment. He ran his incensed eyes over Edith's face and then leaned down until their foreheads nearly touched and their eyes met. "Do you think Argyll is more powerful than me?"

She shook her head in an honest, unstoppable rejection of the marquess's query. "No. I believe you are."

To give herself some space with which to breathe, Edith pressed her palms over Lord Malden's black lapels and started to push him away.

But for some unexplainable reason, Edith remained frozen with her hands on him in a way so intimate, she should pull away. Instead, the way she might a wounded beast, Edith stroked him; slowly, soothingly, tenderly.

"That is why I sought you out, my lord," she murmured and lifted her eyes to his. "But if you will not help me…" *I have no other choice.*

Edith didn't need to speak those words. She knew he understood, just as she knew they were more potent left unspoken.

The shades of gold, reds, and browns that made up his haunting irises blazed like Satan's inferno. "Say it again," he rasped.

This time, it was with true confusion that Edith shook her head.

He gripped her more tightly. "Who is the most powerful?" he rasped.

"You," she said clearly. "You are the most power—"

Growling, Lord Malden covered her mouth with his in a hard kiss that both punished and praised.

She'd only dreamed of being kissed before her sister's death. After, Edith wanted nothing, craved nothing other than revenge. The silly, childish dreams of happily-ever-afters with dashing, charming husbands and tender kisses and future babes faded like a portrait that'd been touched by flame, consumed, and destroyed into nothingness.

In those forever-ago imaginings, the embrace Edith imagined for herself had been gentle and adoring and filled with affection.

Lord Malden's kiss was none of those things.

He kissed her as if he wished to consume her.

He slanted his lips over Edith's softer ones, demanding, taking, and also giving. And this embrace set her afire from the inside out. She'd never known it could be like this. She'd never expected it could be.

In a bid to keep herself upright, Edith twined her arms about

Lord Malden's neck. The husky rumble of his harsh laughter tickled her lips.

She whimpered. Why should her body respond to him so? Why, when he was vile and nasty and rude and everything no person should be, did she want this kiss?

The marquess swept his tongue inside; his hot flesh, like a brand, swept over hers, around hers, in a dizzying primitive dance she could not keep up with.

She'd loathed the scent of brandy on his breath earlier. So why then, should he taste of sweet fruit, flowers, and citrus zest? All she knew was that the taste of him proved headier than had she herself drunk of a decanter until the bottle held nothing more.

Lord Malden continued to taste her tongue and mouth with his. His efforts left Edith dizzy and breathless, and shamefully, even as she should pull away and slap his face, she somehow wanted…more of these feelings he'd roused.

"I like my women to have fire," he breathed against her mouth, and she'd have to be deaf as a doorpost to have failed to hear the disappointment.

He is going to stop.

Good! That was precisely what she wanted.

Except, it wasn't. As a grown woman who had no intention of marrying or falling in love, she'd never experience passion or desire, and when it was said and done and Edith brought down her sister's killer, there'd never be an opportunity beyond this one, with this man.

He stopped. His disgust and disappointment more palpable than the three governesses whose instruction Edith had failed again and again.

With an intuition as old as Eve's, however, Edith reflexively gripped Lord Malden hard by his large, muscular neck.

Lord Malden chuckled; a sound as derisive as it was knowing and triumphant. "Want more do you, wench?"

He kneaded her buttocks; that sensual massage stole her breath and all logical thought. Nay, she'd surrendered all common sense the moment she sought out London's most mercenary man.

The marquess squeezed her so hard he wrung a gasp from Edith.

"I asked: *do you want more?*"

No! That immediate response got stuck on her tongue and went unspoken.

His chuckle became a laugh. Apparently, he required no partner in this exchange for he continued introspective as any philosopher.

"Ah, your mouth isn't capable of the same honesty as this sweet, slim body of yours, wench."

He lowered his mouth near hers and intuitively she tipped her head back for his kiss.

"Do you know what I believe, sweet?" he whispered against her mouth.

Another quiet, derisive laugh shook his frame. "Your body makes a liar of you, even worse than that delectable mouth of yours."

Delectable mouth?

He thought her mouth lovely?

His eyes grew suddenly harder. "I'll give you what you seek if you give me what I want."

A little, animalistic mewl built in her throat.

"Lady Violet Brookfield," he whispered with passion ten degrees warmer than when he'd been kissing Edith.

Lady Violet Brookfield…

Through the mad haze of passion, that other woman's name registered. It wasn't Edith that roused him to that level of lustful state.

A hard, savage glimmer sparkled among the golden depths of his eyes.

That realization left her strangely deflated.

"M-My lord?" she asked shakily, trying valiantly to keep up.

"I'll give you what you crave—revenge against your imagined villain," he said, stepping away from her.

Her imagined villain.

"He did kill her," she said sharply. "He killed my sister."

"Whether he did or not matters not to me. You want him destroyed and I will take him down for you."

She drew back. In other words, he didn't care one way or another whether Edith had the right of it where Mr. Stillson was concerned—which she did. Lord Malden would dispose of an innocent man as easily as he would a guilty one.

Evidence of that—nay, his—ruthlessness sent shivers tripping up her spine.

This is the reason you sought him out, the voice in her head jeered. *You needed a man so menacing, so merciless as to be able to do that which you cannot do.*

"What is it, Miss Caldecott? I have a business to run and scintillating company you are certainly not," he said impatiently.

Edith expected his words would have wounded anyone else.

"You didn't even ask his name," she said. "You've consented to help me—"

"Let me interrupt you, so I may disabuse you of that naïve assumption you've comforted yourself with, sweet," he said, a smile in his voice. "I don't help anyone. I don't do anything unless it serves me and my empire some. Is that clear?"

How odd that cheerful tone could accompany a veiled warning. Edith nodded.

"What is his name?" he asked bored.

"Mr. Eustace Stillson." At uttering that name, hate, no less powerful but rather one that grew ever stronger every day, filled her.

He inclined his head in silent receipt of that name tendered.

Edith searched for some indication he may have heard of or knew her distant cousin; there was none.

But then, if Edith's parents had been deemed unworthy company, certainly a mere Mr. Eustace Stillson, with a fortune from trade and no title, would hardly be someone Lord Malden would even share the same air with.

He was set to destroy her cousin. She'd have him know the man he'd bring to justice was one most deserving of it. That should please her; leave her satisfied and happy.

Lord Malden would help her. Everything she'd set out to do this night, she'd achieved.

"Have you changed your mind, sweet?" He sounded downright bored.

"No!" she exclaimed with too much zeal. A man like Malden would only be repulsed by her eagerness. "No," she repeated, more measured, and in control. "It is not that. I remain committed to avenging my sister."

He folded his arms at his chest. "Why do I get the impression that isn't enough, sweetheart?"

"You don't believe me," she said gravelly.

Lord Malden simply stared.

"You think I'm being fanciful."

"Does it matter if I, of all people, believe you, Miss Caldecott?" he asked, laughter in his voice.

For the first time, he sounded genuinely amused by something.

"No," she murmured. She supposed it didn't.

As he crossed over to his desk, Edith guardedly followed his every movement.

No one: not Lord Malden, her parents, her brother, believed Cousin Eustace guilty of the crimes on his black soul, and she was so tired of being alone in this fight. Edith needed someone to believe her. More specifically, she needed Lord Malden, someone on the outside looking in, to be that person.

He opened the center drawer.

"Here." He tossed something Edith's way.

A black, satin mask similar in style to the ones worn by the patrons in the club hit Edith smack on the chest.

Automatically, she caught the disguise.

"You'll wear this when you're here." His lips turned in a crooked grin that oozed derision. "Not that ridiculously modest scrap you donned that reveals half your face."

Edith turned the mask over in her hands and studied the concealment. Designed of black lace, it gave the illusion of transparency to the covering. However, the modiste who'd hand-designed the covering had fashioned the fabric into alternating rows of silver and black lace.

Edith skimmed her fingertips over the place to cover a person's mouth; the material proved thinner here, but the point just over its wearer's top lip featured a heavier lace.

She frowned. She'd not seen other men and women below with their mouths fully concealed; the mask Lord Malden insisted she take and wear would conceal her lips but also make it harder for her to speak.

Edith caught her lower lip between her teeth and chewed at that flesh—still tender from his brutal kiss.

She found herself horrified but also, fascinated by that restrictive design.

"I see," she said.

"What exactly is it that you think you see, girl?"

Girl, he called her.

Was I ever a girl? With what life in the Caldecott home turned out to be, Edith wondered sometimes.

"This is why you were able to identify me as an interloper," Edith remarked.

The marquess wore his patently ironic, hard half-grin.

"You think *that* is how I identified you? Miss Caldecott, you *look* like a virgin, *move* like one, and have the *eyes* of one." Like it was the most horrid thing in the world an innocent woman stood before him, Lord Malden's elucidation contained more of his irreverent mirth.

He stalked off, and she watched on as he strode in the opposite direction and stopped. Then, his fingers moved quickly as he turned a hidden until now gold dial that was a perfect match to the garish gold wallpaper.

With his back to her, as it was, Edith peered intently across the room.

A moment later, there came a discernable *click*.

Her eyes flared. Why, it appeared to be a safe, large enough for a person to walk through.

Or to be dragged into and locked away, never again seen.

Lord Malden reached inside.

"If I kill you, I get nothing," he said, without looking back.

"My l-lord?" she called over unsteadily.

"You were wondering about this closet."

There came the rustle of fabric and material; the swoosh and flutters came fast, as if he were a modiste searching for the ideal material for an illustrious client.

"I thought it was a safe," she felt inclined to point out, lest he truly take her as a melodramatic sort.

He laughed, a sound so sardonic and empty, she wondered if he'd ever known a reason to smile in this entire life.

"You find that amusing?" she asked quietly.

"You have to be stupider than I think if you believed I'd let anyone near one of my safes," he drawled.

This was the closest to a conventional conversation they'd ever partaken in—which certainly said nothing—or rather, *everything*—about the state of their discourse.

"Oh, I expect you are besieged by any manner of threats," she said dryly. "Ladies by the legions from respectable families who—"

The marquess stalked into the office and the rest of Edith's quip died.

"When you're in my club, you are not to wear *that*, Miss Caldecott." The look he slanted Edith's way could only be described as derisive.

Edith followed his gaze downward and frowned. "A gown? What should I arrive in?" she asked dryly. "*Breeches?*"

Lord Malden unfurled diaphanous fabric draped over his opposite arm she'd previously failed to notice. He gave the material a snap, revealing a sleeveless gown—if it could even be called that.

He pushed the scandalous garment Edith's way and reflexively she took it. Dubious, Edith glanced at the gauzy article. With a plunging bodice, studded with crystals, and sheer black skirts, no respectable lady would ever dare don such a piece.

Edith looked up to find the marquess's impatient gaze on her. "What would you have me do with this, my lord?"

"What do you generally do with a gown, Miss Caldecott?"

She bit her tongue to keep from saying something she'd regret.

"I should say, what would you have me do with this," *bawdy*, "particular one?" she opted for. After all, it was best not to offend a man who easily offended.

The grin he favored Edith with was both disgusted and entertained. "Wear it."

Edith drew back.

She held the garment up. "*This?*" Her question was rhetorical, but she expected even if it hadn't been, Lord Malden wouldn't have answered anyway.

"Thank you, my lord, for the offer." Edith shook her head.

"However, I most certainly will *not* be wearing this," she said as calmly as she could manage.

He quirked his lips. "As I see it, it'd only improve your situation."

"My *situation*," she sputtered. This time she didn't even bother to hold back her outrage. "My lord, no proper, respectable, decent lady would ever be caught in such an abomination."

"But visiting Lucifer's Lair is what? *Proper*? Respectable? Decent?" Amusement dripped from his question.

Seething, Edith tossed the tendered garments back at him. "You find this comical, do you?"

Where she'd caught the dress, Lord Malden let it land in a pile between them.

He narrowed his eyes. "I *do* find it droll that you'd force your way inside my kingdom and ask me to kill your dear cousin—"

"He is not a dear cousin," she spat.

"Yet draw the proverbial line at wearing a prurient gown," he continued over her interruption.

Damn him. Damn him for finding any amusement in her family's situation. And damn her for being so desperate as to need to rely on him for help.

"You are not happy with me," he remarked.

Refusing to let him get another rise out of her, Edith made herself stay stoically silent.

Lord Malden walked a slow, predatory circle around her. "After everything I've agreed to do for you and how even-tempered I've been over your breaking into my club, you'd show such cheek."

She stared incredulously at him. *Even-tempered*? He considered *this* even-tempered.

Edith could no longer bite her tongue. "Lest you forget, my lord," she said testily. "I am not the only one who will make out on this deal. I'm bringing you something you value, as well."

Liar, liar, liar, that voice in her head jibed. *You have nothing to offer, other than a lie.*

Edith may have found a greater sense of guilt if he'd not been such a dastard.

The marquess contemplated her with actual interest this time. "You've found your voice after all, sweet."

"I'm not a coward, my lord," she said, angling her chin up.

In his formidable shadow, however, she'd just forgotten that fact.

His dark eyebrows came together forming a menacing line. "Careful with your tone, Miss Caldecott," he warned, his own coated in steel. "I trust this evening has been a lot for one of your delicate sensibilities. Going forward, I won't be so patient with you."

That courage she'd been so proud of flagged.

This man did not ask for her submissiveness. Nay, Lord Malden knew with the same intuition as the Dark Lord that she—and anyone—who crossed his path would acquiesce to his demands.

"This exchange has dragged on far longer than I've permitted anyone," he said. "Either you wear this gown when we meet here, or we don't meet at all."

The latter wasn't an option.

Trapped. She'd no other choice.

She silently railed at the unfairness of being powerless, dependent upon men who expected women were creatures merely driven by emotion. Her brother. Her father. The Marquess of Malden. They were all the same.

The one difference being, the latter would at least help her, even if it was only on the terms he set forth.

"Very well," she said, regret yanking that acquiescence from her lips.

As she angrily scooped up the naughty articles he insisted she wear, Lord Malden preened like an all-too-pleased subjugator who'd vanquished the lesser warrior who'd dared challenge him.

"We are done here," he said icily when she'd finished. "Tomorrow evening, you'll return at the same time." Lord Malden headed to the door.

Balling and unballing her fists at her side, Edith followed his movements.

Lord Malden stopped at the front of the room. Before he opened the door, he looked at Edith.

"Until our business together is concluded, you have thirty minutes each night. Not a second more. Not a second less. If you're late, that is your time. If you arrive after our scheduled meeting, don't bother coming."

As he spoke, Edith saw all too clearly just how he'd managed to build his business into the successful venture he had.

"And when I am done with you," he said silkily, "that will be the last time we see one another. You will be dead to me, and I shall be dead to you. If we should so much as cross paths, I will not even look at you…"

His voice droned on in her mind.

You will be dead to me…

Gooseflesh climbed her arms.

Dead to him…dead to all…

Dead. Dead. Dead.

That was the fate awaiting her.

For all the ways in which Lord Malden tossed her innocence in her face, Edith wasn't so guileless as to believe she'd reach the end of this intact. She'd not escape unscathed.

For Evie, however, if need be, Edith would give her life.

Edith…do not do this. Please, I do not want you to do this. Not for me. Not for anyone. Live your life.

Edith squeezed her eyes tightly shut and attempted to squeeze out the echo of Evie's voice, as real as if she spoke before her.

Only, it wasn't just for Evie. Mr. Stillson would strike again. Evie had merely been an accidental loss in his evil efforts. He'd not fail in a second attempt to kill Hutchinson. Given the number of years that had passed and her family's complacency, he was no doubt poised to strike. That was why Edith had to act first. She had to succeed. Failure was not an option.

"Miss Caldecott? *Miss Caldecott?*"

Edith stared at the grim line of Lord Malden's mouth as it moved, and then snapped herself from the clamor in her mind.

What had he said? And yet, her response wouldn't matter, as he only truly would accept or demand one.

Edith bowed her head in the obeisant way he required; for the first time, she didn't hate that slavish behavior he expected of all. This time, it aided her.

Lord Malden took in her solemn person with a wolfish glint in his eyes. Then, he yanked the door open and said something to the men stationed there.

Edith strained her ears, but her efforts were in vain as he may as well have whispered so subdued were his tones.

The marquess glanced back and beckoned her over.

Edith hesitated a moment and then made her way to Lord Malden.

"Gruffton will escort you out," he said the moment she reached him.

Edith looked from the stocky guard with his stony expression and unblinking gaze Lord Malden indicated, to the marquess.

With that, the marquess set to work tying the fastenings of her cloak he'd sliced through earlier that night. He tugged her hood up into place.

It was, between the care he took with concealing her identity and the protection he conferred, the first sign of gentlemanliness shown by the marquess and not a very insignificant one, either. Somewhere, buried deep inside, dwelled the man he'd used to be.

When he'd finished, Edith lifted her eyes to Lord Malden's. "I thank you for offering me that protection," she murmured.

"I do not care one way or another what harm befalls you except how it affects our arrangement," he said, instantly vanquishing that wishful thinking on her part. "I'm ensuring you don't go exploring my club any more than you already have."

Had there ever been a man as soulless as the one before her?

As if he'd read her thoughts, Lord Malden favored her with another of his frosty smiles. Then he pointed at the door.

Needing distance from him and all the tumult he turned her to inside, Edith swept eagerly past.

As Mr. Gruffton followed her out of his lordship's office, she felt Lord Malden's eyes upon her.

"One more thing, my dear."

Edith and Lord Malden's guard froze; when the marquess spoke the *whole* world stopped.

She glanced back and instantly gave thanks for even the flimsy protection offered by her hood. His penetrating gaze cut all the way through her.

"Do not make me regret this, sweet."

She bowed her head.

A look passed from Lord Malden to Mr. Gruffton. Then, the guard started Edith back on the path of escape.

A temporary escape, her mind continued to heckle. *You return on the morrow.*

There came that familiar thrill of terror roused by even standing in Lord Malden's shadow, and shamefully, a different thrill as well. One she'd deny to her dying day—which was likely coming all too soon. A taste of the forbidden.

As she took her leave, she felt his gaze boring into her.

Edith had given him one important truth this night. She'd come of her own volition, and not at the behest of anyone who wished ill of him or his gaming hell.

When the marquess, however, learned there was no friendship between Edith and Lady Violet, it'd not matter whether she'd lied to him on behalf of herself or another. For a man such as he would never tolerate being duped.

She wasn't so naïve or hopeful as to believe when this was all said in done, she'd remain unscathed. After years of piecing together her cousin's role in Evie's death, Edith was coming to a reckoning.

She found herself in a race against time to take him down before he discovered she was close on his heels. If Cousin Eustace found out, he'd cut her down even quicker than he'd done Evie.

One thing was for certain—there were some fates worse than death.

And if—*when*—Lord Malden discovered Edith's deception, God help her. She would be praying for whatever end Eustace Stillson exacted on her to spare her from facing the wrath of the Marquess of Malden.

CHAPTER 5

Only a half-wit or reckless man would have let Miss Edith Caldecott leave last evening with only her side of the story and no further investigation into the details about the lady, her family, the Caldecott's history, and the veracity of her reason for seeking Malden out.

As such, late the following evening, two hours before he was to receive Miss Caldecott at his clubs, Malden sat on the gold velvet squabs of his carriage bench, in the seediest side of the Seven Dials, perusing a black leather folder in his hands.

Across from him sat Severin Cadogan, former assassin for the British empire. The imposing fellow had one encounter gone wrong with an adversary in France. It'd seen the once great agent with a scar that ran from his forehead down to his right cheek. That mark greater than any calling card had effectively ended the other man's hope of honest work.

That was, as honest work as killing men and women could be.

As the third-born son of some hateful marquess, Cadogan had since built a career for himself, in the same ruthless profession in England—only this time *not* sanctioned by the government.

The man was rumored to have the soul of Satan, and had the raven black hair and black eyes to suit. With a jaw too heavy and a nose too bold, his face wasn't handsome enough or distinct enough to have attracted notice, which was likely one of the reasons he'd been slated for the work he did.

Cadogan's savage looks roused terror in the hearts of anyone who passed him. Fortunately for Malden, he didn't find himself in possession of that pathetically weak organ. Just as fortuitous, Malden held the former assassin on retainer.

"Here's the information you sought about the dead sister," Cadogan said, in a voice as graveled as broken glass and stones ground together.

Malden accepted the latest sheet and quickly read the contents. *Miss Evelyn Caldecott.*

Sudden onset of illness symptoms, initially consistent with tuberculosis: headaches, night sweats, malaise, body pain, weight loss. Though initially taken as a wasting illness, there was no accompanying cough—

He skimmed the hastily scrawled writings of the document, detail after detail about the deceased Caldecott sister. Etc. Etc. Etc.

A sound of annoyance escaped him. "This again," he muttered.

"It is early yet, but my initial findings do not give merit to the premise the dead girl was a victim of anything other than a sudden illness."

"Of course, they don't," he muttered. "And the brother?"

"You'll find that on the next page," Cadogan said. "He's out of the country more than he's in it and as such, it'll take me longer to dig up information about whether he's ever had any encounters that could have been more. I'll keep searching."

"Don't bother." Not taking his focus from the next page, Malden gave a dismissive wave of his hand. "It doesn't matter."

As he'd informed Edith Caldecott, whether Mr. Stillson was or wasn't guilty of any crime hardly mattered to Malden. As long as the willful Miss Caldecott provided Malden what he wanted, he'd no qualms eliminating who she wanted eliminated.

"You don't know if something matters until it does," the agent said with an intransigence that would have impressed Malden were it turned on anyone else.

Malden snapped the file shut. "I'll be the decider of that."

Cadogan, his scarred face impassive, finally gave Malden what he sought. "To your first and most important question, my lord, as to whether there is a connection between the Brookfields and Caldecotts. The latter family is a sponsor of Marchioness of Guilford's school."

He sneered. Ah, yes. How could he forget?

The barren marchioness and her *Ladies and Gentlemen of Hope*, school for orphans and the most pitiful members of society. That establishment where the lady's daughters, Faith DuMond, ne Brookfield, and Lady Violet worked—worked, like common chits.

Hate singed his veins like a venomous poison that spread throughout, leaving only evil and more evil in its wake. As much as that antipathy strengthened him, in this instant, the potency of that emotion left Malden on the edge of madness, keener for the steady composure of Cadogan across from him.

Forcing Malden to give up the business he'd helped build with his own hands and turned out; a friendship severed as easily as the fragile thread of an artery, DuMond and Argyll would pay for what they'd done.

Revenge against the Brookfields would be a sweet, secondary consolation to go along with his ultimate triumph.

"Is there anything else?" Malden asked.

"That is all. For now. If I discover anything else, I will call on you immediately."

With the clandestine meeting at an end, Cadogan let himself out of the carriage, and slipped as effortlessly as night into the shadows.

Malden thumped a fist on the roof.

His driver immediately set the team into motion and directed the conveyance to the more respectable end of London. As he did, Malden gathered all the papers Cadogan had handed over.

Previously, Malden had merely skimmed the contents which contained unnecessary detail after unnecessary detail. Now, his meeting concluded, Malden read through those previously dismissed but still irrelevant details.

After all, one never knew what might prove useful to one in the future.

Miss Edith Caldecott, with her bend toward tartness and insolence, rose each morning at six o'clock, religiously.

She partook in two plain slices of toast and one boiled egg for breakfast each morn.

While she broke her fast, she did not keep the company of

either her parents or younger sister—not yet on the market—but rather, did so alone.

Throughout her morning meal, she alternately read or took notes in her journal.

From there, when the sun only just began to rise, the lady walked through an empty Hyde Park and disappeared within a wooden copse.

What took place in there behind the trees and brush, however, remained unknown—for now.

That detail, Malden would glean soon enough.

Otherwise, there was nothing peculiar or of interest about the lady. She had no wicked proclivities. There'd been no lovers, which given the fact she moved like a virgin had ever been in doubt. She didn't so much as drink anything at public events.

She preferred to sit on the sidelines of the activity and take the gatherings in.

A memory whispered forward of Edith Caldecott's wide-eyed virginal gaze on Malden's patrons in various states of dishabille.

A voyeur she was, his Miss Caldecott.

And Malden found himself all too titillated at the prospect of her taking in the salacious sights available to view at Sodom and Gomora. He envisioned her astride his lap and her innocent eyes growing heavy with desire and becoming those of a worldly woman as she took in sights far more arousing.

His breathing grew heavy, and Malden again marveled at the sudden allure of a maiden. This was why men took part in the nightly auction Malden now offered his patrons. Miss Caldecott was the very reason.

Or, rather, the idea of Miss Caldecott becoming sexually emboldened.

Perhaps he'd play with her some, after all. In addition to the business they now had together, they might enjoy additional benefits from one another.

As soon as the enticing thought slid in, it as effortlessly slipped out.

Intrepid as she'd been, there'd been a fear and guardedness to the lady. She'd protect her virtue the way a nun would and deny herself true pleasure.

Everything he'd learned thus far about Miss Caldecott supported as much.

She didn't play cards or wager too many funds.

She took only the faintest trace of sugar in her tea.

And that was only the beginning of her and her family's staidness.

The Caldecotts attended Sunday sermons regularly—Satan help them.

They supped together.

Attended formal gatherings *together*.

They…played parlor games—not just as house parties or gatherings, but rather, when they were together, alone. *Parlor games*. For the sake of simply playing. As though there was fun to be had in those inane non-amusement amusements.

He shuddered. God, they were a manner of bucolic family Malden previously believed only existed in the gilded framed paintings adorning noble families' walls. Certainly, they couldn't have been more different than Malden and the duke; two strangers, joined by blood, and from that sanguine connection sprang their power.

There'd been no mother—at least not one he'd a recollection of. She'd died when he'd been just two, attempting to bring the spare into the world.

Malden gave his head a disgusted shake.

In the matter of Edith Caldecott's male kin certainly didn't fare any better.

Neither brother nor father possessed debts that would have resulted in them sending her into Malden's lair. They had no vices. They didn't drink any more than a measured amount of spirits—at that, only brandy. They didn't bugger boys.

In matters of the bedroom, the heir only kept one mistress—how singularly dreadful.

The father didn't keep *any*—how singularly impossible.

The viscount and his son were as staid as their daughter was spinsterish.

In short, Miss Caldecott's story checked out.

No one had sent her to infiltrate Malden's club. The fool had come of her volition.

Malden's findings didn't mean he trusted the chit. He wasn't so doltish as to trust anyone. But he'd verified that Miss Caldecott was indeed everything he'd taken her as—lily-white and hopelessly naive.

Malden's carriage slowed, and he knew even by the slight, intricate maneuvering his driver managed, they'd returned to his club.

The servant guided the team down an alleyway wide enough to accommodate the black barouche. That narrower makeshift street opened up into a vast cobbled courtyard based around the back of his club.

Malden hastily gathered up the notes about Miss Caldecott and stuffed them inside his jacket. The moment his driver brought the team to a stop, Malden let himself out and headed for his club.

While he walked, he took everything in with pride. The outside of his empire bore the same attention to detail and extravagance as the inside. Even the pavement was expertly crafted of tricolor stones—white marble and red and black limestone.

All around him, grooms and servants rushed about, seeing to their respective work in the stables or clubs. Big, uniformed guards carried crates filled with whiskey and brandy to replace the spirits patrons had currently gone through while others hefted barrels of ale and jugs of wine.

Forbidden Pleasures had been a venture thought up and brought to life by three men.

Lucifer's Lair, however, Malden constructed of his own thoughts, money, strength, and resolve.

This was what mattered. No one. Nothing. Only *this*.

And now with Edith's help, Malden would have the sweetest revenge on his former partners.

CHAPTER 6

THE FOLLOWING NIGHT, EDITH RETURNED punctually to Lucifer's Lair.

Ushered in by the same hardened guard who'd escorted her out the night prior, she followed closely behind him.

As she walked the length of the hallway, past the men stationed at various points, Edith's skin prickled. Reflexively, she burrowed deeper into her cloak. Even with the cover the voluminous black garment provided, Edith, wearing the shameful piece the marquess insisted she don, had never felt more exposed than she did in this instant.

She found herself actually relieved when Mr. Gruffton stopped outside Lord Malden's offices and knocked once.

"Enter."

Her relief proved short-lived as the marquess's booming voice answered the guard's call.

In a show of blatant disrespect, Mr. Gruffton stepped aside so Edith could open the door. The moment she entered the guard drew the panel closed hard behind him.

Edith jumped.

A chuckle resonated from the corner of the room. *"Scared, kitten?"*

Terrified.

Edith looked to the Louis XV giltwood chase where the marquess lounged as comfortably within the upholstered folds of his seat as Satan in his inferno.

Even across the room, she caught the mocking challenge in his eyes.

Edith lifted her chin.

"I'm eager to begin, my l-lord." The slight stammer made an utter liar of her.

Another low rumbling laugh from Lord Malden said he knew it, too.

"So eager, you've already wasted," he consulted his timepiece, "one minute of your time."

His reminder of the limitations he'd placed on her compelled Edith to join him. When she reached the marquess, she hovered there.

She'd expected to be directed to the chair opposite his desk as she'd been made to do last evening. Oddly, being asked to join him on a comfortable leather button sofa proved threatening in a different, but even more dangerous way.

Without standing and bowing as any respectable gentleman would, the marquess tipped his head back and continued to stare at Edith with his usual derisive humor.

"Sit, sit," he urged, with a clearly false eagerness.

Edith eyed the sofa warily.

With the way the marquess had positioned himself, he'd ensured there was a farthest point away from him Edith could comfortably sit, without being near him.

Edith went to take one of those places next to Lord Malden.

"Your cloak, Miss Caldecott," he said, with another dark, ironical smile.

"I am comfortable as I am, my lord, but thank you for offering." To show some compliance, however, Edith pushed her hood back.

His gaze lit on her gauzy mask and heat flared in his eyes. The sight of which caused her belly to flutter.

"The cloak, Edith," he repeated. "I'd see if you are an obedient girl or whether you've defied me."

The husky quality to the marquess's latter option possessed a queer eagerness, as if he were titillated by the possibility.

What manner of man did she tangle with?

Edith carefully removed her cloak and held the taffeta article close.

Their gazes locked in a battle she knew she couldn't win.

"Lower it, Miss Caldecott," he silkily commanded.

Silently cursing him to hell, Edith threw her makeshift shield on the back of a nearby armchair.

The marquess proceeded to do a slow, methodical up-and-down search. As usual, she could make nothing out of the glint in his eyes.

"This suits you more, my dear." His voice, thick with desire, did more of those strange things to Edith's senses.

"I'm so glad you are happy." She spoke with a crisp evenness, not knowing how she managed such a feat.

The moment she'd seated herself, the marquess got right to business. "Tell me what manner of revenge you'd have upon Mr. Stillson?"

Edith didn't even have to think. "Slow and torturous." She herself had ruminated over that very question thousands of times. "Like Evie's death.

He sharpened his gaze on hers. "I thought you said hers was quick."

Did he think to trip her up? Did he believe she'd lied about even this? "I said her *illness* was quick. Have you ever watched anyone die, my lord?"

"My dear," he drawled, sounding so amused she itched to slap him, "I don't sully my hands with such tasks." His jaw flexed. "Now, if anyone sought to directly harm me, then I'd end them on the spot, but the world knows that, and it is why no one dares to cross me."

Edith studied Lord Malden. How invincible he believed himself to be, and maybe he was. Because he didn't care about anyone or anything outside of his wants, and as such, he found himself safe from actual pain and suffering.

"I'm not asking if you've killed anyone with your bare hands," she said quietly. "I'm asking if you ever *watched* a person die?"

He went mutinously silent, like a man resenting that he didn't have firsthand knowledge of that question put to him.

"Let me tell you what it is like, my lord," she said, shaking. "It is quiet. The kind of calm and still that comes when a winter storm descends over the land and chases away all sound. Nobody talks:

not servants. Not family. Everyone retreats and sits with their own worst fears."

Edith stared at Lord Malden, but his powerful form became amorphous as the past whispered forward and she became trapped in the worst days of her life.

"The air…" she continued thickly.

It had been the worst.

"It has a specific scent," she explained. "One a person has never smelled before, but so distinct that there's an inherent knowledge of what it is—the smell of death."

Her breath came so loud and fast, it filled her ears and drowned out everything—including the sound of her voice.

Still, Edith needed the irreverent Lord Malden to understand, because maybe if he did, she could reach him. Perhaps then, he'd share Edith's same desire for revenge and she wouldn't be alone in this.

"The world takes their cues from the one who is dying, my lord. They are silent and still and you keep that quiet and remain motionless."

In Edith's case, she'd rarely moved from Evie's bedside. Only when their other siblings had craved time with her had Edith reluctantly pulled herself away so as to share what she'd ultimately known were Evie's final moments.

"You unintentionally adopt every transformation occurring in their bodies—but without the same physical pain." Her throat worked. "There's pain. Sorrow so deep it's as great as the affliction that left your loved one confined to a bed. Then, it is as though the one who is dying awakens from a great slumber. They stir slowly and open their eyes, and for a brief moment?"

A ball of emotion formed in her throat, and Edith struggled to speak. "For one brief moment, you believe they've cheated death, after all, and you feel this profound…"

Edith searched her mind for a way to describe a nearly indescribable sentiment. "*Joy* unlike anything you've ever known or will know until you realize their body remains a shell that their soul merely exists within. The person you love and would give your very life for remains further away from you than had they already gone to the hereafter."

She squeezed her eyes shut. "Their body becomes like that of one who's possessed. They thrash, writhe, twist. And it is violent." Her throat worked. "And so very loud. They scream and cry until their already weak voices grow hoarse, and no further audible sounds leave their bloodless lips."

"Evie! Please, you'll hurt yourself," Edith sobbed and attempted to hold Evie's flailing form. *"I am here. I love you…I love you…"*

"And then," she whispered. "It stopped. She went quiet as she'd never been in life. She took one great, gasping breath and I thought she died in that moment, and in my arms…she was so still."

Her skin pricked and burned and blankly she pulled herself out of her telling and looked toward the silent, unexpressive gentleman before her.

From under thick, golden lashes, Lord Malden stared at Edith.

She blinked slowly; she'd forgotten his presence and that she spoke for his benefit. Somewhere along the way, Edith's telling had become jumbled between the general explanation she shared with the marquess and her own remembrances of when Evie lay dying.

And describing the last days of *Evie's* life and not some overall generalization left Edith feeling splayed open and on full display, exposed in ways that left her vulnerable.

Edith, too much a coward to hold his flinty gaze, got to her feet and put some distance between her and Lord Malden; as if in doing so, she could outrun the remainder of her telling.

"After that great fit," she continued, keeping her voice deliberately blank as his expression had been, "comes more silence and stillness. It's greater than any of the moments of quiet to come before it. You know the end is near. You know you are not strong enough to slay the reaper. He's intent on claiming the person you most love. So instead? Instead, you beg *God* to save them. Everything you've learned about the Lord and Savior is that he is all-powerful. He can move mountains. Walk on water. So, you barter with the benevolent, loving *Creator*." She didn't bother to try and suppress her bitterness and mockery.

"But death comes anyway," she said, tears clogged her throat and added a thick, husky quality to her telling. "And when it happens, it comes not with a scream or a cry or tears, but a whisper of breath and then…nothing."

Evie! Evie! Eeeeeevie! Wails and screams and shouts and sobs of yesteryear reverberated inside her head; each Caldecott's varying expression of grief woven together into a single article of profound sorrow.

Blindly, she felt around for some purchase, something with which to keep herself upright. Her fingers collided with cool, hard wood, and she grappled with the back of what felt like a chair.

Please, please, please, Evie. Evie. Don't. You can't.

Edith squeezed her eyes shut. Only, she had.

"She was so still in death," she whispered, her voice distant in her own ears. "Yet strangely, eerily even more beautiful in her eternal rest than she'd been in her life."

I cannot live without you… Please, stay. Stay with me. Edith's pleas of then echoed around the chambers of her mind now.

The veil of black danced at the corners of her vision.

No!

She dug her fingers into her temples.

Not like this. Not here. Not now. Not with this man who'd deride Edith for her weakness and decline to help her further for her lack of self-control that bordered on madness.

She gripped the solid surface, curling her fingers into the only thing coming between her and falling flat on her face.

"Miss Caldecott?"

Lord Malden's voice came as if down a long, dark tunnel.

"Edith. *Edith.*"

Edith. He'd called her…Edith. Why was he calling her by her given name? She told her brain to tell her lips to make words. To tell him she far preferred the sound of it to the formality he insisted on between them.

"And that is why…" Edith's voice emerged in a garbled slur. "I will have revenge. That is why I will see him pay for what he did."

Then, the demons, as they invariably did, won out.

Edith's hold slackened. She slumped forward and remembered no more.

CHAPTER 7

Cursing roundly, Malden caught the lady before she hit the floor, and swept her into his arms.

"Fainting," he muttered as he carried her limp form over to the chaise. "God spare me from fainting women. As you can probably gather, I despise the wilting sort, Edith."

Glaring, he set her down upon the recamier. "You'd have to be conscious to detect my annoyance."

He fisted and unfisted his hands at his side.

In limp repose, with her slender legs angled in opposite directions, she lay as awkward as a child's abandoned doll.

Between her unnaturally white pallor and listless features made all the starker against the black velvet fabric, Edith personified the imagery she'd painted of a dying woman.

With another black curse, he gently rearranged her graceful limbs, so they were no longer distorted.

Malden seated himself at the very edge of the chaise. "I'll have you know I didn't want these details about you and your sister, Edith," he said curtly.

The details and stories surrounding her life, the things only she knew, didn't matter to him.

Having been born to a bastard of a brutal duke, Malden had made it a point to not involve himself in anything that dealt with the emotions of people around him—that was aside from his two boyhood friends. Those same friends who'd ultimately betrayed him and cast him out.

No, allowing emotion to dominate one's self only left a person weak.

Now, in hearing Edith speak, he found himself compelled, not only by her telling, but the depth of her resolve in seeking retribution—no matter she labored under a delusion. In her large, tragic eyes, he'd bore witness to a depth of pain and sorrow and suffering, the likes of which he'd neither witnessed nor known, nor even believed in—until now. Until her.

That demonstrative showing of emotion ought to repulse him. He should be raring to toss her out on her small, pear-shaped buttocks because he didn't have dealings with creatures ruled by their *feelings*.

And yet…Malden found himself alternately repulsed and inextricably fascinated by her.

Perhaps it was because he'd never witnessed a woman—or for that matter, *anyone*—so candid as to share all their thoughts and weaknesses. The people he dealt with grieved over the loss of fortunes, lands, bad wagers, card matches; never, however, were they moved to tears and a faint by the loss of a person. To do so, they'd have to care about someone other than themselves, and that was simply not the way of the world.

No, lords and ladies—same as Malden—were invariably greedy, self-serving sorts.

He contemplated her.

Edith, with her candor, courage, and this complex ability to love, proved the same as a unicorn or fairy—creatures Malden had previously only taken as mythical beings. But now, the lady's presence proved things he'd taken as fanciful—love and devotion of others—were very much, factual.

The virtually world-shaking discovery left him unnerved.

She unnerved him.

And no one unnerved him. No man, and *certainly* not a woman.

This waif-thin lady, however, was like a complex puzzle whose parts he might be compelled to assemble just so he could understand this new breed of person he'd never before met.

Either way, the novelty of her and her curious ability to care for and love someone other than herself was a distraction he certainly did not need. What he did require, on the other hand, was to get on with their arrangement. She had a man to see dead. He had a debutante to seduce. The last thing he needed was an innocent lady about, befuddling him and presenting a shade of grey into a world comprised of only black and white.

Malden lightly tapped her clammy cheek. "Miss Caldecott. Edith," he said, this time more insistently. "Arise and shine."

Her extraordinarily long brown lashes didn't so much as flutter.

He opened his mouth to call to her, louder this time, but then froze; his gaze locked on her face.

Funny, he'd spent so much time being annoyed with Edith Caldecott he'd failed to note she really was quite—and much, surprisingly—*lovely*. Her small, delicate nose came to a slight point in perfect symmetry and alignment with her daintily pointed chin. She bore a dusting of freckles upon her high, fragile cheekbones, both of which had *also* gone unnoticed until now. Her crimson red lips, slightly slack from her swoon, formed a perfect cupid's bow and fair begged for a man's mouth and attentions.

She'd kissed like an innocent, too. At first.

Lust fired in his blood as he recalled their last night's meeting.

He'd never had a virgin and had never been the caddish sort who harbored a fascination with seducing them. Now, transfixed by Edith's lush lips, he recalled having that mouth under his. Her timid movements, which had become bolder as he'd deepened that embrace, had been proof clearer than any maidenhead of her innocence. And for the first time in his life, he understood all too well why the gentlemen below lined up to partake in a make-believe auction of virgins.

What the hell is wrong with me?

He gave his head a disgusted shake.

Lusting after a virgin in full swoon? He was in desperate need of a good fuck. There was no other accounting for his fascination with the innocent miss, unconscious beside him.

Scowling—this time with himself—Malden straightened and headed for his well-stocked sideboard.

He swiped a silver-plated decanter and glass and carried them both back to Edith.

"I trust you are not one for spirits," he said loudly.

Another mark against her. Not that there need be any further ones.

Malden yanked the stopper off with his teeth and spit the crystal cork onto the crimson carpet. He proceeded to splash several fingerfuls into the glass and then, sitting beside her once more, he slid an arm under her shoulders and guided her into an upright position.

Malden waved the fruity contents of this particular bottle under her nose. That adorable appendage scrunched ever so slightly.

Still, she remained in full faint.

"Arise and shine, love," he said softly.

Oddly, this time, Malden's quiet murmuring, and not his previous shouts, penetrated the that fold of darkness she found herself wrapped in.

Edith's thick lashes fluttered ever so slightly, and then like Giambattista Basile's very own Princess Talia, she awakened from her deep sleep.

She managed to open her eyes. And not unlike his discovery before, up close as they were, he noted her eyes were not purely brown, but rather a hazel comprised of brown with specks of gold, amber, and green.

Confusion clouded those luminous irises, as her foggy gaze took in the room, and then Malden.

He flashed a mocking half-grin. "Good morning, sweeting. Have you enjoyed your rest?"

Edith blinked wildly, and then her eyes flared impossibly wide, and Malden knew the moment she registered exactly who held her.

With a gasp, she struggled away from him.

"Worry not, love," he drawled. "The last thing I have in mind is your seduction."

That droll pronouncement managed to send much-needed color to her wan cheeks but did not quell her squirming.

Did she want to hurt herself? Good. Let her. Why should he care? He didn't. He should let her, but God rot his already black soul for somehow wanting to prevent her from doing so.

It is only because if she again faints on you, the longer you'll be made to suffer her company, and they'd not even gotten on with their business.

Edith pushed her shoulder against his and attempted to leverage herself away from him.

This was really enough.

"I assure you for all the iniquitous proclivities I *do* enjoy, rape is not among them, my dear.

"Now," he said through gritted teeth, "unless you want to hit the floor this time, might I suggest you not fight me as if I'm assaulting you?"

Edith ceased her struggles but continued to watch him with deservedly wary eyes.

Clever girl. Or at least, sometimes, anyway.

He grunted. "Drink."

She eyed his offering dubiously. "I don't drink claret."

"Absolutely *shocking*," he drawled. "My apologies, I do not have tepid *lemonade* to rouse you."

Four little lines furrowed her brow in a display of her confusion. "Tepid lemonade wouldn't rouse a person."

"Precisely." He pressed the glass at her. "Now, drink."

She didn't. "I—"

"I know," he said tersely. "You don't indulge in claret. You're making an exception."

God, she vexed him as no other.

She shook her head. "That's not what I was going to say, my lord."

"It doesn't matter what you were going to—"

"I was going to clarify," she accepted the spirits, "I don't drink claret, *regularly*," she added. "Only on occasion."

He smirked. "Ah, should I fetch you a brandy, then?"

"A whiskey, please, my lord."

She expected *him* to believe she indulged in whiskey?

"Never tell me," he drawled. "You enjoy a glass during a rousing game of whist?"

"I'd hardly describe whist as a rousing, high-stakes game, my lord."

She gave him a peculiar look. "In fact, I'd expect a scandalous, wicked gaming hell owner to have a greater idea of what constitutes a high-stakes game," she said, a wealth of disappointment in words that emerged as if her ruminations were intended only for her ears.

His growl of annoyance was lost as she continued prattling on.

"I enjoy having a whiskey during a round of hazard or Vignt-et-un *and* when I'm playing billiards."

"No doubt you smoke a cheroot, too," he said dryly.

"A *cheroot? During billiards?*" she continued with a like incredulity. "However would a person properly play a game with a cheroot in one hand and a snifter in the other?"

She looked at him as if he'd gone mad. Because she apparently couldn't recognize sarcasm had it been the only thing hanging in her wardrobe to wear.

Edith gave her head a shake. "I don't take my cheroots *during* billiards." She flashed a cheeky smile. "Only afterward once I've trounced the other player."

Her admission conjured an image of the young lady in a dimly lit billiards room and celebrating her big win with a smoke and snifter of fine French brandy; the image so ludicrous, so improbable, Malden barked with laughter.

The sound emerged rusty and hoarse from little to no use, and so rare he barely recognized it.

In fact, he couldn't call forth a time when he had done so. With the harsh childhood he'd known under the duke's thumb and even harsher go he'd had of it in school before DuMond championed him, there'd never been reasons to laugh. It felt odd and strange and yet…he couldn't suppress that levity.

Edith's expressive eyes reflected his own shock.

Good God. Her madness was contagious.

He buried the rest of that unexpected mirth in a sneer. "If you're going to spin fanciful yarns, you'd do well to strive for some believability. You are a terrible liar, Edith Caldecott."

"Yes, I am." Something flickered in her eyes, a flash of fear, perhaps? It was gone too quick for Malden to identify.

Edith's smile faded and she glanced down and their previous absurd exchange turned serious, once more.

"Sip, you sometimes whiskey, always brandy drinker," he said brusquely.

A frown played on the corners of her sweet, curved lips. "I'm not a lia—"

"Take a sip," he snapped.

Edith jumped and that quick jerk of her body sent amber

droplets splashing over the edge. With an impressively withering scowl, the lady raised that glass to her mouth he'd spent entirely too long ogling, and—drank.

And continued drinking; the long, graceful arch of her neck slid rhythmically, as she downed the contents of her snifter with all the ease of a drunken sailor.

Malden's eyes widened and this time, he made no effort to hide his surprise. My God. He'd never believed in love and never would. But if he were one of those fanciful, romantic fellows, falling for an innocent miss who guzzled spirits like a sailor would be the manner of woman he'd lose his heart to.

Edith finished quickly and then held over the empty glass. "Is that good, Lord Malden?" Her eyes sparkled with amusement. "Or do you require I *sip* another glass?"

Her and her tart-mouthed response. No one spoke to him so. That transgression alone should rouse his fury. Instead, his gaze lingered on her mouth for altogether different reasons—salacious ones.

Her lips glistened and gleamed with the remnants of whiskey. Malden was consumed with a savage hunger to suck on that plump flesh until he was drunk off both the spirits and the taste of her.

An imp's smile teased her lips, tormented him. "Nothing to say, my lord?" she bantered.

God, she really was pure as the driven snow. She had absolutely no idea he was rock hard and lusting after her.

"You don't want to know what I'm thinking, Edith," he said on a silky whisper that managed to effectively freeze her innocent smile.

He dared her with his eyes to be brave enough to say the words he wanted her to say.

"Yes, I do," she said softly.

Her impertinence he'd initially loathed, but her intrepidness now fueled his blood. Everyone saw him as one to cower from or bend to. And that this proper, virginal miss should meet him head-on at every turn fueled his lust. It put him in mind of a savage king of the jungle who'd found a worthy mate, and then, with his body, marked her as his.

"I'm thinking about how I'd love to avail myself of your mouth," he said huskily. "How I want to lick and nip that delectable flesh until you're moaning, and then I'll slip my tongue inside as I did yesterday."

Edith's eyes went wide and those lips he now sang praise to parted in a moue of surprise. "Oh," she said weakly.

Malden continued, delighting in scandalizing her with the wicked image he painted for her. "And then, after I drank my fill out of you, I'd kiss you elsewhere." He placed his lips near hers. "Do you want to know where, dear Edith?" he tantalized. "Do you want me to show you?"

Her chest rose and fell in harsh inhalations and exhalations. She offered no words this time, but rather a juddery nod as her confirmation.

And he knew then, this acquiescence had nothing to do with any contest between them and everything to do with her want of him.

Malden, however, would have more than a bob of her head. He'd have her tell him plainly and clearly what she wanted. "If you really want that," he taunted, "then give me the words, Edith."

"I want you to show me where you'd kiss me." Her timorous voice emerged so very faint and husked with desire.

Malden pressed a palm between her legs. The fabric of her skirts crunched noisily in a hedonistic rustle. "I'd kiss you here," he said harshly, and through the thin fabric of her satin dress, he rubbed her in that spot, and in a way he knew she'd love.

Desire clouded her eyes and she bit at her lower lip.

He continued to stroke her until a little whimper she tried to conceal slipped past her lips.

Her hips lifted slightly.

For that unashamed showing, Malden rewarded Edith with more petting.

"And then, Edith, after you came, I'd have you take me between your beautiful lips and suck me until I spill myself down your throat." His voice grew raspy, and he, who'd set out to entice, found himself entrapped in the visual he painted for her.

A little shudder wracked her delicate frame and her eyes slid shut. "No."

Lost in her, his every sense clouded with desire, it was a moment before Malden registered that unfamiliar word, never spoken by a single one of the wantons he'd bedded.

His brows shot up. "*No?*"

"No," she said, her voice entirely too steady for his liking. Not when his body trembled still with an insatiable, inexplicable hungering for her.

Malden gritted his teeth.

"I cannot allow liberties with a man whose Christian name I do not have possession of or permission to use," she said with the piousness of a nun.

His nostrils flared as another wave of lust shot through him.

That is what she wanted?

Did she take him for one of those fellows who protected his given name? To Malden, it was nothing more than one assigned him at birth by his now dying sire. As such, he'd happily tender the damned thing for the pleasure of fucking her.

He grunted. "Edward."

Malden reached for her, but she drew back slightly, contemplating him.

"Edward," she repeated, as if tasting the sound and feel of it on her lips.

Her voice, husky with desire and softly lilting, wrapped around those two syllables, and never before—until now—had the sound of his name spoken in the throes of passion roused him to such a level of hungering.

Granted, no woman had spoken it because he'd not given them leave to do so. Neither had they asked. Only, this woman had.

With an animalistic growl, Edward drew Edith atop his lap and arranged her so that her legs were draped on either side of him, and her skirts climbed mid-thigh. Cupping her buttocks, he pressed her core against his rock-hard shaft and slowly rocked himself against her.

Her body tensed and her eyes closed just as tightly, in a clear sign of a woman who clearly warred with herself.

"Shy all of a sudden, sweeting?" he whispered.

She bit her lower lip. "It is wrong."

He nuzzled at her neck. "Why?"

"Because…good ladies do not go about doing naughty things with men who aren't their husbands."

"Good ladies are vastly overrated," he said, sucking on the shell of her ear.

A little moan spilled from her lips.

His breath came harsher. "For that matter, good ladies also don't go about having men killed, as such, you needn't trouble yourself with false demureness."

He'd said the wrong thing. He knew it the moment the taunting words left his mouth. Her previously pliable, soft body went instantly taut in his arms.

Edith struggled away from him.

She needn't have bothered. He'd already gathered their fun was at an end.

Malden sighed, and, in one fluid motion, caught Edith around the waist and set her on her feet. Bloody hell, she was going to leave him with an erection that would not quit.

"How dare you make light of me, Edward?" she asked, her voice a cross between hurt and anger.

He allowed the lady her pique. This modesty and indignation was precisely why he didn't bother with virgins. In the future, he'd do well to remember that vital detail. Reclining on the chaise, Malden spread his feet wide, and let his legs fall open in lazy repose.

"I didn't give you permission to use my name when you're in a temper, sweet," he said dryly.

"All of this is a game to you," she whispered, her eyes flashing fury.

His earlier fun at an end, Malden fixed a hard stare upon her.

"There are no games in life, Edith," he warned in cool tones.

"What we did just now, Edward? It was a mistake."

"I'd say it's the only right thing you've done since coming to me, sweet."

Color flooded her cheeks. "You are a reprehensible, horrid—"

The rest of her insult ended on a gasp.

Malden jumped to his feet and caught her by the wrist.

"Let us be clear, madam, I've *tolerated* your virginal indignation, but going forward, I will not be so magnanimous," he whispered.

"No one," he tightened his grip in a hold meant to warn but not punish, "absolutely no one questions me or my intelligence. Is that clear, madam?"

Edith gave a short, choppy nod.

Malden released her.

She rushed to the other side of the chaise so that the chair offered a barrier between them.

Malden allowed the lady that illusion of control.

The lady laid her palm protectively over the place where he'd snatched her. She stared at him with troubled eyes.

He frowned.

The sight of her transformation from intrepid minx to affrighted miss let loose an unfamiliar swirl of emotions in his chest. Malden didn't care *who* he terrorized. In fact, ordinarily, he found people's fear of him exhilarating.

This time, however, with this woman, it didn't feel at all satisfying. He couldn't give it a name as he'd never before felt the way he did at this precise moment.

The sooner he was done with her, the better he'd be.

Malden stalked over to his desk and dragged out his chair.

As he sat, he didn't bother to mask his impatience. "What do you want, Miss Caldecott?"

She darted the tip of her tongue out, traced those lips still swollen from his kiss, and effectively pulled his attention back to their lascivious exchange from moments ago.

He narrowed his eyes.

Were he not a master of judging people, he'd have taken that slight movement as one meant to entice, seduce. With this one, however, he recognized that habit as a telltale sign of her unease.

"Miss Caldecott?" he barked.

That drove the lady into movement. She hastened over, and then made to seat herself.

"Did I give you permission to sit?" he asked with deliberate slowness and quiet.

Her fingers froze upon the back of the mahogany chair. Other than that tensing of her hand, she gave no outward reaction to his effrontery.

Leaning back in his seat, Malden steepled his fingers together and stared over the tops of them at a silent Edith. "This won't be long."

She inclined her head.

"Now," he began and, fiddling with the roll lock, he dialed the numbers. "What fate do you have in mind for Mr. Stillson?"

Click. He fished a journal from within his second drawer and opened the book.

As he collected a pen and had it poised over a clean page, he registered Edith's silence.

Malden glanced up and found her looking at him through wide, unblinking eyes.

He sent an eyebrow arcing up. "Is there a problem?"

Edith gave her head a hesitant shake and that back-and-forth bob evolved into a nod.

"And?" he snapped when she didn't explain.

"It is just," she said softly. "I didn't think it would be like this."

He furrowed his brow.

"All of this," she clarified. "It is as though you were creating a shopping list for Cook."

Ah.

Malden joined his hands and laid them upon the unsullied page.

"What did you think it would be like, Miss Caldecott?" he asked, all too happy for her to see his amusement.

"I…" She turned her palms up. "I don't know. Just…I…" The lady drew in a deep breath and tried again, this time to greater success. "I suppose I didn't really consider *how* exchanges such as these go."

Mm, second thoughts. They'd come far later than he'd expected.

He knew beyond a shadow of a doubt he could horrify her enough to have her alter her course for Mr. Stillson. He also knew, however, that in doing so, it would sever his link to the innocent lady with a link to another innocent lady; the latter being Lady Violet, whom he'd have for his wife—and revenge and greater prosperity and power.

Oh, he'd no doubts he could find other ways to meet Lady Violet and wheedle his way into her affections, but he also knew it would make the task of ruining DuMond's sister-in-law longer and more complicated.

"It is not too late, you know," he murmured, this time in the gentle tones he'd learned had a calming effect upon her. He gestured to the chair he'd earlier denied her. "Please, sit," he continued in that soothing manner he'd only ever been able to manage for his mount.

He saw the tension leave her shoulders and a softness return to her face.

Wordlessly, she availed herself to a seat.

"If you wish to end your plans for Mr. Stillson," he said quietly, "I will not blame you. I'll understand. This way of life, Edith," he appropriated her name once more as a way to further slip past her defenses, "my life and the art of revenge and ruination is complicated and ugly."

And were also the reasons he reveled in his existence.

"You are not made for this. Not because I don't believe you are afraid or weak or that you don't want and deserve revenge for your sister's murder," he continued softly. "But if you're so fixed on avenging her, then you cannot truly live, and your sister would not want that."

Her eyes grew stricken and her face went white.

"That is what Evie said," she whispered.

He looked at her, confused. "Evie?" he repeated. "As in, your *dead* sister?

Like she'd only just recalled his presence, Edith blinked slowly and then stared at Malden.

"I…" She shook her head. "Before she passed, I mean."

"Your sister is right, Edith," he said, with a false tenderness meant to further ensure her trust in him.

"I told her I would." Edith clasped her hands as if in prayer and bowed her head over them. "But I lied. It was one of the last things I was able to say to her, and it was a lie, Edward."

Bloody hell. Perhaps he'd gone too far.

When Edith, at last, lifted her head and met his eyes squarely, the hurt, sorrow, pain, and regret that had previously filled their depths had turned glacial and hard.

"He deserves to pay, Edward," she said, with an icy cold he'd not believed her capable of. "And I'll see him pay. I want you to bankrupt him. I want you to destroy his business, claim all the money he's ever made so he has nothing but fear of debtor's prison."

"And what will we do with these funds?"

The lady chewed at her lower lip a moment. Her eyes lit. "We can give the money to Evie's nieces so someday they have guaranteed security other than—"

He snorted. "That hardly seems like fair repayment, love."

She frowned. "*You* want them?"

"I deserve them."

"And you are in desperate need of funds?" she snapped.

Malden smirked. "There's no limit to the amount of wealth and power a man can amass."

"I beg to differ but will not debate the point. My repayment is helping coordinate your meetings with Lady Violet," she astutely pointed out.

"And after I've destroyed him financially, Edith?"

"You'll have him killed."

CHAPTER 8

HE TAMPED DOWN HIS SURPRISE. How icily, how matter-of-factly, she spoke of murder. Even with the request she'd come to him with, he'd not believed her capable of this level of ruthlessness, and that juxtaposition between evil and the purity of her spirit and self enflamed him.

"Do you have a preference for how Mr. Stillson meets his end?"

She worried at her lower lip. "I've…not much experience with the options, other than poisoning."

"Poisoning is sloppy. It requires too many people involved. One has to infiltrate a household, and slip past servants, repeatedly. There's too much room for error. I can, however, decide and handle this particular piece of your plan on my own," he offered that gently so as to not raise her defenses.

Edith nodded slowly. "I would appreciate that, Edward."

Malden inclined his head and stood. Edith took his cue and jumped to her feet.

"I venture we are done…for now, Edith."

Only when she'd collected her cloak, donned it, and began to lift her hood did Malden speak.

"Before you take your leave, when do you plan to coordinate my first clandestine meeting with Lady Violet?"

She froze with that hood halfway in its place. "I'd thought…I'd expected…"

He sharpened his gaze on her face. "Yes?"

Edith angled her head at an almost shy little angle. "I'd thought we would focus first on my assignment and then put all our energies into yours, Edward."

Edward flashed a grin. "My dear, I assure you, I'm quite adept at carrying out multiple deceptions and treacheries at once."

Worry tightened her features.

Good. It would do well for her to be reminded at points that he was a man not to be crossed or questioned.

He flattened his lips, crushing his previous smile. "When?"

"I…what of, not this morning but this coming Thursday? As I want to be sure I allow myself enough time to coordinate an outing."

Malden nodded. "That will suffice. Where?"

"I…" Edith paused and appeared to rack her head. Suddenly, she stilled.

An idea glimmered to life in those revealing irises of hers. "Of course," she whispered. "What of Hyde Park?" she exclaimed. "Lady Violet and I, we adore disappearing into a copse at the earliest morn hours, when few are about and discarding our stockings and boots and running barefoot through the water."

Her eyes sparkled and excitement spilled into her every word. The more she spoke, the more animated she became, and the more Malden found him pulled under the most quixotic spell with thoughts of her, with her shapely lower limbs bare as she splashed about like a child.

"Then after, when the sun climbs higher and visitors to the park begin to arrive, we sit on the edge of the shore and let the warm sun dry us."

Once more, she, like a master artist with a glorious stroke of his brush, painted a tableau of things so very foreign to him.

"And then," her gaze drew in that inward way he'd come to recognize came whenever she found herself lost in both her happiest and saddest thoughts, and now, her most wistful ones, "we toss stones. We love to skip them and see who can manage the most jumps before the rock disappears under the surface."

Her expression grew solemn and sad; all her earlier animation and joy gone.

Malden balled his hands at his side. He *despised* that metamorphosis; loathed it with every fiber of her being. For the sole reason, he didn't have patience or time for the self-pitying sorts. That was why. That was absolutely the *only* reason why.

"Thursday, then," he said harshly, determined to snap her out of that state.

Edith started and looked at him in confusion.

"Hyde Park, the perfect trysting location," he murmured, more than satisfied at the lady's suggestion and habit of frequenting a park, alone.

A troubled glimmer sparked in her eyes. God, she was so transparent.

"You…can't ruin her with *me* about," she whispered, horror wreathed her tone.

"Of course not," he scoffed. "Neither do I intend to merely trap her." He intended to trick her which required a short, ardent secret courtship on his part.

He grinned. That would make the lady's ruin and her family's fury and sorrow all the sweeter.

"We are done here, Edith," he said.

As it was, he'd spent entirely too much time with her. None of their exchanges need be long.

This time, when Edith brought her hood into place, he allowed her to do so without interruption. When she was done, however, she continued to linger there, like one who was reluctant to leave, which was impossible, given who Malden was.

A moment later, she bowed her head and made for the door. Without so much as a whisper of parting, the lady let herself out—and then, was gone.

The moment the panel closed with a click behind her, Malden went and fetched the decanter of whiskey and lady's empty snifter. Pouring himself a glass as he walked, Malden headed over to the impenetrable black velvet curtains that merely existed for show and drew the fabric back.

The same clever mirrored window he'd had specially designed and installed over the casino floors, had also been outfitted in all the rooms which overlooked Bond Street.

As he sipped his whiskey, he skimmed his gaze over the darkened streets and searched for a sign of the lady's conveyance waiting for her to make her exit.

Malden identified a hired carriage some twenty yards from the club. Given the driver's drab greatcoat with a superfluity of capes, and horses that were not of bloodstock, the lady had traveled not with a hackney coachman but rather an inferior jarvie.

Malden scowled. What manner of lady set out on her own, rented a blasted jarvie, and didn't spend coin on the more respectable and efficient mode of travel?

Edith Caldecott did. That was who.

The bloody twit. Was she trying to get herself discovered, raped, killed, or all of the above?

He clenched his teeth so tight, they grated noisily.

Not that he cared, either way. Her business was her business. Her mistakes were hers.

If something were to happen to her, Malden was a man of many sources and resources. He would simply find another means to get closer to Lady Violet. Reminding himself of that, he intently studied that carriage and the general area around it, searching for a hint that someone had accompanied her.

Even though she'd proven naively transparent and embarrassingly forthright, Malden possessed neither of those unfortunate traits. As such, despite the investigator he'd hired and the research he'd discovered about Miss Edith Caldecott, Malden still searched for signs that she worked with another. That reason and that reason alone accounted for his intent to wait for the lady's appearance.

Still surveying the cobblestones below for a sign of her and any potential threat out there, he took another drink.

Malden recalled the last person to place their lips upon the rim of the crystal snifter.

"Is that good, Lord Malden? Or do you require I sip another glass?"

Edith's saucy response raised a relaxed half-grin that he'd deny to his dying day. A unicorn or fairy, indeed. Or maybe a sorceress, because she had him thinking of her and lusting for her when he'd never before wanted anything less than the most skilled Cyprian.

A moment later, the lady appeared.

Malden instantly went on alert. She paused on the sidewalk about Malden's clubs, and as if she knew she was being watched, as if she sensed Malden there, she stiffened.

Her hood shifted slightly in an indication she did a search for any possible foe. Then, Edith, like she was on a damned jaunt through Hyde Park with a maid, footman, and friend about, made for the rented hack.

He grated his jaw. The damned fool. Didn't she have a jot of sense to not look for enemies in the shadows, but instead get herself to safety as quickly as her legs could carry her?

Except, he already knew the answer to that.

At last, after her leisurely stroll, Edith reached her rented carriage. A lanky fellow with a shock of red hair under a tattered cap climbed down, opened the door, and reached his palm out to help her up.

Edith, with more of her customary artlessness, laid her fingers in the jarvie's. The fellow immediately folded one of his palms around hers, and the other he slipped around her waist.

A feral growl started in Malden's chest and got stuck in his throat.

How dare the other man touch her in that familiar way. It didn't matter the fellow was the most common of drivers or that Malden had never been the possessive sort where women were concerned. There were enough to go around, and Malden invariably had his pick of them.

This time, however, this woman, proved different.

Her untried body and his hungering to taint that innocence with his own depravity left him afire and made him want to burn to ashes anyone who dared encroach upon her.

The driver said something. Even with the distance between them, Malden detected the way Edith's shoulders shook with amusement.

"Why not join the fellow for tea and biscuits while you're at it?" he growled. "Am I going to have to accompany you like I'm some goddamned nursemaid?"

The thought should rouse annoyance, instead, it conjured thoughts of him and Edith, alone in a carriage; she astride his lap and her skirts high about her waist as she rode him. Her body moving up and down upon him, in time to the rhythmic bouncing of the carriage.

The driver finally handed the lady inside.

As though she felt Malden watching her and knew the lewd thoughts he had of her even now, Edith paused and glanced swiftly back. That quick movement sent her hood tumbling back a fraction and left her face on full display.

If there'd been any doubt the lady didn't have a duplicitous bone in her body, that carelessness there put all of them to rest. Exasperated, Malden tossed back the rest of his drink.

She scoured the streets with her gaze and raised that searching stare higher…all the way up to Malden's office windows. She went still and remained with her eyes locked on the thick glass barrier between them.

Malden stilled. For a moment, he thought she could see him, which was preposterous, given that pretend window could not be penetrated by any voyeur.

Again, Edith made as if to leave, and then stopped.

He narrowed his eyes on her. "It's decided, you twit," he mumbled under his breath. "You are going to find yourself in all manner of trouble."

Like she'd heard that prediction and found it the greatest of jests, an impish smile teased at her cupid's bow lips. Then, angling her head the tiniest bit so the right side of her profile was displayed to Malden, she winked his way.

He narrowed his eyes. The minx. She *did* know he studied her every move.

After giving Malden a quick, cheery little wave, she disappeared inside the carriage. The jarvie glanced confusedly about, no doubt in search of the mystery person behind Edith's wave. Finding none, the driver gave his head a shake, pushed the door shut behind the lady, and returned to his box.

The moment he did, the burlap sack which had been repurposed as a makeshift curtain parted. Edith pressed her forehead to the glass window and again, grinned.

"Enough," he mouthed, over-enunciating each syllable, even as he knew she couldn't see him.

As if she could though, her smile faded, and her delicate nose scrunched up. Then, like a naughty girl, she stuck her tongue out.

His eyebrows flared.

That insolence, that ability to think she could jest with him. No one ever had.

Malden stared after the slow-moving conveyance until it'd

faded to a distant dot on the horizon. It appeared the lady needed another—but different—warning. If she intended to play a wayward child, she could expect the spanking that would go with it.

His cock, still hard from unsated lust, twitched. Perhaps his accompanying her home after their meetings would not be so terrible, after all.

In fact, a carriage ride alone with Edith Caldecott might prove *quite* diverting.

CHAPTER 9

On Thursday morn, with darkness lingering on the morning sky and the orb of the sun struggling to make its climb, Edith made her way through the peacefully quiet grounds of Hyde Park.

The night's chill still had a slight hold upon the earth and Edith burrowed deeper into the folds of her cloak to find whatever warmth she could.

It did little to help.

Perhaps that is because it's not the cold that plagues you, but the impending meeting with Edward.

Edward who would be expecting to have his first meeting with Lady Violet but would instead only find Edith waiting for him. And then what would she do? And what would she say?

She'd not thought this through.

In fairness, when she'd hastily crafted the idea of a pretend friendship with Lady Violet Brookfield, Edith had believed her portion of the bargain would be made in repayment *after* hers was fulfilled.

She should have known better.

As if Edward would put anyone's wants or intentions before anyone else's.

Edith reached the wooded copse that some years back had become a place of solace and peace. This had been she and her sisters' private playground. With Evie, they'd frolicked here and danced about and tossed rocks and talked about their futures and dreamed about their sweethearts.

Edith hovered there outside the small path that led to the lake on the other side. Several old oaks flanked the makeshift entrance to the quiet, tucked-away setting. Never before had she hesitated on the fringe as she did now. Rather, she was always eager to step inside and allow the trees to swallow her up so she could sit alone, with just her thoughts and reflections for company.

When inside these woods, the world couldn't see her or gawk or whisper about the poor Caldecott girl—as if those people actually cared about the Caldecotts. As if Edith and her surviving family were something more than a curiosity to be examined like they were caged animals in the London Menagerie.

Edith had never revealed the existence of her copse with anyone and never intended to. When she was nestled inside, it was where she felt Evie's presence most.

This time, however, was different. When she stepped inside this day, there'd be a living someone and not mere memories to join her here. For now, she'd invited Edward into this part of her world, and she felt knotted up inside for it.

Last time she'd met with Edward, Edith had been caught up in some moment she still didn't quite wholly understand. For reasons unknown, she'd been consumed by a longing to share the little paradise where she'd used to play and live joyously and freely *with* Edward.

From the nearby lake, a collection of little egrets snorted and squawked at Edith for the liar she was. She briefly closed her eyes. Tucked away as it was, the woods here offered safety and security. But she had not been thinking to plot and scheme here.

No, she knew why she'd suggested this place for her and Edward's meeting.

Edith, in a brash moment of madness, had wanted to share her sanctuary with the jaded, ruthless marquess. She'd wanted him to experience a parcel of earth unknown by man and not corrupted by a material world's influence. Something untainted. She'd wished to offer him a taste of something decent and wholesome that didn't need the strappings of gold and silver to provide a person succor.

No person was born heartless and cold. They became that way; the innocence of their souls altered because of people or traumas that had befallen them.

Edith knew that firsthand.

And when she should be thinking only about avenging Evie and bringing down Mr. Stillson, Edith found herself consumed by thoughts of Edward, the Marquess of Malden.

What had made him so iron-hearted as to think nothing of having a man killed on behalf of another, to advance his alternate goals?

Why, when that should repulse, did it only further intrigue Edith? Why, when he said and did the most lascivious things, did she yearn for his touch and dream of him at night?

In those dreams, there lived none of the fear that should haunt her in the waking and sleeping. There existed only remembrances of his hands as he'd moved them over her or his mouth as he'd kissed her, until she awakened frustrated and aching in that place between her legs he'd rubbed through her gown.

On the other hand, it was certain a man of Edward's appetites and constitution hadn't given her one thought. In fact, he'd likely bedded any number of women in the mere two days they'd been apart.

Such a man wouldn't appreciate this wooded paradise. Likely, he'd sneer and find it uncivilized and resent having muddied his fine, leather boots.

Now, she felt as though she'd come to meet him, naked and afraid.

It doesn't matter if he doesn't like this place. What is important you love this place, Edith. If he is too blind to see and be healed in parts of his soul by the grandeur of it, then he is the one who has lost. She told herself that and wanted to believe it.

But she *did* care.

She'd not had a friend in so long—not that she'd ever call a man like Edward 'friend'—it was just, aside from her surviving siblings and parents, she'd not let anyone into her life, in any way.

"Enough," she mouthed.

Her shoulders straightened with resolve and, taking in a steadying breath, she entered the copse. Immediately, the green leaves of the May trees in full flower and the lighter green leaflets of the common ash blanketed her.

The faintest morning breeze stirred the dense, rich foliage and set them fluttering and swaying in different directions. As they parted and closed, those trees granted the light of the moon, still in the sky, partial entry of the copse. And just like that, the uncertainty and doubt about her decision to bring Edward here began to fade. As did thoughts of revenge and death and danger.

Edith closed her eyes and took in the sounds of nature: the frogs that croaked from their lily pads. The lone high-pitched chirp of a Bar-tailed Godwit which blended with a symphony made by crickets.

She filled her lungs with the scents of this hideaway. The fresh, crisp aroma of spring's new leaves muted the smell of last autumn's now decomposing ones. The traces of soil and dirt in the air conjured thoughts of the days Edith and her sisters spent gardening with their mother.

And those memories, along with the calming effect of this place of refuge, banished the last of her worrying.

CHAPTER 10

MALDEN DIDN'T KNOW HOW LONG it had been since he'd arrived at his and Edith's meeting place. It'd all become confused the moment he'd entered the quiet copse and found her standing there with her head tipped back, her eyes closed, her features relaxed, and her mouth curled in a soft smile. She had the look of an enchanting fey fairy he'd stumbled upon in her previously private, untouched fairyland.

So bewildered, bothered, and bewitched by the sight of her, Malden couldn't even workup a proper annoyance and disgust with himself.

Had there ever been a woman devoid of all artifice and full of such artlessness?

Then, like an unsuspecting doe that'd discovered too late danger was near, Edith's eyes flew open.

She gasped. "Edward."

In the almost light of this new dawning day, he acknowledged he didn't want his given name on her lips, after all. No doubt she preferred using it because it made her less afraid while dealing with a monster. He'd not have her harbor any illusions, lest she get the wrong impression that he was somehow soft.

"Malden," he corrected.

Her previously soft, upturned lips dipped at the corners in the smallest of frowns.

"As I told you, love, only if you allow me a place between your legs will I allow that familiarity."

Her frown deepened. "Then Malden, it is," she conceded.

Good. That was how he preferred it.

He'd not thought allowing her usage of his given name would matter—and it certainly didn't—but Malden now conceded it suggested a familiarity he didn't at all like the feel or thought of, with anyone.

He cast a glance about the area she'd selected for them to meet.

This was where she enjoyed spending her time?

Polite ladies preferred ballrooms and modistes and drawing rooms and music rooms.

Wicked ladies preferred bedrooms and garish, lavish gaming hells.

No ladies preferred being outside amidst the mud and dirt and dead leaves and rocks.

Malden, continuing to take in the wooded area, gave his head a rueful shake, entirely too curious to be disgusted. Every moment spent with the lady, he found her to be more and more peculiar.

All the while, he took in his surroundings, he felt Edith staring intently at him. When he finished his survey, he looked at her.

"Charming," he murmured.

Her eyes lit. "Isn't it?"

"In addition to being a poor liar, you're also not very adept at identifying sarcasm." The moment he said it and her expression fell, he had the strangest desire to call his words back.

I'll not feel bad. I'm not capable of remorse.

Annoyed and unnerved, he doffed the oval-blocked, black leather top hat he'd donned for his first meeting with Lady Violet.

Then he frowned. Caught up—nay, distracted—as he'd been by Edith, he took belated note of a most important detail.

They were alone.

"You'd indicated she'd be here with you at this time?" he asked, tugging out his fob and consulting his gold-encrusted timepiece. For, in order for the scheme to play out as planned, he needed to happen upon *both* ladies.

Edith alone did him no good. Her sole purpose this day was to ease Lady Violet's fears.

At her silence, he snapped his head up. "Well?" He glanced about. "Where is she?" he asked impatiently. He despised anything that didn't go to plan, to the point he didn't tolerate it in anyone he had dealings with.

Edith dampened her mouth. "She isn't here."

"Yes," he said succinctly. "I've ascertained as much. When is she arriving?" He'd need to find someplace to wait until Edith was in position with Lady Violet.

"She isn't, my lord."

My lord.

That was how she *should* refer to him. In fact, moments ago, he'd *instructed* her to address him thusly. How strange to regret hearing the sound of it on her lips.

Maddened at himself, it was a moment before he registered the other words she'd spoken that'd been far more important than how she'd referred to him.

He stared at her. "She isn't?" he repeated. Why, when he never repeated himself, did he find himself doing so constantly with this woman?

"She isn't," Edith confirmed, this time in steadier tones.

Malden shook his head. "What does that mean?"

"Well," she spoke slowly like she was talking to a child, "it means she will not be coming today. Late last evening I received a note indicating she'd be unable to meet as planned and—"

Malden let loose a stream of invectives.

In the face of his frustration and annoyance, Edith went silent and remained in complete control. That bold defiance should have left him furious; instead, it enflamed him.

"Why didn't you send word?" he demanded harshly.

"I don't know," she volleyed. "Perhaps because getting a note to England's worst human being at his even worse gaming hell in the middle of the night without compromising myself and our plan hardly seemed like the wisest way to avoid discovery."

Color suffused Edith's delicate face. Her chest surged and heaved like she was Queen Margaret of the War of the Roses, leading her Lancastrian forces to victory at the Second Battle of St. Albans.

Malden's nostrils flared. Never before had he seen a woman so intrepid, so undauntable. Lust brought his lashes sweeping down into a narrow-eyed gaze.

Edith only lifted her chin in further uncompromising defiance.

That proved his undoing. Growling, Malden snatched Edith

around the waist, dragged her into his arms, and kissed her. Twining her arms about his neck, she met every fierce, angry slant of his lips.

He grunted his approval.

Like two animals in the wild, they mated with their mouths, in a ritual both violent and fervid.

Malden's cock ached, and catching her by the hips, he dragged her closer so she could feel the effect she had on him and the reward he would give her if she but let him.

"Open for me," he demanded against her mouth, between kisses.

She whimpered but instantly acquiesced.

"Good girl," he praised and swept inside to taste of her. "You taste of strawberries and honey. I want a bite," he teased, his voice husky with desire.

He swirled his tongue around hers, intermittently whirling and nipping at that soft flesh, and she boldly did the same to him. His breath and hers came in noisy spurts, mingling in a harsh, ragged symphony.

Malden sucked lightly on her tongue.

Edith groaned low and long, and letting her head fall back, she opened herself to Malden.

He shifted his attention lower, giving her what she sought.

Malden teased her first with a delicate trail of kisses over the graceful arch of her neck until he landed on her tear-shaped birthmark. He lapped that spot, sucking it like it were an actual crystalline drop.

Edith's hips bucked against him, in an angry frustration.

A chuckle shook his frame. "My poor dove, I'm being too gentle, aren't I? My naughty girl likes it rough, don't you?"

Like a nervous kitten, she whimpered and burrowed her face against Malden's shoulder.

He caught her chin firmly between a thumb and forefinger. "Look at me," he ordered harshly.

Hesitantly, his untried virgin lifted her shy eyes and flushed face.

Malden scoured those delicate, elfin angles.

God, he ached for her. She was a fire in his blood. A disease in him. Only when he at last claimed her could he be free of this debilitating hold she held over him.

"There is no shame in desire, Edith. There is just raw, unbridled feeling and the greatest satiation to be had. Let me show you that. Let me give you a taste of just some of what I can give you."

He brushed his lips over the delicate swell of her bosom and then tugged the neckline of her gown low so her beautiful mounds were bare before him.

Malden dropped to his knees before her and then filled his palms with the soft, ripe swell of her breasts. He tested their gentle weight. He'd always preferred his women voluptuous, and until now, had underestimated the alluring feel of the smaller ones in his hands.

Through his examination, he felt Edith's gaze upon the top of his head. "You have lovely breasts, Edith," he murmured. "They are beautifully formed and fit in my palms as if they were made for me."

He detected the harsh, raspy uptick of her breath and buried a smile. Malden, delighting in tormenting her this way, stroked the pads of his thumbs over each rigid peak.

"I love your nipples," he remarked conversationally. "I had thought given the rich shade of brown your hair is and by the paleness of your skin they'd be the lightest shade of brown or beige. This delicate pink is an unexpected, but lovely, surprise." Admiringly, he swept the pads of his thumbs over those erect peaks.

She moaned soft, long, and low, and he reveled in her body's responsiveness to even his slightest caress.

"Now, I'd like a taste of them, Edith. Will you let me?" he asked softly.

He knew she would. Malden knew she yearned for that and far more; things she didn't understand or yet know but would, after he introduced her to the wonders of lovemaking as she so adorably referred to it.

"Y-Yes," she granted in husky consent.

"Yes?" he repeated, continuing to brush his fingers in a rhythmic motion over those overly sensitive buds.

A breathy little moan escaped her, giving her want away.

With feigned innocence, he glanced up.

Edith had her full lower lip between her teeth and bit on that flesh still swollen and moist from his own mouth. "Is that a yes, Edith?"

Then, like a benevolent queen, she brushed her hand over the top of his head and murmured. "Yes, you may."

God, she was magnificent.

Malden brought her right breast to his mouth and then experimentally teased his tongue over one pink, pebbled tip.

Her hips moved in that agitated way that gave her desire away.

His cock throbbed. "You love to see me this way, don't you, love? On my knees like a beggar before you?"

Her keening whimper served as the only answer he needed.

"Do you know, I've never prostrated myself for anyone. Never have I gotten on my knees for any woman, but I am on my knees for you, now. Does knowing that make you happy, my siren?"

She moaned. "Yes."

It was too much. She was too much. She was a fire in him that needed to be extinguished lest it consume him.

With a growl, he scooped Edith from under her back and buttocks and brought her down under him. Their lips met in a fierce kiss; both of them takers and givers of desire. Never had he felt this way about any woman. Her untried innocence was like a wickedly carnal opium he found himself drugged by.

Reaching between their bodies, Malden dragged her skirts and chemise up, until she lay bare beneath him.

"Open for me," he demanded, between each parting and joining of their lips.

Edith, with an intuition as old as Eve, splayed her legs and presented herself to Malden. And Malden, like a green boy with his first whore, scrambled to get a hand to that covetous spot.

Only, he was no untried lad and Edith was certainly no whore, and her rare wholesomeness—and only that—accounted for Malden's own savage, unflagging lust.

He palmed satiny soft curls already damp from her longing. "You're already wet for me," he praised. "That makes me very happy, Edith. Do you want to know how I reward good girls?"

She emitted a broken, guttural sound that sounded very much like, "yes."

"I stroke them here. Like so." He ran his fingers through her thatch. "And now, because you've been so very good for me, I'll pet *you*, here."

With that, he slipped a finger inside the place where she was moist and desperate for him.

Edith cried out softly.

"Uh-uh, love," he chided, gliding his finger in and out of her exquisitely tight channel.

He gritted his teeth. God, she was so tight. He'd never known a woman tighter.

"Parkgoers will be coming soon. The respectable gentlemen out for their early-morning ride. We wouldn't want for them to find us here while you have your first orgasm," he continued to tease, but an overpowering lust robbed his voice of its steadiness and made it hoarse and guttural.

Edith frantically lifted her hips and lowered them in time to the rhythm he knew she'd match when he eventually fucked her.

"Or maybe you would enjoy that, Edith?" he asked huskily. "Putting on a show for them?" Except as soon as he uttered that provocative suggestion, a visceral rage born of possessiveness, like Malden had never before known, swarmed him.

Edith caught him by the nape and stopped the flow of those turbulent, confused thoughts.

She angled his gaze to where she wanted it so that it met her longing one. "I don't want anyone here, Edward," she said, soft as her big, doe-eyes. "I only want *you*."

Her words, coupled with the husky murmur of his name she shamelessly possessed, sent lust firing through him. Like a savage beast, Malden grunted his approval and devoured her mouth.

Edith met each glide of his lips over hers, and each thrust and parry of his tongue with a gloriously increasing boldness. And to honor that wantonness, he returned to worshipping her pulsating core.

"You are so wet for me," he rasped between kisses, while she rode his fingers.

"Mmm," she moaned, her speech dissolved, her body growing more and more tense.

She was close.

Malden slowed his strokes and she keened loudly, but he swiftly buried the telltale cry of desire.

"Please," she implored. "Please."

At those delicious little pleas falling from her swollen mouth, his balls tightened painfully.

"It is better like this, little dove," he said soothingly, even as he ached with an acute hungering, an intensity of which he'd never known. In this moment he couldn't sort out who suffered the greatest for the restraint he demanded—himself or Edith.

Malden petted her with a butterfly softness.

"Your climax will be so much more exquisite for the suffering you're feeling now, Edith," he promised, as much a reminder for himself as for her.

Like someone in the throes of great pain, Edith whimpered, and violently lifted her hips, attempting to steal what he withheld.

He continued to stroke her and tease her. He played with her clitoris.

A hiss exploded from between Edith's teeth, and shoving herself up onto her elbows, she thrust her hips angrily at him, demanding release.

Malden's breath came faster; grew shallower. He'd always been a generous lover, ensuring that his partners were well-satisfied but ultimately, his attaining sexual gratification mattered most.

Sweat beaded his brow, and he fixed his gaze upon Edith's beautifully flushed and gleaming faintly skin. In this instant, her pleasure was paramount to even his own. His shaft throbbed with a yearning to bring her surcease.

"So beautiful," he said harshly, increasing the cadence with which he stroked her.

Edith bit her lip so hard a drop of crimson blood appeared. Growling, he leaned down and sucked the hot bead into his mouth.

"Please," she begged. "Please, Edward," she implored him with her eyes.

He added a second finger to her tight sheath and stroked her with both digits.

She moaned.

"Do you know what you are asking for, Edith?" To draw out her pleasure, he continued caressing her in that place she hurt and yearned for him.

Merciful lover that he was, he increased the speed with which he touched her; and when the rise and fall of her hips grew faster, frantic, and jerky, indicating her rapture was near, Malden added just the right amount of pressure that would send her over.

Edith stiffened. Her luminous eyes widened. Her lips parted in a wide moue and then, anticipating her scream before she could even breathe it into existence, Malden consumed her lips; he swallowed that sound and absorbed it as the hoarse, animal-like groan it became.

His sweat fell from his brow and mingled with the tears that wetted her cheeks.

Malden gritted his teeth to keep from coming in his trousers like a damned callow boy. With his fingers, he worked Edith harder, faster, until her hips tensed and flexed in the last dying gasp of her climax.

She gasped and collapsed upon the forest floor. Her chest heaved like she'd run a race and with wide eyes fixed on the canopy of leaves overhead, a smile filled with wonder graced her lips. Contained within that smile was an innocent's discovery of the wonderment to be found in her body and with the attentions of a skilled lover.

Malden gently kissed her well-worshiped lips. "Good?" he whispered.

The lady would have a difficult time explaining the state of her swollen and bruised lips. The sign of his mark upon her filled Malden with a primal satisfaction.

Her sated smile grew shy. "It was wonderful," she murmured.

He sharpened his eyes on her guileless face. How? How was it even possible for a woman to have his fingers in her and his mouth all over her and still retain this...wholesomeness?

He'd expected now, having a taste of her first little death, she'd look upon him with a worldly woman's eyes. Yet, the mix of wanton beauty climaxing in his arms one instant and blushing angelic miss the next was unexpectedly salacious and sent another swell of blood pulsing to his already rock-hard erection.

Who was this woman that she should have this control over him?

"Let me love you completely, Edith, it will be so very good," he tempted and teased her still-puckered nipple with a little lick. "When I make love to you," he said hoarsely and wound his fingers into the damp thatch between her legs, "it will bring you a level of pleasure that makes your climax here weak in comparison."

She quivered in his arms.

Of course, she wanted him. Now that she'd had a taste of what bliss he could bring her, she'd never be satisfied again unless she had Malden in that place where she needed him.

The first hint of hesitation entered her eyes filled with sated desire. "You said there is no love involved," she ventured haltingly.

Bloody hell. He forgot he dealt with a virgin who harbored ridiculous ideas of romantic love. And worse, where in hell had those words even come from?

Malden silently cursed his slip-up. "No, there isn't." He placed his lips near the swollen tip of her right breast and breathed upon the sensitive flesh.

"But for you, Edith," he murmured, "I'm willing to pretend." With that, he, at last, drew that bud into his mouth and suckled deep.

A little shudder wracked her frame and her hips moved restlessly against his erection. Thank the God he hadn't believed in until now.

"Good girl," he murmured gently so as to not scare her.

Edith tangled her fingers in his hair and, gripping him hard, made Malden abandon a task he found himself immensely enjoying.

Frowning, he slanted a questioning look.

"I don't want to do this… with you."

All his muscles went taut, and he alternately wanted to beat his chest and rage at the false being he'd praised too soon.

"You don't want to do this *with me*?" he growled, which implied there was another man whom she'd give her body to in the way Malden longed to possess her.

A pretty blush trailed up the graceful lines of her cheekbones. "With *anyone*," she clarified.

That explication ought to appease him, and he expected it would if his cock wasn't throbbing from the pain of unrequited lust.

He'd not, however, beg her. He begged no one and he certainly didn't intend to begin now for a tumble with an innocent lady. An impudent, spirited, brave lady, granted, but an innocent, nonetheless.

"Then, what do you want?" he snapped.

And yet, even as he put that question to her, in the form of a demand, there was one certainty—Malden wanted prim, proper, except when in his arms, Edith Caldecott, more than he'd ever wanted any woman before.

CHAPTER 11

The next morning, Malden guided his mount along the quiet streets, and on to the Old Corner Bookshop for his meeting with Lady Violet.

The idea should bring with it a thrill of triumph and lust at how very close he was to having revenge upon DuMond and the Brookfields.

Instead, puzzlingly, from the moment he'd taken his leave of Edith yesterday, he remained plagued by thoughts of their exchange in Hyde Park.

What in Satan's name had possessed Malden to mention the years he'd been bullied to Edith? Or *anything* about his bastard of a father?

Malden had intended to take all those details to his grave so as to not give anyone power over him. Instead, he'd shared those personal pieces of his life with Edith Caldecott.

No, not only *that*; he'd given her information to leverage against him.

Malden gritted his teeth. Why had he revealed so much to her? She was some kind of siren who destroyed a man's logic. That was also the only way to explain how an innocent lady filled him with such lust.

His stallion moved nervously under him. Malden loosened the inadvertently tight grip he had on his reins. When his mount relaxed, Malden continued at a more even pace until he arrived at the morning meeting place.

After he'd handed his reins to a nearby urchin, and let himself inside the Old Corner Bookshop, he took a look about the decaying establishment.

Why had he insisted on meeting *here*, of all places? There were a thousand other locations he might have selected, and yet, he'd chosen *this* one.

Restless, Malden wandered through the shop and considered the wood shelving and aged books upon them. It was as if he'd stepped back in time, some twenty-five or so years ago.

In his mind's eye, he saw a small, frail, bespectacled boy run past, and he followed that tiny figure until he faded into the shadows of Edward's memory.

Malden didn't stop walking until he reached the very back of the shop.

Malden hesitated a moment and then made his way halfway down an aisle.

The same layering of dust that marred the shelves also coated the spines of the books.

He wiped two fingers along one of them until the title was clearly revealed.

Leviathan.

A wry grin formed on his lips.

There'd been a time Malden despised Hobbes's works and his erroneous, cynical views of man. Now he knew the truth—men were rotten to their very core and required, but one man, one king of all. And Malden was the one who ruled over the world, deviant members of the ton, inhabited.

"Good morning, good sir! May I help you find something?"

Malden looked to the owner of that boisterously loud, cheer-filled greeting.

"No." Malden spoke, coolly and succinctly, so as to not encourage further discourse from the fellow as ancient as the books he peddled.

The white-haired shopkeeper adjusted spectacles entirely too small for his face, and apparently by the way the man now squinted at Malden, required a bigger prescription, too.

"You have a familiar look you do, sir."

Malden tensed. "You have me mistaken with another."

Instead of taking proper offense, Malden's words seemed to

amuse the other man. "I don't make mistakes when it comes to my patrons."

Now, that he believed. Given the old fellow couldn't possibly receive more than a dozen patrons at most, over the years.

Malden's jaw worked. "As I said," this time he used the steely tones he employed with all and should have started out by using on this bothersome fellow, "you have me confused with another."

"Very well, my lord." At last relenting, the proprietor bowed and finally hastened on.

A tinny bell jingled in announcement of a new patron.

Edith.

Malden strained his ears. He needn't have bothered.

The proprietor called out a resounding welcome. "Good morning, Miss Caldecott."

He narrowed his eyes.

Miss Caldecott had been here before.

Malden detected Edith's quieter, lilting tones, but he could not make out what she was saying.

Irritated by the length of their discussion, Malden drummed his fingertips upon the cover of *Leviathan*.

At last, Edith, whimsical, wistful, and radiant appeared, wearing a smile.

He ceased his tapping and stared at her. He couldn't recall a time anyone smiling in his presence, let alone, *at* him. It unsettled the hell out of Malden. Knocked him off-balance.

With spritely steps, Edith headed over, snapping Malden from his momentary spate of madness.

He hardened his gaze. "So happy you could join me, Miss Caldecott. I'd begun to wonder if you'd, in fact, come to meet me, or our *dear* proprietor."

At his clear displeasure, Edith's smile dipped, but otherwise it didn't even give her pause. She stopped only when they were a pace apart.

Proud and spirited and stronger than any woman, this one was. That and that *alone* accounted for this near mad, obsession with her.

Edith spoke first.

"Hullo, Edward." Her smile returned; this one softer, and pensive, like she had a secret that belonged to her and only her.

And damned if Malden's hunger to possess all didn't extend to the very thoughts in Edith Caldecott's head.

"I come with, unfortunate news," she whispered, a sultry siren whose lush mouth he remained bespelled by.

Consumed by remembrances of the feel and taste of her lips, and the overwhelming need to claim them now, it took a moment for her words to register.

He frowned. "What?"

Edith trailed her tongue over her lips and drew his focus to that entrancing glide.

"Lady Violet was forced to cancel, again," she tacked that last word on, regretfully. "Her mother required her assistance at the The Ladies and Gentlemen School of Hope."

"And you didn't inform Gruffton?"

Edith frowned. "Considering I received her regrets while I stood in the foyer with my maid, I couldn't very well say 'oh, please wait. I just have to run ahead and let the Marquess of Malden's head guard know the woman he intends to compromise, cannot meet me'."

Again, there'd be no Lady Violet.

He *should* be annoyed at yet another foiled attempt to meet the girl in person.

Delicate fingers grazed his jacket sleeve.

He looked at Edith.

She spoke haltingly. "I am so sorry, Edward. I know you wish to see her. It is just, between Lady Violet having had her Come Out and balancing her work at her mother's school, it's increasingly difficult for us to meet."

Malden should be the only one of their pair with regrets at DuMond's sister-in-law remaining well out of his reach—a feat, Malden knew all too well wasn't merely coincidence. He *should* be enraged at being thwarted by his former partner and false friend.

And yet…

He centered his focus on the woman who *did* stand here before him.

Edith, with her palms clasped before her like she awaited her harsh master to bestow his wrath for her failing in her duties.

He flared his nostrils and breathed in slowly through them.

The sight of Edith so, only fueled his lust, and thoughts paraded through his mind: Edith face down across his lap. Him tossing her skirts up to reveal her creamy white buttocks and then spanking that beautiful flesh until the crimson imprint of his palm stood out, stark upon her skin.

Blood rushed to his cock and obliterated any regrets at Lady Violet's not being here.

Edith stole a tentative—and uncharacteristic for her—peek at Malden.

He kept his features impassive through her timid search.

"There will a time and it will be soon," he said quietly. "For now, you're here."

"I am here," she softly echoed.

In the revealing browns of her eyes sparked an emotion very close to joy.

Malden drew back in surprise.

Surely not at being with *him*?

Either way, her transparency unnerved the everlasting hell out of him. Fear he preferred. Terror in his presence Malden knew what to do with.

He steeled his jaw and hardened his eyes.

"Here, I'd expected this place was new to you," he said on a silky purr. "It appears you've been here before, Edith."

His wasn't a question.

Edith nodded anyway.

"At no point yesterday did you think to mention that detail?"

His interrogating question didn't have the intended effect.

"That I knew a bookshop that you suggested we meet at?" she rejoined.

The teasing smile on her lush lips, moist and plump, were a veritable invitation for him to join her in sin.

"If I had, perhaps we might have talked about how *you* know this out of the way shop," she remarked.

He stiffened. She'd laid a trap and he'd stepped right on in—

the lady sought to gather information about him and how he knew of this place.

"For what purpose?" he snapped. More specifically, how did she think to use it against him.

Edith blinked those silky eyelashes that went on forever with an innocence that fired his blood.

"Why, so we can talk about the shop, Edward."

"*Talk*," he repeated. She wanted to *talk*.

"As in, converse."

"I know what the hell *talking* is," he clipped out each syllable from between tightly gritted teeth.

"I know, Edward." Edith leaned close and whispered. "I was teasing."

He'd spent too much time with her. She'd become comfortable around him.

Malden took Edith gently but firmly, by the shoulders and pressed her back into the shelving. "I do not enjoy being teased, Edith."

He preferred her cowering and timid. That woman he knew what to do with. This undaunted, teasing, question-asking minx, was a different story.

Her eyes grew stricken. "I am sorry."

He stiffened at her instantaneous, all-knowing apology.

Malden tightened his grip. "You are thinking it's because I was bullied?"

When she didn't immediately reply, he squeezed her again, this time harder.

"Yes," she murmured. "Is it not?" she ventured, with more of her breathtaking courage.

"It is not. Teasing implies familiarity." Which Malden allowed no one.

Is it her you issue that reminder for or yourself?

Edith stared at him with those enormous brown eyes.

"Is that clear, Edith?"

"I didn't know yours was a quest—"

"Is that *clear*?" he asked again and gripped her so tight, the pads of his fingers imprinted upon her skin.

She didn't even flinch.

Lust coursed through his veins as much from the sight of his mark on her slender, creamy-white arms and as thoughts of the pain she could take in his bed.

My God, she does not fear me.

Panicked inside, Malden wrenched his hands back and flexed his fingers in a futile bid to erase the feel of her that still lingered on his skin.

"I began coming here after Evie died," she said softly, and it was a moment through the riotous tumult in his head before he registered what she'd said.

Malden stiffened. "Do you think I care?" he taunted.

If that is the case, why then, do you want her to continue?

Edith ignored Malden and carried on with her telling. "We had Evie laid to rest in Leeds at the family cemetery. My sister Elyse and I fought with our parents over the decision to do so."

While she spoke, he stared intently at her.

"We insisted she be buried alongside the swing she'd spent hours upon hours in," she said, her eyes indicated she was somewhere else.

"Our parents," she said softly, "once told my sisters and I that on the day Evie was born, our father had the swing hung from the ancient oak tree that overlooked the lake so the first of his precious daughters could eventually soar. Evie loved that swing. Of all of us, she used it most. She deserved to go there. It was where she was happiest."

Edith's gaze grew wistful and more distant, and he was grateful she did, so she could not see the rabid intensity with which he stared.

Her eyes darkened like the ocean amidst a turbulent storm.

"Evie made it a point to avoid the grounds that held the Caldecott ancestors. Despite mine and Elyse's protestations, that was the land eventually chosen as her final resting place."

At last, that dazed state cleared, and then Edith gave a small little shake of her head as if to further dislodge any remaining cobwebs.

She looked fully at Malden.

"We remained in the country for a long time and I was so glad. When I was there, I felt closest to Evie. We'd wanted to escape from the anguish of living in the place where Evie had taken her last breath, but eventually, we had to return," she said, with what Malden expected was the same level of regret she'd felt during the actual time she now spoke of.

Edith lifted her gaze to his. "And when we did, Edward? Everything came back as if Evie had only just left us. The sorrow that surrounded our townhouse. And the *stares*. The bloody, unceasing stares."

Acid dripped from her bitter lips. "They followed us wherever we went. People looked and whispered, and some talked openly as if *we* were the ghosts Evie had become."

He should have known Edith then. He'd have happily killed anyone who dared look at her. It'd have done her good, as well as the world on the whole.

Malden stilled. Where in blazes had that protective instinct come from? And good God, how did he ensure he never felt that way for her or anyone, ever again?

"I made it a point to find all the least frequented parts of London and I made them mine, Edward," she called to him, speaking through his unease. "That is how I discovered this bookshop."

Edith smiled like she'd shared with him the happiest moment in her life and not the most tragic one.

She wandered to the very end of the aisle until she'd reached the timber frames plastered over the walls, and then sank to her haunches. "I'd settle myself right here."

He knew the moment he lost her, again.

Edith plucked an aged, warped leather volume from a shelf and contemplated the title.

"These were the books you read, then, Edith?" Were they still?

His serious dark-haired lady whipped her head up; the suddenness of which set several chocolate brown tendrils free of her thickly braided plait.

As if he were a stranger or fellow whose presence she'd forgotten all about, Edith stared at Malden with vacuous eyes.

"Hmm? No, no. I used to sit here because I wanted to hide. I didn't care what books were here. I didn't read these." She held the one that had sparked the quarrel aloft. "I didn't read *anything*."

The image she painted, of her, bereft and alone, in hiding, from the pain she'd felt at the loss of her sister, caused a queer *tightness* in his chest, and he shifted in an attempt to dislodge that ache.

His efforts proved unsuccessful.

Edith seated herself fully on the floor.

"One day, Mr. Tarrington found me here," she said, her telling weaved in and out, between her past and Malden's.

"…ah, you've found my favorite corner of the bookshop, young sir…"

"He did not ask me what I was doing. He simply offered to gather books I might be interested in," she murmured.

"…If you tell me what you might enjoy…"

"And bring them for me to read here," she finished softly.

"…I will bring them to you…but I truly believe you would enjoy these immensely, sir…"

His heart thumped hard against the walls of his chest. Her telling, near identical to his, left Malden all confused in his mind.

She'd roused distant memories he'd not thought of until this moment; memories he didn't want to relive.

Disquieted, Malden grunted. "Perhaps we—"

But Edith wouldn't allow him freedom from the exchange. Tears sparked in her eyes and the sparkling drops of her misery managed to break through his past's unwanted hold.

"I didn't *want* to read anything, Edward." With shaking fingers, she toyed with the corners of her page. "I didn't want to do anything. I just wanted to… die," she whispered.

Every muscle fiber in his body jumped. He wanted to snarl and make her past despair a battlefield opponent to be slayed.

"That way," she continued through his riot of emotions, "Evie and I could be together, and I wouldn't feel this wretched agony tearing me asunder. I wanted it to end."

Edith's small, narrow shoulders moved up and down, swift from the force of her breathing.

Seething, Malden stared at her bowed head. A visceral rage rolled in slow, consuming undulations and a hungering to vanquish the demons that'd haunted her then and now.

His fingers curled into sharp fists at his side. No one tormented the one who belonged to him.

And gazing upon her, he conceded in this moment the fight

he'd been fighting. No longer. She was his. He'd be the first man to possess her body completely. She'd not be Malden's wife, but she would be his lover, and he would offer himself all the same as her protector, her warrior, her master. There came no fear at this knowledge, just a sense of rightness.

Edith drew in a slow, ragged inhalation and then lifted a haunted gaze—one that seared through Malden and saw beyond him to the moment she relived in her mind.

"But I couldn't do it," she whispered.

He sank to a knee, joining her on the floor. "Of course, you couldn't, love," he murmured.

A woman hellbent on revenge and achieving it by any means was too strong to let sorrow and loss defeat her in life and usher in an early death.

The distantness of Edith's eyes grew weaker and weaker until they were stone-cold sober.

"I couldn't die, Edward," she said softly, "but I wanted that which was closest to it. I asked Mr. Tarrington for stories of real ghosts and books about death and dying and I'd come here…"

A wry grin tipped up her berry-red lips and lust ran through him, at the thoughts he had for her delectable mouth.

"This is where you now mock me for reading ghost stories," she murmured and trailed her fingertips over the bottom shelf.

He should.

Normally, he would.

This time, Malden couldn't work himself up to that deserved response. Why? Cruelty and wryness was his way. So why did both escape him now?

Edith stole a glance about and then motioned to Malden.

He stared at her.

She gave another wave of her hand.

"What?" he asked, perplexed, a new state he found himself uncomfortably living in because of this troublesome minx.

"Sit. I want to show you something."

"I'm not sitting on the floor," he sputtered.

She laughed softly. "Because you're too powerful to do so?"

He growled. God, he couldn't determine if she fascinated or infuriated him.

"Yes," he said coolly. "That is precisely why."

Edith gazed up at him, and he'd have liked to see those eyes lifted to him, while she was on her knees and his shaft buried in her mouth.

Edith flashed him a beatific smile. "Fine, then sit *with* me, Edward. In *my* corner of the bookshop."

If she knew the lascivious thoughts churning in his brain, she'd not be wearing that angelic look or issuing invitations for him to join her.

Or, maybe she *would* and this was the reason he found himself enthralled by her.

"That is still the floor," he said tersely.

"No, it is not. It's different."

"How?" Malden snapped.

What the hell was wrong with him; he was having this child's quarrel with her, and what was worse? He actually *wanted* answers to the word chess she now played.

He waited for her to crow but when Edith spoke, she again proved how different she was from the sordid lot of people in Malden's world.

"You see," she began.

Malden fought the need to jam his fingertips into his temples. He saw absolutely nothing anymore. He should resume wearing the spectacles he required for distance viewing.

"This is *my* space, and *you*, Edward, make everything yours. You said, there is nothing too small or too big that you won't add to your empire. Your only goal is to expand your power and possessions."

She offered him another smile. "As such, you need to claim a spot here, if for no other reason than because *I* own this space." Edith lifted her shoulders in a little shrug that marked an end to her justification.

Her very *sound* justification.

That explained then, why he finally took a seat.

He gave her a lascivious once over. "It occurs to me, I can think of any number of naughty things we might do down here."

"Here?" she said, so aghast, he scowled.

"The truth is, Edward, this space doesn't belong to just me," she murmured, tracing the initials ED C which she'd, at some point, marked into the wood.

Edith ran her fingertip along the engraving beside hers. "It belonged to this person, too, and when I came here, to read my books about ghosts and the afterlife, I felt less alone."

His palms went moist and sweat slicked his skin. All the while horror lent his heart a sickly beat. Through the loud buzzing in his ears, her words came faint, as if from down a long, empty corridor.

ED MM

Edith traced the same fingers she'd moved over her initials along these three others.

She stopped, and he knew the moment she knew. Edith's stunned gaze flew to meet him.

"Edward DeVesy, Marquess of Malden," she breathed.

"No."

"It *is* you," she whispered, digging in with a defiance that made him want to beat his chest and roar at that challenge.

With an understanding dawning in her eyes, Edith looked around. "This is how you knew of this place. This is why you suggested we meet here because you have been he—"

A low growl rumbled from deep within his chest.

The remainder of Edith's revelation faded. She must have seen the intent in his eyes, for she rose unsteadily.

Narrowing his eyes, Malden let her have the handful of inches she'd not yet claimed between her and the wall. All the while Edith went, she watched him warily. He stared goadingly at her in return. The bold, fearless way in which she held his gaze sent the blood rushing to his cock.

As he'd known it would, Edith's back met the wall. A primal triumph filled him. Her sanctuary had now become her prison, and Malden, like the beast he was, stalked her the rest of the way.

With less than a pace between them, Malden stopped and hooded his gaze.

"You know nothing of what you speak," he seethed.

She lifted her chin. "I do and you know it."

God she was fearless.

Malden gripped her hips in his hands and dragged her close so she could feel the long line of his erection.

Her throat jumped.

"My innocent, naïve, girl," he crooned, as he rubbed himself in slow, smooth circles over the flat of her belly.

"Edward," she whispered. "Mr. Tarrington will find us."

It didn't escape Malden that the lady didn't speak another protest than that one.

"No, he won't." Malden cupped her fine, pert arse and gave both globes a none to gentle squeeze. "The old man is as ancient as his books. He hasn't had sound hearing for decades."

With that promise, he placed his lips along her neck and alternately kissed and suckled her satiny-soft skin. He breathed in the scent of her, filling his lungs with the heady aphrodisiac that was her innocence.

He brought a palm to rest on the wall above Edith's left shoulder and made his body a prison with which to keep her.

The gracefully long column of her neck moved, wildly.

"And what if those initials do belong to me, hmm?" Malden kissed the shell of her ear. "What does it matter? The boy who came here is dead."

"He i-isn't."

Her response came so throatily, his cock ached.

"Oh, fortunately, he is." Malden slipped her breasts free of their constraints and raised one delicate swell close to his mouth. "He was a good boy, Edith," he remarked casually. "Proper. He would have made you a very good husband."

Her breath hitched and she rocked against him; like the possibility of her and Malden united in life, was one she loved.

"But he would have bored you," he said, matter-of-factly, smoothing the pads of his thumbs over her nipples.

"H-He wouldn't." There was a faint pleading in her whispered words.

"Oh, but he would," he insisted happily. "He wouldn't suck your nipples in public, like this." Malden drew the pebbled peak into his mouth and gently suckled.

She moaned softly and moved herself against him.

Malden smiled against her breast. "Yes, you are a good girl, Edith. You are *my* good girl."

He sucked harder this time.

"A *g-good girl* doesn't allow men to take shameful liberties at a bookshop," she rasped.

"Ah, yes, kitten," he whispered. "But we know we are the only souls here…"

He dangled that as the temptation it was meant to be, and, collecting her skirts, he slowly raised the hems higher and higher. "We are fire and ice, Edith."

That was why he needed to consume her, or else, be destroyed by her.

At last, he kissed that fascinating teardrop birthmark and then lightly suckled. She'd bear *his* mark this day.

Edith moaned softly as he trailed a path of kisses lower and lower. "Fire and F-fire." She tangled her fingers in his hair.

He joined his gaze with hers. "You seek to avenge the death of a sister you loved. Me? I will happily destroy a man, for no reason and do not believe in that emotion you call love. But let us not debate it," he said, willing to concede a fight for the pleasure of getting his hands all over her.

Malden slipped his hand between her legs and grinned at the hot wetness that greeted him.

"My good girl," he purred.

"I'd wish you'd stop c-calling me that. I'm n-not, you know," she insisted, her voice husky with desire.

"You, love, are the most virtuous woman I know." No, that wasn't altogether right. Of *anyone* he'd encountered, taken to his bed, had dealings with, she was the purest of them all. That rarity accounted for this obsessive infatuation with her.

Malden bent to claim her mouth.

Edith spoke, freezing him when he was but a breath away from taking what he wanted. "Given the people you keep company with, my lord, that is not at all surprising."

Malden bestowed the tender kiss upon her lips that she so deserved.

He may as well have made love to her mouth for the way she rocked her hips and softly moaned. With her body only recently awakened to passion, even the slightest touch and faintest whisper of a kiss, was heightened.

Malden gripped her hip in his left hand and squeezed. The soft, crunching noise of her satin skirts enflamed him.

His. Before they were done together, she'd belong to him. And then perhaps after, he'd make her his mistress so he could possess her until he tired of her.

"My innocent, Edith," he said, cementing his ownership of her.

The desire ebbed from her gaze, and he growled his displeasure as she retreated.

She rested her palms upon his chest and solemnly searched her gaze over his face. "If you knew the things I've done. You would hate me."

This, again.

To hide his laughter, he kissed her.

Or, he attempted to.

Edith turned her head so that intended kiss fell upon her cheek.

Annoyance tightened his gut and all amusement disappeared. "What is it?" So that he could get back to doing all manner of wicked things to her in the dusty bookshop.

"The only reason you desire me is because you think I'm innocent," Edith said, her soft contralto as entreating as her eyes. "But you need to know, it isn't real."

Panic filled the sharp planes of her face. "The very reason I've come to you is to see a man killed, Edward. That is not the act of a good woman and should tell you everything you need to know about me."

She chattered like a sinner who confessed her sins to a man of the cloth and not the evilest soul in England.

Her expression fell. "I have told lies. We are not different, you and I." Her voice caught.

He trusted *she* believed that.

"I am tired of talking, sweet," he breathed against her lips, and then kissed her with the tenderness he knew she needed in this moment, until her reservations melted away.

Malden renewed the attention he paid her beautiful breasts. Pressing the silky flesh together, he simultaneously, kissed and licked both of her nipples.

Edith moaned softly, and then promptly bit her lip.

He pressed against her temple. "Moan for me," he coaxed, reveling in each slow, undulation of her hips as she rocked against him. "He'll never hear."

The tinny bell jingled announcing another patron.

"Ignore it," Malden whispered at her temple.

Edith's lashes fluttered. "We can't," she murmured.

He scoffed. "I can do anything, and, as you belong to me, you too can do whatever you wish, whenever you are with—"

A cheer-filled cry shattered the otherwise quiet of the bookshop. "Hullo, Mr. Tarrington!"

Horror filled Edith's eyes. "Oh, my God."

Frantic, she shoved Malden hard.

Malden stumbled at that unexpected push and frowned. "What the—?"

"Emmy," Edith whispered at the same time, Mr. Tarrington called, in happy return.

"Miss Caldecott!"

Malden froze.

Emmy? Miss Caldecott.

"Your s—?"

"Sister," she mouthed, in confirmation. Her hands shaking, Edith shoved her skirts back into place and smoothed her palms over the front of them.

"…you…my sister…" The other Caldecott girl was asking.

"Arrived some time ago," Mr. Tarrington boomed, even louder than usual.

Malden would have wagered his gaming hell and all his land holdings the shopkeeper did so to announce the young lady's arrival. And all these years later, Malden recalled just how much he appreciated the old chap.

"Splendid," Miss Caldecott piped in.

"Wait!" Mr. Tarrington shouted, his voice cracking slightly. "Uh…uh…"

All the while, the older man stalled, a pale, Edith attempted to tuck her flyaway tendrils back into place.

Taking mercy on his lily-pure lady, Malden made quick work

of rearranging Edith hair until he'd gotten it to the same place her maid had sent her out.

She wrinkled her nose. "You are quite skilled with a lady's hair, my lord."

"Quite," he purred. "And as you have ascertained," Malden gave her a wolfish look, "skilled in a great number of areas where women are concerned."

She pursed her mouth.

Ah, his little dove was jealous. That possessive bent should repulse. The last thing he wanted or needed in his life was a clingy, pouty miss. And yet, Malden found himself enjoying her ire—*immensely*.

"Would…like me…escort… Miss Caldecott?"

Alas, Mr. Tarrington had stalled the young lady as long as possible. It'd been a valiant effort and Malden intended to make an anonymous and sizeable donation to the establishment to ensure it remained open. It'd be a sin to lose such an ideal trysting spot.

"That isn't necessary. I know…to find…"

Edith bolted.

Malden caught her by the ribbons at the back of her dress and reeled her in like a prized catch.

"Wait, Miss Caldecott!" From across the shop, Mr. Tarrington again called out, his voice croaking like a frog, this time. "There is…thing…would…"

Edith trained those entrancing eyes on Malden.

"What are you *doing*?" she whispered.

"A parting kiss before you go, love," he said huskily.

Edith's eyebrows shot up. "You are *mad*."

"Oh, I assure you, I am very much sane," Malden promised in silky tones. "The only thing that plagues me is a lusty appetite."

"And any warm body will do, I suppose," she said under her breath.

"Indeed." Malden brought his lips up in a lewd half-grin. "Fortunate for you, dear Edith, you happen to be that warm bo—"

Edith went up on tiptoe and kissed him hard on the mouth, knocking the rest of Malden's words free. It started too soon and ended too quick, and yet the unexpected kiss from this innocent woman, left him randy as a damned schoolboy.

"There," she muttered, and taking advantage of Malden's distracted state, Edith bolted.

He narrowed his gaze upon her until she disappeared around the corner, without so much as a backward glance.

"Edith!" That elated greeting came nearer.

"Emmy, whatever are you doing here?"

Only a deaf man would fail and note the high-pitched and very guilty quality to Edith's reply.

"What am I doing here? Whatever is wrong with you, Edith?"

Malden could all but see the frown in the young woman's voice.

"We always come here together, which was why I am more than slightly offended you've come without me…"

"I…I…"

Malden could hear Edith's thoughts frantically churning.

Malden shook his head. *Come on, love, say something.* Alas, there came more hemming and hawing. God, she really *was* rot at prevaricating. He really *should* be far more repulsed than rueful at the reminder.

Edith's long, regretful—and Drury Lane Theatre worthy—sigh filled, what Malden expected to be every corner of the Old Corner Bookshop. "I fear you have found me out. I came in search of a gift."

"Oh, Edith!" The other Miss Caldecott squealed. "Is it another ghost tale?"

"Shh," Edith said frantically.

His lips formed an uneven smile. *More* ghost tales. It was another—albeit—unnecessary reminder of just how innocent Edith Caldecott, avenging sister, in fact, was.

"…later, I promise," Edith was saying. "…Gunter's—"

The rest of that mention of the ice shop was met with an even wilder squeal. There came the echo of retreating footfalls, the whine of door hinges in desperate need of greasing, a tinkle of that old bell, and then the Caldecott girls were gone.

Malden didn't linger.

He made a beeline for the wide front windows. He found the

pair of sisters as they made their way down the street. Edith had an arm looped around her younger sister's shoulders, and they walked in lockstep, their bodies bent close as if together they'd blocked out the world's scrutiny.

He'd never seen two people so close. He'd never believed family could be that way. And it was because of that momentary stupefaction it took Malden a moment to register the lords and ladies moving all around Edith and her sister.

As the sisterly pair went, people stopped and stared. Others whispered behind their hands, and some didn't even bother to feign politeness and spoke without hiding their mouths.

If it weren't for Edith's earlier revelations, he might have believed her immune to the looks.

But she *had* shared.

An unholy, blinding rage tightened his gut and a bestial rumble started in his belly, swelled in his chest, and spilled past his lips. Compelled, like the animal he'd become, Malden stormed through the shop.

An always merry Mr. Tarrington greeted him with a wave. "Leaving so soon are you, my—"

Malden's growl drowned out the rest of those kindly words of farewell.

He shoved the door open with such ferocity and speed, the chain of the ancient bell broke and gave one more chime before it hit the pavement and met its final resting spot.

With an angry shout, Malden thumped a fist against his chest. All stares that'd once been on the Edith and her sister, shifted to Malden.

Malden fixed his rabid stare on each man, woman, and child.

Unlike where they'd brazenly stood in watch and wait for the Caldecotts, this time, Polite Society's *finest* knew they found themselves in Satan's company. Lords and ladies averted their gazes and dashed to the opposite side of the street; they tripped and stumbled all over themselves to put distance between them and Malden and his wrath.

A quiet settled over the street, a calm at odds with the energy pumping through him, and Malden glanced around. From an adjacent shop window, his gaze caught on the primordial, savage beast with its crazed eyes and wild hair, reflected back.

Me. I am that beast. I lost control because of Edith Caldecott.

There'd never been a doubt he was a monster, but it'd never been a woman who'd robbed him of his restraint and left him mad.

Malden scraped an unsteady hand through his wild hair.

What is happening to me?

CHAPTER 12

When Malden arrived in his clubs, his staff was clever enough to cut him a wide swath.

He kept his icy gaze directed forward.

Gruffton approached. He'd be the only one who'd ever dare do so.

Having worked together at Forbidden Pleasures, the ruthless guard had proven himself loyal to Malden and for that loyalty, he'd been rewarded with the role of his right-hand man.

Gruffton fell into step alongside him. "Received a request for—"

"Not now," he said, not breaking stride. "I'm not seeing visitors."

The guard fell back.

Malden stomped upstairs. The minute he reached his office, he pushed the door shut hard behind him and made for his desk.

With a rote familiarity, he spun the number dial on the lock.

Click.

Yanking the drawer open, he grabbed a cheroot and friction match. After he'd lit the thin scrap, he raised it to his lips and took a deep draw.

When he inhaled, he noticed his hands trembled.

Now, I'm bloody shaking. What the hell was happening to him?

After several long, slow inhalations and exhalations, Malden regained full control of his emotions.

Malden headed over to the viewing window overlooking the kingdom he'd built.

Instead of the rush of satisfaction that came in seeing the floors teaming with patrons, he felt a bizarre restlessness.

Somewhere between first meeting Edith and now, the balance Malden achieved over his mind, sexual urges, and self-control had been upset.

He stood here, his thoughts consumed by a young lady whose only experience in carnal pleasures had come from Malden's own hands.

He took another drag from his cigarette and exhaled the smoke from the right corner of his compressed lips.

It was just lust, this deepening obsession with Edith.

Why was he all knotted up over his unceasing preoccupation? He needed to fuck her. Only then could he purge her from his mind and put his attention back on the woman deserving of his focus.

He'd partaken in the taste of Edith's innocence and sought to consume her lily-whiteness, being the first to possess her body in every way. And when he, at last, had his fill, he'd be free of this all-consuming desire for her. He'd leave her, skilled and hungering for sex, and ready for the next man she let between her legs.

But a new tableau whispered forth.

Of some man petting her thatch in that way she adored and then rutting between her legs. She'd beg her lover because Edith's need for pleasure always proved greater than her pride.

Reflexively, a blinding rage shot through Malden and brought his fingers curling so tight his cheroot snapped in half.

Knock-Knock-Knock

With a curse, he stomped on the smoldering scrap. "I told Gruffton I'm not accepting visitors."

"It is, Gruffton, yer Lordship."

"Then, you should know better than anyone I don't take to having my orders ignored."

There came a pregnant pause.

"Yes, my lord. But Oi think ye'll *want* to see this particular guest."

Enraged, Malden opened his mouth to take Gruffton to task for his presumption but caught himself.

He'd want to see this guest. A guest, which indicated the person was one whom Malden had current dealings with. And there was but one whom he found himself consorting with.

With a volatile energy thrumming in his veins, Malden was across the room in several long strides. He turned the lock with such haste, his movements were sloppy, and he growled at that latest, weakness.

As Malden, opened the door, any frustration and fury with himself, however, were superseded by an eagerness to see—*Not Edith.*

Like a bloody lackwit and hopeless to quell the feeling, Malden stared blankly at the pair now facing him.

Gruffton eyed Malden concernedly.

On the other hand, the *guest* escorted here stood with his hard, scarred face assembled into an impenetrable, emotionless mask, Malden resented him for.

Instantly sobered, Malden schooled his own features.

Cadogan inclined his head. "I've discovered some information you'll be most interested to know."

Mr. Stillson, the man Edith believed murdered her sister. And either way the man responsible for the sorrowful look that lived in her eyes and on her person. Malden would be all too happy to have the man killed.

Malden suppressed a growl. "Stillson."

"Miss Caldecott."

"Evie Caldecott," Malden clarified, with a nod. "Yes?"

"That is the second eldest *living* Miss Caldecott—Miss *Edith* Caldecott."

It was a moment before Malden registered the name the assassin uttered. Edith's name falling from the ruthless mercenary's lips felt wrong. The right to speak her given name belonged to Malden and Malden only.

Gruffton and Cadogan exchanged a glance.

Giving his head a slight, imperceptible shake, Malden motioned with his hand and urged Cadogan inside. After he'd entered, Malden, without so much as a word for Gruffton, pushed the panel shut.

Cadogan didn't waste any time. "Given the assignment you put to me, I took it upon myself to compile a list of each Caldecott and their individual and familial connections."

Folding his arms at his chest, Malden inclined his chin. "And?"

"In so doing, I've collected information about every social event they've ever attended over the past decade."

As the assassin spoke, Malden listened intently; mentally noting every detail shared.

"Considering the possibility that there *was* poisoning involved and the viscount *was* the intended target, I've researched the brother's frequent travels, and the nature of his business. Any travel companions he had. Friends. Foes. All of it."

Malden narrowed his gaze on the stoic man opposite him. "What did you find?"

"The brother has one best friend, a man by the name of Lord Jeremy, the Earl of Mauley, who is loyal to the family. Other than that, it's yielded nothing of note."

"At this time," Cadogan added, "I've also taken an accounting of the people and families each Caldecott is friendly with; organizing them in terms of close friends, casual friends, mere acquaintances, as well as enemies."

The man was thorough and detailed and quick. That's why the assassin was the best at what he did, and it was also why Malden hired him.

"My efforts haven't turned up many who carry antipathy for the family," Cadogan was saying. "Pity is a common sentiment they receive and have since the eldest girl's death. But I have not turned up any malice carried for the Caldecotts." He paused. "That is, not any that is different than Polite Society's usual scorn."

Restless for the other man to get on with whatever it was he'd uncovered, Malden forced himself to be patient through the detailing. Whatever it was that'd brought the investigator here, and led Gruffton to defy orders, hinted at something of import.

"Which brings me to the reason for my visit."

At last.

"Just what do you know about Miss Caldecott?" Cadogan murmured.

All Malden's muscles went taut. He wasn't deaf. He heard the hint of more on the other man's query.

He narrowed his eyes. "I haven't hired you to ask me questions," he snapped. "What do *you* know about Miss Caldecott?"

The assassin's features remained harsh and immobile. "A lot and I believe you *want* to hear it now."

CHAPTER 13

THE FOLLOWING MORNING EDITH SAT with her boots off, her skirts hiked about her knees, and her toes kissing the edge of the Serpentine. She absently trailed her big toe over the placid lake and traced a circle upon the water. Ripples fanned out from where her foot touched and disturbed the previously still surface.

Edith found her gaze drawn to the spot on the forest floor where Edward pleasured her. Even as her eyes slid closed, she heard him and saw him as clearly as if she were living in the moment now.

"You have lovely breasts, Edith... They are beautifully formed and fit in my palms as if they were made for me."

Edith trembled.

She remembered his touch.

"You're already wet for me... That makes me very happy, Edith."

Her breath caught and warmth settled between her thighs. In a bid to alleviate that sharp ache, she shifted and squirmed. Her efforts were in vain.

Only *Edward* could give her body what she craved.

It was him, her body needed.

Nay, it was him, *she* needed and wanted.

Edward had cracked open a window, and she'd had a glimpse inside, at the secrets he'd guarded as closely as the royal guards do the King of England. Now, she wished to be for Edward that woman she'd spoken of at the bookshop; the one who could teach him about love and show him a different world than the sorrowful one he knew.

The blanket of leaves overhead stirred in a quiet, graceful dance.

Edith opened her eyes and saw him as he'd been when these very same branches had swayed above her and Edward.

"Do you know, I've never prostrated myself for anyone. Never have I gotten on my knees for any woman, but I am on my knees for you, now. Does knowing that make you happy, my siren?"

Her heart quickened.

No, a man as powerful as both God and king of the world they inhabited would neither bend nor bow to anyone.

And yet, for her, in this sacred sanctuary, he'd done just that.

After only a short while knowing Edward, she had done the most scandalous things with him and let him do the most wicked things to her.

Perhaps had she been a young debutante and not a grown woman of twenty-four and firmly on the shelf, she'd be consumed with shame. She'd not only *allowed* Edward those liberties, she'd loved each and every sinful second of the things he did.

Edith drew her knees up close to her chest and looped her arms around them in a light hug.

The thing of it was, for all the places he'd touched Edith and made love to her with his mouth, what she and Edward had shared at the Old Corner Bookshop proved even more intimate.

Their exchange hadn't just been sexual in nature. He'd shared with Edith painful stories about his past and, in so doing, he'd opened himself to her.

Since Edward had discussed his connection to that ancient bookshop, she couldn't help thinking about the boy he'd spoken about, a small, unloved child, beaten and bullied by not only his peers but his monster of a father.

Just like Edith, he'd gone to a dusty, shadowy bookshop few patrons frequented so he could hide from the world and lose himself in a different one, on the pages of books.

Edith picked up a stone and sent it skipping over the water.

She followed its flight as it bounced, one-two-three-four times before it disappeared under the surface.

She'd allowed Edward intimacies she'd never permitted another man, and never would. How could she after having known the level of exquisite pleasure she'd had in his arms?

For Edward, on the other hand?

"...The only thing that plagues me is a lusty appetite."

Edith happened to be just another woman in a long line—that would continue to grow if it hadn't already—of lovers. Edith herself had viewed firsthand the exquisite beauties who lived in or patronized his gaming hell. Were he merely a man in need of a female body, he had any number of far more beautiful options awaiting him now and long after they parted ways.

Her throat worked painfully, as she recalled other words he'd spoken.

"...And any warm body will do, I suppose?"

"Indeed...Fortunate for you, dear Edith, you happen to be that warm body..."

Miserable, Edith pressed her hands over her face.

For all his sneers and jeers and scowls, there'd been no soul she felt closer to than Edward de Vesy, the Marquess of Malden.

All the original fear she'd felt in his presence had faded, as she'd quickly discovered, despite his ruthlessness, Edward wasn't a man who'd harm a woman.

And many of the things he'd said hadn't been cruel, but harshly spoken and forthright.

She'd just...failed to see the difference—until now. Why, Edward hadn't even been wrong in the charges he'd leveled against Edith's father and brother. The men in her family *had* failed Evie, just as they now failed Edith.

What'd begun for her as a terrifying partnership with London's most ruthless, most powerful man had become, in such a short period of time, *more*.

Edward was the one person Edith felt she could truly rely on to bring closure to and justice for the Caldecott family.

More than that, at every turn, Edward revealed glimpses of a tender side—one he masterfully concealed from the world.

When she'd fainted, he'd tenderly roused her. When they'd been in this very spot and she'd been a world away in her misery, he radiated not annoyance, but concern she might swoon. He gave her pleasure without expecting or asking for any himself.

Even those times he gripped Edith tight, there was always an underlying gentleness to his touch.

She'd come to care for Edward and could maybe even love—

Edith blanched and she forced the rest of that silent thought to go unfinished.

Drawing in a jagged breath, she closed her eyes briefly. Until she was an old woman at the end of her life, alone in her bed, she'd recall what she'd shared with Edward de Vesy, the Marquess of Malden.

If you survive that long, a voice whispered.

And she *wouldn't* if Mr. Stillson got to her before she got to him. Not if she didn't let her vendetta go.

"I need to do this," Edith said, her voice sounding weak to her own ears.

Do you? Or would you rather build a future with your Lord Malden?

Build a future with Edward?

"He isn't *my* Lord Malden," she spoke softly and regretfully.

But he could *be…*

At that improbable wish, she picked up another small rock and hurled it as far as she could. The projectile hit the river with a satisfying thump.

Edith released a quiet, frustrated, shout.

There couldn't be a future between them.

Why, not? That insistent query knocked around her mind.

"Why not?" she said under her breath. "Oh, there's just the small, minor, detail that he intends to ruin and marry Lady Violet." *And then there is the teensy, tiny matter of you lying to him.*

No, there'd never be anything more than *this*, a relationship borne of treachery and built on Edith's lie about her connection to Lady Violet.

But for one moment, she let herself *imagine*—what if. She closed her eyes and imagined a life *with* Edward.

All their walls would come down. They'd share pieces and parts of their lives they'd never shared with anyone else. And they, two people who from life's cruelty didn't laugh and smile, would learn to do so—her, again, and Edward, for the first time—because of one another.

He'd only been part of her life for a few short days, but she knew—a life with Edward at her side would be…

"Magical," she whispered.

Edith made herself surrender the impossible dream.

Even if he could come to care for her, a man as proud and powerful as the marquess would never forgive, or for that matter, let go unpunished, a woman who'd betrayed him.

Tears filled her eyes, and one slid in a hot, windy path down her cheek—followed by another and another. Edith angrily swiped them away, but there was only more to take their place.

"I'm c-crying." She half-laughed and half-sobbed.

The only tears she'd believed herself capable of shedding were ones for Evie.

Now, here Edith sat, weeping about the fact that with her rash decision to lie to Edward to secure his help, she'd ended any possibility of something more with him.

But maybe, just maybe, he is capable of forgiveness.

Edith went motionless.

My God, what is wrong with me?

Here she sat, thinking about *Edward* when the only thing, the absolutely *only* person Edith should be focused on was Mr. Stillson.

And Evie.

Edith stilled as an ache invaded her heart.

Here she sat lamenting what could not be with Edward and hadn't thought of Evie since that first meeting when she'd swooned in Edward's office.

The air stirred.

"…I don't want you to be sad anymore…"

Her heart thumping erratically, Edith whipped her head right and then left.

"E-Evie?" she called softly.

For this moment, she felt her eldest sister's presence here clearly, in a way she'd only once had before. After a dream she'd had in the middle of the night, several years earlier, when she'd been pouring over her notes and fallen asleep in the music room.

"Is that you?" Edith held her breath and waited.

The answer to her call came in the form of rustling leaves and the warbling call of a black grouse.

"I want you to live again…I want you to experience it all."

Edith went motionless; her sister's whispered words from that long ago dream floated into the now.

"*Evie, surely you aren't simply saying we forget what happened to you?*"

Those long-ago murmurings merged with the present and formed a distant echo that swirled around her mind so Edith was trapped between then and now.

"I have to do this, Evie," she said softly, reminding herself, reminding her sister.

"*Hand this information over to someone who can and will research so that you and Emmy and Hutchinson and Mama and Papa are safe.*"

Edith found herself slipping further and further away.

She'd found a man more formidable than anyone, and where the Caldecotts had proven weak and powerless, with Edward, Edith felt invincible.

"I found someone," Edith murmured, her tongue heavy.

"*…Is he a sweetheart we didn't know about? You are blushing…*"

"He is not a sweetheart," Edith spoke into the quiet of her sanctuary. *But I would like him to be.* "He is helping me," Edith reminded herself and her words came from far away. "Nothing more."

"*You must let go, for the both of us…*"

A darkness appeared at the corners of her vision, and Edith blinked furiously. All the while, knowing it was to no avail.

"*…If you are only focused on avenging me, you are not truly living… You have to live.*"

An inky darkness crept across Edith's vision.

Her eyes slid shut, and everything went black and there was nothing more.

"Good morning, *La Belle au bois dormant.*"

La Belle au bois dormant.

Edith tried to make sense of those foreign words.

She'd heard them before. But where or who had spoken them, escaped her.

Edith fought through her stupor.

"Time to awaken, *La Belle au bois dormant.*"

There it was again. *La Belle au bois dormant.* Why did this man refer to her so?

In search of light and needing to look upon the owner of that rich baritone, Edith fought to open heavy eyes. She yearned to reach the owner of that darkly compelling voice, but an unrelenting torpor continued to keep her under its hold.

"*Edith.*"

She forced her lids open.

Edward knelt over her, a smile on his face.

"Edward," she murmured dreamily, and her eyes drifted shut once more.

It was as though out of her earlier musings, she'd summoned him to her side. He'd come here, to this place he knew to be special to Edith because he'd known he would find her here. All the hopeful thoughts she'd carried, made themselves present once more.

With a languid smile, Edith again opened her eyes and stilled. The seeds of apprehension sprouted in her belly and from them, the flowers of foreboding grew.

In the time she'd come to know Edward, Edith had learned the varying types and meanings behind each of his smiles: The one where he fought amusement as he might a battlefield foe. The crooked, hungry grin that graced very pleased lips whenever he touched her.

This smile he now wore was the blank, merciless one from when she'd invaded his clubs and he'd first looked upon her as a stranger.

Unsteadily, she forced herself onto her elbows, until she sat upright before Edward. The fact he'd made no attempt to help her did not escape Edith.

Edith's mouth went dry, and she swallowed several times to bring moisture back so she might speak.

As if Edward gathered the struggle Edith encountered, he removed a flask from within the front of his jacket and uncorked it. "Brandy this time, to fortify you."

With Edith's brain still hazy from when she'd fallen unconscious, Edward's cheerfully—cheer as false as his current grin—spoken words repeated in her mind.

This time to fortify you.

To fortify you *this* time.

How the transposed order of a few simple words contained so very different meanings.

At her hesitation, Edward wagged the silver cask under her nose and jolted Edith from her ruminations.

"Whiskey, I believe, is your spirits of choice." He gave her a cryptic look. "That is, unless you were lying."

Unable to meet his unswerving gaze, Edith glanced down. With fingers that trembled, she took Edward's offering.

"But you would never do that," he said in cloyingly sweet tones, that froze her when she had his flask to her lips.

Edward stared intently at Edith, but through his otherwise opaque gaze, she caught the knowing glint there, and her heart dropped. "You would never be so stupid as to feed me falsities, Edith."

Did he know?

Edith dampened her mouth.

Edward made a tsking sound. "Here I thought you darting your delicious tongue out and biting at your lips, bespoke fear. All the while it merely was your tell."

With that, she had confirmation—*he knows*.

Of course, he'd figured it out before she'd gotten revenge on Mr. Stillson. *Do you truly believe a man of Edward's reputation would not verify the veracity of your claims?*

Edith's eyes slid shut and *this* time she raised Edward's flask to her lips without hesitation. She drank and drank and continued drinking until a calming warmth permeated her entire being.

Some of the dread eased.

But more remained.

His horrible, mirthless chuckle rumbled in the copse and Edith made herself open her eyes.

Edward remained bent over her, making her feel so very small. "What do you have to say to me, Edith?" he asked harshly.

She bit her lip, and then recalled his charge from a moment ago, and made herself stop. "Please, Edward—"

"You have no leave to use my name, madam." Edward stared down the bridge of his aquiline nose at Edith like she was trash at his feet. "You never did."

The evidence of his loathing hurt like a physical ache inside.

He narrowed his eyes upon her. "If I were capable of admiring a person, then I confess, your singular focus on revenge would certainly earn mine. But I do *not* suffer liars. Which begs the question, Edith, what should I do?"

Catching his angular chin in hand, he rubbed that bone. "What, should, I, do?"

She knew him and it was why she knew he toyed with her and sought her fear. She'd be damned if she gave it to him.

And by the way a vein at his temple bulged, Edith's stoic silence enraged Edward.

Edward contemplated her and she continued to keep still through his scrutiny.

"Do you know, for your crimes, I believe I'll destroy your beloved sister and stupid parents, and absentee brother for your crimes. And," he said, so conversational in his disparagement and threat against her family, "I am going to find the utmost joy in their," he swept a derisive gaze over her person, "and *your*, demise. Immensely."

Rage and fear brought Edith flying to her feet. She barreled over and grabbed Edward by the satin lapels of his black wool jacket.

"Do not," she rasped, hating that hers emerged as an entreaty and not a threat, "hurt my family."

"Do whatever I will to you, though?" he jeered. "No pleas on your own behalf?" Edward caught her curled fists in his and moved them free of his person as effortlessly as he might brush dust from his sleeve.

He did not, however, release her.

"My *good* girl will make herself a sacrificial lamb." His eyes hardened. "And for *who*, sweet Edith? Your loyal, *loving* family?" he sneered. "The same *loyal, loving* family who doesn't believe you and hasn't helped you in any way, and who lets you go off on your own, all hours of the day and night so you can have your itch scratched by London's wickedest lord?"

She wrenched free of his hold and stood there, her breath coming in hard, noisy, painful spurts.

Only, he wasn't done with her.

"Though," he murmured, like a philosopher pondering the existence of man, "I haven't fucked you yet."

She flinched. It was her latest mistake with the Marquess of Malden; he sensed weakness the same way a huntsman smelled blood upon its prey.

Edward took a slow walk around Edith. As he did, her skin burned from where his eyes bore into her. She made herself keep her gaze directed at the branch of an old oak she'd climbed a lifetime ago.

At last, Edward stopped his predatory stroll and looked down the noble bridge of his nose at her. "I've sampled enough of you to know you aren't worth my efforts or my lenience."

Her body went hot and then cold with shame. How crude and how vulgar the marquess spoke of something that'd been so very special—special to *Edith*, anyway. Anguish in knowing how little she mattered and how effortlessly he'd destroy her and those she loved, threatened to consume her.

Edith balled her hands into fists; her nails left crescent imprints upon her palms. "How cruel you are," she whispered.

He chuckled and the mockery in that laugh raked over her skin like shards of broken glass and the pain left, just as agonizing.

"Ah, yes, but isn't that why you sought me out, sweet? To use me for my evil." A muscle rippled along his jawline. "No one uses me, Edith. No one lies to me. No one makes a fool of me. You are about to learn why."

She stared at his granite-hard features; this man beautifully carved by the hands of God, but possessed of Satan's dark, empty heart.

Edward found strength in weakness and thrived off fear and sadness, and she steeled herself with the reminder of his ruthlessness.

"You will not go near my family," she said quietly.

He arched a brow. "Won't I?"

Absolutely, he would. There was no limit to his evil.

"I will, Edith," he purred. "You know it, and you know how much I will enjoy every moment of your ruin."

A welcoming anger shot through her. "How dare you!"

His gloriously long eyelashes swept low. "What did you say to me?" he whispered.

Desperation and sorrow made her brave, or careless, or stupid. She tossed her head back.

"You heard me, *Edward*. I said, 'how dare you'."

Edward drew his lips back, baring his even, gleaming, white teeth.

Edith didn't back down.

"*You*, of all people, have a singular intention of obtaining revenge against your former best friends and partners because they…what? Forced you out of your business after you'd nearly gotten Mr. DuMond's wife *killed*."

His dark eyebrows flared ever so slightly.

"Yes, I know that," she said. "I do my research, too, *Edward*. And what did you do for me, anyway?" she spat. "You've spent more time seducing me than helping me."

"You loved every minute of it, sweetheart," he taunted.

She'd loved it and craved it. But that was not the point.

Edward reached for something inside his jacket, and she flinched, expecting him to draw a knife or pistol.

Edward froze, a hard smile on his lips. "You think I'm going to hurt you, love?" he withdrew a small notebook. "I should. Alas, I will not, as much pleasure as it would bring me to do so, you would enjoy it even more, and you don't deserve any of the climaxes I've given you."

Edward hurled the book at Edith's chest. She caught it, glanced at the small notebook, and then back at this cruel man she'd come to love.

He nudged his obdurate jaw Edith's way. "And as I told you, I'm capable of doing far more than two things at once." His features were a study in icy hatred, and she hurt all over, inside and out.

The unadulterated hatred blazing from his eyes sawed her heart in half, and breathless from pain, Edith, to hide her tears, gave all her attention to the notebook. She fanned through the pages; the words marked in pencil were blurred through the crystal sheen that marred her vision.

When she'd blinked enough, and the markings became clear, she stopped.

"They're debts," he snapped.

Edward needn't have bothered elucidating, she saw.

"After only recently accepting an offer of membership to my club, he's in thirty-five thousand deep at just my club. Turn the page," he barked, and Edith jumped.

Pages and pages containing vowels he'd snatched from her sister's killer.

Edith's mind whirred.

"So, my dear," he said, and snapped her attention back to him, "all the while, in between having my hand up your skirts and my fingers in your hot quim—"

Edith winced at that vulgarity.

"I was overseeing *my* end of our arrangement." A hard smile formed on his lips and a cruel glint lit his eyes. "And what were *you* doing? Using me for my services." He scraped a lecherous gaze up and down her person. "*All* of them."

She bit the inside of her cheek.

"Not that I didn't find *some* enjoyment," he remarked matter-of-factly. "I've never had a purse quite so tight as yours before. I would have fucked you, too. But now, you won't have that gift you crave even now."

How crude he made something that had been so very beautiful.

"I wish to thank you for the damage you've done to Mr. Stillson's finances," she said quietly.

He laughed at her; a derisive sound that hurt. "What I did? I didn't do it for you. His wealth is mine."

"You won't help me?"

Edward drew back and then laughed again. "My God, the ballocks on you." His false mirth ended. "I'm done giving you anything, Edith."

"I see."

She glanced about this place that had once been her sanctuary, that had just died as swift a death as her sister.

To hell with him. To hell with his cruelty and condescension.

Steeling her shoulders and her heart, Edith pulled her spine back. "I do not need you."

"Of course, you don't," he mocked. "You've proven so capable in your getting revenge for some imagined crime—"

"It isn't an imagined crime," she raged, hating him most for not believing her than for all the slights against her.

"That you struck a deal with me," he finished.

No, he was correct.

Around them, a soft spring breeze filtered through the copse; and upon their branches, the delicate leaves swished back and forth.

Edith hugged her arms around her middle and forgot him. It'd never been about him, anyway. She'd just made the mistake of letting her heart get involved. She'd lost focus. Along the way, she'd failed her sister.

She'd not make that mistake again.

Edith let her arms fall to her side and looked at Edward. "I do require help, but I certainly don't need yours."

He laughed.

"You think you're the only person—"

"If there were someone else you could rely upon, I'd trust you'd have gone to that person and not—"

"The Duke of Argyll," she stated calmly.

Edward's entire body jerked. Rage eviscerated the handsome angles and plains of his face, transforming them into a horrid, savage mask of ugly.

"What did you say?" he whispered.

Edith's heart hammered. She'd gone too far. She'd evoked the name of his mortal enemy. But she was too far along.

She edged her chin up a notch. "The Duke of Argyll," she repeated.

His nostrils flared.

"I should have sought him out." *Instead*. She let that dangle there, and by the narrowing of his eyes, he'd caught the unspoken word. "He is a gentlem—"

"*Gentle*man?" Edward's laughter cut her off and wonder of wonders he was capable of real mirth. "*Argyll?*"

"Given, he's affable and charming—"

"Oh, sweetheart, if you knew the *half* of his sins."

"Yes, well, I am in need of someone to kill the man who killed my sister, so I'm not looking for a *wholly* good fellow." Edith lifted her shoulders in a little shrug. "Just one who is good enough and not so self-centered and pigheaded as to be unwilling to help a woman who is in need of his assistance."

A mottled flush hit his cheeks. "You wouldn't dare."

And it was a testament of the hate which had grown between once best friends that Edward heard not the insults Edith hurled at him but and only Argyll's name.

Edith held his steely gaze.

"Look at me, Edward," she said quietly. "I sought *you* out. I deceived *you*. Do you *truly* believe I *wouldn't* turn to Argyll, or for that matter, *anyone* who can help avenge my sister's murder?"

Then, Edward, master of emotion that he was, reigned in his fury.

"God, Edith, with all the time you've spent with me and in my arms, how are you still *this* naïve?" he asked, his antipathy, agonizing.

He favored her with a pitying look. "I know the man as well as I know myself so let me spare you a visit to Argyll's and share a thing or two about the *gentle*man. He has a room, a cell of sorts, where he does all manner of sexually deviant things to his bed partners. He binds them. Where I serviced you, he will be selfish."

He held her eyes with his. "You will be a body to him, and at that, I suspect a very bruised body. Everything is about his wants, his pleasures."

"I have some familiarity with the former," she said, unable to keep the bitterness from creeping in.

Edith needn't have worried about Edward detecting her pained regret, he continued with his warnings.

"He will expect repayment." Edward looked pointedly at her neckline.

As in the form of her body.

So what if he did? She'd already given of herself to this man, who'd broken her heart completely, and so there could be no feelings left to feel.

"I know what you're thinking, sweet," he said with smug frostiness.

"You couldn't even begin to guess, my lord," Edith murmured.

For he didn't know anything about love and so couldn't begin to fathom the thoughts in her head.

"You are thinking I've schooled you for other men."

Edith curled up and shriveled inside. *This* is what he believed she'd contemplated?

"I know what you are trying to do, Edward," she said, shakily. "You are trying to scare me."

His lips curled up in a sneer. "If that scares you sweet, you have *no* idea what truly awaits you with Argyll."

Edith shivered.

Neither she nor Edward moved. They stood motionless, upon the same earth where Edward had shown her such bliss.

Even with the vile insults and words he'd hurled, she hated herself for remembering every beautiful moment she'd spent in his arms.

"I want you to vow you'll not hurt my family, my lord," she finally said.

He looked at her like she was half-mad, and maybe she was for daring to stand up to him.

Edward approached, stalking her, toying with her. "And just how do you intend to stop me, sweet?"

He'd shown her the pleasure her body was capable of, and he'd also taught her not to bend in the face of fear.

Edith strode the rest of the way to meet him with bold, confident steps.

Shock and desire sparked in his eyes.

"You may know my secrets and sins, Lord Malden," Edith lifted her chin, "however, *you* forget, I'm in possession of secrets that could destroy your plans for revenge—your intent to target Lord Rutherford's's sister-in-law."

From between perfectly even, bone-white teeth, Edward hissed. "Are *you* threatening *me*?"

Despite her attempt at bravery, the rage which poured off him in waves sent Edith retreating a step.

She forced herself to dig in.

"No, Edward." Taking a deep breath, she shook her head. "I am reminding you, we *both* hold damaging information that would be ruinous to each of us. Let that be e-enough," she said, choking on emotion, "and this th-the last time we see one another."

Edith squeezed her eyes tightly shut. What was wrong with her? Edward proved himself to be the beast the world professed he was. He should be the last person she'd ever wish to cross paths with again. Why then did the realization this would be the last they met bring with it the crushing weight of loss?

It is done.

We are done.

In the whirlwind of just a few days, she'd gotten lost in the lure of his seductive pull.

But it was over.

Edith opened her eyes and found Edward continued to study her in that impenetrable way. How had she failed to note how very close to black the sapphire depths of his irises, in fact, were?

Bowing her head in silent acknowledgment of what they'd shared—even though it'd meant nothing at all to him—Edith headed for the tree-lined walkway that led her away from Edward.

"You are wasting your time, sweet," he called out. "I know Argyll's taste in women. *You*, my dear, are *not* it."

"I've heard that before from you." Keeping her head held high, Edith kept marching and refused to let him get the rise he sought out of her.

And then, she stepped out of the shadows made by her former sanctuary in the woods, and into the sunlight.

CHAPTER 14

MALDEN, STOOD BEHIND THE GILDED pulpit at the center of his kingdom with his hands clasped behind him and surveyed the casino floors. Set several feet above the action, it allowed him a full vantage over his domain.

Since he'd parted ways with Edith three days earlier, he'd put all his attention back firmly where it needed to be.

His gaze landed on the current *auction* unfolding; on that stage courtesans were charlatans who feigned chastity all to satisfy the desires of depraved men who hungered to debauch a virgin.

With a critical eye, Malden assessed the latest *innocent* prize to be won, a blonde beauty, attired in a lacy negligee that left nothing to a man's imagination. On the surface, the prostitute had all the mannerisms down; bowed head, hands clasped before her as if in prayer.

After having had Edith in his arms, and rousing a true innocent to her first climaxes, he recognized just how dreadful a showing these stage actresses put on. Their lips were too rouged, their mouths, too coy. The sway of their hips too seductive.

Malden hardened his jaw. The entertainments he offered, the shows the prostitutes here put on, and the services they offered, were top caliber or they were sent elsewhere, leftovers for lesser clubs like Forbidden Pleasures.

He did a search of the clients taking part in the evening's debauchery. They sat perched on the edge of their red velvet chairs, straining toward the actresses on the stage. By the way his depraved patrons salivated and their hands flew up over and over, driving the bids, higher and higher, they remained oblivious to the mediocre show being put on.

Bored by that poorly pretending virgin, Edward looked away in disgust.

Maybe it was not the fault of the experienced Cyprians. Would Malden before, even with his connoisseur's eye, have noted the failings that gave them away if it weren't for Edith?

Edith who, in contrast to the women he kept company with, wore her innocence like that glorious, chaste, Greek goddess, Artemis.

"…I want you to show me where you'd kiss me…"

And just like that, all his previously relaxed muscles went taut.

"I don't want anyone here, Edward…I only want you…"

His breathing grew harsher and faster.

He'd never wanted to fuck Edith more than when she'd turned into a raging spitfire who'd gone toe to toe with him, and that he never would, made him gnash his teeth like a beast who'd been thwarted of his meal. Only if he were to possess her body could he be rid of these thoughts of her.

But to do so, would give her the greatest of pleasures, none of which she deserved for her sins.

He'd left her with an ache that'd go unfulfilled, and every day would grow stronger and stronger. And *each* and *every* single day of her miserable virginal life, she'd be left with her unrequited desire as a reminder of the lies she'd told him.

What he'd not anticipated, however, was that mindless lust would take on a lifelike force in him and grow *each* and *every* day.

"My lord?"

At Grufton's unexpected intrusion, Malden growled. "What the hell is it, Gruff—"

"The lady has moved."

Malden stared at his most loyal henchman a moment before those words actually registered.

The guard doffed the cap he'd taken to covering his bald head with. "Caught word she had the jarvie waiting. Same fellow, driving.

The jarvie?

Then, it finally hit Malden what the other man was saying.

He released a quiet curse.

"When?" he demanded, already quitting his place at his pulpit and heading for the door directly behind him.

Gruffton followed in close pursuit. "Near a quarter an hour ago."

"A quarter of a fucking hour?" Malden thundered the moment they were alone.

His head guard's pallor turned white. "I've got Dailey following her. He'll report back when she returns from wherever it is—"

Malden stopped in his tracks, gripped the guard by the front of his jacket, and shoved him against the wall.

"I didn't want fucking Dailey to report back," Malden whispered. "I wanted any information on where the lady lands brought to *me*, immediately."

Gruffton's giant Adam's apple bobbed wildly. "Didn't want to bother you with—"

Malden stuck his nose in the other man's face. "You may have proved your loyalty to me before, but so help me God, if you ever gainsay my orders again…"

Malden tightened his hold upon Gruffton. "If you so much as presume to think about it, I'll personally throw you out on the street and make sure you never work a fucking day in your life. You will die alone, an old man on the streets, with your body eaten by rats and only the memories remaining of your greatest mistake in life. Am I clear?"

Gruffton gave a quick, uneven nod. "Y-Yes, my lord," he stammered.

With a long string of black curses, Malden released his servant and headed a quick clip for the courtyard stables.

The head guard called after him. "Do you want me to tell you when Davies sends word where she's—"

"I know where she's going," Malden bit out.

Oh, he knew.

Fury roiled in his gut and rage nearly blinded him. She'd betrayed him once before, but this day, she'd committed a grave and mortal sin. And when Malden had his hands on her, he would make Edith Caldecott regret ever having transgressed him.

Fueled by a near-carnal bloodlust, Malden, after a mad ride

through London, arrived outside an all too familiar townhouse. As palatial as Malden's own future ducal estate in Town, this edifice, with its ornate columns and gilded moldings was impressive in its own right.

It'd also been a residence Malden once visited…and often.

When he arrived, Malden kept to the shadows and his gaze trained on the limestone manor in Mayfair. Aside from a pair of floor-to-ceiling length windows being lit, the townhouse remained, otherwise, bathed in darkness.

The occupant of this particular household kept as late hours as Malden and only returned when dawn approached. He wouldn't be home at this time. But the Red Riding Hood who sought out the duke didn't know those details about the latest wolf she'd gone to for *help*.

Malden fisted his hands at his side.

Oh, he'd make her regret even the idea of seeking Argyll out.

And then, the rattle of carriage wheels infiltrated the absolute quiet.

Edith.

Unlike the previous times when the driver had dropped his passenger off outside Malden's gaming hell, this time the fellow all but drove to the front like he escorted the lady of the house and not some scandalous chit sneaking about.

Without assistance, Edith let herself out of her hack with a haste that hinted at her eagerness to see the duke.

"Look at me, Edward…I sought you out. I deceived you. Do you truly believe I wouldn't turn to Argyll, or for that matter, anyone who can help avenge my sister's murder…?"

A low growl formed in Malden's throat and remained stuck there like some kind of monster's graveled warning.

He no longer doubted she would. He'd underestimated Edith two times too many now.

Edith paused on the pavement. Just ten yards away, Malden stood close enough to detect the stiffening of her spine; she, the prey who'd just sensed her predator. Her deep satin sapphire hood shifted, as she angled her neck a fraction.

She felt him here. The same way her scent was imprinted on Malden, so too had he imprinted upon her.

On a silent tread, Malden started for her.

Then, like a quick, little rabbit, Edith picked up her pace, scampered for the tall black gates that stood open in welcome of visitors and took the eight stone steps quickly.

Edith knocked.

With a silent curse, Malden retreated to the opposite side of the street.

The lady shuffled back and forth on her feet. Even with her hooded frame and back to him, he knew she was biting at that plump lower lip of hers.

Malden's lashes grew heavy, and his prick became hard as a pike.

Open the door already, he silently railed at Argyll's lax servant.

As soon as the man turned her away, the sooner she'd return and find him waiting. Edward would claim her mouth—and then *all* of her.

But before he did, he'd turn her over his knee and spank her.

Malden's breathing became labored.

At last, Argyll's loyal butler finally answered the door.

Dixon, wizened and white-haired as the old fellow had been since Malden was a lad of thirteen, ducked his head out.

The moment he clapped eyes on Edith's delicate figure and the quality of her cloak, his bushy eyebrows shot up.

Malden waited for Edith to be turned away—which she would.

That was another difference between he and Argyll.

The duke had a gaggle of sisters. As such, Argyll may be a depraved, dark, lord like Malden, but he had to keep up at least some façade of *proper gentleman*. He didn't have the luxury of entertaining cloaked women in his family's household.

Malden, on the other hand, didn't have the burden of people reliant on him. He was free to do what he pleased, whenever and however, he pleased.

Finally, the servant closed the door in Edith's face.

Triumph filled Malden.

Edith's shoulders sagged.

A moment later, the door opened a second time. Only it wasn't Dixon who appeared.

Malden's body turned to stone.

Argyll.

By the way the duke still sported a raven black wool evening coat with its buttons undone, he'd recently returned from Forbidden Pleasures.

Affable, roguish, and in possession of a countenance that'd earned him the hearts of ladies and wicked wantons alike, the duke's effortless charm had previously left Malden drolly amused.

Now?

Fury sent Malden's hands folding into reflexive fists.

Now, Malden wanted to charge like a savage beast and take his former friend apart at the limbs.

While Edith spoke, the duke listened.

She must have stopped talking because Argyll contemplated Edith for a long time.

Don't you fucking dare, Argyll. Don't you fucking—

And then, the duke, because he'd always done precisely as he wished or pleased, did just that—he motioned Edith inside.

In the speed with which she complied, she showed none of the fear of Argyll that she had in her first meeting with him.

That realization should bring with it a thrill of satisfaction.

It *should*.

Instead, as Edith disappeared from Malden's line of vision, a visceral rage threatened to consume him. For he knew, Edith was easy prey for a man of Argyll's experience.

The duke lingered at the threshold, and like one who sensed an enemy lurking in the shadows, he ducked his head out.

By the casual grin Argyll wore, he appeared all too eager for a battle.

Oh, and there would be. For a beast, born of that bastard's betrayal, *did* lie in wait.

Malden would rip Argyll apart for having even breathed the same air as Edith. Then, he'd steal her away and claim her body as he should have done long before she'd gone to Argyll.

The duke shut the door.

Lust and bloodlust comingled, leaving Malden hard. With a razor-sharp focus, he locked his gaze on that gleaming emerald green panel between he and Edith.

Were Malden to force his way inside like some crazed madman, it'd reveal a weakness to the last men who could see any from him.

No. Malden? He'd wait.

With that, he headed for Edith's hired hack.

CHAPTER 15

A GILDED CHARLES BALTAZAR CLOCK TICKED away; a steady, recurring tapping sound made all the louder by silence and the wee morning hour.

Edith should be afraid.

She stood in the office of London's most notorious rogue; a man rumored to have seduced young and old alike, who had left a string of broken hearts throughout England, and dueled men for the pleasure of having their wives as his lovers.

Waiting in silence as long as she'd been and contemplating his pink and green floral Aubusson carpet, the duke revealed not even a scintilla of impatience.

Where an aura of sin and darkness surrounded Edward, the Marquess of Malden, the Duke of Argyll possessed a soothing air of calm and lightness that made fear of him an impossibility.

Instead, she found herself riddled with guilt for appealing to Edward's avowed enemy for help—which was preposterous!

She'd been determined to avenge Evie, by any means possible. It had become Edith's sole purpose for living.

Edward had withdrawn his support and ended their connection. In the cruel parting words, he'd volleyed and how easily he'd cut Edith out of his life; he couldn't have been clearer—she didn't matter to him.

And yet, knowing all that still did nothing to erase the feelings of guilt.

Edward had snarled and mocked and hurled insults throughout the course of their first meeting. The duke patiently waited for Edith to speak; a perfect gentleman, he did not press her.

Why, he didn't even check that gilt French clock, as he was *well within* his rights to do. His responsibilities extended from a dukedom to a number of sisters and a business he personally ran. Plus, the hour was late.

She should go.

"Pretty, isn't it?"

That casually spoken question brought Edith's head flying up.

"Your Grace?" she asked hesitantly.

"The rug," he murmured, his voice a pleasing baritone not at all graveled and angry and harsh.

Edith immediately shifted her focus back to the carpet in question. Previously, she'd but absently stared at it while lost in thoughts of Edward.

For the first time, Edith, from deep within the protective folds of her hood, actually considered the article.

At the center of the flatweave Aubsson rug bloomed embroidered pink peonies, roses, camellias, and dahlias, interspersed with green chrysanthemum, carnations, and gladioli.

Amidst the rainbow of flowers, it was easy to envision oneself within a gloriously wild, beautiful gardens.

"It is very lovely," she said softly.

Though, the duke's exquisite carpet would never be considered a match for the heavy, masculine furnishings.

"Not precisely fit for a gentleman's office," he drawled, unnervingly following her thoughts.

Her cheeks warmed. "No. I didn't—"

The duke waved his hand. "Oh, you didn't have to say anything. I'm well aware of the incongruity. Alas, my sisters insisted on picking my carpet and I allowed them that choice. I'll let you in on a secret, miss."

The duke cupped a hand around the right side of his mouth and spoke in an outrageously loud whisper. "I'm helpless to deny them anything." His kindly eyes sparkled. "Though, I suspect they well know it."

They both smiled.

Despite herself, the evidence of the Duke of Argyll's brotherly devotion warmed her, in a further betrayal of Edward.

How very playful the duke was. Between his handsome-to-the-point-of-beautiful features and irresistible charm, Edith certainly understood his appeal among the fairer sex.

But, in a world where men shielded ladies from everything, Edith far preferred the way Edward spoke to her the same way he would any man.

The duke also proved to be more patient than she deserved.

Where Edward had snarled and mocked and hurled insults throughout the course of their first meeting, the duke, a perfect gentleman let Edith set the pace of their meeting.

"I want to thank you for seeing me," she began softly.

"My pleasure. Though, I would be remiss if I failed to point out I don't technically *see* you." He nudged his chin at Edith's hood.

Her cheeks warmed. "No. I know. Forgive me."

With shaky hands, she made to lower her covering.

The duke closed the distance between them in three quick strides.

"*…He has a room, a cell of sorts, where he does all manner of sexually deviant things to his bed partners…*"

The Duke of Argyll caught her gently by the wrists so that his hands formed tender manacles about her.

"*…He binds them…Where I serviced you, he will be selfish…You will be a body to him, and at that, I suspect a very bruised body…*"

Gasping, Edith attempted to wrestle free.

The duke instantly released her.

"Hey, now, love." The roguish gentleman immediately lifted his large, tanned hands and stepped away.

Edith eyed him warily.

He spoke in the kind of soothing tones he might use with a skittish mare. "There is no need to be afraid. You don't have to show yourself if you are uncomfortable doing so."

I needn't reveal myself to him if I'm uncomfortable doing so?

A strained giggle bubbled from her lips. Given the favor she needed of him, she would be required to reveal far more than her identity.

Edith lowered her hood.

Surprise filled his sun-bronzed features. "Miss Caldecott."

She started. "You—"

"Know you?" he finished the remainder of her question. "I know you, love. Over the years, we've attended several of the same events."

Where she'd been invisible to Edward, the duke had seen her.

But then, people tended to, just *not* for the reasons Edith wished.

"Because of my sister," she said woodenly. The fact her sister had died happened to be the only reason *anyone* knew Edith lived.

The duke folded his arms at his chest in a lazy way that would have stolen any other woman's breath.

"*Because* you looked as miserable attending the functions as I myself did," he drawled.

A disarmingly boyish grin tipped his hard lips up at the corners.

Instead of the duke's grin doing the wild things to her heart and belly, that Edward's hardest, most cynical smile wrought, it reassured and calmed Edith, further.

The duke gestured to a leather button sofa near a French-styled marble fireplace, adorned in floral carvings.

"Please, make yourself comfortable, Miss Caldecott."

"Never tell me," Edith ventured. "More of your sisters' influence?"

"*You* have guessed correctly."

His blue eyes sparkled. "But you mustn't let a soul know that where my sisters are concerned, I'm the worst softy, or you will thoroughly ruin my reputation," he said, ringing a laugh from Edith.

The duke perched a hip on the arm of the sofa.

"Please," he repeated, this time, all seriousness and still without Edward's impatience.

Where Edward left Edith all tangled up in knots, the duke evoked in her, a tranquil calm, which made it easy for her to join him.

Taking a breath, she just came out with it. "I have come to request your help with a *personal* matter."

"Has someone hurt you?" he asked with such offense on her behalf, Edith was confused a moment, that maybe they knew one another better, after all.

"No," she assured him.

Only, that isn't altogether true. Between Evie's death and Edward stomping all over your heart, you carry invisible scars the world cannot see.

The gentleman must have heard something unspoken in her murmuring.

He leveled an utterly penetrating stare on Edith.

A chill ran along her spine.

If that scares you sweet, you have no idea what truly awaits you with Argyll…

For a sliver in time, Edward's warnings paralyzed her.

Stop. That is what he wanted to do.

Edith regained her footing. "My sister was killed," she said, without preamble.

The duke's eyebrows flared slightly.

Edith proceeded to tell him everything: from the sudden onset of Evie's illness and its coinciding with Mr. Stillson's visit, to Edith and Emmy's suspicions.

When she'd finished, the duke's exquisitely defined features were a study in intensity and revealed none of his earlier relaxedness. Just a pace away, Edith could make nothing out of the opaque mask he now wore.

His Grace did *not*, however, look scornfully upon her.

"Who else have you shared this with?"

"The rest of my siblings, my parents, and…" *Edward.*

His Grace stared at her questioningly.

"And that is all," she demurred.

She fought the urge to squirm under his incisive gaze.

He straightened from his relaxed pose. "And what is *their* opinion, Miss Caldecott?"

This again! She'd been foolish to think a man, also a stranger, would believe her when the men in her own *family* did not. She lived in a world where men were too blind to see the truth before them, all because it fell from a *woman's* lips.

"I know how this sounds, Your Grace." A bitter laugh bubbled from her lips. "Trust me, I *know.*"

Edith marched over to him and tipped her chin back to meet his stare.

"I *know* what you are thinking," she said calmly. "You believed

I'm just another melodramatic woman, a lady maddened by grief." Edith touched a palm to her breast. "But I am not, Your Grace. I—"

The duke placed two fingers against her lips, silencing the rest.

Then, with a deliberate languor, he proceeded to run the pad of his thumb, back and forth, over her lower lip.

Edith's breath quickened. The duke possessed the expert touch of a rogue, and despite her earlier apathy, the whispery softness of his caress brought with it a welcome warmth.

The ghost of a grin on his hard lips indicated he knew the effect his touch was having.

"…Argyll is not unlike me…"

Recalling Edward's warning, Edith hastily stepped away from the raffish duke. The backs of her knees collided with the sofa, and she tumbled back into her earlier seat.

Argyll turned away.

Panic pounded in her chest.

He is showing me the door.

She opened her mouth to call for him to stop, when Argyll took a path to his well-stocked sideboard, instead.

The gentleman contemplated the many crystal bottles lined up before he ultimately settled on a gold-rimmed decanter and snifter.

With both in hand, the duke returned to Edith and slid his powerful frame next to her on the sofa.

Unlike Edward who tore bottle Stoppard's out with his teeth and spit them on the floor, the Duke of Argyll, all urbane sophistication, carefully removed that plug.

After he'd poured a drink, he wordlessly offered it over to Edith.

She stared at the glass.

"Come, Miss Caldecott," he said gently. "Think of it as liquid fortitude. Something *also* tells me you are in fact, a lady who doesn't turn her nose up at indulging in spirits."

Edith lifted startled eyes to his cobalt blue ones twinkling with amusement.

He winked.

Unnerved by his accurate assumption, Edith accepted the

drink, took one sip, and then another, until the velvety fragrant burgundy spirits ushered a soothing warmth through her previously tense body.

"Are you familiar with the tale of Julius Caesar?" he asked.

That unanticipated question brought her up short.

She nodded slowly. "Yes, Your Grace. My sisters and I took particular delight in putting on performances—"

"I am aware," he said without recrimination, which he'd certainly be well within his right to expression.

She expected the entire world knew of the notorious Caldecott Recitals; an annual event where the *ton* gathered to witness the ghastly musical performance put on by Edith and her sisters.

Edith grimaced. "Not *those* performances," she said.

He smiled encouragingly.

"We would perform plays and act out scenes. Tired of the books our governess insisted we read, we would sit outside our brother's lessons and listen quietly as he was forced to read aloud. Though we did not hear all of it, and our brother closely guarded his volume because he knew how desperately we wished to read it, and delighted in tormenting us."

Edith registered the duke's stupefied look and realized she rambled.

She cleared her throat. "Among our favorites to act out was Caesar's death scene in Shakespeare's work." God, how had she ever been entertained by any plot featuring the death of a character?

She glanced up.

Intrigue filled the duke's almost-too-sharp-to-be-perfect features.

"Did you and your sisters perform the only major scene with Caesar's wife?" he asked. "Or have you heard it, perhaps?"

She shook her head. "No."

"On the fateful night before Caesar was assassinated, his wife Calpurnia, had a dream. '*Caesar was a statue which like a fountain with n hundred spouts did run pure blood; and many lusty Romans came smiling and did bathe their hands in it.*'"

Enrapt, Edith hung on the duke's every word.

"She begged him not to go to the Senate," he spoke in solemn tones. "She told him of her nightmare—"

Edith moved to the edge of her seat. "But he went anyway," she whispered.

"On the contrary," the duke said, sliding closer so his thigh touched hers. "Caesar was so moved by his wife's sorrow, he promised her he'd not attend, but then his dearest friend, Brutus, urged Caesar not to be swayed by silly omens. And the rest, Miss Caldecott is now history," he concluded. "Do you know what I am trying to say, Miss Caldecott?"

Edith shook her head. Had she not consumed those strong spirits so quickly, she expected she might.

"Sometimes, Miss Caldecott, there is only intuition to guide us. Those who do not trust those feelings inside one's gut, are certain to a similar doom as Caesar."

And then through the slight fog of drink, she finally understood the morale of his telling.

Oh, God.

Tears filled her eyes, and she closed them. He didn't think her mad. He did not dismiss her outright.

"Given the unconventional nature of our early morn meeting, might I use your given name, Miss Caldecott?"

Perhaps it was the—as His Grace called it—liquid fortitude of his fine brandy, or maybe it was the simple fact that the favor she'd put to him required some level of closeness with the man, but she found herself volunteering without hesitation.

"Edith."

"Edith," he murmured.

Those two syllables rolled off his tongue, smooth and sensual and that the duke could manage that feat with Edith's marm of a name was testament to his formidable charm.

Her gaze lingered on his hard symmetrical lips that may as well have been carved to perfection by Michelangelo himself.

The thick fringe of his pale blond lashes swept low but did little to conceal the heat radiating from the depths of his irises.

"Edith," he repeated, like he'd tasted something delicious and wished for another bite.

She warily studied his smooth movements, and even with the

haze left by drinking too fast, she recalled every cautionary tale Edward had shared about his former friend and partner.

For the veneer of gentlemanliness to the duke, the fact remained: Argyll possessed a reputation as black as sin and engaged in business no respectable gentleman *would*.

"You have a lovely name," he murmured in a husky, musical baritone.

The duke's whispered words filtered in and out of past remembrances of a far different man.

She closed her eyes and imagined another.

"You have lovely breasts, Edith… They are beautifully formed and fit in my palms as if they were made for me…"

Her breath caught and that place between her legs stirred.

"It is a beautiful name, for a beautiful woman…"

Through his lilting murmurings, Edith's first meeting with Edward resurfaced in her mind.

"…A marm's name to go with your marm's looks…"

This is what the world warned of and whispered about the duke—he possessed a charm to rival Satan in disguise, out to snatch a soul.

Snapped from her memories of Edward, Edith giggled and swiftly took another long sip to hide the rest of her amusement.

Her time with Edward had taught her dominant males didn't take well to anyone taking them anything less than seriously.

The duke eyed her bemusedly. "I've said something to amuse you, Edith?"

"It is just, I'm well aware of what my name is, Your Grace," she drawled.

After all, she'd been saddled with it her entire life.

"Gregory." Amusement added another glimmer to his eyes. He folded his arms at his broad chest. "And do tell?"

"A marm's name, Your—"

"Gregory," he insisted.

The duke hooded his lashes. "*Your* Gregory, if you so wish it. Who has given you reason to believe your name is somehow less, Edith?" he asked softly.

Warning bells went off. This had been a mistake.

With unstable fingers, Edith set her empty glass down and

made to stand. "It doesn't matter," she whispered, hating that her voice cracked.

But the duke caught her by the wrist and kept her seated there.

"That someone hurt you, matters a great deal, Edith," he said with a quiet insistence and indignation on her behalf, and she found her reservations flagging.

She could not be angry at Edward for having spoken the truths he had to her. Hurt, but not angered.

The duke took her hands in his larger ones, encircling them with warmth.

"Whoever is responsible for that sad little look in your eyes," he murmured, giving her a gentle but firm squeeze, "is a man undeserving of you."

Edith forced her lips up in a semblance of a smile. "What gives you the opinion that it was a man?"

He scoffed. "*Of course*, it was a man. It is *always* a man. We're not a clever species, you know. In fact," he leaned in and whispered, "we are the absolute worst."

His playful banter drew a laugh from her. When her amusement faded, he contemplated her through darkened eyes.

"You never did tell me what it is you'd like me to do for you, Edith."

Before Edward, she would have missed the duke's clear double entendre.

It was enough to raise warning bells.

But there was also no one else to turn to.

Edward's harsh rejection and hateful words hit her all over again like a kick to the stomach; the pain as great as it'd been in Hyde Park.

Strong fingers caressed her chin and pulled Edith from the misery of her thoughts.

The duke guided her gaze to his. "Edith, you've come to me in the dead of night, without anyone to accompany you?"

Edith glanced down at her lap. "I've come alone."

At his protracted silence, she looked up to find the duke studied her with hard, searching eyes.

She blinked and that cynical glint was gone, so Edith wondered if she'd imagined it.

His Grace let his hand fall to his side and went about pouring Edith another drink.

This time, Edith took his gift of libations without reluctance.

They sat in silence for a bit. While they did, Edith sipped from her snifter.

"We've now ascertained you did not come to me so I might duel a fellow for besmirching your name," he said after she'd consumed the contents.

Picking up the bottle, added to her glass a third time. "Which begs the question of what service I may provide you with, Edith?" he asked, handing over another glass.

She stared into the blurry contents of her drink.

This is bad. All of it.

Oddly, that understanding existed in a faraway corner of her sluggish mind.

Edith took another drink. A welcome warmth chased away her reservations.

"I would ask you to help me avenge my sister's death, Your Grace."

She shared the rest: her plans for her bastard of a cousin—all her plans.

"You needn't bankrupt him as I've already—" Edith blinked slowly.

I shouldn't have said that.

"Who have you gone to before me, Edith?"

Even foggy from drink, she still detected the steel underlying his words.

She hesitated. She'd deceived another man and that had cost Edith his support and…the gentleman altogether.

Her throat tightened painfully.

Tears filled her eyes and blurred the remaining brandy in her glass.

"Ed—the Marquess of Malden." Her throat tightened.

Silence met her announcement.

Betrayal. It is yet another betrayal of a man you care too deeply for.

Except, unlike Edward who frothed at the mouth and spit with rage at the mention of his former friends, the duke's features remained remarkably even.

"Did he decline to help you?" he asked.

"No." She shook her head. "I…managed to secure his cooperation. He bankrupted him—" Edith grimaced. "Or, he was in the process of doing so—"

His neck notched up a fraction. "And?"

"And when he discovered my betrayal, he…He quite clearly indicated I was dead to him, as was his vow to help." Edith's lower lip quivered and to hide that telltale tremble she downed the remainder of her drink.

Argyll rubbed a palm over his mouth.

"Edith," he began, and she tensed, already hearing the gentle let-down coming. "I cannot simply have a man killed."

My God, it hadn't occurred to her she'd now given two men her revenge plans, which included murder. If they were to reveal her intentions to the world…

Fear left her mouth dry.

Edith gave a juddering nod and set her glass down at her feet.

"I u-understand," she stammered. "I'm s-sorry, Your G-Grace." She jumped up, but her legs swayed under her. "If you'll excuse me."

What was wrong with her voice? And *legs*?

Edith managed to get herself all the way to the entrance of Argyll's office.

"Allow me to finish, Edith," he called out.

Heart hammering, she made herself face the duke.

He strolled over on sleek, languid strides—they were Edward's steps, and she imagined a time when Edward and the duke practiced those languorous steps.

At some point during her quick flight, he'd shed his jacket and now remained attired in nothing more than his shirtsleeves, trousers, and boots.

Why can't he be another? Pain knifed at her heart. *Why can he not be the man I truly yearn for?*

The duke stopped less than a pace away from Edith. "I will not have a man killed unless I myself confirm he is guilty of those crimes."

"I…understand…" she said, her voice thick.

And she did. Edith herself loathed the idea of seeing a man

dead, but grief and mindless rage at what he'd done to Evie compelled her—as did the understanding that her cousin had attempted to kill Hutchinson—one day he would succeed.

"I don't believe you do," the duke said gently. "I will have a thorough investigation conducted. I'll get you definitive answers to confirm what you know to be true so that we both have the facts laid out before us, and then…I will handle him so you, and the rest of your family, need never worry about him again."

Edith's breath caught. Joy left her light as she'd not been since Evie's passing.

"…let me spare you a visit to Argyll's and share a thing or two about the gentleman…Everything is about his wants, his pleasures.

Edward's taunting voice continued to echo around her mind.

"He will expect repayment…"

Her stomach churned.

The duke had offered everything Edith wished for—and more. And, among all the things she'd learned in her short time with Edward, he taught her, nothing was for free.

"I…cannot thank you enough," she said, her voice hollow.

A question filled the duke's eyes.

I'm going to be ill.

Unable to meet his gaze, Edith laid her palms upon the lapels of the duke's jacket.

The hard wall of muscles bunched under her hands and as she slid her unsteady fingers over his chest, the searing sense of betrayal threatened to consume her, and she wanted it to. So that way, she needn't do the things she'd shared with Edward, with this man.

The duke captured her wrists again in a gentle vise.

"Hey, now, love," he murmured. "What are you doing?"

Her cheeks warmed. "You will, of course, expect repayment."

"Repayment," Argyll repeated dumbly. He stared at her. "*What?*" he asked, so thoroughly befuddled, Edith's tension eased—*some.* "Edith, are you *offering* yourself to me?"

Argyll blanched.

If her blush grew any hotter, she was going to catch fire, and in this particular moment, she very much welcomed the idea of such a fate to get her out of this.

"*You are wasting your time, sweet…I know Argyll's taste in women. You, my dear, are not it.*"

"I'm not your type," she whispered, recalling Edward's warning. How was it she found herself both relieved and panicked?

Confusion lit the duke's eyes.

Suddenly, he recoiled. "Egads, Edith! That isn't it. I would *never* have you that way. I would never have *any* woman that way."

Hope filled her breast. "You wouldn't?" she whispered.

He laughed. "*God*, no. Do I strike you as *that* kind of gentleman?"

"No," she exclaimed.

"Or one who needs to force a woman, Edith?" he sounded and looked visibly insulted at the mere possibility.

"No, Your Grace."

She chewed at her lower lip. "It is…I'd just thought—"

The duke stilled; his expression grew more serious.

"Malden," he muttered.

Refusing to confirm that correct assumption he'd made, Edith glanced down.

"Edith, look at me."

He possessed the manner of voice to compel an angel to give his soul to Satan.

"First, for the love of all that is holy, given the nature of our meeting and discussion, would you *please* refer to me as Gregory."

She lifted her gaze to his and nodded. "Yes, Gregory."

The duke—Gregory—moved his gaze over her face and then gripped her lightly by her shoulders.

"I am not Malden," he said gravely. "I've known him my entire life. I know the man he was and the man he's become, and I am not, nor have I ever been, nor will I ever *be,* him."

Hearing him speak, even in the veiled way he did, about Edward only deepened this agonizing sense of betrayal against a man who didn't even deserve her loyalty.

"I would never force you, Edith," the duke said, pulling her out of her sorrowful musings. "*Not* because I don't desire you." His eyes darkened. "I do, but because I'd *never* take something from you or any woman that you didn't want to give."

He pushed her cloak back and took her shoulders in his hands.

Then, he edged her sleeves down enough to allow him to caress the pads of his thumbs over the skin he'd exposed.

With the duke being of similar height, build, and coloring as Edward she could almost imagine the duke was that other man; the one who set her body ablaze with nothing more than a look.

And oh, how she wished it *was* Edward.

"I require no repayment," the duke said. "I would, however, very much like to kiss you, Edith."

Edward's voice reached through her clouded state.

"*…Nothing is free…*"

Edith stiffened, but the duke continued that butterfly-soft, soothing massage of her shoulders.

"I suspect you would like me to kiss you, Edith."

All the brandy she'd consumed had turned the duke's husky baritone, hypnotizing, and in her mind, she envisioned Edward.

"*…because you've been so very good for me, I'll pet you, here.*"

Her breath hitched.

"*You're already wet for me…That makes me very happy, Edith…*"

She dimly registered him cupping her by the nape.

Edith braced for Edward's hard, greedy possession of her mouth and whimpered.

Only, the kiss bestowed this time was a gentle taking and agonizingly chaste.

A frustrated moan spilled from her lips.

Why did he not give her what she yearned for?

Edward stilled in her arms.

Dazed, she lifted her heavy lashes, and found, not Edward, but, another man, looking back.

Her head felt heavy, and she couldn't make sense of the gentleman gazing at her.

Raw lust blazed from his eyes.

The duke.

Edith gasped and made to step away, but the Duke of Argyll tugged her into his arms with a force that brought her body flush with his. Where before he so tenderly kissed her, now he pillaged her mouth.

Edith remained passive through his kiss. He clearly possessed the same level of skill and experience as Edward, so why did this embrace feel different?

Where Edward tasted of the woody, spicy hint of cinnamon, the duke bore the fragrant sweetness of brandy and strawberries.

The two men tasted as different as they were in temperament.

And maybe those differences between the two men accounted for Edith's thoughts drifting back to Edward while a different man kissed her.

It was as though the duke sensed Edith's indifference.

Her lack of responsiveness seemed to enflame rather than offend him.

Gone was all gentleness he'd shown Edith earlier. The duke gripped her neck and angled her neck to deepen his kiss with a force that stole her breath. He slipped his free hand under her buttocks and squeezed the flesh savagely, hard enough to bring tears to her eyes.

This embrace, *this* harkened to that of another man—the man she yearned for. The one she so pitifully wished wanted her in return.

And at last, Edith allowed herself to surrender fully to her wild imaginings.

Edward pressed her against the long, rigid line of his shaft, then rotated his hips against the flat of her belly in that way she so adored.

"Good girl," he praised, his voice harsh.

"Good girl… You taste of strawberries and honey. I want a bite…"

He shifted his demanding lips elsewhere and moved them down the curve of her cheek, lower, until he found the birthmark at her throat, he'd sucked so many times.

Edward nipped hard at the flesh, ringing a gasp from her, but this was the violence she'd come to expect from him.

Edith moaned.

"Edward," she entreated.

He tugged her hairpins free. Edith's curls cascaded down her back.

"I can be whoever you want me to be, love," he whispered, his voice smooth. "But I know I can make you forget all about him, if you'll let me."

Those words and that husky voice yanked her back to the moment.

Edith gasped and pushed herself from the duke's arms.

With a dawning horror, she touched her fingertips to her swollen, and bruised mouth.

"I didn't…I shouldn't…oh, my God," she whispered.

She'd not wanted this man. Not truly. Yes, he possessed the talents to rouse a lady to desire, but…

Besieged with hysteria, Edith whipped her attention over to the empty snifter and bottle of brandy that'd begun as full, now three pints lighter.

Her pulse knocked loudly in her ears.

"…You will be nothing but a body to him…"

"Edith," the duke said quietly.

Edith swung her panicked gaze to him.

With a gentle smile, the duke lifted his palms. "As I said, I'll not force you. You are free to—"

"Why would you expect nothing in return?" she demanded, her words angry and slightly slurred.

"You don't know me and yet you'd invest your time annn' money into helping me avenge my siiister?"

The duke let his arms fall. The façade lifted as a hardness settled in the duke's previously affable demeanor.

"You aren't giving me *nothing*, Edith."

"…Everything is about his wants, his pleasures…"

Her heart thudded sickeningly in her breast.

The duke's cobalt eyes darkened to a shade nearly black. "I'd be helping *you*, a woman Malden wronged. Where he likely demanded your soul in exchange, I will ask for nothing, and not even for the very good reason, I *need* absolutely nothing."

"That hardly seems like fair repayment, love."

"And you are in desperate need of funds, my lord?"

"There's no limit to the amount of wealth and power a man can possess."

With a sleek panther's strides, the duke approached and jolted her from remembrances of Edward's *largesse*. She couldn't sort out whether too much drink or those languid steps he'd undoubtedly practiced accounted for the slowing of time.

The duke stopped.

"It would bring me the utmost pleasure to show you the man you cried out for earlier is wholly undeserving of you; that a man *can* be powerful and ruthless, but tender and caring, too…" He paused. "Especially for a woman he hopes to make his."

With her mind increasingly dulled from drink, it took a moment before the duke's erroneous assumption sank in.

"And," he continued, "Malden will despise that you've come to me. It will eat him alive."

"Nooo, it *won't*," she said, unable to keep the bitterness from her voice. "He is incapable of caring or loving." He'd told her that enough—and now showed Edith, as well.

"That is true," the duke acknowledged. "But he knows *I* am capable of those sentiments and will hate me all the more for it."

The icy glint in his gaze and the hardness to his features revealed the very reason he had agreed to help—to hurt Edward.

Her throat moved spasmodically.

I cannot do this…

"You speak of claiming me, Your Grace, but you've never met me before this evening," she whispered.

Even as Edith spoke the words, she knew it was folly to quarrel with the man who'd offered to take down Evie's killer.

Instead of offense being taken, an amused glimmer sparkled in his eyes.

"You braved the wrath and ugliness of the Marquess of Malden, you were rebuffed and turned away. Instead of wilting, you bloomed brighter. You came out this night, alone and sought me out." A wry grin formed on the duke's mouth. "Which given my reputation, I expect proved daunting for a proper lady."

"Does a *proper* lady seek out not one but two of London's most terrible gentlemen?" she asked before she could call back that challenge.

"No," he agreed.

That seductive grin was gone quickly, replaced with a more boy-like one she expected he reserved for his sisters.

"That is why I'm enthralled by you, Edith." His lashes swept low. "Make no doubt about it, you are very much a lady, and yet you've done remarkable things no other woman would, out of love and loyalty to your sister, and *that*," he added, placing additional emphasis on that word, "is something I both understand and admire."

The duke's solemn deliverance meliorated some of the knots in her stomach at working side by side with Edward's enemy.

Argyll drifted closer. "You have been doubted, mocked for what you know to be true about your late sister's death. Instead of being cowed, you have sought help elsewhere from men who, with our power, are in a position to help. Your resolve, determination, courage, and strength are all qualities I would see in the woman who becomes my duchess."

Just like that, the earlier calm receded, and Edith's chest tightened. She took a step away from the duke. Her back collided with the door and set the white-painted oak panel rattling.

Everything inside her balked at working side-by-side with Edward's former best friend.

In her mind, Edward fought for mastery of her.

All memories of Edward, the Marquess of Malden, however, proved as strong as the man himself.

"They were best friends, men I saw as brothers. They provided me protection and put an end to the misery I'd endured. Not me. DuMond and Argyll…And ultimately, they proved just how close that bond was by casting me out, for trying to protect DuMond from mistakes he'd made…"

She bit her lower lip still bruised from the kiss of Edward's arch-rival and welcomed the pain—for having allowed the duke's embrace.

The duke must have sensed her wavering.

"It is your call, Edith," the duke said.

"…Edith…I do not want you to obsess over my loss…"

"As I said, I've never forced a lady, Edith, and never will. Not in the bedroom, and not in any way—none at all."

Argyll's current utterances reached faintly through Evie's past ones.

Her sister's voice, however, demanded to be heard.

"…What I am saying is, hand this information over to someone who can and will research so that you and Emmy and Hutchinson and Mama and Papa are safe…"

Edith shut her eyes tight.

I am, Evie. I gave it over to Edward. He didn't want it. Now, I'm putting this information in the hands of the duke...

"Give it to me, Edith," the duke's murmuring came as from down a long hall. "Let me take this burden and make it mine."

Can you truly trust a man as hellbent on revenge as the man you've fallen so deeply in love with your heart will never recover?

Edith, with her head clouded by confusion, spirits, and old memories along with new ones, couldn't make sense of whether that query came from within or instead spoken from the great beyond, by her sister.

"*I don't want you to be sad anymore...I don't want you to lock yourself away inside mourning me. I want you to live again...*"

Suddenly breathing became a chore, the darkness pricked at the corners of her eyes.

Edith wrestled with the clasp at her throat, loosening it. She registered the garment sliding off her shoulders and falling around her feet.

No. Not here. Not now. Not with this man.

Then she recalled Edward the first time she'd lost consciousness with him.

And where she'd never before been able to break the spell of blackness when it appeared, the memory of Edward's tender side as he'd cared for her, kept her from falling over the abyss into nothingness.

"*If you are only focused on avenging me then you can't truly live...*"

"As I said, it is your choice, love," the duke said quietly.

"Don't you think I *know* that?" she cried, her strident imploration rang around the duke's office.

Edith sagged against the door.

He cleared his throat. "My apologies," Argyll murmured. "I—"

"I wasn't talking *tooo* you," she said weakly, her voice trembling. "I...I was..." Edith closed her eyes and took a breath in slowly through her nose. "I was talking to myself," she finished lamely.

Now, he knew he'd welcomed into his midst a madwoman—just one more private, with more personal secrets, she'd let him in on.

Strong fingers brushed her chin and the duke's gentle touch brought Edith's eyes flying open.

"Edith," he said. "I am no stranger to loss. I, too, lost a sibling, my eldest brother, and also the heir to the dukedom."

Her lips parted slightly. She'd never known…

"It has been so long, some twenty years ago, as such, no one really recalls," he murmured, unerringly able to read her thoughts. "All this to say, I know something of grief. I know the power it has over us. It is an invisible pain that slowly consumes a person. As such, you will never find judgment here."

He took her hands in his and gave them a slight, encouraging squeeze. There was no overt suggestiveness to his touch, nor the veiled anger of before when he'd spoken about Edward.

And all the reservations and guilt—about coming to this man, Edward's one-time friend—receded as born of his admission came a kindred connection. For there had once been good in the duke. He'd championed the marquess when Edward needed it most.

"Thank you," she said softly.

He released her hands and was immediately all business.

"In order for us to speak freely about the information you've collected and discoveries I've made, we'll be required to meet."

He will expect repayment…

Edith tensed.

"I will not, however, allow you to run all over London at this ungodly hour and put yourself in harm's way," he continued, in a stern voice she expected was the big brotherly one he used on his younger siblings. "As my sisters reside here, I do have to be mindful about not having women sneaking inside all hours of the night."

"I'm sorry," she said on a rush.

In her yearning for revenge, she'd selfishly not thought about the duke's younger sisters.

"No apologies necessary. Were it not for my sisters, I'd welcome mysterious cloaked visitors any time of the day." He waggled his eyebrows, ringing a laugh from Edith.

Then, he was all seriousness once more. "As learned during my lessons when I was the spare being trained for a military career, you and I are best served hiding in plain sight. Coincidental meeting at various events that I'll ensure we both receive invitations to. I will plan to host a ball which will allow us our first opportunity to convene."

She struggled to keep up with his rapid-fire planning.

When he'd finished, the duke picked up her cloak and draped the garment over her shoulders.

Then, in what felt like a lifetime since she'd arrived, and an eternity since she'd last seen Edward, the duke escorted her to the foyer.

The same aging butler who'd granted Edith entry sat upon the deep padded, velvet, hall bench. He struggled onto his feet. With his back bent by age and time, the old man took a slow, laborious step toward the door.

"You may retire for the night, Dixon," Argyll interjected before the other man could take another step. "I have it from here."

Dixon gave an unsteady bow.

Edith watched until the old servant had gone.

"I've insisted the good fellow take a nice retirement with the generous compensation I've provided," Argyll explained, as he headed over to handle the servant's duties.

Under a rake's veneer, the duke's generosity and kindness toward his servants bespoke the heart of a good man.

"I cannot ever thank you enough, Your Grace," she said softly.

He slid closer. "Do you know how you can repay me, Edith?" he whispered.

She managed to shake her head. Warning bells chimed once more.

"You can stop calling me 'Your Grace' while we are in private, at least," he said dryly. "And discreetly while in public."

"Thank—"

"Eh-eh," he scolded. "*Gregory*, I insist."

Edith nodded. "Good night, Gregory."

"Good girl," he praised.

"*…My naughty girl loves it rough, don't you…?*"

The duke with his affable charm and devotion to family and servants and willingness to help without requiring anything on

Edith's part, should have snagged him at *least* several corners of her heart.

So why then, as seemingly perfect as the Duke of Argyll was, why, as she drew her hood up into place, did her thoughts belong to another?

Argyll drew the door open for Edith.

The moment she stepped outside, her skin prickled.

She did a sweep of the streets and found them empty and silent as they'd been when she'd arrived thirty minutes?—A lifetime?—ago.

Edith took a step to leave.

"Edith," the duke murmured, his voice sotto voce. "One more thing."

With infinite tenderness, Argyll reached up and drew Edith's hood higher into place. After he'd finished, he shifted strong, capable fingers lower, then deftly retied the enormous black ribbon that served as her cloak's fastening.

"Until later, Edith," he murmured.

As Edith hurried down the long walkway, framed by boxwoods, her nape prickled from the feel of his eyes upon her.

Before she exited through the gates, she paused and stole a glance back.

Argyll with his arms folded loosely at his chest, and his shoulder dropped against the doorjamb, had the look of an angel, watching over her.

He gave a small waggle of his fingers, and even with the distance between them, she caught the gleaming whites of his even-teethed smile.

She'd triumphed. She'd secured the help she needed, and from a man who wasn't cruel—or he had been, overtly—just not to her.

Why then, while hurrying to meet her hackney, did Edith have a sick feeling about the deal she'd made?

CHAPTER 16

Forty-three minutes.

To be exact, it'd been forty-three minutes and a handful of seconds since Edith disappeared inside the Duke of Argyll's residence.

Malden knew, because he'd counted each and every single bloody one of those seconds.

The innocent Miss Caldecott hadn't been summarily shown the door as Malden expected. Though, in truth, the moment Argyll greeted Edith, looked her over, and motioned her inside, Malden knew she wasn't coming out.

At least, not until after he'd had his hands all over Edith and her skirts up and bent over his mahogany desk.

Malden gritted his teeth.

I should have stormed the bloody residence.

He should have barreled inside, hunted Argyll down, and torn him apart with his bare hands. And then when he'd finished, with his teeth shred the remains of his former friend who'd dared encroach upon that which belonged to him.

But Malden hadn't.

Instead, he'd sat upon the lumpy, thinly padded bench of Edith's rented conveyance, and waited for her to return from her meeting with the scrupulous-on-the-surface rogue.

Malden clenched and unclenched his hands.

I don't care.

And why should he? Fidelity and possessiveness of a woman bespoke weakness.

I don't care if he fucked her.

Except, his anger spiraled higher.

Malden had wanted to be the one to claim her. He'd been the first to initiate Edith to the joys of debauchery and now some other bastard—*Argyll*—of all men, had more than his fingers in her hot quim.

Like corrosive poison, rabid jealousy spread through him and destroyed every logical thought in his head. It ate away at every corner of his brain until all that remained in its place was an indescribable madness.

Filled with a restive fury, Malden peered through the crack in the crude curtain, once more.

While Edith made her way back to her carriage, Malden's gaze was not on her, but rather the one who watched her with heavy eyes; ones belonging to a well-sated man.

Where before Argyll sported a raven black jacket, at some point, he'd shed the garment, as well as his cravat.

As if Argyll's earlier exertions robbed him of the ability to stand on his own two legs, he rested a big shoulder against the doorjamb.

A low, guttural, barely human sound erupted from Malden.

For, he knew precisely what led to the *charming* duke's current state of dishabille.

Rage turned Malden's breaths into short, raspy spurts; the kind of inhalations and exhalations made by his sickly—and hopefully soon dead—father.

Edith paused and stole a glance back at Argyll's house. Did she even now fervidly recall the things the duke had done to her?

Malden clenched his teeth so hard, pain shot all along his jaw.

Edith climbed inside the rented conveyance, shut the door, and then seated herself.

"Hullo, sweet," he drawled. "Have you missed me?"

Edith's ragged gasp ricocheted around the carriage.

Malden smirked. It should so happen he could enjoy himself, *after all*.

"E-Edward." His name fell as a breathy, uneven whisper of sound from her lips.

"In the flesh, love." He hardened his eyes. "Or, were you expecting another, hmm? The Duke of Argyll, perhaps."

She didn't emerge from the shadows of her cloak, and though Malden couldn't see her expression, he studied the lady close enough to detect the light rippling of her blue sapphire covering.

Another wave of resentment rolled through him.

"Let me *see* you," he ordered, harshly, his breath somehow more ragged than hers.

Edith hesitated.

"Now, Edith!" he barked.

His once brave warrior queen hurried to comply. With unsteady fingers, she pushed back her hood.

Malden fell back in his seat.

Edith's dark curls hung loose about her shoulders and peppered between several of those luminous strands were the handful of pins that remained after Argyll's efforts.

Then, he homed in on Edith's mouth. Her bright red, swollen lips left little doubt as to what she'd been up to.

With a primal shout of fury that likely resonated through the quiet streets, Malden punched the ceiling hard, over and over.

Edith's already pale skin turned a ghastly shade of white.

The driver erroneously took the cue to drive, and Malden let him.

As they pulled away from Argyll's, Edith didn't put up a fight. She offered no protest. She just sat, with her hands joined as a single fist in a grip so tight, she'd drained the blood from her knuckles.

Malden ran a critical eye over Edith, solemn as he'd never seen her—which, given the business that brought her to him, was saying something indeed.

He grimly contemplated that mouth, which before this night had belonged solely to him. Now, by the sight of those puffy red lips, they'd not only been sampled but devoured by another.

All the while, he fought to rein in his spiraling emotions, Edith remained vacuous as a child's overly-loved porcelain doll. Never, not even when she'd spoken of her sister's alleged murder had he seen her this way—haunted, tormented.

How bloody ironic. Time and time again, he'd told Edith he wasn't capable of feeling anything, but here he sat crazed because she'd been in another man's arms.

As if she felt his eyes burning into her, Edith burrowed deeper into the corner. She gave Malden her shoulder and denied him a full view of her well-used mouth.

He studied her as untwined her hands. With the tip of her index finger, Edith teased her curtain back.

He flared his nostrils.

For all the deliberate and unceasing attention Edith gave that bloody window and the way in which she ignored Malden, the lady may as well have been alone on a carriage ride through London.

The rickety hackney rolled over uneven cobblestones and jostled Edith so those glossy dark brown curls bounced and swayed about her shoulders.

His gaze snagged on the reddish love bite at her neck.

He froze. Unblinking, all his attention centered on that place where Argyll had left his mark upon her.

A burning sensation started in Malden's stomach and rapidly fanned to his chest and every corner of his rotted soul.

So, this was jealousy.

"Ah, sweet," he said nastily. "I see Argyll wasn't as gentle as I expected him to be. I trust he learned quick that you don't like to be treated like a lady."

When his attempts at getting a rise out of her failed, he gnashed his teeth. *How dare she?* How dare she sit opposite him and remain in cool possession of herself and her emotions?

Malden worked himself up to the question he alternately needed to ask but didn't want an answer to.

The query exploded harsh and sharp from his lips. "Did he fuck you, Edith?"

In an unhurried way, Edith returned her beautiful brown eyes to Malden's. Where before those expressive depths sparkled and glittered with rebellion or mirth, unrestrained desire or fury, now they contained an eerie emptiness.

A shiver traversed his spine.

"Edith," he urged, this time, forcing down some of his anger.

In deadened tones, she returned his question with one of her own. "Would it matter if he did?"

"No," he lied.

He thought he caught her wince. It could, however, have merely been a trick of the dim light from a passing streetlamp.

Her finally having spoken, however, revived Malden and restored him to his detached, contemptuous, and welcomingly familiar, self.

"As I told you," he continued in frosty tones, "fucking is fucking. I'm just curious whether Argyll's sampled more of you than I did."

This time, there was no mistaking the wound his words had inflicted. Sorrow and hurt bled from her eyes, yet the sight of her suffering from vile things *he* said didn't make Malden feel stronger.

Nay, for the first time, something shifted and left Malden with an unwelcome sensation in his chest—a sentiment he neither wished nor intended to consider too deeply.

Edith retwined her hands in a lone, pale fist that hinted at the death grip she had upon herself and gave all her attention to her lap.

He frowned.

Warning bells chimed faintly at the back of his mind. This desolate figure bore no resemblance to the woman he'd spent unexpectedly glorious, debauched days with.

From his first meeting with Edith to their last in Hyde Park, whenever Malden spoke in that vulgar way he just had, she'd blushed or recoiled. In the dead of *this* night, she remained eerily detached, laconic, but for a few pithy words.

His unholy fury forgotten, Malden stared at her through new lenses.

He saw the glaring details that jealousy had previously blinded him to. Everything he'd overlooked before, became crystal clear: her lack of fire, her vacant eyes. Her lack of fight.

He closed his eyes and recalled the few words she had spoken.

Would it maaatter if he did...

When she'd put that question to Malden, there'd been a slight slur to Edith's speech; one that hadn't been there even when she'd consumed two healthy-sized glasses of whiskey in Malden's offices.

I'll kill him.

His fingers curled reflexively into claws.

His breathing came lower, slower, more ragged.

And after he killed Argyll? He'd rip the bastard's still-beating heart from his bloody body, and then feast upon his remains.

"Edith?" he repeated her name a third time, gentling his voice, in a way he'd previously thought himself incapable of, before Edith.

But then, Malden's life would now forever be divided into two points: everything *before* Edith and everything *after* that portentous night she'd stormed his club.

She gave no indication she heard him.

A pit formed in his stomach.

Something *had* happened to her.

Argyll had *done* something to Edith.

"Did he hurt you, Edith?" How did Malden manage to ask that question so calmly when black, murderous rage fired in his veins?

She hesitated for a while. In fact, he thought Edith might deny him an answer so that the question would ultimately fester in his brain, slowly eating him from the inside out, until it destroyed him altogether.

Finally, she gave a slight, nearly imperceptible shake of her head. "*Nooo.*"

No.

Her answer should have done away with Malden's intolerable and unceasing fury. But her denial came not as a succinct single syllable, but rather a garbled *three*.

Carefully, Malden switched seats and joined Edith on her bench.

He made to lean close to gauge whether there were spirits on her breath, but he needn't have bothered. A strong, fruity scent of whatever Argyll had given her hit him.

Malden released a black curse.

"He got you drunk," he said bluntly.

Edith spoke so quietly; Malden barely heard her. "Brandy. Not like when you gave me whiskey."

Tears filled her eyes.

His queen had never cried and now she would because of Argyll.

His heart wrenched.

Argyll was a dead man; he just didn't yet know it.

Malden would kill the duke dead, resurrect him, and then kill him all over again.

"I hate brandy, but I drank it," she slurred, pulling Malden away from welcome thoughts of all the ways in which he'd make Argyll pay.

"I was able to tell you I like whiskey, but I couldn't tell him," Edith said.

She'd blame herself.

He ran his gaze over her.

"What did he do to you?" he asked as calmly as he could. "I need you to tell me, Edith."

That way Edward could tuck each bloody detail away to ensure he meted out a suitably horrible redress for each and every offense.

"I don't want to talk about it," she said, her words all rolling together, and filled with anguish.

"Tell me," he demanded, needing an answer, for the not knowing would torment him.

Then, he heard her.

"He touched me."

His gut clenched.

I don't want to know.

"Where?" Malden grated out.

Edith hesitated and then reached around, gesturing to the curve of her buttocks, which, prior to this night, had only been in Malden's hands.

"And he…k-kissed me." Her voice caught.

With each detail she revealed, a preternatural fury the likes he'd never before known—not for his abusive father, not for the merciless bullies who'd tortured him—began to consume him.

She'd come to him innocent, and in less than a handful of days apart from her, someone had taken that from her—and Malden.

"It is my fault." However many drinks Edith had, caused her words to roll together.

"It isn't," he said, calmly, even when inside the savage beast roamed and demanded to be set free.

"But it is," she whispered, so forlorn she made him ache in a way he'd never believed he could. "I am bad, just like you said."

"You're not," he said sharply. He'd never known a soul possessed the good this one did. "You're *my* bad girl, in the very best ways."

"You don't understand," she cried out. "I…I *enjoyed* his embrace."

Stunned, Malden jerked like he'd been shot—and he found he would have preferred that fate to *this*.

"I wanted it to be you, Edward. I *imagined* it was you." Edith broke down sobbing and curling herself into a ball, making herself as small as possible against the wall of the carriage.

Like an outsider looking in from afar, Malden stared blankly at Edith as she wept.

He'd been wrong. Whatever answer she'd given him about her meeting with Argyll had been destined to shake Malden to his core.

A pulling sensation knotted his gut and wrought a queer feeling in his stomach he'd never before known. The twisting and twining of his insides so repulsive, he wanted to never be victim to it again.

He despised Argyll and until Malden died and took his place in hell, he would forever burn with fury, knowing Edith had enjoyed another man's embrace.

But Malden, the king of vice and more debauched than Caligula, wouldn't let Edith feel guilt for her body responding in the natural way it had.

Argyll was an experienced lover. The duke knew every way there was to know around a woman's body. Edith had been no match for his skills.

And I'm the one who sent her there…

The knowledge of *that* would also be something Malden had to live with, forever. When he'd discovered she'd lied to him to secure his cooperation, he'd been too blind to see he wanted Edith anyway. His discovery, however, had come too late. And the muscles in his chest, close to that place where that detestable organ rested, spasmed.

Malden attempted to rub the muscle ache away, but his efforts proved futile.

He stared at the woman who'd absolutely obliterated his self-control.

Her gasping, heaving sobs had dissolved into a soft, even more sorrowful weeping.

He had to say something.

Were he Argyll, Malden would have been armed with all the right words and soothing promises. But Malden wasn't that man and never would be.

"It is just lust, Edith," he said matter-of-factly, giving her that same reminder he had throughout their brief relationship. "Everything he roused in you was your body's automatic response."

His words were intended to alleviate any sense of guilt. Instead, she turned her face flush from crying, still damp with the tracks of her tears, and looked at Malden with something akin to horror.

Unnerved as he'd never been with this woman, and in a way he'd not experienced since his boyhood years, Malden fought the urge to squirm.

Something was expected of him here. But what the hell was it?

Except, that question would go unanswered.

For as if he'd spoken and said all the worst things, Edith gave her head a small shake and put all her attention back on that crack in the curtain.

He realized the back-and-forth sway of the jarvie had come to a stop.

Marden parted the fabric that covered his window to ascertain where the driver had brought them.

Edith's street.

Even without directives, the fellow had known to bring them to the lady's home.

Malden returned his attention to a so very silent Edith. With her fingers shaking, she attempted to straighten her hair.

Her visage blurred.

In his mind's eye, Malden envisioned the moments that had brought Edith to her well-loved-looking state: Edith locked in the duke's embrace. Argyll tugging her pins free and letting those luscious strands cascade around them like a chocolate waterfall. Argyll sliding his hands around the curve of her waist, and filling his palms with her lush, curved buttocks, and drawing her against his erection.

Malden's breath grew harsh and angry. He willed that stream of vile thoughts to cease, but they continued coming.

Then, Malden saw what hadn't happened this night, but, what, as long as Edith worked with Argyll, would eventually come to be. The always infuriatingly dashing duke, burying himself to the hilt inside her, at last giving Edith what she'd craved—and what Malden wanted to be the one to show her.

It was too much.

His lip curled back in a reflexive snarl. "I'd expected a charming rake like Argyll would at least have set you to rights."

Even before Malden uttered those snarky words and witnessed the way her slender body jerked, like he'd struck her, he knew he was a bastard for them.

"I'll do it," he snapped.

Edith cast a confused little look over her shoulder.

"Here," he made himself say, this time, more gently.

She sat motionless while Malden cared for the tangle made by another man.

"Thank you," she whispered.

He grunted.

When he'd finished, he had her face him so he could assess his work. Malden ran his gaze over her face and still-swollen lips.

He briefly closed his eyes and imagined the kiss that had made them so and wanted to snap and hiss and rage.

But more, when he opened his eyes and found Edith staring at him with that sad-eyed expression, he wanted to vanquish *that* look, the way he could one of his living, breathing foes.

Her lower lip quivered.

"I look terrible," she whispered.

"No," he said gruffly. Helen of Troy, Cleopatra, and Phryne could have formed a triumvirate and still not rivaled Edith Caldecott. "You look…" *Magnificent.* "Fine."

As if in supplication, she bowed her head, and reached for the door handle.

"Edith," he said, staying her.

"Did you speak to…*him*," Malden couldn't even get that poisonous name out, "about us?"

She hesitated and then dampened her lips in a way that answered all he needed to know.

The only question at this point was whether or not Edith would lie to him for a second time.

"I did."

Even as her admission in the affirmative portended an escalation in the war between Malden and his former partners, the fact she'd given him truth filled him with a terrific satisfaction.

When he spoke, Malden did so in equanimous tones, so as to not close her off any more than she already had. "What did you tell him?"

"He asked who else I'd brought my information to," she said, this time without any faltering. "I thought about lying but remembered…" Edith glanced down at her joined hands. "What it cost me when I withheld the truth from you."

Malden studied her bent head.

"And what exactly did it cost you, Edith?" he asked quietly.

A lone tear slipped down her cheek, and he reached out to brush that drop away, but there was already another one there to take its place.

Funny, he'd always been repulsed by tears. He'd taken them as a sign of weakness. And even as they were, what was it that set everything and everyone apart from this particular woman? For, as he pulled out a kerchief and tenderly brushed that dampness away, it wasn't disgust but more of that odd tightening in his chest. Like a vise had been clamped about his lungs and gripped and ungripped those organs so breathing became a chore almost not worth fighting.

Malden relinquished his handkerchief to her, and her fingers immediately curled tightly around it the same way they might had she been handed the King's crown.

When she remained there, tugging agitatedly at the corners of the fabric, Malden shifted so he sat across from her. He placed his larger hands over her two far smaller ones and dwarfed those delicate digits.

"Edith?" he urged.

She picked up her gaze, her eyes red and swollen from crying. "You."

That lone, breathy syllable floated throughout the dead-silent carriage.

Malden's heart thudded against his ribcage. *Me?*

Stunned, he yanked his palms away.

At his silence, Edith resumed fiddling with her fabric. "It's silly, you know?" A soft, melancholy chuckle escaped her. "I didn't *really* lose you, because I never ever *had* you. I just …" She lifted her shoulders in a tiny shrug.

He scoured her face.

She just *what?*

She'd wished he'd wanted her?

Imagined something more with him?

What was it?

And why in hell did the answer to those silent questions suddenly seem more important than even his feud with DuMond and Argyll?

Edith made to leave again, and this time he didn't keep her from doing so.

This time, however, she hovered.

She finally spoke. "I know we won't see one another again after this."

Did he detect regret in her voice?

Or, God help me, does that regret belong to…me?

"Before I go, I wanted to tell you," she said, through Malden's tumult, "the only reason I sought out the Duke of Argyll is because I have nowhere else to turn."

Malden balled his hands tightly. Desperation was what had brought her into his life and also what had driven her from it.

Edith clasped the handle and opened the door a fraction, but instead of leaving, she turned, and this time did give him one last look. "I wanted it to be you, Edward," she said softly. "I wanted it to be you."

With that, Edith let herself out of the carriage and out of his life.

As she went, and Malden followed her flight, a hollow sensation settled in his chest.

Me, I'm the one who drove her into another man's arms.

Not just any man—*Argyll's.*

Edith expertly weaved in and out of the shadows with the stealth of London's most skilled pickpocket.

Only when he'd confirmed she'd made it through her family's tall, pink-painted gates did he knock the ceiling. The driver had been clever enough to bring Malden and Edith here without distraction, the fellow would be smart enough to return Malden to his horse.

On the return back, restless, Malden shoved the curtain all the way open. Staring out at the eerily silent and empty streets, he considered everything Edith had shared. She'd said fewer words this night than any of the previous times they'd been together, but somehow, she'd managed to say so much more.

No one truly wanted Malden. Oh, people wanted him, but not for any reasons that didn't have to do with him, as a *man*.

From the moment he'd drawn his first breath, Malden served but one purpose: for his father, the King, and the world—to be the future Duke of Craven. Proper young ladies craved a connection with him because he was a duke. All Polite Society sought his company because he'd be the next Duke of Craven and they sought his favor.

"You bloody fool," he muttered. The only reason she'd come to Malden in the *first* place, was because she needed something he could provide her.

But did that change along the way…? a voice whispered at the back of his mind. Of course, it hadn't and even if something had, it wouldn't matter to Malden. He dragged a hand through his hair.

For with Edith's parting words, she'd been clear—when it came to solving her sister's murder, Argyll would do as well as Malden…but she *wanted* Malden.

His eye twitched.

The hack rolled to a surprisingly smooth stop, and he gave his head a hard shake. For now, Malden needed to table whatever the hell this was going on inside him. He had a *meeting* and required all his wits about him.

He angled his neck left and cracked the muscles, and then swiftly bent in the opposite direction and cracked the right.

The moment Malden jumped down from the hackney, he broke into an all-out sprint. All the while, despite his attempts to bury thoughts of Edith, she lived, real as life, inside his head.

He kissed me.

Malden growled and quickened his pace.

That didn't matter. She shared their association with Argyll.

He touched me

The lady could tup whomever the hell she wished, but Argyll had been a bridge too far. And there could be no doubting the debauched duke would come 'round to fucking her.

Malden took the stairs two at a time.

"…*I enjoyed it…*"

A thick, black curtain of rage briefly blinded him, but it didn't slow his forward movement. Without breaking stride, Malden threw Argyll's doors open and stormed the enemy's lair.

The negligent servant who'd been asleep on the job, scrambled up from his bench. "Halt!"

Malden knew the moment the fellow recognized the identity of his nighttime intruder.

The second butler gasped. "My l-lord! F-forgive me." Red patches filled his gaunt, and previously ashen, cheeks. "H-His Grace has given instructions you are not to be granted entry."

"Oh, I'm sure he'll make an exception this one time," Malden sneered. "For the sake of old friendships and all."

An enormous Adam's apple bobbed in a neck so slender, it looked a chore to hold his head up. "H-He said we are to speak with him before—"

With the other man still rambling, Malden stalked off. He didn't give a shite what orders Argyll's lackadaisical staff had been given.

"My lord!" Argyll's second butler entreated. "You cannot—"

That was where the other man was wrong. Malden could do and intended to do whatever the hell he wanted.

While the servant raised a belated and entirely too-late hue and cry, Malden jogged through corridors as familiar as his own.

When he reached Argyll's office, he threw the door open so hard the elaborately carved oak panel hit the wall, then bounced back.

Malden shot a hand out to keep it from hitting him in the face.

He did a sweep of the office and found *him*, the smug, faintly amused figure lazily reclined on the sofa, with a drink in hand and in the same state of dishabille he'd been when Edith took her leave of him.

Argyll smiled icily. "Malden, my *good* man."

His former best friend lifted his glass in salute, and caught Malden's focus, bringing it to the lone, empty snifter, resting beside a nearly empty bottle, on the table.

"…Brandy. Not like when you gave me whiskey…"

"To what do I owe the unexpected pleasure of your company…?" Argyll was saying as he, unhurriedly, came to his feet.

Through the dull buzzing in Malden's ears, he couldn't make out anything more. He dimly registered an army of servants arriving at the door, and Argyll ordering them gone.

All the while, Edith's revelations flooded his brain and left Malden suspended in this peculiar state, where reality remained frozen.

As Argyll's footmen left and shut the door behind them, the duke's lips moved, but Malden was upside down, underwater; everything above the surface came muted and muffled.

Those hated, hard lips that'd claimed Edith's as previously only Malden had.

"You all right, chap?" Argyll's voice came from down a long, distant hall.

Even separated from the moment as Malden found himself, his brain detected the duke's jeering tone.

Argyll's mouth curved up in a mocking grin.

That same mouth which had marked Edith's creamy white skin, and worshipped the birthmark, Malden got hard just thinking about sucking on.

Crazed, Malden ripped his gaze away from a face he'd never hated more than he did in this moment.

Get control of yourself, man.

His pulse continued to hammer like a drum.

It'd always been so easy, so why now did madness hold an unbreakable grip on him?

Dragging a shaky hand through his hair, Malden did a small circle to get himself back from a precipice of insanity.

Only there was no reprieve in sight. For Malden's unblinking stare locked on the arrow-shaped hairpins scattered about the hardwood floor. Those brass-plated fasteners lay, pointing Malden to the very spot where Edith had known the pleasure of Argyll's embrace.

The duke had filled his hands with her buttocks and driven her body against that wall and plundered her mouth.

"But I wanted it to be you, Edward…I imagined it was you."

Malden came whirring back to the moment, and every sense came alive, stronger, and more acute.

He looked upon the man he'd once considered a brother and let show all the loathing and contempt he now carried for him.

Growling, Malden stormed over.

Whatever smug words Argyll had been speaking, abruptly cut out.

The duke tensed.

Malden went sailing past him and made straight for the glass Edith had drank from. He grabbed the empty snifter and brought it to his nose.

The aromatic hint of Malden's entirely too fruity brandy clung to the snifter, along with something else—a strong, pungent, smell.

His fingers curled reflexively around the glass.

Opium.

Edith, who believed her sister died by poisoning had consumed an opium laced drink Argyll gave her.

"I enjoyed it. I…I enjoyed his embrace…But I wanted it to be you, Edward. I imagined it was you…"

"You bastard." Malden, speaking with a calm he knew not where it came from, held the glass out toward Argyll. "You *drugged* her." Malden gave him a scornful once over. "Here, after all these years knowing the *great* Duke of Argyll, and I'm only just learning, you're relying on drugs to get them more easily into your bed."

Argyll flashed a smug smile. "Whatever you need to make yourself feel better about Edith enjoying the things I did to her, old *friend*."

With a roar, Malden hurled Edith's snifter and amidst the explosion of crystal and tinkling of shattered glass, he charged Argyll.

Anticipating the coming attack, Argyll brought his fists up but proved no match for Malden's bloodlust.

His sharp right, rear hook, connected solidly with the duke's granite-hard jaw.

Impressively, the other man kept his feet and met Malden with a lead uppercut.

The force of the blow sent Malden's head ricocheting.

Argyll smiled a bloody-mouthed smile and came at Malden again.

This time, Malden anticipated the duke's move; sidestepping Argyll, Malden leaped atop the same sofa Edith sat not just an hour ago, and, with a bellow, launched himself at Argyll.

They landed with Argyll taking the brunt of the impact. As his back collided with the floor, all the breath was expelled from his lungs.

Taking advantage of Argyll's stunned state, Malden punched him in the face over and over, until his blood splattered Malden's face and mingled with the sweat that rolled from Malden's forehead.

Malden's quick, panting breaths struck an off-rhythm score to Argyll's.

All the while Malden beat his former friend to a pulp, the satisfying sound of flesh striking flesh, filled his ears and drowned out Edith's telling in the carriage that'd haunted him since she'd whispered it into existence.

Suddenly, and simultaneously, Argyll reared his head back and at the same time he brought his forehead colliding with Malden's, the duke got a knee up and hit him between the legs.

With a low, death-like groan, Malden collapsed in a heap. Gritting his teeth, he writhed in agony.

Argyll took the upper hand and proceeded to return Malden's earlier favor.

The fight between them was a well-matched one, but in the end, Malden delivered a sharp left hook, that sent Argyll's head reeling into the hardwood floor.

Spent from battle, both men collapsed beside one another, shoulder to shoulder.

Aside from the quick, ragged breaths each drew, they may as well have been the two boys they'd once been, lounging at the late Duke of Argyll's well-stocked lake after a day spent swimming.

As his heart rate began to come down, Malden stared at the wood-paneled ceiling overhead.

A low grumble sounded from beside him, and Malden turned his head.

Argyll's entire body shook. Tears seeped from the corners of his eyes.

"This is r-rich," the duke managed to get out.

"What?" he snapped.

"Here, I believed you'd sent poor Miss Caldecott with her outrageous story to try and have a window into my life and dealings."

Malden's stomach muscles tightened.

This time, Argyll didn't fight his laughter. "It's why I plied the lady with drink and opium and had her in my arms to assess whether she was as innocent as she let on. Th-that was an unexpected perk of my research," he said, between great, big, gasping breaths.

As the other man's words began to sink in, Malden sat up slowly. His heart thudded a sick beat against his ribcage.

Far steadier, just as he'd been throughout their entire exchange, Argyll shoved himself up onto his arrogant ass and spit blood upon the glass-littered floor.

"Even after Miss Caldecott left, I marveled at her performance and looked forward to our next meeting. All the while…all the while, you truly *do* care for her. Oh, my God, this is too good to be true." It was as if a dam burst. Argyll clutched at his side and roared with laughter.

A sick feeling settled like a pit in his gut. In his fury and rashness, Malden had proven an area of weakness and left him ripe for attack.

Winning the battle for self-control, Malden stood and took his time before speaking. "I do not care about Miss Caldecott," he said coolly.

Which was true. Malden didn't. He wanted to possess—

"Then I'm free to fuck her?"

A demoniac rage flashed through him, but a detail the duke let slip, managed to restrain him.

"*I'm free to fuck her…?*"

Not: "*Then I'm free to fuck her…again?*"

"You can do what you will with Miss Caldecott," Malden said icily, lying all the way through his teeth, and depriving the other man of getting another rise out of him.

Edith Caldecott had belonged to Malden from the start. Over his dead and decaying corpse would Argyll lay claim to her.

"Just didn't want me to have her then, old friend?" The duke sounded downright disappointed at failing to receive the reaction he'd wanted. Argyll dropped his voice to an overly loud whisper. "From one friend to another, let me, let *you* in on a little secret. In the future, Malden, if you want a woman, I'm the last man whose arms you should send her running to."

Malden curled his hands so tightly, his nails sunk deep into his palms.

Amidst the broken glass and blood-spattered floor, Malden and Argyll, both stood there. Once friends, now mortal enemies, they stared at one another with matched hate and contempt burning from their eyes.

"You know," Argyll began soberly. There was a time I would have died for you or killed for you." His voice was devoid of all the earlier malevolence that'd greeted Malden since his arrival.

Malden's peeled his lip back in a sneer. "I had two best friends, men who were like my brothers. You and DuMond. You chose DuMond."

"What did you want me to do, Malden?" he shot back. "Sever my friendship with *him* because he cut you out of his life after you nearly got his wife killed?"

Malden sneered. "The same wife who broke into our club, stole our secrets, and shared our business with the world."

"You speak so very easily about having DuMond's wife disposed of," Argyll mused. "I find it ironic coming from the man who rushed my house and launched an all-out attack because of a woman he *doesn't* care about and who you *don't* mind if I fuck."

Malden fought his body's natural recoil. What was the other man suggesting?

No, Malden knew. The duke was the manner of stupid fool to believe in romantic feelings.

When Argyll glanced away first, Malden started to leave.

"Malden," Argyll called out, stopping him before he'd even reached the door.

Malden angled a glance back.

The duke narrowed his eyes. "I believe you've taken the kindness I've shown you over the years as a sign of my weakness. A word of warning—I'm ruthless to my foes. You are now among that number. The next time you enter my residence, or if you so much as think to harm a hair on any of my sisters' heads, I will take immense pleasure in destroying you."

It was Malden's turn to laugh. "Destroy me, will you?"

Argyll curled his lips into a subhuman smile that served as an answer and challenge to Malden's mockery.

This time, Malden quit the duke's residence without looking back. Battle lines had been drawn and now, redrawn. The fight between him and his former partners had escalated to an all-out war.

Two certainties remained.

One: Malden would emerge triumphant.

And two: Edith couldn't have been more wrong when she'd predicted she and Malden would never see one another after tonight.

They would meet again—and *very* soon.

CHAPTER 17

In the weeks since Edith and Edward severed their connection, Edward's monster of a father died and went on to join the Devil in Hell.

The Marquess of Malden went on to become the new Duke of Craven.

And it was all anyone in Polite Society spoke of and wrote of, which meant, for Edith, there was no escaping thoughts of Edward.

With his father's deserved passing, everything had certainly changed for Edward. When a man ascended to the ranks of almost royalty as he had, his obligations, holdings, and level of power and influence all grew.

While for Edith, *everything* remained the same.

"Two young dukes," Emmy marveled aloud.

It was all anyone talked about, and that unfortunately included Edith's sister—the fact that not one, but now several, young, handsome, wealthy dukes were available.

Seated on the carriage bench, next to her father and across from her mother and sister, Edith made a show of staring out the window.

This way she didn't have to take part in a discussion she had absolutely no desire to take part in.

"Imagine not one, but two, handsome, respectable dukes who are all in want of a duchess," Emmy continued. "Only one of them appears to be of any interest, and it isn't my dear sister's beau."

Edith's beau, as in the *Duke of Argyll*. Given the times he'd paid call to Edith and the number of outings they'd had, what other conclusion was her sister—or anyone for that matter—to have drawn?

She gritted her teeth.

What he'd promised would be chance, casual meetings or dance sets were actually visits that more than resembled an *official* courtship.

"*Only one* of those dukes is respectable," their mother was saying. "And the other is the Duke of Craven. From everything I've read, the new duke is as horrid as the late duke."

Edith made herself sit motionless as her mother carried on with a cataloging of the late duke's offenses. "High-handed and arrogant..."

Confident. Confident would be a far more apt descriptor of the indomitable duke.

"Cruel."

"I've sampled enough of you to know, you aren't worth my efforts or my lenience..."

Of their own volition, Edith's fingers curled tightly on her lap.

"...as horrid as his father," her mother said again.

Her words shifted in and out of focus, with those uttered in confidence to Edith, by the new Duke of Craven.

"...The duke didn't love me at all. Nor I him. The old bastard loved but two things; his dukedom and beating me to turn me into a man worthy of inheriting the kingdom after he passed..."

As horrid as his father...

As horrid as his father...

Edith cried out. "He is nothing like—" *His father.*

Her family stared at her as if she'd gone mad.

"The Duke of Argyll," she finished weakly. "He is nothing like the *Duke of Argyll.*"

Nor was that really a lie. Edward and Argyll were nothing alike. One set her heart aflutter—or he had, before he'd broken it. The other left her more annoyed than moved.

Edith's sister gave her a peculiar look—and one Edith most certainly deserved.

The viscountess on the other hand, fairly beamed. "Listen to your older sister, Emmy. Defending the *honorable* duke, as she ought."

The *honorable* duke who'd plied her with brandy and done things he oughtn't with an intoxicated woman.

Edith bit her cheek hard.

The viscountess gave a quick clap of her hands. "I'll not have Edith's night spoiled."

"It is not my night," Edith said tersely.

She may as well have saved her breath.

Her mother continued. "There will be no further comparisons between the dukes. Any similarities between them end at the title 'duke'."

How dare her mother find *Edward* wanting? She didn't know how badly Argyll and DuMond hurt Edward.

"They were best friends, Mother," Edith snapped. "Do you recall *that*?"

The viscountess gave her head a confused little shake. "I don't—"

"You used to pine for an invitation to gatherings attended by the future Duke of Craven," she took relish in pointing out. "How many times did you say, a man such as he would make any one of your daughters a fine match?"

Color filled the viscountess's cheeks.

"Edith," her father said warningly.

Edith ignored him. "In fact, I rarely heard you breathe a word about the Duke of Argyll being a respectable match for any of your daughters."

"That was before, Edith. He's clearly…reforming his ways."

For Edith? Did her mother truly believe that?

Edith snorted.

Her mother's lips moved but no words came out. "Edith, where is this coming from?"

The viscount, and peacekeeper of the family, finally interjected. "There'll be no further talks of The Duke of Craven."

Having the support of her husband, seemed to revive the viscountess. "Precisely. He is scandalous and outrageous and," she lowered her voice to a whisper, like it wasn't just the Caldecotts present, "he owns a *less* than respectable establishment."

That was the understatement of the ages. What would her mother say were to have visited Edward's club and witnessed the debaucheries in action?

For the first time in weeks, Edith burst out laughing.

Her mother frowned. "You find that amusing, Edith?"

"I find it amusing you should mention only *one* of those duke's less than respectable establishments, Mother."

The viscountess blushed.

"That is different," she mumbled.

Edith made her expression serene. "How so? Have you been to those club—?"

Emmy's laughter drowned out the rest of Edith's jibe.

The viscountess gave each of her daughters a stern look. When her attempts at quelling their devilry failed, she cast a desperate glance her husband's way.

A dutiful as always, the viscount took his wife's cue. "I said, there'll be no more talk on the Duke of Craven or scandalous establishments," he spoke with a rare firmness that always managed to silence the Caldecott siblings. "Am I clear, girls?"

Emmy—and a more reluctant—Edith, nodded.

The rest of the way, Edith contemplated the window but barely saw the passing landscape.

When she'd first entered society, she'd seen Edward from afar. She'd marveled at the urbane gentleman; so self-possessed, handsome, and sought after by all, she'd secretly wished he'd look her way.

Only, he hadn't.

And he'd not remained society's darling; the man all mamas and papas wished would make a match with their daughters. Now, no sane—or desperate—parent would let their respectable daughters within a thousand yards of the 'gentleman'.

As such, the title of most eligible bachelor had been usurped by the Duke of Argyll. Possessed of a title just a smidge below royalty, dashing looks, and affable nature, the gentleman could have any woman he wished.

And with the 'whirlwind courtship' he'd launched, Argyll had done a convincing job of letting Polite Society believe Edith was that woman.

Edith fought off a bitter laugh. The duke had gone and taken his plan for 'hiding in plain sight' meetings to discuss Evie's murder to a very public courtship.

Where Edith expected he'd put in an appearance at the same respectable affairs she attended with her family, he'd done not only that but also *unexpectedly* paid morning visits and escorted her on carriage rides.

All of London's Polite—and Impolite—Society believed Edith and the duke to be on the cusp of marriage.

Edith should only be grateful. During the time she'd spent with the duke, he'd centered their discussions and the information he shared on Evie's murder. The men he'd hired had even begun to make headway with a druggist in the Eastern side of London.

All the while, Edith knew the truth. She'd made a deal with another devil. The duke had provided Edith with precisely what she'd desired. In exchange? He'd tricked her into a public relationship, all for the sole reason of infuriating Edward.

She'd come to both men naïve, but she was not stupid—at least not anymore.

The moment she'd left the duke's and entered her hired hack to find Edward sitting in wait, she'd learned in an instant, from his volatile reaction, the depth of the rivalry between the two former friends.

She'd become another weapon in their war—where she remained, unfazed by the duke turning her into a pawn, but the fact she was nothing more to Edward than that, hit like a blade to the belly.

Edith took a shaky breath.

Her father's quiet murmuring pulled Edith from her musings. "What is it, poppet? I should think being courted by a fellow such as the duke would see you with more of a smile, and yet, it did not escape me this past week that you look as glum as if he'd stolen your puppy."

She offered her best attempt at a smile "I don't have a puppy, Papa."

"No. If I thought it might make you happy again, I'd certainly fetch you one."

He gave her a little wink, then his expression grew somber.

"Do you know, Evie looked forward to her London Season like no other young woman I've ever known before. Not any of my three sisters. Your mother," his expression grew wistful, "we ran into one another whilst escaping a tedious affair and commiserated over how much we detested *ton* events. But Evie, she wanted a Season."

Her throat moved painfully. *This* is what her father thought accounted for her misery? But then, why shouldn't he? These past years Edith had been swamped by grief and all of it had stemmed from the loss of her eldest sister.

Instead, she'd not properly thought of Evie in…too long. Now, all her thoughts, sleepless nights, and wandering daydreams belonged to another.

"You know, your sister would have wanted you to be happy," he said quietly, mistaking Evie's silence for guilt. "She would have wished for you to dance until your toes hurt and fall in love—"

"I know, Papa," she said, more sharply than she intended.

Edith felt immediate guilt at his stricken state and briefly closed her eyes. She didn't want to think about falling in love, because God help her, she'd already fallen for the absolute last man she should. She'd betrayed him, and he'd responded as he ought, and now it was over.

Edith drew in a slow breath and tried again. "Forgive me, Papa. I know what Evie wants for me."

"Nothing to forgive, poppet," he said gently, giving a little wave of his hand. Fortunately, the carriage rolled to a stop, sparing any further discussion on the matter.

Edith was last to descend from the carriage. Her father tucked her hand in the fold of his sleeve, and as they walked, her earlier reprieve proved short-lived.

"I want you to walk into the duke's ballroom and embrace the night as the one you've been so deserving of." The earl's throat moved. "And also, one I should have known long before now, that you not only deserved but also desperately needed. I've been remiss, my girl."

"No," she insisted. "You have not."

They'd all been lost in their sorrow.

"Ah, but I have. Let's not quarrel over anything else. I expect tonight should be a magical one for you."

Later that evening, standing with Emmy at her side, in the crush that was the Duke of Argyll's ballroom, Edith found her father couldn't have been more wrong.

The only magic she hoped to find in this grand, austere ballroom with its hundreds of guests, and roar of conversation that nearly drowned out the orchestra, was the kind that could make Edith disappear.

Alas, she had two sets with the duke which guaranteed Edith would be at the center of attention.

Just then, the orchestra's lively country set concluded.

The haunting strains of a waltz filled the duke's ballroom.

Edith's gaze was drawn to a dashing couple who stood at the center of it all—Lady Faith and Lord Rex Rutherford.

The lady with her midnight black coils, elegantly wound like a coronet about her head, and the dark-haired, dangerous-looking fellow couldn't have been more striking.

And yet, for the beauty of that pair, it was the way they gazed at one another that held Edith enthralled.

This was Edward's former best friend. The man who'd betrayed him, and Edith despised him on sight. And yet, as the marquess moved his wife through the sweeping circles of the waltz, Edith watched them with a mix of envy and sadness.

How very much in love they were. The marquess and his wife gazed upon one another like there wasn't another soul in the room.

This is why Lord Rutherford had been unable to forgive Edward.

Edward, of course, wouldn't have understood and never would—because he didn't believe in love. And he'd insulated himself in such a way, he'd ensured no one *could* love him.

Except, I did.

Tears pricked her lashes. *Because I'm a stupid, pathetic, pitiable fool who fell for a man so guarded, I don't know if a pickaxe could get him free of his armor.*

"He is quite handsome."

Edith blinked slowly and glanced over.

Sipping away at her tepid lemonade and casually considering the other guests, stood Emmy.

Her youngest sibling motioned with her glass, and Edith followed that less than subtle point to not the Marquess and Marchioness of Rutherford, but the gentleman beside them.

Gregory, the Duke of Argyll. Currently partnering his sister, the sibling pair danced alongside his friend and business partner.

"I...yes," Edith allowed.

Argyll said something to the other man, that drew a laugh from Lady Rutherford, and a scowl from the lady's husband.

"He *seems* quite dashing," Emmy remarked.

"He does." Because he was. Between his smooth tongue and the way in which he looked at a woman like she was the only one in the room, it was no secret why he was a breaker of hearts.

Edith, however, seemed to be the only one to recognize that rakish façade for what it was.

"Do you love him?" Emmy murmured.

Edith promptly choked and attracted curious stares from those around her.

Emmy pressed her drink into Edith's hands.

As Edith sipped, her youngest sister slapped her on the back.

"Given his whirlwind courtship of you, I daresay mine wasn't the manner of question to elicit *that* reaction," Emmy drawled when Edith could breathe again.

A playful twinkle or teasing note would have been far easier than that mature, omniscient observation from her sister.

Answering in the affirmative would put an immediate end to her sister's questioning.

Edith hedged. "What woman would not be more than half in love with His Grace?" She could not even lie about loving Edward's former friend. That would be a betrayal too far.

"With his arrogance, slimy smile, and overtly rakish demeanor, the better question is what women *would* love him?" Emmy asked, not missing a beat.

Edith's eyebrows flared. Slimy smile? "But I thought—"

"I approve of him? I *did*, but that was when I believed you loved him," Emmy whispered. "Nor, sister dearest, does it escape me that, one," her sister lifted a finger, "your reaction in the carriage, and two," she stuck up another digit, "you have not answered my question."

"I…" Edith fumbled and tripped and searched for a response.

"If you have to think so long, allow me to spare you, Edith, you don't." Her sister's gaze became sharply probing. "Which begs the question as to why—"

The rest of Emmy's unwanted query was thankfully absorbed by the thunderous round of applause that fell over the room as the waltz drew to a close.

"Saved," Emmy muttered. "For now."

Edith followed her sister's focus to the Duke of Argyll. With his sister in the care of Lord and Lady Rutherford, Argyll now headed Edith's way.

His long, confident strides were so very Edward's, that if she closed her eyes quickly, she could almost imagine it *was* Edward walking her way.

And yet where Edward had the menacing prowl of a predator that didn't hide his savageness, there was a lazy languidness to the duke's steps which were, no doubt, meant to trick unsuspecting prey.

When the duke reached them, he swept a respectfully low bow to Edith and her sister. "Miss Emma Caldecott."

"Emmy," her sister muttered.

"Miss Edith Caldecott," he continued, after shooting the youngest, unimpressed, Caldecott girl a wry glance.

Edward's former friend gathered Edith's fingers and slowly raised them to his lips for a lingering kiss. "I hope you're enjoying yourself, Miss Caldecott?"

Emmy spoke before Edith could. "Ah, so many guests a person can hardly breathe, in a room sweltering hot, what isn't to enjoy, Your Grace?"

Edith shot an elbow out catching her sister in the side, even as the duke turned all his attention on her cheeky sister.

"Your Grace," Edith began to make the younger girl's apologies.

A grin twitched at the duke's lips. "It is fine. Having sisters, myself, I'm more than accustomed to spirited young ladies."

"Are your sisters also accustomed to you speaking in front of them as if they aren't present?" Emmy asked, deadpan.

Even as embarrassment brought Edith's eyes sliding shut, the duke barked with laughter. Fortunately, their mother, from where she'd been conversing with Lord and Lady Guilford, caught Edith's expression and hurried over to collect her youngest daughter.

Edith's mother whisked a scowling Emmy off several steps to allow the duke—and Edith—a reprieve from the younger girl's temper, and granted Edith and the duke some perception of privacy.

Hiding in plain sight, he'd called it.

"I'm sorry for my—"

"Worry, not. She is spirited—like her sister," the duke murmured. "That is a good thing. It will serve her well in life."

Edith made a show of studying the dancers completing the steps of a quadrille. While she did, she felt the duke's eyes upon her.

"She's cross with me," he said quietly.

Edith glanced at him.

"Your sister," he clarified.

Edith scoffed. "She does not even know you, Your Grace."

"That is true." He paused. "Which, given the fact she doesn't, leads me to only one conclusion…"

Edith didn't ask because she knew he intended to tell her.

"She is cross with me on her beloved sister's behalf. Have I done something to offend you, sweet?" the duke asked, entirely diverted.

Sweet.

That was Edward's endearment. Hearing it slip so smoothly from this other man's tongue, felt like a further perfidy on Edith's part. Not interested in playing any more games with any more men, she gave him a level look.

"I'm not stupid, Your Grace. I understand what is at play."

"What exactly is that?" Argyll dropped a shoulder against a nearby pillar and angled his broad, muscular body in a way that shielded them some from the world's view. "You must enlighten me, dearest."

"You've coordinated our meetings to raise Society's," *And Edward's.* "—notice."

"And?" he drawled, more than faintly amused.

"You're playing a game with Lord—" Except that was no longer the title by which to refer to him. "The Duke of Craven."

"*You* asked for the meetings," he pointed out.

She gritted her teeth. "Yes, but—"

The duke hammered her. "Have we not met several times a week to discuss your concerns? Have I not supplied you information about the druggist with a reputation for being bribed for the right amount?"

Yes, he'd done all those things. So why then, could she not shut her mouth?

"I'd thought…"

He dropped his voice and spoke in a seductive whisper. "You thought what, Edith? That we'd meet somewhere private, after hours, as we did that first night you came to me?" he asked huskily. "That we'd find private drawing rooms and clandestine spots to meet. Is that what you did with Craven?"

She blushed.

For the first time since she'd entered into a partnership with this other devil, the duke let his mask slip and revealed the malevolence that dwelled under the veneer of a charmer.

The duke, with the discretion only a cunning and utterly unscrupulous rake could, grazed his index finger just under the fabric of her sheer puff sleeve. "I'd be all too happy to oblige, Edith."

Unnerved by him but unaffected by his touch, Edith eyed him evenly and remained motionless.

Argyll chuckled. "God, you are such a bloody surprise."

Edith detected the flare of interest in his eyes deepen.

"I do not wish to be a pawn in your and Edward's game," she said gravely.

His expression grew serious.

"Very well, Edith. I'll square with you. It does bring me the utmost pleasure and satisfaction to know I'm meeting with the last woman Malden would have me anywhere near."

"You're wrong," she said quietly. "The only reason for any anger he may feel—"

"*May* feel?"

"Is a product of this enmity between you."

"But that does not mean," he continued, ignoring all mention she'd made of Edward, "I do not want you, Edith. I'll confess, initially, I did consent to aid you in your investigation because I sought to understand the connection between you and Malden."

The duke shifted so close, Edith had to crane her neck to meet his eyes, a strategy she knew to be deliberate.

"Then," he continued, "I did pay those public visits for the very reasons you suspect."

He moved his gaze over her mouth, and then lower, to the deeper-than-she-usually-opted-for bodice of her gown.

"Now, I find myself spellbound by the thought of you and your intrepidity. I would very much like to make you my duchess, Edith," he said, his voice thick with desire.

Edith resisted the urge to snort. She expected some other—most *any other*—woman would have believed that rather convincing show.

When she met his offer with only silence, he gave his blond head a rueful shake. "You're bad for a gent's pride, love."

Edith flashed a wry grin. "As I don't devote myself to making powerful men feel better and bigger, I'm afraid to inform you I do not feel properly chastened as you'd intended."

This time, the earlier tension faded away, and Edith and the duke shared an honest smile.

"We've spoken enough about Craven," he said, motioning a servant over.

A handsome, crimson-clad footman circulating with a tray of champagne glasses, promptly appeared.

Argyll availed himself to one and started to reach for a second. "Miss Caldecott?"

The memory of that night in his offices hit her like a kick in the gut.

"No, thank you," she demurred.

The duke lifted his shoulders in a little shrug and then took a drink of his spirits.

Since Evie's death by poison, Edith was careful to not drink in public places. The time she'd let down her guard with the Duke of Argyll served as a cautionary tale, and she'd not make the same mistake twice.

While he sipped, Argyll scanned the ballroom, as if he sought better company or someone in particular who was decidedly not Edith.

She stared past the duke. In her mind, she saw Edward as he'd been the night she'd first met with Argyll.

Upon learning the duke had plied her with brandy, rage, the likes of which she'd never witnessed, had possessed Edward. He, a man who was impervious to all, had turned crazed.

As the duke drained the remaining contents of his flute, Edith forced herself to stop thinking about Edward.

A different, and just as dutiful servant appeared with a tray to relieve his master of his empty glass. Instead of availing himself to another, this time, Argyll waved the footman off.

"I have information for you, Miss Caldecott, regarding the druggist." The duke's pronouncement came so hushed that over the din of the other guests, it barely reached her.

Hope blossomed in her breast.

"Your Grace?" she whispered.

Argyll continued to speak from the side of his mouth. "The man I've hired has managed to track down an underground operation that is being run in St. Giles."

The duke did a glance about.

"We should discuss this somewhere else, Miss Caldecott," he said, mutedly. "If you can meet me in…"

Argyll's voice and whatever it was he now said, faded from focus. A shiver tickled her nape and teased her spine.

Suddenly a buzz filled the ballroom.

The duke's gaze slid over the top of Edith's head to the reason for the commotion at the front of the ballroom.

Argyll whistled quietly between his lips. "Well, I'll be damned," he said, with his earlier amusement restored, and this time filled with more of that frosty hardness he made no attempt to conceal.

Edith followed his gaze to the avenging figure striding down the marble staircase with all the ease and comfort of one who owned the household.

Her breath hitched.

Edward.

Edith had longed for him more than was proper and definitely more than he deserved, but her heart didn't care about those *unimportant* details.

When he reached the landing and began his walkthrough, the crowd parted with the deference they'd reserve the King, and a king in his own right, the new Duke of Craven.

All the while he made his march, Edward's gaze remain fixed on Edith.

With his presence alone, Edward brought the world to a stop: the orchestra ceased its playing, the dancers stopped their twirling, and a great hush descended over the members of Polite Society gathered in the duke's ballroom.

With every step that brought him closer, her heart beat faster and faster.

She'd not seen him since that night in the hired hackney when he'd returned her home, and she'd never thought she'd come face to face with him, again.

Her heart contracted.

What is he doing here?

And then, at last he reached Edith.

It seemed the whole world held their breath, in anticipation of the one who'd break the still.

Narrowing his eyes, the Duke of Argyll looked from Edward to Edith, and then back again to Edward. "The ballocks on you, Craven."

The fact that not a single horrified gasp went up at the duke's language was a testament to the crowd's fascination. Edith remained as transfixed as the rest who watched Edward and Argyll the way they might a riveting production at the Royal Theatre.

She dimly registered the Marquess of Rutherford approaching from Edward's left.

Edith sprung to action. She hurried to place herself between Edward and his greatest enemy.

Finally, gasps filled the ballroom.

The Duke of Argyll positioned himself at Edith's side in a placement that could only be seen as the possessive move it was.

"Old friend," Argyll said, with a frosty geniality. "To what do I owe the honor of this—?"

Edward took a step so quickly, that even the Duke of Argyll stumbled. However, Edward bypassed the other peer and wrapped an arm around Edith's waist.

Then, to the stunned cries and shouts of the Duke of Argyll's guests, Edward covered Edith's mouth in a kiss that marked her ruin.

CHAPTER 18

The following morning, with a man of the cloth in tow, Edward, the new Duke of Craven climbed the front steps of Viscount Drayton's residence.

The moment he'd disembarked from his carriage, all eyes of passersby and less than discreet neighbors in windows had been upon him and the vicar.

Craven raised his hand to knock when the door was immediately opened by an ancient-looking butler.

Before he could hand over a calling card, the rheumy-eyed servant greeted him with a bow and stepped aside so Craven and the vicar could enter. "His Lordship indicated we might be expecting you and asked that I usher you to his office the moment you arrived."

Craven masked his surprise.

What in hell *was* this?

In all his preparations for his morning appointment, not in a million years had Craven expected he'd be greeted by the Caldecott butler as if he were a close friend of the Caldecotts come to call, and before Craven could even request a meeting, subsequently invited to join the viscount in his offices.

"If you will follow me, Your Grace?"

Craven looked at the man he'd dragged along this day. "This will not take long."

While the man of cloth helped himself to a seat on a foyer bench, Craven joined Edith's family butler on the walk to meet the viscount.

His skin prickled from the sense of being watched, and he looked up.

A young lady stared down at him with impressively cold eyes. Then, even more impressively, she held Craven's gaze, made a slashing motion at her throat, and jabbed a finger Craven's way.

At that unexpected show of spirit and fearlessness from the girl, Craven grinned.

"It seems all the courage and strength in the Caldecott family has been reserved for the daughters," he called up.

"Indeed." She narrowed his eyes. "You'd do well to remember it, Your Grace. I've lost one sister, I'm not afraid to kill for another."

In every way, she possessed Edith's spirit.

A thought slipped in, an imagining of a different young girl; one with Edith's luscious chocolaty curls and intrepidness.

"Your Grace?" the butler's gentle prodding brought Craven crashing to the present.

As he resumed his walk, he attempted to reign in his fatuous musings.

Craven well-knew, following the epic scandal he'd caused in the middle of Argyll's ballroom, Edith's father was certain to issue a duel.

With that being the inevitable response from Viscount Drayton, after Craven returned from the scene of Edith's public ruin, he'd spent the remainder of the night preparing for his appointment with the older man.

Now, his razor-sharp focus for the impending meeting had become all dulled by thoughts of a girl babe he and Edith might have. Why, there'd not even been a thought about his future son and heir.

Good God, what in hell gripped him?

When the servant finally brought Craven to a stop outside an arched oaken doorway, he'd, at last, managed to set his thoughts to right.

That restraint proved all too short-lived.

A quiet, familiar voice sounded from behind Craven. "I have it from here, Thomas."

Edith.

Edith, pale as he'd ever seen her, not even one of the times she'd been at full faint, and with large, dark circles under her eyes, stared subduedly at Craven.

His body stirred, and oddly enough, so did the place in Edward's chest where his heart ought to be.

Thomas passed his worried gaze between the pair, and then reluctantly took himself off.

"Commanding the head servant as if you are the head of household," he purred. "Why does that not surprise me, my love?"

"Why are you here?" she quietly asked.

"I think that should be fairly clear, sweet." He strolled closer. "I'm here to do right by you."

She remained expressionless. "You wouldn't even know what that means, Your Grace."

The sound of his new, more powerful title falling from her lips should arouse Craven. Instead, strangely, he found himself missing the effortless way she'd once spoken his given name.

"My love is mad at me," he said amused.

"I'm not your love. It couldn't be clearer; you aren't capable of the sentiment."

Did he imagine the flash of sadness in her eyes?

"I'll not have you kill my father."

"Would you rather duel me instead, sweet?" Amusement crept into his voice.

Somehow, her wan cheeks went even whiter. "You would make light of this?" she whispered.

For all the depraved behaviors he'd displayed with and around her, and all the villainous plans he'd revealed to Edith, she'd still ask her current question with such shock and anguish.

The evidence of her suffering shouldn't bother Craven, either way.

It shouldn't.

Unnerved as he'd never been, Craven gave her his back and knocked on the viscount's office door.

A moment later, Edith's father appeared. "Come in, Your Grace," he murmured. "Come in, please."

Please? The man would beg for Craven's company.

Surely Edith recognized her father's ineptitude and would be grateful to be free of him. Only, as Craven cast a glance her way, he found the place where she'd previously stood, empty.

"Your Grace?" the viscount ventured haltingly.

Giving his head an indecipherable shake, he followed Edith's father into the room.

"If you will?" the viscount said, leading them toward his desk.

Instead, of claiming a place at the head, Edith's father angled one of the leather-armed chairs at the foot of the neat, mahogany desk, and settled himself into those comfortable-looking folds.

Craven took the indicated seat and cagily eyed the man opposite him. What man abandoned his position of power in exchange for a cozy leather seat beside his enemy? Either Edith's father was a master tactician or an old, bloody fool.

Given the ease with which Edith had slipped out of this very household, again and again, and dashed all over London, Craven felt more than comfortable staking his life on the latter being true.

The viscount steepled his long fingers together. "I would offer you spirits, Your Grace, however, given the earliness of the morning hour, I must forego that offer."

"Considering I ruined your daughter in the middle of the Duke of Argyll's affair, you should have already gathered, I'm not one given to follow social niceties," Craven jibed.

"No, that is…true." The viscount took a deep breath. "Would *you* care for spirits?"

Spirits? A muscle ticked in Craven's jaw. He may as well have lifted Edith's skirts—which he had any number of times before—and tupped the lady in front of the *ton*, for how ruined Craven had left her, and the bloody sod was offering him *refreshments*?

He let his silence serve as his answer.

The viscount took the cue. He dropped his hands to his lap. "May I begin, Your Grace?"

Craven had only ruined his daughter, made their family a laughingstock, and still he'd ask Craven's *permission*. What upside down world did he find himself?

"Please," Craven said, layering a wealth of mockery into that word, that by the viscount's smooth expression, the dolt didn't even hear.

An easy smile formed on the old man's mouth. "Each of my children was born near the late afternoon hour, or during the early nightfall. And *always* at a certain mealtime."

That unexpected direction Edith's father took knocked the prepared warnings and threats he'd intended to give, from his head. Were Craven listening to any other man, he'd have believed that'd been a successful ploy to do just that.

"My son, Hutchinson, arrived just at sunset, and as we sat down to the evening meal. Elyse, just as the viscountess and I sat to partake in our afternoon meal."

Sadness overtook the viscount's previously relaxed features. "E-Evie," his voice caught.

Edith's father turned his head momentarily and coughed into his hand.

And Craven, who prided himself on being imperturbable, needed to glance away from the other man's display of emotion and reminded all over again why he'd forbade himself from loving anyone.

"Evie, well, she arrived at dessert. The footman had just put down a plate of baked custard before my wife. Custard is the viscountess's favorite dessert and one she craved even more during her pregnancy. My wife insisted," Edith's father held up a finger for added emphasis, "*insisted* she'd not have the babe until she finished all her custard. She had half before Evie began to make her entrance."

This time, the viscount's remembrance of his late daughter's birth roused a healthy laugh, and staring at him as Craven did, he felt like a theatergoer watching a stage actor.

And yet, hearing Edith's father speak so fondly and laugh as Craven's bastard of a father certainly had never done, Craven found himself, from this glimpse, understanding why Edith defended a father who did not deserve defending.

Disquieted and needing all his wits about him, Craven spoke coolly. "I am not sure what any of this has to do with my reason for being here."

The viscount's amusement faded fully. "It has everything to do with your being here, Your Grace. Do you know what time my Edith arrived?"

My Edith.

Edith belonged to no man—not even the one who'd sired her—*except*, Craven.

This time, too proud to admit he wanted that detail about Edith's first moments on this earth, he forced boredom and mockery into his voice. "I'm guessing a mealtime hour."

"Given my others, well, one would certainly expect so," the viscount mused.

He shook his head. "No, Edith, was nothing like the others. In the part of the morn, where one's not sure whether to refer to it as night or day, when the whole slept, Edith arrived quickly. She didn't make a sound; not so much as a cry."

The viscount held his thumb and forefinger a hairsbreadth apart. "Just the tiniest, faintest little squeak, and I feared we'd lost her because I'd never known a baby could be so quiet when coming into the world."

The viscount spoke with all the wonderment and joy befitting the proud new papa he'd been that long time ago.

"But her eyes, Your Grace, her beautiful eyes were wide open, and they darted, back and forth, like she'd come before the world awoke because she wanted to see it all. She wanted to experience every moment."

Of its own volition, Craven's mind went to each and every late night and early morn visit he'd had with Edith. It would seem that'd always been Edith's hour.

The viscount rested a hand on his right knee and leaned forward. "And I wanted all that for her. I wanted the world for her. I knew as women, my daughters would not have the same freedoms my son enjoyed, and so when I saw her tiny little gaze darting out, my wish that day was that she'd find a man who loved her and who saw her as a friend and partner and who explored all the sights the world has to offer and experienced all the moments Edith's heart could desire."

Ah, now Craven understood. "And I'm not that man."

The viscount shook his head. "You are not that man."

Regardless, Craven was the man who would marry her.

"You ruined my daughter and…" The viscount's voice cracked. "I do not even know wh-why."

An admission that also indicated how little Edith's father knew of the going-ons in Polite Society.

The older man took in a shaky breath. "I know what is expected of me. I know I sh-should call you out at dawn and duel you to defend her honor."

Yes, that was precisely what the viscount should do. Had it been Malden's daughter handled so in a ballroom, Craven wouldn't have bothered with a duel. He'd have gone straight to murdering the bastard with all of society witnesses to the evil he'd do the dastard.

At the very least, Edith deserved a father or brother or husband who'd destroy anyone who wronged her.

Craven would be that man for her.

"You've left me in a pickle, Your Grace. You are a young man. I, on the other hand?" The gentleman lifted his hands, palms up. "These are old like me. Everything I do is slower. My reflexes. My movements. If I duel against you, I'll lose."

A vein pulsed in Craven's temple.

My God, *this* was the man Edith and three sisters relied upon for safety? It was a wonder the lady had survived as long as she had. For the first time, he truly considered the suspicions and fears which had sent Edith into his life and considered them in a new, more distinct light.

"Your fear of dying is greater than your devotion to your daughter," Craven snapped.

Had he felt any guilt for his actions last evening—which Craven decidedly did not—there were none at all, knowing he'd be rescuing Edith from such a man.

The viscount grimaced. "You don't understand."

Oh, Craven understood perfectly. Edith deserved a man who'd fight for her and battle her enemies, both real and imagined.

He should be relieved instead of annoyed that he'd meet no resistance.

"As I see it," Craven said coolly, tired of the man's maudlin excuses for why the viscount would not fight for Edith, "your son, Edith's *older brother*, is the one who *left you in a pickle*, my lord."

Craven didn't relent. "Perhaps if your son and heir spent more time watching after his sisters, mother, and weak father, we wouldn't be sitting here."

Fortunately for him, however, there hadn't been a protective older brother about.

The other man's face twisted. "You don't understand. After my daughter's death, my son—"

Craven cut him off. "I don't need to hear excuses for why your *son* ran away after he failed you and Edith, my lord, or why you living is more important than your daughter's honor."

He reached inside the front of his jacket and withdrew a thick, folded sheet.

Craven held it out for the other man to take. "I'm marrying your daughter."

The viscount's eyes slid shut and a paroxysm of grief twisted his features. "Edith, she is special."

"Given how special she is, you should have had the foresight to watch after her more carefully than you did," Craven said, without any remorse for the older man's feelings.

Confusion filled the viscount's eyes. "I don't…" He shook his head. "How could I have watched her any more closely than when she was at the center of a ballroom?—surrounded by nearly all of Polite Society."

Craven flattened his lips.

In his rage, he'd forgotten the viscount knew nothing of Edith's late-night jaunts all over London.

When her father still made no attempt to accept the official document, Craven dropped it on the other man's lap. "I've secured a marriage certificate from the King. I have a vicar waiting in the foyer. I'm marrying your daughter *now*."

A look Craven recognized so very well from his dealings at first Forbidden Pleasures and now Lucifer's Lair filled the viscount's every feature—desperation.

"Her dowry," the viscount began.

Ah, so they'd entered the negotiation stage.

"Your Grace, I would have my daughter retain control of some aspect of her life; see that she has money to care for herself should she—"

"As my wife, she'll want for nothing, but she may keep her dowry. What else, Drayton?"

"I'd beg you not to hurt her. She is—" Tears filled the older man's eyes. "Please, do not hurt her."

"I don't hit women," Craven said bluntly.

"There are other, even worse, ways to inflict pain upon a person, Your Grace," the viscount said quietly, like an elder imparting sage advice.

"Next?"

"I would ask you to allow Edith to remain with her family—"

"Absolutely not. From this day forward, I'm her family."

Family.

That word percolated in Craven's mind.

He'd never had a family in the sense the world thought of it. No different than an animal or beast in the wild, Craven had been sired. There'd been no affection, no emotion, no love— just the understanding that when the sire died, there would be another beast to carry on in his stead.

But Edith? Edith was made different. She cared deeply and loved her siblings and parents mightily, and whatever children they had, there was no doubt in Craven's mind that she would care for them and love them in that same way.

His thankfully now-dead father would have despised knowing that weakness would infiltrate the de Vesy bloodlines.

Maybe that's why Craven reveled so deeply at the idea of Edith bringing that light to the de Vesy line.

"There is nothing I can say to persuade you?" the viscount entreated.

"Nothing."

The viscount took in a deep breath. "Very well. It is settled."

It was settled—Edith would belong to him, in both name and body.

And Craven suspected their lives entwining this way had been ordained from the moment she'd crafted a plan to enlist his help.

CHAPTER 19

Before a vicar who was a stranger, her parents, younger sister, and a silent, menacing fellow who'd arrived as the duke's witness, Edith and Edward recited their vows and were married not even thirty minutes after he'd arrived to speak with her father.

Standing at the last family portrait that'd ever been done of all the Caldecotts together, Edith stared blankly up at Evie's smiling visage. Their conversation from that long day, that'd become an all-out sisterly quarrel, echoed in her mind.

"Will you just cease? I don't want a grand wedding, Evie…"

"Can you not talk about this some other time," Hutchinson groused. Edith and Evie ignored him.

"Bah, of course you do. Flower petals, Edith! You must have flower petals and white iced wedding cake and parlor games when you marry…"

"You have that at your wedding, Evie."

"Will you girls cease bickering?" the viscountess implored.

Edith trailed a fingertip around Evie's silhouette, never actually touching the canvas, so as to not mar this last rendering of her sister.

She smiled sadly.

In the end, she'd had precisely what she'd told Evie she wished for—a small affair, with few guests, and no fanfare.

Only, what she'd never imagined was that Evie wouldn't be present, or Hutchinson or Elyse; that'd be just a rushed ceremony between Edith and a cold-hearted man who felt not an iota of love or true regard for her.

Why, there'd not even been time enough to prepare a proper wedding breakfast.

Emmy sidled up beside Edith and pulled her away from her melancholic thoughts. "You know, I might choose a better hiding spot."

She glanced over and found Emmy's gaze locked on the portrait in the same way Edith's had been, until her youngest sister's arrival.

Her sister had correctly surmised Edith was taking advantage of her belongings presently being packed so she could avoid Edward.

Not that you'll ever be able to avoid him again, after this moment...

"I can sneak you out the back entrance," Emmy ventured, with a sisterly loyalty that brought a tremulous smile to Edith's lips.

"I know you can." Just as Edith knew, Emmy didn't speak in jest; that she would help her make an escape if she so wished it. "I also know he'd find me anyway, wherever I may go."

"Hmm."

At that non-committal sound, Edith looked over. Her youngest sibling had put all her attention back on the portrait.

"What?"

"It is just, strange to me, that a man you do not know, and who never had any interactions with you before the Duke of Argyll's ball, should be so very determined to keep you in his life," Emmy remarked, with a wisdom beyond her ears.

"I..." Edith dampened her mouth. "I may have met the duke before," she confided.

Emmy spun; with fake shock stamped on her features. "No." The younger girl slapped a hand against her breast. "That is *impossible*. I cannot even fathom last evening was not the first you'd met."

Despite the hell that'd been these whirlwind days, Edith managed to smile. "You knew?"

"That you'd been going off to meet someone, and that certain someone was the new duke?" Emmy raised an eyebrow. "I may have had an idea when I saw him emerge from the same corner of the bookshop you always love to visit."

Then, just like that, the floods opened, and everything came tumbling forth—the reasons she'd sought Edward out. The things he'd made her feel. The agony of his rejection. His rivalry with the Duke of Argyll.

For so long, Edith had shared so few with anyone—nay, *no one*.

Since Evie died, each of the Caldecotts, in their own way and to varying degrees, ceased sharing their thoughts and feelings and worries with one another. In fact, Edward had become the unlikely someone, and an even more unlikely confidante, she *had* shared so many parts of herself with.

Now, Emmy was here at her side, and it felt so very good to have a sister back in her life whom she could talk to. Why had she waited until now?

Because you've been so consumed in avenging Evie, that you stopped seeing the family you still had all around you.

When she'd finished, Edith took in a shaky breath.

Emmy looked back and forth, from their approaching mother to Edith, and then, silently mouthing, 'I love you', the younger girl slipped off, allowing Edith and the viscountess time to speak, alone.

Between her mother's eyes red and swollen from crying and her pallid expression, she bore the same look she had as when she'd lost one daughter to death.

With a heartrending look, Edith's mother claimed her hands. "My girl," she said, her voice breaking. "My girl, my beautiful girl."

That mantra she'd often and only uttered for Edith, a special saying that'd belonged to only her third-born, brought on another onslaught of tears. Knowing her mother would be shattered at the sight of them, Edith launched herself into her arms, the same way she'd used to do as a child, and buried her face against her shoulder.

Only, this time, in a reversal of roles, Edith's mother wept. "I don't know why he did this to you," the viscountess said, between her copious tears. "Why? Why?" she implored, sobbing her question to no one.

Edith, determined to be resolute for her despairing mother, adopted an unaffected tone. "The Marquess of…"

Only, that was no longer Edward's title.

"The Duke of Craven," Edith amended, "is a sworn enemy of

the Duke of Argyll, and I suspect, the Duke of Craven, in order to thwart what he believed were any intentions on the duke's part for me, he…ruined me."

She may as well have saved her breath.

Her mother continued speaking quietly to herself. "It does not make any sense. What man would do this?"

Edward would do this. No, Edward *had* done this.

Powerful, ruthless, and ambitious, he'd think nothing of tying himself to a woman—as he had Edith—all to enrage his former friend and rival.

The jest, however, was on Edward.

What would Edward think were he to know the Duke of Argyll hadn't *really* wanted Edith? That the only reason he'd given an illusion of a courtship was because Argyll thought he could use Edith to vex Edward?

In the end, Edward in his quest to one-better the Duke of Argyll, found himself stuck with Edith in marriage, until death did part them.

A panicky giggle gurgled in her throat.

Edith's mother mistook that shrill laugh as a cry, and it was as though that erroneous sign of Edith's misery grounded the older woman.

The viscountess stroked the back of Edith's head and made soothing sounds. "It will be all right," the viscountess murmured. "It will be all right, my girl."

Only, Edith wasn't a girl, and she knew it wouldn't be all right, ever again. Still, she didn't say as much, because it mattered more that her mother had those assurances for herself than be reminded of the grim reality awaiting Edith.

Not unlike her marriage to Edward, nothing good would come of it.

There came a light cough.

As one, Edith and her mother looked to where the viscount now stood. At some point, Edith's father had joined them. His eyes were even more tragic than they'd been the first weeks of Evie's death.

"H-His Grace is impatient, Edith. He has asked that I come collect you, or…or he will come along and fetch you himself."

It was time.

"It is time," Mother said raggedly.

Edith, flanked on either side by her parents, made the suddenly too-short walk to the foyer.

The double doors sat open, while servants carrying Edith's packed belongings, bustled past the previous footmen and maids who'd already deposited their loads.

Edith's gaze, however, remained fixed on the tall, austere gentleman who stood at the center of it all—Edward. At the present moment, he examined a golden, carved watch fob.

As Edith approached from the east corridors, she used the moment to study the man, who by the laws and society's dictates, owned Edith in every way.

As he took in the time, his angular features were a study in impatience, and seeing him as he was, Edith could almost believe he was an eager groom, desperate for his new wife's company, and not this cynical, unfeeling man who wouldn't care whether she lived or died.

He finally glanced up from his watch and his gaze collided with Edith's.

No eager, besotted bridegroom stared back.

Impatiently, he tucked his timepiece away. "I don't like to be kept waiting, wife."

Edward delivered that icy censure, the same way he might do so to an indolent servant. "You would do well to remember that in the future."

Edith lifted her chin a notch. "Then, you should have found a more biddable woman who worried about such things, Your Grace."

The viscountess gasped.

"Have a care, Edith, please," her mother implored, while at her side, Edith's father kept his entreaty to the silent type he now did, with his eyes.

Instead of the anticipated and hoped-for rage, amusement filled Edward's eyes.

Edith spoke with a frost to rival her husband's. "His Grace won't hurt me," she directed that assurance she gave at her husband.

"He cannot." He'd already hurt her far beyond anything else he might do.

"It is time, wife."

It is time.

Edith took a step to go when a cry rang out.

She looked up as Emmy came racing down the stairs.

Without breaking stride and her downward momentum carrying her, Emmy flung herself at Edith, nearly taking them both down.

And they would have certainly fallen…had Edward not shot a hand out to steady Edith and her sister.

Emmy wrapped her arms around Edith and sobbed. "I cannot b-believe I've n-now lost a-all my sisters."

Fighting tears, Edith held her youngest sibling close and stroked the back of her head. "Shh. I will a-always be here."

"N-No. You'll b-be with him, and I *hate* him for taking you."

Edith glanced over the top of her sister's soft, golden curls at Edward. His expression hard and his eyes even harder, Edith couldn't detect so much as a glimpse of compassion for her grieving sister.

Damn him for his difference. What manner of man would she be made to spend the rest of her life with?

Edith continued to hold her sister until her tears faded to a watery hiccough, and then after she dropped a kiss atop the younger girl's head, Edith turned to her parents. She hugged them both and then remained briefly in a comfortable, loving triumvirate of Caldecotts.

It is time…

Edith took in a steadying breath and forced herself to step away from her parents.

And then, after she'd said her final goodbyes, Edith left the childhood home she'd grown up in, and made for the carriage that would take her to the residence where she'd remain forever.

Edith wouldn't look at him.

Craven couldn't care less.

Or, he *shouldn't*.

But as Lord and Lady Drayton's servants saw to the final preparations, Craven, seated opposite his bride, found himself *missing* the spirited minx who'd challenged him in her family's foyer. He'd take her snapping, hissing, screaming, hell, even woeful, rather than this absolute *nothingness*.

His jaw rippled. Nor, for that matter, was he a man who took well to being ignored—and certainly not by this woman.

"My bride is angry at me," he drawled, in attempt to get a rise out of her.

She didn't disappoint.

Edith swung a fury-filled gaze on him. "As though my *husband*, cares either way *what* I'm feeling," she spat.

She'd be wrong on that score. The sight of her holding her young sister and fighting back tears had ravaged him. He'd decided in that moment he, unaffected by everyone else's misery, didn't like the sight of his wife in pain.

However, he'd cut his arms off before admitting that weakness.

The carriage dipped in an indication his driver had taken his place upon the box. There came the snap of reins and a moment later, the servant set the conveyance into motion.

"You should thank me, you know."

She pursed her mouth like she fought to ask the question he wanted her to.

"Just what exactly should I be grateful to you for, Your Grace?" she said between tightly clenched teeth. "Denying me a choice? Forcing me out of my family's loving home, and into yours, where I'll know neither light nor love?"

Hearing her speak so ardently of her bloody family and her love for them, sent a furor through him.

Restraining himself when he spoke, Craven flashed a mocking half-grin. "Your *loving* home where your sister was killed, and your father failed to properly watch after you? Correction, then. That would make two reasons for which you're grateful to me, sweet."

Edith gave him a long, sympathetic look and he wanted to rage. How dare she put that pitying stare on him.

"My father is not a violent man. He loves his family more than anything. He doesn't have the vices you've built an empire around," she said quietly. "As such, I'll not resent him for failing to believe such evil exists and that it should, in the form of a relative, creep into his household."

After delivering that matter-of-fact chastisement, Edith returned her attention to the window. With that, Craven found himself summarily forgotten for a second time.

The hell he would.

"You didn't want to know the other reason you owe me your gratitude, Edith?" he purred.

She gave Craven a once over. "Considering the wrong conclusion you'd reached regarding my family, it didn't even cross my mind."

The ballocks on her. God, she was magnificent.

"Argyll had every intention of compromising you that night of his ball, love," he said bluntly.

Edith remained wholly nonplussed over that revelation. So much so, he wondered whether she'd in fact heard him.

Annoyance roiled inside.

"Remember how he gave you brandy to drink, sweetheart? It was tainted. He intended to have a certain servant come to the two of you with a tray of champagne flutes, and, then after you drank, suggest you meet elsewhere so you could discuss his findings about your sister's death."

Surely that'd rouse a furious response, not with Craven, but the bloody bastard who'd slipped opium in her drink.

"You *ruined* me based on the assumption that I preferred you to Greg—*eep*."

Her words ended on squeak as Craven gathered her wrist and brought it close to his mouth.

"Pretend all you want, dear wife," he breathed. "Pretend you are unbothered that the man you turned to after me laced your drink with *opium*," he jeered.

Edith trembled; her features quavered.

Craven dropped a hard, angry kiss upon that place where her wrist met her hand. "But I know you, Edith de Vesy."

With a growl, he dragged her onto his lap, so her legs hung on either side of his lap and filled his hands with her saucily curved buttocks.

He kneaded the flesh, molded the lush globes in his palms.

Edith's eyes slid shut; a tremulous sigh spilled from her lips.

"Let me be clear, wife," he growled, bringing her heavy lashes fluttering open. "I've been very patient with your temper and insolence."

Craven cupped her by the nape and drew her face closer, so their lips nearly touched. "But I'll not tolerate talks of Argyll," he snarled. "Or you pretending it isn't me you want between your legs."

Craven ground his lips against hers.

Equally savage, Edith gripped him by his hair and returned his kiss.

Enflamed, Craven captured her chin hard in his hands and squeezed, so she parted for him and then he plundered her mouth. They violently tangled their tongues; he and Edith each warring for supremacy.

She moaned long and low and he drank of those reverberations wrought by her desire.

His hard cock twitched. God, how he wanted her, and now, she was his, which meant he could bury himself inside her now and whenever he wanted.

As if she'd read his silent, triumphant revelry, she bucked her hips wildly.

Craven shoved her satin wedding dress higher up around her waist. "My naughty girl has missed this," he rasped between kisses.

I've missed this.

Since his last time with her, he'd existed in a constant state of pained arousal. Now, he'd finally be able to claim her and purge her from his blood so he could think clearly, once more.

He grazed his fingers over Edith's soaking entrance when suddenly, she laid her palms against his chest and edged herself out of his embrace.

"Stop," she ordered.

Before he knew what she'd intended, Edith scrambled from his lap.

She proceeded to right her skirts.

He gritted his teeth.

For the first time in their relationship, Craven found himself on the other side of his innocent wife's self-control. He fought to exercise restraint, even as every part of him ached to have his hand in that place he'd yearned to touch since he'd cast her from his life.

A perfectly composed Edith, on the other hand, stared serenely back. "There are matters we must first discuss.

"Matters?" he snapped impatiently.

"Our marriage. There are certain rules I will be laying out for you to obey."

Craven stared at her. "Rules? As I recall, not even an hour ago, only one of us vowed to obey, and I'm decidedly not the one," he snarled.

Edith took in a slow breath. "No, you are correct. But then, that is the world, is it not? Women, we are expected to give our husbands our obedience, fidelity, and even become property to them. Wives do not get the same."

"No, you don't," he said bluntly.

She flinched slightly.

Craven nodded his chin. "I'm listening."

"You got what you wanted," she said quietly. "I'm now your wife. You've triumphed over the Duke of Argyll. I, however, have received nothing in return."

He scoffed. "You have received everything: the safety and security your family could not provide you. Wealth to rival Midas'. I'll drape you in diamonds and the finest silks. I'll have a crown commissioned dripping in gemstones befitting your role as my queen."

Sadness flickered in her eyes. "I don't want any of that, Edward. Those are things you believe are important, but they are not." She paused. "At least, not to me."

That brought him up short. All people craved wealth and power. His wife was an oddity and rarity.

"What *is* important to you?" he asked, truly befuddled.

A small smile teased her lips, and his chest shifted. It'd been so long since he'd seen that beautiful curve of her mouth.

"Happiness…laughter…having a husband who would be my friend and partner," she said solemnly, slowly.

Her answer only further confounded him. "You wish for happiness but do not want jewels or gowns," he repeated.

Edith sighed. "I want to be married to a man who I can talk to, Edward."

At hearing Edith speak, with a finality and in that pitying way, his frustration redoubled. He'd limitless wealth and power, and now to be told, he couldn't offer her something she desired left a sour taste in his mouth.

"We *are* talking, wife."

This time, she pressed her palms over her face and laughed.

Rage would have filled him, had she not chosen that moment to reach across the bench and twine her fingers with his. "Not just talking, Edward," she said, applying a light pressure to his hands. "But rather, sharing parts of ourselves."

Fortunately for Craven, he was spared from the embarrassment of asking further questions about a discussion he'd absolutely no understanding of.

"I want to have a relationship where my husband and I are open with each other, and share our greatest joys, our greatest sufferings, and our hopes for the future and our children," she quietly explained. "I want him to know which season I love most and share his favorite with me."

It was on the tip of his tongue to point out that a season was just a season and didn't really require so much thinking around them, but the more she spoke, however, the words flew fast from her lips.

"I want to be married to a man who knows my favorite soup is summer pea and that I adore Haricot lamb with carrots so very much that it is the meal my mother has had Cook make for every one of my birthdays since I was five years old. Or how I sneak into the kitchens first thing in the morning and help myself to bread and butter pudding whenever it's been on the day's menu."

All the anguish that'd marred her features these past days, reappeared. "Oh, Edward. We are of two different planets. Those items you speak of? They are just that—material possessions. What I want, are intangibles; gifts that cannot be physically touched, but that are more valuable than all those personal effects combined. Love, affection, warmth, and they are gifts you cannot give me.

"I understand it is not your fault," Edith continued. "I know the blame for your warped view of life and love is a product of your father's doing and the company you've kept. I can't change that." Regret spilled from her expressive eyes. "You've forced marriage upon me, Edward." She set her jaw. "But I will have some say in our union."

He smirked. "Very well. What do you want?"

"I will not make love with you. We will not consummate our marriage."

The world came to a screeching halt, just as his carriage came to a stop. An obedient servant was there and began to draw the panel open.

"Don't you dare touch that bloody handle," he shouted.

It closed the remaining crack.

All Craven's focus was fixed on his blasted, insolent, infuriating, stubborn minx of a wife. She sat serenely, her hands folded on her lap, as if they discussed the weather, and not her barring him from her bed.

"Absolutely not," he gritted out. "I'm not capable of abstinence." Especially, not where she was concerned. He wouldn't finally have her, only to give her an oath of chastity.

Again, a smile teased her lips. "It wasn't a question, Edward."

"You think you're the only woman? Sweetheart, I've got any number of them who'll happily spread their legs for me and do even more than that."

"Indeed." Edith inclined her head another fraction. "Which is why denying you a place in my bed should really not make you cross. Given your work and reputation, there are certainly more beautiful, skilled lovers you can turn to."

Craven gnashed his teeth. He didn't want experienced and goddamn it, Edith was a fucking dark-haired goddess with soulful eyes. He wanted to lay between her legs, and her legs only.

"Is that what you want, wife?" he taunted. "For me to bestow my attentions on another woman? To have my mouth on her and all over her, and my fingers in her quim, the way you love?"

Edith winced.

She darted her tongue out and traced the seam of her lips in a way he now understood. He absolutely reveled in that tell-tale glide of that flesh which told him she loathed the idea of him taking a lover. Well, good for her, not another woman could satisfy his craving for her. The devil he'd ever give her the upper hand by revealing it.

"No," she finally said, quietly.

She glanced briefly down at her interlocked fingers. "I would far rather have your fidelity."

"You'd have my fidelity, but not allow me to bed you? God, wife, you are contrary." Craven couldn't help it; he laughed.

Only when he'd reined in his amusement did Edith again speak.

"I will not give the gift of my virtue to a man who robbed me of choice. If you want a place in my bed, you must earn it, Edward. And as you said, you can very easily find your pleasure elsewhere, but as long as you do, I will never belong to you in that way."

Craven saw red. He wanted to toss his head back and roar and rage. *Earn* a place in her bed? How the hell was he supposed to do that? God, she was maddening.

"I can force you," he snarled, a savage beast, made desperate by his unlikely master's control.

She nodded. "You can. But you won't."

"How can you be so confident, wife, in a man who ruined you?"

"You wouldn't resort to force. You aren't capable of it," Edith said with a calm he resented her for. "I saw how enraged you became when you discovered the Duke of Argyll used drink to weaken my defenses."

Even the maddening image she painted of what had almost been with her and Argyll, sent Edward into a near frenzy.

She spoke on through his private tumult. "A man who'd become offended and furious at a man drugging me to ensure my cooperation is not a man who goes about raping women."

"Perhaps I only did that, because that man was Argyll," he shot back.

Her expression grew thoughtful.

"Maybe," she allowed. "But I don't believe that's the case."

God, he hated that she was not only right but that she knew it, too.

"So, what do I need to do to bed you, *wife?*" he snapped.

Her lips twitched. "You can begin by being faithful to me and showing me you are a man deserving of that gift, husband."

Had she been bitter and vindictive Craven might have stood a chance at rebuffing her outright. But this soft, almost gentle amusement of hers held him captive and spellbound.

With that, queen that she was, Edith let herself out of the carriage, and, without so much as hesitating at finding her new home a gaming hell, she marched on ahead, leaving Craven staring after her.

Edith spoke about his hopes for the future…

Strange. For Craven's entire life, his answer to that question would've been clear and constant. Aside from revenge against the ones who'd wronged him and a hungering for power and a desire to be feared, he wanted nothing.

He still craved those aspirations, but now, there existed the face of a person who shared his future, and his imaginings of life with Edith had nothing to do with power, revenge, or a desire to be feared.

She also spoke of a family, children born of him and Edith. Where Edward's childhood had been as merciless as the rest of his life, any sons and daughters he had with Edith would be nurtured in a way he didn't understand and should be repulsed by. Except, instead, he was…intrigued.

Sweat slicked his palms and forehead.

As Craven, who'd attained a level of strength and power as to fear nothing, found himself besieged with absolute terror for being tempted and entranced by thoughts of a bucolic family with his glorious wife.

CHAPTER 20

LATER THAT EVENING, CLOSETED AWAY in elegantly designed, masculine chambers very clearly belonging to her husband, Edith fought the urge to weep.

Tears were decidedly not a promising start to a new marriage.

But then, what bride would have managed anything *other* than a good cry at such a first day of marriage?

Forget her husband, there'd not even been a kindly or unkindly housekeeper to escort Edith to her new rooms. Instead, an older, angry-looking servant, with a gun at one hip and a knife in the other had escorted Edith through eerily darkened hallways.

Aside from his name, he'd uttered not so much as a single word; Edith's attempts at a friendly conversation were met by his annoyed grunts or silence.

The man, Gruffton—a perfect name for such a dour fellow—had quickly taken his leave, and Edith had since paced from wall to wall, wondering if her husband would come to her. Yet, given his reaction to the ultimatum, she knew very well where she'd driven Edward.

"You think you're the only woman? Sweetheart, I've got any number of them who'll happily spread their legs for me and do even more than that..."

She'd only been further reminded of that detail when they'd arrived, and a courtesan, Vivian, had been waiting to help Edith into her white cotton, modest nightshift, and wrapper.

After the taciturn woman had gone, Edith found herself truly alone...where she'd stayed that way the remainder of the evening.

This time, a tear did slip out, and she let it fall.

A man with Edward's appetites would not abstain. He'd turn to any one of the experienced women he'd mentioned who'd welcome them in their beds and between their legs, without any questions asked or any promises expected.

She closed her eyes and desperately fought off thoughts of where he was and what he currently did, but her efforts proved futile.

"Is that what you want, wife?… For me to bestow my attentions on another woman? To have my mouth on her and all over her, and my fingers in her quim, the way you love?"

Images slipped forward, of Edward stroking one of those breathtaking beauties between her legs. Of him, worshipping some other woman's breasts, and suckling the tips until he drove his ladylove mad.

A sob built in her throat.

Stop!

Taking in a shuddery breath, Edith pressed her forehead against the stained glass window. The colored glass carved of the Craven coat of arms, a white dragon and lion standing as fierce protectors on either side of the seal, distorted the fashionable streets below.

A painful little laugh spilled from her lips. Only her husband would be the manner of gentleman to open the most debauched club in a fashionable end of London and boldly plaster his coat of arms at the zenith of the debauched palace for all the world to see.

Knock-Knock-Knock

That firm thump at the door slashed into Edith's lamentations, and she swung her gaze to the front of the room.

Edward.

There came another round of rapping, this time, more impatient and annoyed.

Edith dashed across Edward's chambers, swiping away her tears as she went. With her heart pounding in eager anticipation of seeing him, Edith drew the panel open.

"Oh," she said dumbly.

The big, burly servant who'd escorted her above stairs some seven hours earlier, stared back with clear annoyance and even clearer loathing.

Her cheeks warmed. Well, that certainly wasn't the way to earn the fellow's friendship.

"Cook prepared a meal for you." Gruffton stepped aside and allowed a quartet of equally big, angry-looking fellows in.

To keep from being trampled, Edith hurried out of their path.

One man, tall, dark-haired, scarred, and menacing carried a table through the entryway, and promptly set it down at the center of the room.

"His Grace has the most unconventional maids and footmen," Edith teasingly noted.

Gruffton didn't so much as crack a grin. "They're guards," he said in a flat, faint Cockney. "Every man or woman employed in the living suites is trained to kill and protect the duke and his property."

She'd have to be blind to see the mordant look he leveled on her.

A shiver raced down her back. For whatever reason, this particular guard had taken a dislike to her and had made it his mission to scare her.

After all the other guards finished setting the table and delivering various trays, they took their leave so that only Edith and Gruffton remained. If Edith was to live here, she'd not allow this man or anyone to make her afeared in her own home.

"You don't like me, do you, Mr. Gruffton?"

The armed guard gave his freakishly broad shoulders a shrug. "Don't know you."

"Well, I am the duchess, the Duke of Craven's wife, which I expect means something."

From down the length of his crooked nose, Gruffton sneered at Edith. "I've been with His Grace since he was a boy out of university and was there when his partners betrayed him. You wearing the title duchess and being his wife doesn't mean a thing to me," he said, making no attempt to hide his loathing.

Gruffton likely thought she'd be offended, but Edith could not. The old, but still fierce-looking man had been loyal to Edward from the start. When Edward's former friends and partners cast him out, this man remained faithful.

Edith inclined her head. "That is fair, Mr. Gruffton," she said.

"You do not know me and therefore shouldn't be expected to extend the same loyalty to me that you do Edward."

His heavy features remained apathetic. "Ye need anything else?"

Oh, he was going to prove a difficult one to bring 'round.

"No," Edith murmured. "That will be all, Mr...".

The allegiant servant left and closed the door behind him.

"Gruffton," she finished, giving her head a wry shake.

Well, Edith's day first day living at Lucifer's Lair, as the Duchess of Craven, could only be considered an unmitigated failing.

Edith made her way over to the lonely table of one that sat in the middle of her husband's rooms. She sat down heavy on the hard, mahogany, Chippendale chair, and dropped her elbow upon the table.

The crystal candlesticks flickered upon the gold tablecloth.

She passed her gaze over the small tureen, solitary dinner-sized, covered platter, the smaller silver one beside it, a single bowl, a lone glass of claret, and a small pitcher of the wine. Collecting the champagne flute, Edith stared into the deep, almost burgundy contents, and then lifted her glass towards the long, wax, tapers.

"To the two of you," she said to the lone pair on this, her and Edward's wedding day.

Tears again threatened and she bloody hated them.

Edith downed the fruity-flavored claret and grimaced. She didn't care—or shouldn't care—that Gruffton despised her. But knowing she'd traded a home with a loving sister and friend, servants who were like family, and parents who loved Edith beyond measure, for a new home with a man wholly indifferent toward her and guards who hated her and where she didn't have a single friend in this godforsaken place, well, she *did* care.

Edith poured herself another drink, and when she'd filled her glass to the top, she'd left the crystal pitcher nearly empty.

Morosely, she sipped of her second claret, and with her spare hand, lifted the lid of the tureen. A subtle hint of saffron wafted in the air.

Dumbly, Edith set aside her champagne flute. Her hand trembled and she had to steady her grip. Her heart beat a quick rhythm in her breast as she stared unblinkingly down at the bright green contents.

Summer Pea Soup.

She didn't move for a long moment. It could be a coincidence, and yet—

Edith hurriedly set down the porcelain lid and jumping to her feet, she quickly grabbed the handle of the large silver dome.

"Haricot lamb with carrots," she whispered.

For the first time this day, the tears that filled her eyes and clogged her throat were not those of sorrow and regret.

With happy tears blurring her vision, Edith lifted the other lid, already knowing what she'd find.

Bread and Butter pudding.

Her eyes slipped shut and warmth weaved throughout her person.

She'd not caught a glimpse of her husband since she'd left him in the carriage and assumed all the worst things. Now, seeing the attention and care he'd shown in the meal he had prepared for their wedding night—even if it was just for her—sent warmth weaving throughout her person.

More light from Edward's romantic gesture, than even the sweet claret, Edith put the lids back on their proper trays, and quit her rooms.

Gruffton stood some five or so yards from Edith's—Edward's—chambers. The minute the door opened he shot one of his already familiar, hostile glares Edith's way.

Edith smiled in return.

Not even the reminder of the surly lot who made up her new family could squelch her happiness.

"Mr. Gruffton," she greeted, giving him a cheerful wave.

"What do you think you're about?" he shot back, in return.

That drew her back, some. But Edith found her voice in an instant. "I'm exploring my new home, and what are you up to this fine—?"

"It ain't your home," he cut her off. "It's His Grace's kingdom."

Edith didn't let her smile falter. "Given I'm Edward's wife, I expect that makes me the queen of his empire, eh?" she said, with a waggle of her eyebrows.

He narrowed his eyes.

Not that she expected he'd be amused.

Edith took a step to start past the old guard, but he put himself between her and the path she intended to travel.

"You don't have leave to go snooping around His Grace's property; not without an escort."

Snooping? Not without an escort?

She'd allowed it would take some time for Grufton to understand Edith posed no threat to Edward or his club, but neither would she countenance him making her new *home*, a prison.

"Mr. Grufton," she said firmly, "I appreciate you are faithful to my husband and that you look after his interests as you do. I'm *also* aware of the reason for the breakdown in His Grace's friendship with Mr. DuMond. However, I never set foot inside this club with any intention of stealing my husband's secrets, nor do I intend to, or would I ever."

He gave her a scathing once over. "You done, duchess?"

Edith pressed her lips together, refusing to say something that would only complicate an already arduous road to an uneven truce.

"Not yet," she said. "I'd ask for directions to my husband's offices."

"Craven doesn't allow people in his offices."

Edith favored him with another one of her most winning smiles. "Ah." She held a finger up. "But I am not just any person. I'm his wife."

She had him there and by the vein bulging at Mr. Grufton's temple, he knew it, too.

With those directions in hand, Edith made a friendly goodbye and went in search of her husband. When she arrived at his office, she found two familiar guards who'd served as sentry during one of her earlier visits positioned on either side of the panel.

Unlike the anger and disrespect she'd found with Mr. Grufton, these particular guards each gave deep bows that would do in any ballroom. The taller, leaner man, with chestnut hair cut short, and angular features slightly too pronounced to make him classically handsome spoke for the pair. "Your Grace, can we be of some service?"

"Hawley, is it not?" she asked, and then glanced at the other slightly shorter but powerfully built fellow beside him. "And Cannon?"

Both men just stared.

Edith resisted the urge to squirm.

She made a clearing sound with her throat. "We had the pleasure of meeting before I was the duchess."

"I recall," Hawley said.

Edith tried to make sense of either man's expression, but it was as if stony features were required of those in her husband's employ.

"I am wondering if I might see my husband?"

"His Grace isn't in his offices, Your Grace," Hawley confirmed, and given the slight glint of pity in his hazel eyes, mayhap he wasn't so very skilled at impassivity, after all.

Her toes curled sharply into her arches until her feet ached. "I am aware of that," she lied, and the glimmer in both men's gazes indicated they knew it, too.

"I would like to wait for him to arrive," she finished lamely.

For though she didn't have a single idea where her husband spent their wedding night, what she could say with absolute confidence was he'd seek this room out long before he came to Edith.

The guards exchanged a look with one another, and she wanted to scream in frustration at how little control she had not only of her life now, but something as small as her new household.

"Given you know my husband as you do," she said, her voice sharper than she intended, "I expect you can trust His Grace would not have married a woman and brought her into his club and home, if he did not trust her."

That did the trick.

Keenan reached and pressed the handle so Edith could enter. Almost fearing he'd change his mind, or worse, that Gruffton would come running and bar her entry, Edith hurriedly stepped inside and closed the door quickly behind her.

She wandered deeper into her husband's imperial workspace. As she did, she touched her gaze on each corner of the room. Everything from his immaculate desk to the neatly kept, well-stocked sideboard, and crimson settee as they were the night she'd first visited, it was like she'd returned to the time of their first meeting.

Edith stopped at the viewing window, and unbidden, she looked upon the sinning at play on the floors of her husband's clubs.

The memories here proved too great, and she didn't even try to fight them off.

"…I'm thinking about how I'd love to avail myself of your mouth… How I want to lick and nip that delectable flesh until you're moaning and then I'll slip my tongue inside as I did yesterday.

"And then, after I drank my fill out of you, I'd kiss you elsewhere… Do you want to know where, dear Edith? Do you want me to show you?"

Closing her eyes, she bit her lip. Even with all he'd done, Edith shamefully wanted him still.

A deep voice interrupted her wicked musings. "My beautiful bride has come looking for me."

Edward.

The sound of his low, mellifluous baritone did strange things to her belly. Feelings she didn't wish to feel because of him just speaking something as simple as her name.

Unable to face him, she instead held his gaze in the window, with hers.

"I did," she confessed. "I wished to thank you."

"Thank me?"

The reflective mirror showed his approach.

She nodded. "For the dinner and dessert."

His cheeks flushed with color. "It was nothing."

How vulnerable he was at being thanked for his kindness, and this glimpse of his more vulnerable side, stirred her heart.

"It wasn't nothing, Edward. Not to me, and you know that," she said softly.

Her husband reached the point just beyond her shoulder and stopped.

Her body went shamefully alert and aware as it always did at his nearness.

Edward however, proved the model of indifference. He folded

his arms across his broad chest. "Do you find yourself in need of anything, wife?"

Him. His affection. Her family. A proper maid. But Edith had refused to take hers along. She'd not require an innocent young woman to live in this den of sin.

"No, Edward."

He followed her answer with another quick question. "Has Gruffton proven unhelpful?"

She'd not have described the taciturn guard, as *helpful*. Unkind, disrespectful, and rude came to mind more when thinking of Edward's faithful friend.

At her hesitation, Edward narrowed his eyes. "Has Gruffton treated you with anything less than respect, Edith?"

The steel in his voice indicated if Edith answered in the affirmative, he'd fire the fellow in an instant—long relationship between them, be damned. She'd not, however, become a source of contention between Edward and his right-hand man.

"No, Edward," she tendered another lie. "Mr. Gruffton has been a model of courtesy and politeness."

He said nothing for a long while. Edith's heart hammered away at his nearness.

"Do you know what I think you're really doing here, Edith?"

She shook her head.

He cupped her hair and lifted the curtain of curls off her nape, leaving her neck light as he exposed her skin to the soft sough of his breath.

"I believe you're here for your wedding night," Edward murmured.

"I told you there will be no wedding night," she breathlessly reminded him. "Unless you've come to force me, after all?"

"As you pointed out, I'm not a man who needs to force a woman."

"Ah, of course, because as *you* pointed out," she said sardonically, "women beg to be your lovers."

"Yes, there is that." He kissed her nape. "Do you know what else I believe, wife?"

Had someone put to her a question of her name, Edith couldn't think of a single logical thought or answer.

"I believe you stare out at this window, drinking in the sights of people fucking down below."

"No!" she exclaimed, that denial ripped fast from her throat.

He laughed, and that cynical rumble contained a wealth of knowing that she hated him for.

Malden gripped her by the ties at her waist and used it like a fishing line to draw her in until she was caught between his body and that viewing window.

He touched his lips to the sensitive shell of her ear with such tenderness she could almost believe he cared about her. Inch by inch, he drew her night skirts up until he'd bared her from the belly down.

The cool night air soothed the places where his touch burned her.

Her head fell back.

"I believe you'd like for them to see you," he whispered like temptation itself.

The hard ridge of his shaft against her buttocks and the ache between her legs sharpened not at the words he spoke, but at the evidence of his desire for her.

"It is all right if that is your wish, Edith."

Edward pressed a palm against her right buttock and guided her so the thatch of curls shielding her womanhood kissed the glass. He rocked his hips in a slow, circular rhythm that sent her own undulating in an erotic dance against the window.

Intermittently, they'd thump the window. Edith closed her eyes and fought the compulsion to see whether the world below knew the wicked games at play here.

"Look." Edward sucked on the lobe of her ear. "See for yourself what they see—or don't see."

Edith squeezed her eyes shut all the tighter and gave her head a firm shake.

And then, not satisfied until he had her humbled and surrendering, Edward slid the same hand that had been squeezing her buttocks and slipped it between her legs.

She knew what he'd find there, as surely as he'd known what he would find—Edith wantonly wet for him.

"Should I stop?" he made to withdraw his touch.

Unable to repress an animal-like moan, Edith's thighs reflexively clenched around him.

Edward laughed.

Edith closed her eyes; both shamed and grateful to have him in that place where she ached.

He slipped his fingers through her damp curls and into her sodden channel.

All the while Edith lifted into his expert touch, the window reflected her husband's smug smile.

She silently cursed her body for betraying her but could not bring herself to stop.

Edward dropped a kiss along her temple. "This is your clitoris," he said, teasing that over-sensitized bud between her legs.

She bit her lower lip hard to keep from crying out, knowing that loss of control was precisely what he craved and sought.

"You said no—'what did you refer to it as'—making love, I believe?" There was a teasing quality to his voice. "But I'm going to make love to you in a different way that doesn't break any of your rules, Edith."

Then, Edward, with a fervent tenderness at odds with his granite exterior, turned her around so her back rested against the window. He slid to his knees and like a devoted servant, knelt before her.

From underneath heavy lashes, Edith stared confusedly at him. "Wh-What are you doing?" she asked, her voice so breathless it barely produced sound.

But the same way as her husband knew everything, so too, did he hear everything. "What am I doing, sweet?" he placed a tantalizing kiss along the inside of her right thigh.

Edith shivered.

"I'm going to put my mouth here." He briefly palmed her curls. "And then," he tantalized, "then, I'm going to slide my tongue right in your slit." He slipped a long, tempting finger inside her.

Edith whimpered. How deft he was in his mastery of her body. She bit the inside of her cheek hard to keep from arching into his touch.

Edward paused and stole a glance up at Edith.

His dark blue eyes bore a smug, all-knowing glint. One that indicated he knew the fight she fought with herself—and also, that it was a futile one.

"I love the smell of your desire for me." Her husband closed his eyes and breathed deeply of her. "Sweet and salty. Oh, Edith, your juices will taste so delicious as they coat my tongue."

Edith moaned. She wanted to resist but her body mocked her with her need for this man and this time, she lifted her hips.

He chuckled and she hated him as much for this laugh as she had his earlier one.

"But that doesn't answer the question you're thinking but stubbornly fighting yourself to keep from asking…what," between each word, he lightly sucked at that over-sensitized bud as a punctuation, "am. I. Going. To. Do?"

A low, agonized moan filled her throat and got stuck there so it emerged more like the purr of a contented cat.

"I am going to lick you, Edith." As he delivered each promise, Edward demonstrated just what it was he meant. "I'm going to suck you."

And as before, he drew her clitoris into his mouth, but this time was different. This time he sucked powerfully.

Edith cried out. Her body hurt. But it was like no physical pain she'd ever known. Rather, this relentless need burned and throbbed, and she couldn't manage so much as a word to beg her husband for surcease.

Edward wasn't done with her.

He gripped her hard under the buttocks and drew her flush against his face. "I'm going to eat you," he rasped against her soaking curls.

"I am going consume you, Edith deVesy and leave you so sated you'll never even *think* about having another man in your bed."

How could he believe she'd want anyone other than him? She bit her lower lip hard from asking that question, knowing he'd revel and preen were she to do so.

"You are mine," he said, in a harsh avowal that made it clear she was his, and then, just as he'd promised, he buried his face in her.

Edith cried out; her hips took on a will of their own, as did her hands.

He ate her. Licked her. Nibbled and sucked as if he feasted upon something delicious. And she, like a woman possessed, lowered her palms atop his head and tangled her fingers in his satiny-soft, thick blond hair and held him there where she wanted him… where she needed him.

He laughed; that low, rumble, vibrated against Edith's mound.

Each expert stroke of his tongue brought her higher and higher, in a dizzying eddy of passion that erased logic and pride and reality and left Edith existing in a place of hot, wrenching desire.

She gritted her teeth and gripped his head harder. She ground herself against him; all the while hating him for having this power over her and hating herself *more* for being so very in love with a man so indifferent of her.

As if he'd heard Edith's unspoken lamentations, he taunted her.

"You love this, sweet," he crooned, between each maddening glide of his tongue.

She did. It was wrong and naughty and depraved, and she wanted it to go on forever and ever.

"Tell me or I shall punish you and stop."

Then, because he excelled in hurting her, Edward ceased his attentions and moved his mouth just out of reach.

Edith cried out; she grabbed his head and attempted to force him back to where she needed him, but she was no match for his strength. He continued to withhold what Edith craved.

Her wail of misery merged with his cruel, victorious laugh.

Then, his mirth faded and that harsh, hard look settled over his features and iced his eyes. "Tell me you love this, Edith. Tell me you want my mouth on you. In you. And I'll give you what you crave. What you need…"

"I love your mouth on me," she shouted, and again the reverberations of her cries danced around the room, twisting and twining with his primal growl of approval.

As promised, Edward put his mouth there and devoured her. He consumed Edith like she was both the first and last meal he'd ever feast upon.

She wept. Her pride lived no more. Though, perhaps that deep sense of her own self-consciousness and dignity ceased to be the moment he'd entered her life. And with him coaxing her body to one of those glorious surrenders only he could bring her, Edith found she didn't care.

She wanted him in this way.

*And you want him in other ways, as well…*a voice broke through the blanket of desire clouding her senses, to taunt her with that reminder. *You do not just want to know pleasure in his arms. You want to know him. All of him. You want to be part of his life and more, you want him to want to be part of your life.*

Terror cut into mindless passion and Edith fought those cruel, incessant reminders.

Determined to shut out those regretful musings for what wasn't and what would never be, Edith gritted her teeth and buried herself more deeply into the exquisite pleasure he wrought over her body.

Stop. You knew precisely what you were getting the day you consented to marry him. At least you have this.

This should be enough.

Let this be enough.

And it should be. It could be.

He wielded his tongue like a brand marking Edith on the inside as his and only his.

The pressure between Edith's legs built; the ache became keen, unbearable.

Sweat beaded from her brow and slipped a windy path down her cheek like tears born of desire.

She bit her lip.

Close. She was so very close.

As if knowing that, Edward reached up and filled his palms with her breasts. He tweaked her pebbled nipples; he caught them between his thumbs and forefingers and squeezed to the point where pain became confused with pleasure.

A low moan spilled from her lips.

Edith, like a vincible animal without hope of anything but surrendering to her all-powerful mate, rocked her hips wildly. Her movements frenzied and her buttocks thumped hard against the window.

"This is what you hunger for," he said, with the guttural, harsh praise of a man who mightily approved.

"You ache to have the world at your back, bearing witness to your depravity," he said, his voice hoarse and graveled with desire.

But *Edward's* lust, was just that—*lust*. It wasn't that way for Edith. Not truly.

Edith stared down at Edward through lashes heavy from her passion. She studied him as he so carefully devoted himself to this act—not even just her pleasure.

For Edward, any woman would do. How many times had he reminded Edith she wasn't special—not to him. How often had he told her that what she referred to as lovemaking, he called fucking, and that it meant absolutely nothing to him.

And she hated that her heart should hurt so.

And what did it say about Edith that she should want a relationship with him still?

As if he'd sensed Edith's sudden distractedness, Edward glanced up.

His nose remained buried in her quim and his mouth busily attending her, but his eyes contained a frown of annoyance and an endearingly boy-like question there.

Yes, a proud man so arrogantly aware of his talents in the bedroom would never take to a woman's indifference—certainly not his wife's. A wife, which by his own admission, he'd never wanted. That stark reminder had an even more sobering effect.

Like a cat, he came to his feet. Edward, in one fluid motion, had her spun about so her breasts and belly were flush to the clever windowing. That cool glass was like a balm upon her weeping center.

Edward placed his lips at her nape and with a tenderness that threatened to shatter he kissed her there.

Her eyes slid closed. How was it possible for him to be so beautifully gentle and yet feel absolutely nothing for her?

Nay, that wasn't true. He did feel *something*. The long, hard ridge of his shaft pressed against the low of Edith's back was proof of his desire. But she wanted more than that base emotion.

Edward reached around and slid his fingers through her thatch.

Her thighs trembled and reflexively her legs parted for him because she would never not want him like this. He'd never not be able to rouse her body to heights both exquisite and excruciating.

"Look," he commanded sharply, his hot breath fanned across her neck. "See them down there."

Edith swept her gaze over his empire; she knew what he wanted her to see—couples in the throes of lovemaking. Men on their knees as Edward had just been, servicing some masked beauty the same way Edward had serviced Edith.

Those women with their fingers tangled in their lover's hair, gripping them as Edith had done Edward.

Despite a keen sadness and disgust, her body shamefully responded to the libidinous sights before her.

"You want them to watch you as you watch them now," he predicted. "You want them to see me on my knees servicing you like you are my queen and I'm your lowly servant bowed to your whims and pleasures."

He was like a master artist who deftly painted that shameful scene.

She bit her lower lip, but the window revealed Edward's cocksure grin.

"I've a button," he murmured like sin itself against her ear. "The curtain can lift and then everyone can see you, Edith." He nipped her lobe. "Should I show them? You've watched them. Turnabout is only fair play."

"No!" she gasped; his laugh drowned out Edith's horrified response.

A cool emptiness filled her heart, slipped to her belly, and spread through her being. She stared blankly out; the libidinousness at play now an amorphous blur before her.

That is what he believed she desired. He thought this was all he needed to give her and expected he could have her whenever he wanted and however, he wished.

Because no one said no to Edward, the Duke of Craven. When he set out to seduce a woman, no woman could resist his advances.

And if she gave into him now, Edith was no different. She'd never belong to him. Not in that way. Not in the only way he wanted her to belong to him. Edward would see her the same as he saw every woman on the floors of his club so driven and controlled by hedonistic wants there existed no love, no light, no joy not related to the carnality within them.

He wouldn't see her as a woman whose heart beat with hopes and dreams and love. He'd see her as a body that was his for the taking and pleasuring, and nothing more.

And Edith wanted, no, she *needed* to be more than that to him—and that was enough to scare the everlasting hell out of her.

She'd be his equal to him in marriage and in life or nothing at all.

"Tell me what you see?" Edward enticed, slicing through her ruminations.

Again, Edith did as he commanded, but this time, she just did that and looked. His kingdom lay before them like the notorious sinful city of Sodom and Gomora—a den of iniquity and vice and sybaritism; that lost empire deservedly destroyed in the Lord's righteous anger.

For there shouldn't dwell a place where such pleasure existed, without the living, breathing heart coexisting.

Her vision cleared, coming into sharper focus, and when she could at last see, she clearly saw. This wasn't what she wanted.

Oh, her husband's adroit ability to rouse her body to the great peaks of desire he'd taken her to, yes. Edith wanted him. She didn't want to be part of the same ribald show his patrons belonged to. She wanted only him.

"Don't be shy, love," he urged. "What do you see?"

What did she see?

With Edith's mind at last free and clear to see what she wanted and the world around her, she looked out.

Edward lightly nipped the place in her neck where her pulse now settled into a calmer, more even rhythm.

Edith knew what he wanted her to say. He wanted her to speak of all the salacious things she bore witness to. He wanted to corrupt her.

Didn't he realize she'd come to him in the first place, corrupted by life's evil?

"The Duke of Rothesby," she murmured.

Her husband continued licking, biting, and kissing that flesh a long moment more, and then he stilled.

Edith angled her head and made a show of studying the gentleman on the floors below. In so angling her neck, she dislodged Edward's efforts.

He growled like a dog who'd had his bone snatched from him.

"He really is quite handsome," Edith murmured, contemplatively. And he was.

Raven-black hair and a tall, powerful physique that hinted at a love for athletic pursuits, the Duke of Rothesby was one of London's most eligible bachelors for reasons that had little to do with his powerful title—though that undoubtedly added to his appeal for many women.

Edward's entire body went on alert—his spine snapped erect and his muscles, whipcord straight.

Ah, so King Edward, Lord of All, chafed at the idea of any man receiving praise—even if it was due praise.

In an act she knew would rouse his fury, Edith touched a fingertip to the window to that spot where the duke sat. She made a show of tracing his strapping frame.

"Hmm," Edith left that to dangle there, deliberately baiting.

Like a trout who'd got a taste of blood deliberately placed in the water, her husband took that bait.

"What?" he snapped.

Ah, he didn't like ceding control. Or maybe it was just that she'd managed to resist his potent charms and gave all her focus to a different man. Perhaps it was an equal combination of the two. After all, Edward, in publicly ruining Edith for having dared to seek out his former partner, the Duke of Argyll, had proven himself a possessive man.

He certainly didn't love her. But he did not want anyone else to have her, either.

Edward growled his impatience.

"Forgive me," she murmured. "I found myself," she made a show of looking once more at the Duke of Rothesby, "distracted." Which wasn't altogether untrue. She *had* been preoccupied by her own musings.

"Were you?" he sounded like he'd just chewed glass.

It'd been Edward, however, who'd occupied her thoughts—as he always did—and not the duke below. She'd sooner bite off her tongue than admit as much.

"I couldn't help noticing; His Grace does not seem to mind."

"Mind what?" he snapped.

She paused and cast a glance Edward's way. "What did you call us? Slender, gawky brunettes."

He spoke through gritted teeth. "I did not—" Her husband caught himself and his mouth tensed. For, he had said just that.

Edith took advantage of his momentary silence and motioned to the gentleman currently sporting the less-than-ample brunette on his lap. "He strikes me as an…attentive lover."

As if the Duke of Rothesby took an actual verbal cue from Edith, he tenderly lifted his partner's breasts and kissed those rouged peaks one at a time.

Edward's eyebrows dipped; his already granite-like features went ten shades colder. "What are you saying, *wife*?"

Who would have imagined that title could carry such vitriol and emerge from a man's lips as an epithet?

There was also a dangerous warning in his question; one that suggested Edith proceed with caution as she tiptoed toward a line too far.

She arched an eyebrow. "Do *you* like to watch people making love, husband?"

"There's no love involved," he said bluntly. A muscle rippled along his obdurate jawline. "Fuck. It's just old-fashioned fucking."

"Fine. Do you enjoy watching them fuck, Edward?"

At her crude words, his eyes blazed like a fiercely burning fire. "You know I do."

"You speak often about letting other men see me as I find pleasure, but I suppose I should ask, husband—is that what *you* want?" she turned that question on him, her voice even. "Would you like to watch the duke fuck *me*?"

The rigid planes of his face froze, like a wintry cold that iced over an arctic steppe.

For the first time, she'd managed to silence her husband.

"Perhaps that is a wedding gift you seek, a present I can offer to a man who wants for nothing?" she ventured haltingly, all feigned innocence. "Having one of your most powerful patrons fuck me. He could see to the bothersome business of my virginity."

A muscle in Edward's cheek jumped; his hard mouth, however, remained implacable.

"I'm sure I would not mind terribly," she murmured. "Why, I expect, given his skill, I would even enjoy—" The rest of that challenge ended with a gasp.

Edward held her wrist in a vise-like grip where gentleness converged with strength.

"No man," he whispered. "*No man*, will touch you. Not without having their hands cut off and fed to them thereafter for that transgression."

As if burned, he released her as quickly as he'd grabbed her.

Unnerved by the force of emotion in his eyes, Edith rubbed absently at the place where he'd touched her.

She did not, however, look away. To do so would be conceding some level of defeat in this exchange. Instead, she held Edward's gaze squarely with her own.

"You ask if I'm aroused by what I see, Edward," she said. "And I am.

Desire blazed to life in his eyes.

"That is what these displays of debauchery are intended to do though, aren't they?" she continued. "My body's reaction is no different than all the other voyeurs. It's nothing more than a physical response. But…that is not what I *really* want, Edward."

He looped an arm around her waist and pulled her close once more. "Then tell me what you really want?" he asked harshly. "Tell me so—"

"So you can bed me?" she asked without inflection.

He had the look of a sullen boy who'd had his hiding spot in a match of hiding seek discovered too quick.

Edith smiled sadly. "You can't give me what I want, Edward."

"Oh, I absolutely can, sweet. Of that, there is no doubt."

He nuzzled her neck; lightly nipping and gently sucking at that flesh. The pull of his mouth grew more intense. Despite herself, despite her resolve to not succumb to him, of its own volition, Edith's head tipped sideways, as she unwittingly opened herself to his ministrations.

With a primitive grunt of satisfaction, Edward guided her, so she faced him once more.

If you succumb to him now, he will never respect you. He will never see you as his equal, his partner.

He'd always believe he could sway her thoughts and control her body with his quixotic touch.

Edward lowered his mouth to claim hers, but Edith turned her head so his kiss collided with her cheek.

"I won't do this, Edward," she said quietly. "I will not let you have me this way." And with all the weight of a thousand stones bearing down on her, she made herself step out of his arms and away from the embrace she longed for.

"You will," he snarled. "There will come a day when you surrender to me in every way, Edith de Vesy. You will be begging and pleading and crying for my touch and I will make you scream in ecstasy as you surrender to me."

"Yes," she allowed. "Undoubtedly you will. But today is not that day. And only the tomorrow when you come to actually care about me and offer me more will I fully surrender in your arms."

Before Edith did something pitiable like give herself to Edward, she turned on her heel and left him seething behind her. Only when she'd stepped into the hall, did she remember the stoic guards on alert, who'd likely heard everything.

Edith, her entire body burning with mortification, took quick flight. She didn't stop running until she'd reached her rooms, and even then, she barreled past Gruffton who didn't so much as glance her way.

Only after she'd closed the door did she relax. Edith leaned against the panel and took in several deep breaths.

She'd not survive this marriage. She was no match for her worldly, formidable husband. Her cause of death was certain to be a broken heart. He—

Edith's thoughts trailed off. Her gaze locked on a folded envelope perched against one of the candlesticks. Like a moth drawn to the flame, Edith's legs carried her over. Only when she'd reached the note, did she register the familiar scrawl.

Unable to quell a happy cry, Edith tore into the page so quickly, she ripped the parchment.

She frantically ran her gaze over the page.

My dear sister,

I pray you are well and hate so very much that you have not had the happily-ever-after we all wanted for you and one another. If you need me to kill him, I will…

A watery laugh burst from Edith's lips.

The other reason I'm writing is because I was today approached by a different duke.

Edith's smile faded. Her fingers tightened on the page. A different duke.

Argyll.

Fury tightened in her belly. How dare he approach her sister. She herself would kill him. Emmy was the manner of innocent, a man like Argyll would destroy in a heartbeat.

He explained your connection and indicated he's found himself in possession of new information that will be helpful to you. He asked that you meet him on the morrow.

Edith frantically ran her eyes over the rest of the letter, taking in the address. When she'd finished, she crushed the note in her hands.

She seethed. How dare he?

She may not possess the worldliness of he and Edward, but she well knew the game Argyll played here. He'd involved her sister, using Emmy to get a message to Edith inside her husband's home.

Edith hurried over to the fireplace and tossed the note into the flames.

She'd meet the Duke of Argyll, and make it clear he wasn't to go near her sister or Edith and Edward ever again.

CHAPTER 21

The moment she arrived in St. Giles and disembarked from a hired hackney, Edith knew…

I've made a mistake.

The dull ache at the back of her head and throbbing pain at her temples that'd plagued her since she'd awakened this morning, were the incessant reminder, she'd failed to heed.

Though, between not telling Edward about the note she'd received from Emmy, sneaking out of Lucifer's Den when he'd gone to his next shift on the casino floors, venturing to the Rookeries without an armed guard by way of hackney, she'd made any number of mistakes.

Now, Edith did a survey of desolate streets that even the morning sky appeared reluctant to visit. Thick fog rolled across grimy, broken cobblestones of Carrier Street, like ghosts of the poor, desolate souls who now haunted the streets that'd once been so unkind to them. The sun which'd risen some time ago was shielded by the thick, grey clouds it hid behind. Dilapidated buildings, endless alleyways, and meandering courtyards made it a place not even constables would visit.

Standing amidst the Rookeries, Edith understood why.

And yet, once again, Edward had left her with no choice but to set out on her own. He'd not expressed any intention of helping avenge Evie's death. He didn't care what she did or who she kept company with.

That is, as long as it isn't the very man whom you now go to meet, the voice in her head, taunted.

A figure stepped from the shadows of a nearby alley, ringing a gasp from her. And she silently cursed herself for not having her wits about her in the crime-filled streets.

The gaunt stranger with a jaundice, pock-marked face, flashed a toothless grin. With an unsteady gait, he started toward her.

Backing away quickly, Edith angled a look toward her hired hackney.

The hired hackney, which, at the moment was pulling away.

Panic built in her breast.

Even with his long, uneven limp, he moved fast, and his strides grew longer—as did the unearthly smile on his lips.

Heart pounding, Edith turned and ran. And collided headfirst with a wall.

Before she could fall, strong hands caught Edith's shoulders and steadied her.

All the air left her on a swift, painful exhale, leaving Edith momentarily dazed.

A familiar blackness plucked at the corners of her mind, but the peril she'd face if she surrendered to one of her blackouts here in the Rookeries, proved stronger.

Her breath coming in fast, raspy spurts, Edith glanced about. The dangerous stranger who'd been approaching had crept back into some other alley.

Through a mindless terror, she registered the gentle touch of the man still holding her in a strong, steady grip, and guiding her safely across the street, and onto the pavement.

Edward?

No, a *different* duke.

"Your Grace," she said woodenly.

"I'd thought you might not come, my dear." The Duke of Argyll favored her with a blindingly bright smile. "Or if you did, to arrive with a guard. At the very *least* an armed servant."

She should be elated it wasn't her husband. If it were him, she'd have witnessed his wrath on full display. Funny, she'd prefer an enraged Edward before her, than the glib, grinning duke who continued to hold her.

"Your husband has been lax," the duke said.

Edith wrenched herself from his loose hold, though the moment she displayed resistance, the Duke of Argyll released her.

"Your opinion of women is so low that you take my being here as a failing on my husband's part and not a testament of my capabilities."

His eyes shone with lust. "God, you're fiery. I hate Craven all the more for stealing you from me."

Stealing her?

"I was never yours," she said frostily.

The duke quirked his lips. "Ah, yes. But given everything you revealed during our first meeting together, you were never really Craven's either."

As he'd no doubt intended, the duke's barb landed its hit striking Edith square in the chest.

Knowing Edward had never wanted her and never would, would always hurt. She'd not, however, give him the satisfaction of responding to that taunt.

A terrific hatred for the Duke of Argyll consumed her. At last, she understood the power her husband found in loathing his former friend. Edith nourished herself on the diabolical sentiment.

Alas, as Torriano wrote, *honey draws more flies to it, than doth vinegar.*

"I've come here this morning to make it clear to you, Your Grace," she began quietly. "I do not want you to contact my sister, for any reason. I'll not have you use her as some kind of emissary between us."

He waggled his black eyebrows. "Jealous?"

The arrogance of him.

The restraint she strove for, slipped. "Jealous at the idea of my sister with a man who'd stoop to drugging a lady who went to him for help?"

The duke smiled. "Ah, the opium was merely there to loosen your tongue and inhibitions to speak freely about Craven and your relationship with him. You and I, however, know your eager little moans and even more eager kiss, had nothing to do with any *drink* I gave you that night."

With a leer, he ran his assiduous gaze over her person.

Revulsion snaked around her belly. "Lies," she hissed.

He met her rage with laughter. She was spiraling, which he undoubtedly intended.

Edith reined herself in. "I'll say this but once more; do not go anywhere near her," she repeated.

"Do you know what I think?" the duke drawled.

"I don't care what you think."

He continued as if she hadn't even spoken. "You were so good at convincing yourself the reason you came today was to warn me to steer clear of your darling sister, that you actually *believe* it."

She met his supposition with mutinous silence.

The duke, like Atilla, pressing his vantage, continued coming at her with his derisiveness. "But you and I both know, the real reason you're here is because your *doting* husband—"

Edith winced.

"—doesn't give a shite what happened to your sister, my dear. Craven finding out answers about her murder doesn't benefit him in any way. As such, he'll never look into it. You came today, because you desire what I've uncovered and you absolutely hate, not only me but yourself, for wanting anything from me."

The duke's face hardened in a way that transformed his almost unworldly handsomeness into a thing of ugliness. Reaching inside his greatcoat, he withdrew a small, ivory envelope, and held it out—daring her to abase herself, testing her.

Edith fought the urge to reach out.

In the end, the pull proved too great.

Tamping down a curse, Edith snatched the envelope from his long, glove-encased fingers.

The duke roared with laughter.

Edith stuffed the envelope inside her front pocket. As he'd correctly surmised, she despised him but, in this instant, she hated herself even more.

After his amusement died down, he shifted closer, so his body formed a protective shield between Edith and the dangerous streets of St. Giles. "There's so *much* I can give you," he said huskily. "There's so much I can show you if you let me."

Repulsion filled her. "You'd bed your former partner and best friend's wife?"

He grinned. "I was referring to meeting the druggist."

Heat consumed her cheeks.

"Also," the duke dropped his voice to a whisper, "the operative word to your early question? 'Former', Edith."

At his possessive ownership of her given name, Edith picked her chin up. "Thank you for the information you've provided," she said, loathing the idea she was in debt to this man. "However, I will not be going anywhere with you, Your Grace," she said coolly. "Furthermore, you are now to refer to me as 'Your Grace'."

Her husband's nemesis inclined his head. "The title of duchess suits." He gave her a lascivious once over. "However, I'd rather my title be the one affixed to you."

Edith narrowed her eyes. "If my husband heard you speak so, he'd kill you."

"He'd absolutely try to, anyway. But then, he's not here, *is* he?" he murmured.

Guilt sat like a stone in her stomach. Edward would see her being here as a betrayal.

As any true huntsman would, the Duke of Argyll spotted his mark.

"Knowing Craven as I do—far longer than you ever have, by the way—he'd *also* be displeased were he to know his bride ran off to meet his former friend and partner, at that, *alone*."

At her side, Edith made fists with her hands but refused to take his bait. The duke's taunts reminded her she needed to end this cat and mouse game he wished to engage her in.

"You've been warned—do *not* go near my sister, ever again." She set her jaw. "For that matter, do not approach any of my kin, or you will regret it."

"*You're* threatening *me*?" he sounded positively delighted at the prospect.

She shook her head. "It's no threat, Your Grace. It is a promise."

Another lazy smile formed on his lips. "Do you *truly* believe you can hurt *me*?" he drawled.

"I'm not so naïve as to believe that I, as a woman, have any real control of anything in this world, and I'm certainly not capable of taking on a man with your power and strength."

He preened under that *praise*.

"My husband, on the other hand," she continued, "would, could, and *will* be all too happy to utterly destroy you."

"Craven?"

The Duke of Argyll laughed and she ached to drag her fingernails down his face for insulting her husband with his mirth.

"My dear, he couldn't hurt me if he tried, and I'm able to say this with confidence as I've known him since he was a pathetic, sniveling boy. In fact, there couldn't be a more apt title for your hus—"

Edith let her palm fly with such force, she sent the duke's head flying back. She welcomed the sting of her hand striking his smug face and delighted in the way he flexed his jaw from the pain she'd inflicted with her blow.

"You knew my husband in the past," Edith said calmly. "But I know the man he is *now*. I know the lethality and ruthlessness Edward is capable of. It's also why I'd stake my life on the fact that you would never stand a chance against my husband."

"We may agree to disagree," he murmured. "The fact remains, for Craven to even try, you'd have to confess to him that you and I have met."

How she hated him for being right.

By the fiercely triumphant glint in his eyes, he'd read her thoughts.

He inclined his head. "Craven deserves neither you nor your loyalty."

With that, he shot an arm up. As if he'd conjured them of the fog, a pair of barrel-chested, swarthy men materialized from the shadows.

Edith gasped. Gathering her hems, she turned to run.

"Calm, my dear," the duke called after her in droll tones. "These are two of the finest guards at my club. I anticipated you'd not welcome my company, more's the pity," he said, sounding genuinely regretful. "I brought them to ensure when I left, you'd be safe in St. Giles."

"Thank you," she said, reluctantly. How was it possible to be grateful to a man she detested?

He inclined his head in acknowledgment. "You see, Edith, unlike your husband, I look after the women in my life."

God, he was infuriating. "I am *not* in your life," she said between clenched teeth. "Furthermore, I'll not let you disparage my husband because of my actions. I'm a grown woman, capable of making her own decisions, and, wrong or right, that is what I did today."

"Fair enough," he allowed. "But I trust you'd far prefer to have a husband who gave an actual damn about you, and who made himself your partner in this dangerous undertaking."

That is precisely what I want and will never have.

As the duke took himself off, strolling the streets of St. Giles like he took a walk through Hyde Park, Edith fought the urge to cry.

CHAPTER 22

When Craven would normally be on the casino floors at this hour, he now sat remained closeted away in his private offices, going over the papers on his usually tidy desk.

For the first time since he'd opened Lucifer's Lair, he didn't find himself pouring over the club's records and ledgers.

Instead, he waded through the lengthy report, Cadogan had brought 'round when Craven had been in the middle of his marriage ceremony with Edith. The folder marked urgent had been left amongst the pile of the daily ledgers.

Craven scoured page after page of the investigator's notes, that'd gone unread, until now—in-depth information pertaining to Edith's cousin, Mr. Eustace Stillson.

Cadogan had managed to find a link between Stillson's brother-in-law, Lieutenant Joeseph Havish in Bath, and a druggist in London.

That connection between the latter two which began several months after the lieutenant returned from the Peninsular War, with a nearly life-ending injury. Havish survived but developed an addiction for the medicine previously used to treat his suffering, and also a financial collapse.

Craven moved his head back and forth, reading so quickly, his spectacles slipped. Not taking his gaze from the findings, he pushed his glasses back into place.

The lieutenant's debt and reliance upon opium led to a split between Havish and his sister's family. His financial state also put an end to all visits with the druggist first, in May of 1821. Then, somehow, Havish found the means to start visiting the druggist for a short while in 1822.

All connections between the men didn't resume again until 1831.

Craven set aside the page in his hand and reached for the first one Cadogan delivered weeks ago.

There it was.

1831.

Edith was right—Stillson was coming for her brother, heir to the viscountcy.

Craven remained locked on a detail in the middle of one page.

Evie Caldecott

Date of Death: 26th*, April 1822*

He stared blankly at the name and date etched in black ink.

He saw them, as if for a first time, and in a new light.

Before, the date of Evie Caldecott's death had been just an extraneous detail he'd breezed over. Now, in his mind, that moment in time was everything *Edith.*

Craven recalled the first night he'd seen Edith—for despite his initial lie, he *did* remember her.

He'd pointed her out to Argyll, and that night, learned her name.

She'd looked as miserable as he'd felt, and he'd been so damned curious about *her.*

Cynically, he'd assumed it'd been her lack of suitors or dance partners. He'd silently wagered himself betting on it, all the while knowing he'd never have the answer to his question.

But now he did. The misery etched in her features wasn't because of something as inconsequential as a longing to dance—as would've been the case with nearly every other woman.

This very date on the page signified absolutely *everything*. It marked the moment Edith's beloved, young, healthy sister was cut down. It signified the exact day Edith surrendered herself to sadness and threw herself into finding answers and justice for her eldest sister.

It'd been what brought Edith into Craven's life.

If it *hadn't* been for Evie Caldecott's death, would Edith and Craven ever have known one another?

But Craven knew the answer.

They wouldn't have even breathed the same air. Most certainly she would've been happier and with a chap who gave her sweet words and tender caresses; that man would be the partner and friend Edith yearned for in a husband.

In short, that faceless stranger would give Edith things Craven would never be able to.

And Craven, selfish bastard as ever, wanted her too much to even care about anything other than the fact she belonged to him.

Giving his head a clearing shake, Craven picked up the previously discarded document and got to work re-reading Cadogan's notes.

There'd been a stretch of years where the lieutenant had ceased visiting the druggist. Craven's eyes homed in on the date Havish started seeing the druggist again.

He worked his gaze over the page, searching for how long those particular payments continued and, Craven froze.

29th, April, 1822.

Grabbing the sheet with the details pertaining to Evie Caldecott's death, he held the two documents side by side.

His head spinning, Craven continued looking back and forth between the pages, studying them.

Three days after Evie Caldecott's death.

Stunned, Craven tossed aside the notes and frantically sifted through the piles that'd previously been neglected, until now—he landed on a sealed envelope. This one also marked urgent and in Cadogan's hand.

Craven tore into the seal, opened the letter, and hurriedly read the investigator's lengthy note.

Knowing the significance of my findings, I've done my best to meet you in person with these important discoveries, to no success. As such, I leave this here.

Based on the information I provided you with earlier in the week, I paid a visit to the Lieutenant. The gentleman proved more than forthcoming and was all too happy to share every detail in Mr. Stillson's role in securing laudanum and opium, among others, from his former druggist, in the months leading up to Miss Caldecott's death.

Stillson was all too happy to fund Havish's opium habit, as long as he had need of his brother-in-law's man. Though, the lieutenant could not personally confirm his brother-in-law purchased poison to kill the future Viscount Drayton, he did establish a link between the timing of Caldecott's death and Stillson's visits.

Following my appointment with the lieutenant, I met the druggist who, though not initially cooperative, under some duress, confirmed his relationship with Stillson. Even more important to note, Stillson recently began purchasing from the druggist again.

~A

When he'd finished reading, Craven, unblinking, stared sightlessly at the page.

Edith had been right all along. Not that he was surprised. His wife was as clever as she was courageous and fearless. And Craven? He'd gone about getting the information he now held in his hands with the same indifference he did anything that didn't pertain to his club.

He scraped an unsteady hand through his hair.

Along the way, however, Edith had turned him upside down as no one—not his father, not DuMond, Argyll, or Latimer, or anyone else, had ever managed to do.

From the moment she'd set her innocent feet inside his club and office, the truth was there, all along. She'd be his queen, and he, her king. Except, Craven had fought it for so long, he'd failed to care for and guard over her.

Never again. Before they'd ever even met, she'd been destined for him and him, for her, and Edith knowing that indefatigable truth, was long overdue.

The moment he stormed from his office, Craven collided with Cadogan. The steely investigator's harsh features set in their usual, menacing mask.

"I've got information and it won't do to leave in a note," Cadogan said, in cunningly bland tones, Craven would've taken exception with—if the apathetic bastard hadn't been right.

Craven motioned the other man inside and made to follow him.

A harsh shout sounded from down the hall.

"Your Grace!" Gruffton bellowed.

Craven looked at the panicked guard. "I'm not dealing with club business at the moment. See to it."

An out of breath Gruffton stopped quick at the door.

Never once, not even when their relationship with Argyll, DuMond, and Latimer unraveled had he witnessed the man anything but a model of calm.

"Her Grace is gone," he said, his chest heaving.

Craven stared blankly at the older man. What had he said?

"Antonson believed she was visiting her family, but the moment her carriage deviated…"

There was a vicious humming in Craven's ears that left everything jumbled and distorted.

Cadogan's calm, matter-of-fact statement, knocked Craven back to the moment. All his senses and nerve endings went on sharp alert.

Gruffton, red in the face from the investigator's interruption glared angrily at the investigator.

Craven, however, cared as little about the old guard's wounded pride as Cadogan appeared to.

"Her Grace is attending a meeting at Carrier Street," the investigator quietly informed Craven.

While the investigator quickly rattled off Edith's whereabouts and the meeting he suspected she sought this day, Craven stared at the other man's mouth as it moved.

His wife had gone to Carrier Street—in St. Giles.

Every revelation of the lady's incautiousness this day should fill Craven with an unholy fury. But an old emotion he recognized all too well from his younger years, one he believed himself incapable of feeling ever again formed low in his gut—fear.

Sweat slicked Craven's palms.

Nay, this, it wasn't the dread of a boy about to face a beating or bullying. Rather an all-consuming, unreasoning, senseless, terror held Craven in a relentless grip.

With a primordial growl, he broke into a sprint. "My goddamned horse," he thundered.

"Already seen to it, Your Grace," Gruffton called, struggling to keep up.

Not so much as slowing the furious pace he'd set, Craven

skewered the old guard with a glare. "Do you expect some kind of fucking praise for getting my bloody horse when you lost my duchess?" he hissed.

Mottled splotches filled Gruffton's heavily wrinkled cheeks.

When they'd reached the courtyard, Craven and Cadogan each took the reins of his respective mount from a pair of waiting stableboys.

Gruffton yanked his cap off. "I can serve ye better if I join ye," the servant spoke so quick, his words slipped deeper into the harsh Cockney that'd become less distinct over the years.

From astride his horse, Cadogan peered sharply at the all-but-groveling servant.

The last thing Craven gave two shites about, however, was Gruffton or anyone else.

"You are to stay and attend the club, and if anything goes wrong, by God, you'd better flee, because I will hunt you down for all the mistakes you've made this day."

Just as if any harm befell Craven's wife: if anyone touched a hair on her head, if anyone so much as brushed against her on the sidewalk, Gruffton would not only be without work, he'd find his life swiftly cut short.

Craven kicked his horse forward. The moment he turned onto a still quiet Curzon Street, he gave the ornery stallion the freedom to enter a full sprint.

All the while, to keep his thoughts from running wild, he kept his gaze ahead.

Back when Forbidden Pleasures had existed as only an idea between, he and his former friends, to the time it'd become a thriving, lucrative casino, Craven had made the journey from Grosvenor Square to the Rookeries any number of times. Never had a single one of those rides felt as bloody ceaseless as the one he made now.

Because Craven knew those streets. He'd witnessed every possible evil that existed in the world, alive and flourishing there in the Rookeries. Murders. Thefts. And worse.

Vomit burned the back of his throat, and he swallowed to keep it back.

They eventually reached the uneven, grimy cobblestones, no

lady should ever travel upon but had now been walked along by his wife. Craven combed Carrier Street for any hint of her or his damned carriage.

Cadogan drew his chestnut horse alongside Craven. "The lady hired a hackney."

Craven's entire body tensed, and Apollo jumped nervously under him.

"She hired a hackney," he gritted out.

The other man nodded. "Follow me." Without waiting to see if Craven followed those orders, he set out ahead.

All the while Craven seethed. Edith hadn't even gone by his bloody carriage, which also meant she was out here, somewhere without the benefit of any of his men; all important details, Gruffton had declined to share.

Dead. Gruffton is dead man.

A handful of minutes later, Cadogan brought them to a stop outside a surprisingly neat, red brick front building; two stocky, well-built fellows stood outside.

As Craven dismounted, Cadogan performed quick introductions between Craven and two of his underlings, who took their horses.

Listening while the men provided the assassin an update on Edith's whereabouts, Craven skimmed the area. Searching for her, kept him from going mad in thinking of what might have happened to her.

One of Cadogan's men pointed down the street and Craven swung his focus that way.

A lone hackney sat in wait.

An indescribable whisper of awareness stirred the air around him.

Without even hearing the rest of the directions, Craven headed for that carriage. Every step that brought him nearer, the more he felt Edith's presence. She'd imprinted upon him, and that intertwining of his dark soul with her lighter one, guided Craven closer to her.

Then, she was there—as he knew she'd be—she darted out of an alleyway some fifteen yards from him.

A relief so profound, the likes of which he'd never known, left him nearly dizzy, and elated.

Eager to get to his wife, so he could thoroughly kiss her and then rail at her for having put herself in mortal danger, he broke into a jog.

Craven knew the moment she sensed his presence the way he did hers. Halfway across the street, she stopped in her tracks. Except, instead of facing him, she angled left.

A figure bolted from the same alley she'd slipped out of.

His wife, sensing the threat bearing down on her the same time Craven noted it, snapped erect.

Time existed in a peculiar state where the world continued in its usual quick blur, while Craven found himself trapped in slow motion.

"Edith!" Even as he thundered his wife's name and barreled towards her, the tall, wiry, bald street tough was closer.

That managed to give her pursuer pause. Except, the sound of Craven's voice also froze his wife. Even with the now ten yards separating them, he caught the way her eyes widened in shock and relief.

Only, he wasn't deserving of her confidence.

The street thug grabbed Edith by the shoulders and dragged her on with him. Crazed with savage bloodlust, Craven's raw, animalistic roar swallowed all the other sounds from St. Giles. Undeterred, the man who'd dared put his hands on Craven's wife, kept her trapped in a solid grip; she twisted and writhed and the sight of her like a trapped animal, frantic to escape.

Amidst her struggle, Edith's eyes found Craven's. There was a pleading in those glittering depths, that would haunt him as long as he stalked this earth.

Abruptly, her assailant stopped.

Craven's gaze followed the other man's to the carriage barreling down on him and Edith. For an instant, Craven believed fear held the bastard frozen.

Except, Edith's attacker carefully followed that quick-moving carriage, and then dove out of the way, leaving her frozen like a small deer to be trapped.

Craven reached his wife a hair before the runaway unmarked

barouche. His breath ragged, he launched himself at Edith and knocked her to the ground. A second later, that carriage went barreling past.

With those threats fleeing, Craven leveraged himself off Edith's slender frame. Her hair hung in a sad, messy tangle upon the stone earth; sections of her lush brown curls lay within a grimy puddle. Her already porcelain white skin faded further to the color of death.

Edith's lashes fluttered open, and her tearful eyes landed on him.

"Edward," she whispered nothing but the two syllables that made up his name. There'd never been a sweeter sound than that of her voice.

But the pain-filled, little moan she released, tore up a corner of his heart that apparently still existed.

Frantic, Craven yanked his jacket apart, sending buttons flying all over the cobblestones. He shrugged out of his jacket and lay the black garment on the ground.

With painstaking care, Craven scooped Edith up and brought her so she lay upon the makeshift blanket his jacket made.

He gently explored her limbs and searched for signs of breaks or blood. "Are you hurt?" he demanded, his question emerged harsh and angry.

Edith gave her head a small shake. "No," she whispered. "I am just sore from where I fell."

It would be more accurate for her to say from when he'd taken her down. The fact it'd been *Craven* who'd caused her pain ravaged him. He wanted to howl, snarl, and hiss like an injured beast.

The danger of the moment now passed, and his heart settled back into its normal, steady rhythm, Craven narrowed his eyes upon Edith. Finding anger and feeding that unholy, but very welcome sentiment, he stood so that he towered over his wife's prone frame.

The flash of fear he'd not seen her direct his way in so long appeared as a glimmer.

Good. He seethed. With the threat now passed, the chit should be afraid. She should be *very* afraid.

Still, when he bent and helped his vexing wife on her feet, he did so carefully.

Edith dampened her mouth.

Ah, that telltale gesture that came only and always from his wife when it involved her lies. The reminder of her first deception stirred his anger.

Rage swirled like the flickering flames of a slow-building fire.

"Edward," she began.

Where her uttering his name in her sweet, dulcet tones had before soothed, now hearing it fanned Craven's fury.

"I know I've—"

Craven glared the rest of that thought into silence. "Not a word, wife," he bit out. "Not a single, bloody word."

At an opportune moment, the carriage bearing his gold-painted ducal seal drew to a stop near them. The guard riding upon the back of the conveyance jumped down and opened the door for them.

Reticently, Craven lifted his wife inside and set her down on a crimson upholstered bench. Without so much as a single glance, he slammed the door shut behind her, and marched over to where Cadogan stood waiting.

CHAPTER 23

EDITH SAT ON THE QUEENLY bench of Edward's carriage and stared at her husband and the three forbidding men he conversed with.

What did you expect? she bitterly reminded herself. Had she truly believed he wouldn't find out she'd left his well-guarded gaming hell and snuck off to St. Giles to meet the Duke of Argyll?

Her stomach muscles twisted painfully. She hated herself for deceiving him—again.

He'd never forgive one betrayal, let alone, *two*.

Edith knew just how deep the antipathy her husband had for the Duke of Argyll, and she'd gone and let her single-minded focus on catching Evie's killer, come first.

"You would hate that, Evie," Edith whispered; her gaze locked upon her stoic husband who remained in a tense, somber exchange with that trio. "You told me to let it go. To live and be happy."

Except Edith hadn't believed she could be happy after Evie's death. So what had she gone and done? Instead of attempting to build a life with Edward and devoting herself to breaking down those protective fortresses he'd erected to keep himself from hurt, she'd remained fixed on revenge against Mr. Stillson.

Sitting there, when it was too late, Edith finally accepted, she'd never not love Edward. She'd fallen head over heels for a man who wouldn't let himself love or be loved. He'd certainly never give his heart to a woman who'd gone behind his back and met with his sworn enemy.

Just then, Edward finished up his conversation.

Edith looked away before her husband could find her staring forlornly out at him. He joined Edith inside, and without waiting for the servant, he slammed the door shut. The spacious carriage suddenly felt very small.

Without a word, he sat on the bench opposite her.

A moment later, the conveyance sprung into motion. Her clear, crystal pane reflected his visage; one that had become so beloved to her.

Edith hurt. From the tips of her toes to the deepest part of her soul, she ached.

They shared the same carriage, but and with their bodies angled away from one another, and his gaze directed out his window, they may as well have been worlds apart.

Never once had she struggled to speak with him. Now, her tongue had gone heavy and her mouth dry and if she weren't so emotionally replete, she would have wept.

The quiet between them became an unbearable, suffocating weight.

"You could have just left me," she said softly.

He looked at her in bafflement.

"When the carriage was coming." Edith clarified. "Then you wouldn't have to bother with me any—"

"Are you bloody serious?" he hissed, with a chill so deep, gooseflesh rose on her arms.

"I…" She chewed at her lower lip. "It's just—"

"You believe I'd let you die?" Grimly, he predicted the rest of Edith's thought.

The telltale glint in his eyes indicated she should proceed with caution.

"Let us be clear, wife," he said, in high dudgeon. "I protect what is mine and make no mistake, you are mine, no matter how much you may hate it."

I should hate it, but I don't.

How pathetic he'd think her.

"Is. That. Clear?" he enunciated each savage syllable.

There was a soreness in her lungs and throat that made speech impossible. Edith could only bring herself to nod.

Her stomach still roiled the same way it'd done since she'd set out this morning. Every inch of her ached from the force with which she'd hit the ground when Edward saved her.

All that pain was nothing, compared to the inflicted by the incandescent rage in Edward's eyes when he looked at her.

She needn't have worried much. As briskly as Edward directed his attention to Edith, was as quickly as he glanced away.

Tears filled her eyes and knowing he despised them, Edith turned her focus out her window, lest he happen to see them.

What did you expect? He saved you because he cares about you?

He'd made it clear time and time again he'd no feelings for Edith that were anything other than annoyance, disgust, and at best, indifference.

When it became clear her husband had no intention of saying anything further, Edith again spoke.

"I know what you are thinking, Edward."

His laugh, as grating as broken glass, filled the carriage.

He gave Edith his flat, implacable gaze. "You have *no* idea, wife."

Oh, she did. Because whether he believed it or not, she understood him. From the personal moments in his life he'd shared with Edith, she *knew* why he'd become the man he had. Just as she knew, somewhere deep inside, that young man who'd visited old bookshops and loved to read, still lived within him. From the tender way, time and time again, he'd given her pleasure, without every taking any for himself to the dinner he'd had prepared for her on their wedding night did not fit with a ruthless man, incapable of caring for anyone.

She also knew, however, a man as proud as Edward, with a hate so deep for the men who'd been the last to hurt him, would never not be anything less than enraged at learning his wife went to St. Giles to meet the Duke of Argyll.

"I deserve your anger, Edward," she said quietly.

He passed a heated, hooded gaze over her. "Yes, you do," he said, his deep baritone a blend of desire and rage. "I'd spank you, except you would enjoy it, and you don't deserve any pleasure—not this day."

Edith bit the inside of her cheek. *What did you expect?*

"The only reason I went to meet him was to warn him to stay away from Emmy, but I now know I should have come to you and—"

The penetrating glint in his eyes stopped the rest of her words. "Who did you meet?" he asked on an incisive whisper.

Oh, God. "I..." *He doesn't know.* Her already ill stomach churned like she rode a small boat on the choppy North Seas.

"Edith," her husband said in warning tones. "I asked you, who you met this morning."

He didn't know. But he needed to.

She was tired of lying to him and keeping secrets and, even knowing the aftermath to follow, she just wanted to finally be open with him, and have a relationship where they talked. Today's meeting, however, was all tangled up with past ones, back when Edward turned her away, and she'd gone to the Duke of Argyll.

Edith tried to sort out where to begin, but the pain in her head made the task a chore.

She dug her fingertips against her temples to dull the ache there.

It didn't help.

Edith let her hands fall back to her lap. "After..."

Only she didn't want to refer to it as the day he'd rejected her. Even if that's what it'd been.

"Before we were married," she amended. "The night I saw the Duke of Argyll...."

Having dispensed with his jacket, Edith caught the way Edward's biceps tensed at her mention of his nemesis.

This conversation had been inevitable and was just as destined to never have been easy.

Determined to get through the telling as quickly as possible, Edith found her voice. "He offered to look into the details about my sister's death. At the night of the ball, the one where you—"

"I know the ball you're speaking of," Edward snapped.

She cleared her throat. "Yes, well, he'd asked to speak with me alone."

"Of course, he did." He narrowed his eyes. "*Did* you at any point?"

"No!" Edith exclaimed.

She took a breath. "I've never been alone with him aside from that night I paid a visit to his townhouse."

Angry color filled the harsh plains of Edward's cheeks. "Why do I suspect that isn't entirely true?"

She grimaced. Because it wasn't. He, of course, knew the end of her current story before she even told it. Still, he sought to make her suffer by telling him anyway. Well, little did he know, she both intended to and wanted to.

"No, you are right. But that evening, and all the outings with him prior, whenever I was with His Grace, I was never without a companion or my sister as chaperone."

His face remained blank like he hardly cared either way.

Edith may have believed him, too. That is, if it hadn't been for the night, she'd found Edward in her rented carriage outside Argyll's residence and witnessed the rage her husband had flown into.

"I received a letter from my sister, Emmy, last evening," she said, hushedly. "It was left on the dinner table in my rooms. She let me know His Grace met with her, privately."

The faintest frown lines appeared at the corners of Edward's mouth.

So, he didn't like the idea Argyll approached Emmy any more than Edith did.

There was something fortifying in knowing she and Edward shared something—even if it *was* something as simple as their rage for a common enemy.

"He wished to meet with me in St. Giles to discuss something he'd discovered about a druggist there. The reason I went, was to warn him to stay away from Emmy."

Edward looked at her so long she wondered if he'd even been listening.

Eventually, he spoke.

"You know, Edith, you said that so convincingly, I think you actually believe it. You, a woman who'd encountered so many obstacles in avenging your sister, that you came to *me* and Argyll, suddenly thought yourself capable of meeting one of London's most ruthless men and having success at warning him off?

Just as she'd prided herself on knowing him, he knew Edith, just as well—maybe, even more.

"No, you are right," she granted. "There was a part of me that knew were you to discover he'd approached my sister—"

"Which I would have."

"Which you would have. That it would further escalate the enmity between you and the duke and possibly lead to a physical altercation—even a duel—between you and Argyll."

"And you were more worried about me squaring off against Argyll than you were about your sister?" he asked cuttingly.

I...was. Edith's face buckled. When had her love for this man grown so deep that protecting him had become just as essential, as caring for her sister?

Surprise flashed in Edward's eyes. He clearly saw the truth there. By the next words from his mouth, however, that truth meant nothing to him.

"And at no time did you risk your bloody life meeting Argyll in St. Giles because you sought out information he'd dangled over you since his ball?"

Edith hesitated and then shook her head.

He peered down the length of his nose at Edith. "That is what I thought, *wife*."

"You haven't exactly made me feel as though I could come to you, Edward," she said entreatingly. "You've been abundantly clear that finding out answers about Evie's death or avenging her doesn't matter to you. That any attention you put into it was squarely contingent upon what you received...or as it so happened, *didn't* receive from me."

A shadow fell over his eyes.

Edith searched his face. Surely, she'd not *hurt* him with the truth?

She immediately had her answer.

Edward laughed; a vicious, mocking expression that caused her to flinch.

"You'd put this on *me, wife*?" he snarled.

"I'd put this on *both* of us, Edward: me, for not coming to you and you, for not being someone whom I feel I can turn to."

He jerked as if she'd stabbed him.

"You feel you can turn to Argyll and not me?" he whispered with a pain she'd never before heard from him.

"No." Edith dragged her hands through her messy curls. "That isn't what I'm *saying*."

"That is what you just said, Edith."

The throbbing in her head grew more incessant.

"But it's not how I feel." She thumped a fist against her rapidly beating heart. She abhorred the Duke of Argyll for what he'd done to Edward and for using Edith as a pawn in their fight. But she hated herself more for ever having gone to Argyll in the first place.

Edward flashed a snide smile. "How is it you *feel*, dear wife?"

"How do I feel?" she whispered. "How do I *feel*?"

Suddenly, it was too much.

"I can't tell if you actually want to know how I feel or whether you're just mocking me with that question," Edith cried. "I'm sure it's the latter, but…I don't know what you are thinking most of the time, Edward."

Her chest burned from the explosive force of her emotion. "I can't tell if you merely dislike me or completely loathe me, and I hate it."

Tears filled her eyes and this time; she was too tired to wipe them away. "I hate it because I want to know everything there is to know about you. All the parts of your past that you hold onto so tight. What *you* like to eat. What truly brings you happiness, *other* than your club. And do you know what agony it is to *love* you, a man who looks at me with so much disdain?"

Edward's brows lifted.

He shook his head and opened and closed his mouth, but no words came out.

Her shoulders shook with the force of her tears. "I didn't even care you publicly ruined me, because I'm so pathetic I yearned to be yours as long as you wanted to marry Lady Violet," she cried.

The color washed from Edward's cheeks.

She'd managed the impossible—she'd silenced Edward de Vesy, the Duke of Craven.

"How that must repulse you." Edith sobbed so hard, her chest heaved hard enough and painful enough to rip her open. "To be stuck with a wife who has no pride when it comes to loving you."

Edward scraped a hand through his hair. "I could *never*."

"Love me?" she asked with an embittered laugh. "I *know. God*, how I know. Does it bring you some kind of perverse pleasure—"

He cursed. "That wasn't what I was saying, Edith. How could you possibly believe I'm repulsed by you? From the start, I have not been able to keep my hands off you."

"Ah, but that is just fucking," she said, her voice faded to a watery whisper.

His face reddened.

"Do you *truly* believe I'd have as my duchess a woman I don't admire?" he demanded.

"I don't know, Edward." She glanced down at her empty hands. "You were willing to take Lady Violet, a woman you'd never met, as your wife, to get revenge on Lord Rutherford. As such, I didn't really think it mattered one way or another how you felt about your duchess."

At last, her body didn't have another tear to shed.

She stared wistfully at an ashen-faced Edward.

"Edward, do you know what's the saddest part of all?"

He hesitated, and then shook his head.

Edith flashed him a sad smile. "If I died today, I couldn't say either way if you would be glad, I'd gotten my comeuppance or whether a small part of you might somehow miss me."

"Edith," he said gruffly, and faintly chastising.

Edward tugged a handkerchief from his jacket pocket. Ever so gently, he wiped away from Edith's cheeks, the remnants of her grief.

When he'd finished, he handed the embroidered fabric to her. "I don't dislike you, Edith."

Somehow, she managed a wan smile. "I am positively warmed, Edward."

Her husband dragged an unsteady hand through his hair. "Edith, I was *never* going to be the man who could warm your heart or be all the things you want a husband to be."

He sounded a cross between angry and desperate.

She stared forlornly at his tear-soaked kerchief. "Maybe not."

All the tears she'd cried made her voice emerge, deeper. "What makes it unbearable, Edward? Is that you won't even try."

Their carriage rolled to a stop outside Lucifer's Lair.

A guard hurried over to greet them. Edward stepped down; so steady and assured and fully in control of himself, she envied him.

He took his handkerchief back and stuffed it back inside his coat.

Without a word, he caught Edith by the waist and set her on the ground.

When they arrived inside the club, Gruffton was there to greet them at the entrance of the private suites.

"Your Grace. There's been no problems here. If—"

"Leave us," Edward cut the other man short.

Edward's most loyal guard looked back and forth between husband and wife and dropped a bow.

"A bath and meal have been prepared for Her Grace." With that, he let himself out.

Then, to Edith's befuddlement, Edward escorted her, not to her bedchambers but to his office.

After they'd entered, Edward pointed to one of the chairs at the front of his desk.

"We're going to talk, Edith,"

She wanted to snap and snarl and defy that high-handed order, but between her emotional outpouring in the carriage and the peril she'd encountered in the Rookeries, Edith didn't have the energy to fight.

The moment she sat, Edward, as was his way, perched on the edge so she was forced to look up at him.

Edith's neck muscles, still sore from her collision with the street, ached to the point she could not meet his gaze—even as she wanted to.

She felt his eyes on her.

"You are hurt," he said softly, his voice, faintly accusing, as if he were bothered by her pain.

"I am just sore," she said tiredly.

Her husband shouted for the guard stationed outside.

"I want a bloody doctor summoned immediately," Edward demanded.

"I don't need a doctor, Edward."

Both men ignored her.

"Yes, Your Grace."

After Aveyard took his leave, Edward came around the back of Edith's chair.

Then, she felt the warmth of his powerful hands as he rested them upon her shoulders. Gently, he began to gently massage Edith.

Applying a firmer pressure that was as exquisite as it was torturous, Edward kneaded knots she hadn't even known were there.

Despite hurting all over, his touch brought soothing magic to the muscles he rubbed.

A little moan bubbled past her lips.

"Too hard?" he murmured with a concern that threatened to break her in the best possible way.

"No." She closed her eyes. "It is perfect."

She'd believed there couldn't be anything more glorious than the passion he stirred in her. But *this*, touch, one fueled by no other desire than to ease Edith's pain, sent a soft, beautiful heat to her heart.

Edward reached up and pressed his fingertips into the point at the base of her skull.

She groaned.

Her husband immediately lightened his pressure.

"Please, don't stop, Edward." He knew right where to touch and the just amount of pressure she needed.

In silent acknowledgment, Edward returned to his previous level of intensity. He continued to glide his strong hands over all the parts that still hurt: her skull, her neck, her shoulders, and lower, to her back.

It was only after he'd stopped did she realize, she'd dozed.

"Better?" he asked quietly.

Her lashes heavy, Edith forced her eyes open and lifted her head to meet Edward's tender gaze. "Much."

Even though the soreness from her fall remained, whenever he touched her, his hands were as much an elixir as the impassioned way he gazed upon her.

The moment was broken.

Collecting the chair next to Edith's, he turned it so he was angled in a way where she needn't strain her neck, and seated himself.

"I am your husband, and you are my wife," he began. "As such, you were correct in the carriage. There will be no secrets between us. They end here, and they end now."

Shock brought her brow flying up. He'd credited Edith with being right, and had not just demanded she be truthful, but that they both be honest with one another?

Perhaps she'd hit her head harder than initially thought.

Edward got to his feet and collected a number of folders and papers on his desk. He took a moment to neatly arrange them and then retook his seat next to Edith.

"You don't know what these are," he said, lifting the now tidy pile up. "Obviously, you do not, because I've not shared them with you."

Edward set the stack on her lap.

Edith glanced at him. He motioned for her to look.

Feeling his intense gaze upon her, Edith opened the top file, and read…and continued reading.

With every page turned, more and more she saw how extensive her husband's efforts had been to solve the mystery of Evie's death. Even after that horrible day in Hyde Park, he'd continued with his research.

She read through a page worth of lengthy details about Mr. Stillson and stopped. When she first met Edward and asked him to destroy Mr. Stillson, Edward spoke so sadistically, and was so blasé about murdering her distant cousin, she'd believed him.

Yet, by the dates on the papers and the information assembled, Edward sought confirmation of Mr. Stillson's treachery, before ending his life. And instead of being disheartened he'd not already seen to Mr. Stillson, she found herself contented in knowing Edward wasn't a man to exact punishment without proof.

When she got to a note marked urgent, she froze.

Here it was, inked in black and confirming that which Edith and Emmy had always known—the proof Mr. Stillson killed Evie.

There did not come the rapid thrill of knowing she'd outwitted him, and he'd now pay the price, as he'd already begun to when Edward bankrupted him. Rather, it felt like an anti-climactic end to a tragic chapter. Evie had been right. Proof of Mr. Stillson's evil wouldn't make Edith feel better, because it could not bring Evie back.

What her late sister hadn't anticipated—or for that matter, Edith herself—was the peace closure brought.

And it had been Edward who'd gifted her this priceless treasure.

A fresh wave of tears brimmed her eyes.

In the end, when her parents and brother failed to believe her. When the whole world had never bothered even looking for answers, Edward had been the one.

When she finished, Edith reassembled the notes and lifted her blurry gaze to his. "Thank you." The force of her emotions left her throat tight.

He fell to a knee beside her.

Edward, a man so powerful as to never prostrate himself, knelt before Edith, and for reasons which had nothing to do with desire.

"Here now, you never have to thank me for caring after you and vanquishing your enemies," he murmured, wiping a tear from her cheek.

His tenderness only made the drops fall faster and harder.

"I d-didn't know," she said, her voice broke. "All along I believed you'd only helped me because of our arrangement and that you'd stopped when you learned I'd lied to you, and all along you were still intent on destroying Mr. Stillson."

Guilt swarmed her.

"You didn't know because I didn't tell you." Edward's quiet murmuring brought Edith's head up.

Edith studied him carefully.

What was he saying.

His eyes blazed with emotion; emotion that was *not* rage.

"I loathe to my very *core* you met Argyll." Her husband punched a fist against his chest. "I hate you felt you could go to him and not me—"

She couldn't bear this.

Edith exploded to her feet.

"It was never about feeling like I could turn to him," she said beseechingly, willing him to understand. "You were right, Edward. My family was right. Avenging Evie has become such an obsession, it's consumed me."

"Edith," he began gruffly.

Needing to explain, she shook her head. "I have to say this, Edward."

Emotion choked her voice. "I didn't even realize what I've become. I've thought more about my departed sister than I have my living family members."

Edith took a deep, pained breath.

Edward tried again. "Edith—"

"Mm. Mm. I am still talking."

As he'd done moments ago, Edith thumped her chest. "You are my family now, Edward, but in ways, I've been no different than your father."

His face darkened. "You are *nothing* like him."

"But I have been. I came to you, asking you to kill a man." Horrified by her own ruthlessness, she dropped her voice.

A muscle rippled along Edward's squared jaw. "A man that deserves to be killed."

"Yes, he does. But even more important, you are a man who deserves to be loved and not used as a weapon of war."

Yet, that is precisely what she'd done.

Her throat spasmed. She'd been the worst sort of hypocrite.

Edith raised her eyes to his. "I passed judgement on you, Edward, for being singularly possessed by a need for revenge, when all along, *I'm* the one whose been all-consumed with destroying Mr. Stillson for years. You taught me that."

Edith took one of his hands in both of hers. She pressed their linked fingers against her chest.

"You matter more to me than revenge, Edward. I don't want you to murder for me, or anyone. I just want to show you the light and love you've been missing all your life."

Edward slipped his hand from hers.

At that rejection, Edith bit the side of her mouth.

Then, Edward brought that same palm up and tenderly cradled her cheek.

"I *hate* that you went to Argyll instead of me. But what I hate even more, Edith, is myself. I made you believe I wouldn't stand at your side and take down your foes."

He flexed his jaw. "In fact, I haven't given you any reason to trust in me." He flexed his jaw. "That stops now."

What was he saying?

"I can't give you love, Edith," he said, regretful-sounding.

She hated, with everything she'd discovered about Edward today and this new, sweet side of him he'd revealed, that, all she could feel was a crippling grief.

"I cannot give you the tender words you want and deserve. I can give you children." His lashes swept low. "And I will, Edith. We'll find divine pleasure in my efforts."

His was a husky promise, that sent heat rushing to her center.

Edward's expression grew resolute. "But I can and will ensure that as my queen, you and our children will always be safe from harm. I vow to you, going forward, I will be honest with you. I'll not keep anything from you."

"And," He held her gaze with his piercing one. "I pledge to be faithful to you."

Edith's heart missed a beat.

"What?" she whispered; desperately afraid he was mocking her with that improbable vow.

"When I saw that carriage bearing down on you, Edith…."

Edward squeezed his eyes shut and sucked a shuddery breath in through his teeth.

When he opened his eyes, his tumult showed within.

"I thought I'd lose you, Edith," he confessed. "In an instant, I realized—my ruining you, my marrying you, my obsession with you has nothing to do with Argyll or revenge. All of it was because I wanted *you*."

Edith hugged herself to hold tight the euphoric joy brought by each declaration.

His features softened in a way that, until now, she'd not believed they could.

"It took me some time to figure it all out, Edith, but I now know. My desire for you is unwavering."

Edward held Edith gently at her shoulders. "I cannot even *think* about having another woman in my bed or in my life, because, *you* are the sun, and everyone else just lives in your shadow."

A sob caught in her throat and Edith caught it in her fist.

"Please, love," he implored, dusting the tears from her cheeks.

That this proud, dauntless man who declared himself too strong to beg, now did so, because of Edith made her cry even harder.

He groaned. "Your tears cut me up inside, love."

And with that humbling admission from her always proud husband, Edith knew—Edward did not love her *now*, but, someday, he *might*. Given his upbringing she just needed to be patient.

Edward drew her into his arms, and she all too happily went.

Welcoming the weight of his arms he wrapped about her, Edith cuddled against his chest, and breathed deep of the sandalwood cologne he must have dabbed on sometime this morning.

Now, she knew.

Sandalwood. A soft smile played with the corners of her lips. The fragrance he favored was a blend of woody and sweet.

She'd learned just one of many details to come about the man she'd married.

Light in ways she'd never been since her family fell apart, Edith drifted in a place between dream-state and reality.

"You aren't to leave the club, Edith."

With her mind still dazed, it took a moment to register what Edward said.

Edith turned a watery smile up at him.

"After the day's events," she said softly, "you have my assurance the last thing I intend to do is go on any jaunts about London."

His expression remained grave. "Not *just* today, love."

An unpleasant thought formed. "How long?"

Edward remained beneficently calm.

That made one of them.

"Edith, you have all the information at your fingertips which shows Stillson not only murdered before but that he's begun visiting the same druggist he did at the time of your sister's death.

"Now, after this morning, we also know," he continued in more of his newfound equable manner. "You were lured to St. Giles, by Argyll, grabbed by a stranger who held you and *waited* until a carriage came barreling at you, and then shoved you at the conveyance. Given we cannot say at this time whether it was Argyll or Stillson who attempted to end your life this day, the only way to ensure your safety is by you staying here."

His continued use of 'we' in reference to her and Edward, should warm her. It should, and she suspected it would have, but for those last three words: *you staying here.*

She pushed herself away from his arms. "And what if you don't ever have the answers to that question, Edward?"

"Edith," he gave her a faintly amused look, "do you *truly* believe I will not have answers to that question, and end either one, or *both,* of those men?"

She glanced down at all he'd managed to gather in a short time about Evie's murder.

No. When driven, her husband, if he wished it, could reverse the course of the earth's spinning.

"I've sent a team of guards to your family's residence, as well, as to your older sister, Lady Elyse, her husband, Lord Burgess, and their new babe. I've already hired an investigator who is in the process of verifying your brother's whereabouts and finding him and his location so he could be warned of the threat."

Edith started. He'd provided protection to Elyse's young family? Which meant…

A smile teased her husband's mouth. "You didn't believe I was aware of your sister's name and family? Or, for that matter, your entire family?"

A blush stole up her already warm neck. He was trying to make it impossible for her to stay angry.

"I…I…" She shook her head. "No," she managed to say, because they'd established there would be honesty between them. "I wasn't aware."

Edward trailed a palm over her hot cheek, and she closed her eyes and leaned into the feel of his touch and the soothing words he spoke.

"I know everything about you, Edith," he said in hushed tones. "Even more than you know."

There'd been a time when that admission would have emerged as a threat and not the gentle explanation it was.

"Edward," she framed his face with her palms, "I know you want to see me safe, but locking me indoors, will not guarantee that."

He scoffed. "Of course, it will."

She'd have laughed if the urge to scream hadn't been that much greater.

"I might choke on my meal."

"Stop it," he cut her off before she completed the last syllable of that word.

Needing him to see, Edith didn't relent. "I might fall down the stairs and break my neck."

His face darkened. "You're too graceful and too strong to let a stair get you."

Her lips twitched. "There can be an enemy within as—"

Flames blazed from his eyes.

She'd gone too far.

"I'm not s-saying you were the enemy, Edward."

Restored to full menace, he leaned so close their noses nearly brushed. "Oh, but I was, Edith. You'd do well to remember that."

She knew he said that because he'd unsettled himself with how much of his feelings he'd let her see.

Their breath melded and twined, and she yearned for his kiss—which did not come.

"You are mine, Edith, and you'll do as I say."

He'd managed to knock her from the cloud she'd floated upon since they'd entered his office.

"I am your wife, not your *prisoner*." Squaring her chin, Edith stood, marched for the door, and yanked it open.

Edward followed her out into the hall.

"Where the hell are you going?" he demanded.

Edith didn't break stride, just carried on her march to her rooms. "What, need I account for my every action, too, my master?" she said, without looking back.

The guards, six more than usual, and who flanked the length of the hallway, each looked down at the floor at the same time.

Edward didn't speak another word until he'd followed her inside her—*his* bedchambers. She gritted her teeth. It was all his.

Even I belong to him.

Edward pushed the door shut behind him. "As much as I love hearing you refer to me so, sweet, if you do so in that tone and in front of anyone again, you'll regret it." His whisper contained a warning.

"What will you do, husband?" she asked, tired all over again. "Beat me?" He'd never.

Nor did he attempt to lie.

"No, love." He narrowed his eyes. "I'd take you against the wall and make love to you until you were crying out, begging for me, so the witnesses can see for themselves who is really in charge."

The image he painted was so deviant, so wicked, that instead of repulsion, wetness flooded her center. She squeezed her sore legs together and prayed he did not see that rustle of her skirts.

That pressure did little to ease her suffering.

He narrowed his eyes. "Have I made myself clear, Edith?"

She nodded shakily. "Yes, Your Grace."

"Say my name," he ordered.

Damn this dominating side of him, which she alternately loathed and loved.

"Yes, *Edward.*"

After she gave him what he wanted, Edward turned to leave.

Pride wouldn't let that be the last words she spoke to him. "Tell me, husband," she called out. "Will you lock me in?"

He spun so quickly, and with such fury blazing from him, Edith stumbled back a step. "Is this a goddamned joke to you, Edith?" he bellowed, his temper broke when she'd believed it never could.

She kept her composure. "Of course, it isn't. I do not, however, like the idea of being a prisoner in my own home. How long?"

He growled. "Until I say."

She loved him. She trusted him to care for her in every way. But she would not let him believe he could restrict her movements and order her about.

Edith shook her head. "That isn't good enough, Edward."

CHAPTER 24

That isn't good enough, Edward…

After everything that had—and almost had—happened to Edith this day, she'd still fight him. God, he hated how her courage in the face of his fury, enflamed him.

"What did you say to me?" he whispered.

Her chest rose and fell fast like she'd run a race. "I said it isn't good enough, Edward."

She took several long, and slow breaths. "You have my assurance, I will not behave recklessly, that I will take two—nay, three, guards with me whenever I go out, but I cannot be made to remain here indefinitely."

"Is that a fate worse than death to you?" he asked coolly.

"Of course, not," she murmured, in what he'd come to think of as her governess tones.

His self-control broke. "Goddamn it, Edith, you were almost killed today," he thundered.

"I meant it earlier when I asked you, Edward," she said, and had there been an accusation rather than confusion in the look she gave him, it would have been easier to take. "Would it truly matter if I die?"

Of course, it would. *Then, tell her, you fool. Telling her will make me a bloody fool.*

Craven dragged a hand through his hair, and as he did, he realized his hands shook. Unnerved and off-balance, he sought to get himself to rights.

Edith mistook his silent tumult as his indifference towards her.

"In fact, as I see it, my death would be quite convenient. Given no amount of money will ever be enough, you'll have my dowry. You'll have triumphed over the Duke of Argyll by having me, and then be immediately freed from having a woman you never wanted as your wife."

He drew back. Is that really what she thought?

What else would she be thinking?

Except, that is precisely how he'd viewed the lady who was now his wife. At first. Somewhere along the way, something had changed, and she'd come to be a woman whom he not only wanted to possess, and…God help him, care about.

All Craven knew was when he'd seen that carriage barreling down on her, and he'd been too far away to reach her, time had stood still, and terror the likes of which he'd never known held him in its grip, and hadn't let go of him since.

Edith smiled sadly. "I thought so, Edward."

He stared vacantly at her proudly retreating form as she wandered over to the porcelain bathtub, still emitting steam.

The words exploded from him. "I was afraid," he said sharply, just as she reached the tub. "I was terrified out of my bloody mind you'd be hurt." *Or worse.*

Edith spun to face him; her eyes formed big circles and a little more of surprise rounded out her beautiful lips.

He'd managed to stun his bride.

Well, that made the two of them.

"There. Are you happy, Edith?" A harsh, acerbic laugh scorched his tongue. "I, the ruthless, unfeeling, Duke of Craven nearly went stark, raving, mad when I saw you—"

Edith stalked over, and twining her arms about his neck, leaned up and kissed him, cutting short the rest of Craven's humiliating admission cut short.

He froze and before she had time to think about the pledge he'd made her, Craven gripped Edith by her nape and plundered her lips; with his tongue, he made sweeping, swirling motions around hers.

Edith swiftly caught the rhythm of the savage dance and circled and tangled her flesh with his.

Hungry for this woman as he never had—and never would—

any other, Craven struggled with the tiny rows of buttons down the back of her gown.

"Too many bloody buttons," he rasped out, between a long kiss that drugged and sent his lust spiraling.

Edith laughed softly against his mouth, a sweet, merry sound of her innocence. Instead of being repulsed by his bride's wholesomeness, Craven found his grip on cold impassivity, slipping further and further out of his reach.

In this moment, he couldn't care. He needed to be inside her. He needed to hear her screaming his name in surrender and then spend himself within her hot, welcoming heat.

With a guttural growl, Craven wrenched the back of Edith's dress apart. The pearl fastenings came loose with a satisfying pop. Even as the fabric rent, tiny pearls hit the floor like a thousand little pings and then rolled about her rooms.

Shoving her tattered bodice low, he drew back enough so he could, this time, without the threat of discovery, look his full upon her.

Worshipfully, Craven filled his palms with her beautifully formed breasts. He gently kneaded and stroked her. The already pebbled tips grew tighter.

"So perfect," he extolled.

Craven caught her nipples between his thumb and forefinger and lightly pinched her. Moaning, she undulated her hips against his.

"Shall I kiss them, Edith?" he tempted.

With a whimper, she dropped her head back, in silent surrender.

"I do not think I shall make you say it this time," he mused, maddening the both of them, with the slow game of torture he played. "Do you know why, my love?"

Keening softly, she arched and writhed against him.

"It's because I want to taste them so badly, my wife."

Instead of taking that bud quickly into his mouth and suckling as he wanted, Craven, wanting to drive Edith insane, took his time kneading and massaging the delicate mounds.

"Edward," she moaned his name.

This time, he gave her a taste of what she craved. He teasingly licked that sensitive peak, then drew another moan from Edith.

He flicked his tongue back and forth over the tip until she began to pump her hips.

"E-Edward," she whispered, her voice breaking. "I c-cannot."

No!

His muscles bunched.

"Please, do not make me stop," he panted, wanting this woman bad enough to beg. He'd go mad if she did. "Let me make love to you."

Edith grabbed one of his hands, and he wanted to rail at the gods for denying him what he craved.

But then, Edith brought one of his palms to her right breast, and he reflexively curled his fingers around that satiny-soft flesh.

His breath grew harsher.

Looking at him through a glorious fringe of long, sooty eyelashes, she held Craven's gaze.

"I cannot bear it if you will not kiss me here, too," she said huskily, but shyly. Guiding his finger with her own, Edith moved the digit over that tip in the way she sought.

"I am all too happy to oblige, dear wife." With that, he closed his mouth around the swollen bud. The rasp of his own harsh inhalations mingled with Edith's, encouraged him on. Craven suckled deep and hard.

Edith cried out.

He wrapped an arm about her waist to keep her upright and shifted his attentions to the tip of her previously neglected breast.

Craven sucked and nipped until Edith was reduced to incoherent murmurings.

His body throbbed with a need to claim her.

It was too much.

Despite Edith's agonized protestations, he wrenched away.

Devouring her mouth, Craven lifted Edith in his arms. She immediately wrapped her legs around his waist, so that her center lay flat against his belly.

Craven cupped the round globes of her buttocks and sculpted that plump flesh with his hands. Edith moaned and rocked her wet core against him.

"Good girl," he gave that harsh praise for her knowing precisely what he'd wanted her to do. Then to further reward her, Edward reached under her and slipped a finger inside her sodden channel.

Edith released a long, agonized moan and rocked against him in a more frenzied way.

The moment he set her down on her knees on the bed, he pulled her gown up and off and tossed it aside. Before that satin article had even hit the floor, he ripped apart her chemise, so it fell in a puddle under her, and she lay naked before him.

All the times before this one, he'd only partially seen Edith's bared body, and never naked. Now, tugging his cravat free, he drank in the sight of her.

She lay like Botticelli's rendering of The Birth of Venus come to life. Her chocolate waves fanned around her waist and shoulders. From the curtain made of those glorious silken locks, her pert breasts peeked through.

Craven shrugged out of his jacket and tossed it to the floor.

Her wholesome, wide-eyed gaze followed his every movement.

"God, you're beautiful," he breathed, as he hopped up and down on one foot, tugging off one boot and then the next.

Modest, where every other woman he'd been with before her had been conceited and preening, a delicate pink blush rushed from the tips of her hair to her delectable toes.

Craven straightened, and, holding her eyes with his, he reached for the waistband of his trousers. Spirited as she'd been from the night they'd met, Edith didn't look away. Instead, she leveraged herself up onto her elbows and stared back with a boldness that blended with her timidity.

Craven shoved his pants down and kicked them aside so that he stood naked before her.

Edith's gaze went to his rampant erection. The blush covering her body turned a shade of crimson bright enough to burn the lady up.

"Don't turn shy on me now, love," he said, in a husky dare as he came down over her.

Parting her legs with his knee, Craven lay himself between the only place he needed to be. With his gaze fixed on her flushed face, he eased himself slowly inside her, fighting for restraint.

"You are so goddamned tight," he gritted out, sweat falling from his forehead.

Her lashes fluttered open. "I'm sorry," she whispered, her husky tones filled not with pain, but desire.

A painful laugh escaped him. "You should only be sorry about how bloody good it feels, Edith." His breathing came in harsh, angry spurts he'd given up on attempting to control long before this moment.

At his words, another one of those innocent smiles brought her lips, swollen, wet, and red from his kiss, up at the corners.

And God help him, it was too much.

"Forgive me," he rasped and filled her with a driving thrust.

"Edward!" Edith gasped but did not buckle or break. Nay, instead, she arched with abandoned longing.

"God, you are magnificent." Edward kissed her hard.

They began to move as one.

"Tell me how much you love this," he demanded.

In answer, she moaned and lifted her hips, taking him deeper. He scoured his eyes over her flushed and gleaming face. Her body glistened with the magnificent shine of their passionate efforts.

Craven took her by the hips and punishingly pinned her in place. Clenching his teeth, he began to move, even as she could not. He thrust into her over and over again, until his beautifully defiant bride thrashed her head back and forth.

"I love it so much, Edward," she screamed.

Rewarding Edith for her submission, Craven released his hold.

Edith moved like a crazed tigress freed of its cage. Never missing a beat, she rocked beneath him, tipping her hips up to meet each of Craven's downward thrusts.

Their rhythm grew frenzied; fast and frantic, they strained against one another.

With each, rhythmic push, he delved deeper and deeper inside her, and the more and more control he lost. All the while, he studied her features soft and intent all at the same time.

Edith writhed against him. "Please, Edward," she begged, for the surcease Craven deliberately withheld.

He answered.

Low, throaty, incoherent sounds spilled from Edith's throat. His balls tightened, and Craven gritted his teeth, fighting the urge to spill himself inside her.

When she released a shuddery gasp and sank into the mattress, Craven still fought his climax, wanting to prolong this moment.

He tightened his hold upon her hips once more, leaving his marks upon her.

"So. Good," he said between gritted teeth, pounding into her.

He placed his mouth over that fading bruise at her nape and suckled of her tear-drop birthmark leaving his mark in place of the existing one there. "Mine," he gutturalized.

Then, he felt it. Edith stroked her palms tenderly along his back, and leaning up, she whispered against his ear. "Yours."

Yours.

Her soft, heartfelt avowal broke his self-control.

With a guttural shout, Craven lost himself in a white-hot eruption. Anchoring her in place, he emptied himself inside Edith, coming in long, undulating waves, as he'd hungered for since their first meeting.

When she'd rung every bit of cum from him, Edward gasped. Replete in ways he'd never been after sex, he collapsed, caught himself on his elbows, rolled onto his side, and brought her with him.

Their breaths came in the same, ragged, sporadic spurts.

As if she sought to get even closer to Edward, Edith burrowed against him, so her buttocks rested against his soft shaft.

He instantly began to harden.

Edward took her right earlobe between his teeth and sucked that delicate, satin-soft flesh. "Be warned, wife," he whispered. "I'm exercising restraint right now because it was your first time, and I took you harder than I should have. But I'm going to see you are well-loved and regularly."

A sleepy smile played on her lips. "Well-loved," she murmured, almost dreamily. "You said love has nothing to—"

Edward kissed her.

Yes, he'd never referred to what he'd just done with this woman as anything other than 'fucking', but Edith was different; everything about her was.

Knock-Knock-Knock

He ripped his mouth from hers and cursed. "Get the hell out!" he thundered.

A small laugh shook Edith's body.

"Your Grace, the doctor is here."

"Her Grace is fine," he shouted. "Better than fine."

His guard on the other side of the panel relented.

Frowning, Edward glanced at Edith. A healthy color filled her cheeks. "Are you fine?"

"Nothing more than tired from—"

Edward gently cupped her mound, and her assurance faded to a pleased little sigh. Edith moved against his hand. He took her mouth in another hard kiss.

Knock-Knock-Knock

For bloody sake. Edward wrenched away.

"It is just, *should* I ask the surgeon to *wait*—"

Leaning over the side of the bed, Edward grabbed his boot and hurled it across the room. It hit the door with a solid *thwack.*

This time, the guard took the correct cue and quit hounding them.

Flipping over onto her other side, so they faced one another, Edith ran her long fingers through the light matting of hair on his chest. "You needn't be so surly, Your Grace. He was just doing your bidding."

"No one's bidding matters more than that of my glorious queen," he murmured, cupping one of her breasts.

Edith laughed.

Edward nibbled at her neck. "My queen is amused?" he asked between bites.

"My how my status has improved," she said teasingly. "I've gone from marm to queen."

He glared. What a bloody fool he'd been. "You are no marm," he gritted out.

"But you said—"

"I know what I said. I was wrong," he mumbled.

Edward made to bury his face in her neck, but Edith evaded his amorous advances.

He growled.

"What was that?" she asked, on a breathless laugh.

"A grunt."

"It sounded more like a growl than a grunt, but what I referred to were the words before the growl."

"Grunt," he muttered.

Edith pinched the flat disc of his nipple, and he winced.

His minx of a wife waggled her eyebrows. "Ah, *someone* doesn't like it rough."

Roaring with laughter, Edward rolled Edith under him. He made to tickle her at her sides, but the serious look in her eyes erased his smile. She stared at Edward like he was a complicated puzzle she could not solve.

He frowned. "What is it?"

"I've never heard you laugh like that," she whispered.

Until now, he'd never had reason to. Until her.

And it scared the everlasting hell out of him.

Sweating for altogether different reasons—ones far less enjoyable than bedding his glorious wife—Edward scrambled out of bed. Padding naked across the room, he fetched his garments, one by one.

"Edward?" Concern laced the question she'd turned his name into. "Where are you going?"

Hopping on one leg, he stuffed his other one into his trousers. "I'm going to ensure you're not a prisoner here, Edith."

After he'd pulled his pants and drew his shirt on, he noted Edith's silence.

He looked at the bed.

With a sheet drawn protectively about her lithe body, at the center of the mattress, a stricken Edith sat back on her heels. "No."

Her denial so whispery soft, barely reached him.

Of course, she understood what he spoke of.

"I'm handling it, Edith."

Clutching that sheet around her, she scampered over. "I don't *want* you to handle it."

Edward took his wife tenderly by the shoulders and stooped so he could meet her eyes with his.

"That's all you've wanted," he gently reminded, without recrimination.

Edith's enormous black pupils gave her an eerie look. "Not anymore," she panted. "You, Edward. I want *you* more. I love you," she cried, her respirations uneven.

He shrank from that confession. "Edith," he said hollowly. "I have to go."

As he let himself from their rooms, Edith's weak cries followed him into the hall. And running from his new bride, Edward discovered he'd been wrong—he *was* the same weak, coward he'd always been.

CHAPTER 25

EDITH HURT ALL OVER AND inside in different ways.

The brief surcease from her misery had come only when Edward soothed her with his words and then, made love to her.

Naked, Edith hugged her arms around her middle and stared at the door Edward had drawn quietly closed behind him and hurt a thousandfold more than any of her suffering this day.

She didn't know how long she stood there staring, trembling from a cold that spread fast within her. Tears wound silently down her cheeks, offering the lone hint of warmth to her being, which only reminded her of when Edward sweetly brushed them away.

This agony cleaving away at Edith's heart had only a little to do with Edward running from her profession of love, and everything to do with terror of his impending meeting.

Even as she believed Edward to be mightier and more formidable than any man, and did not doubt he'd emerge triumphant against anyone, it was altogether different knowing even now he went to square off in a battle where only one man would emerge the winner.

And I involved him in this.

Time and time again, Edith had been reminded by the words of her late sister, her brother, and her parents that she was buried in the past. She'd ignored them. She'd been single-minded in her intent. The idea of avenging Evie sustained her.

Only, to discover too late, revenge? It was hollow. It brought Edith no great sense of triumph or victory. Yes, Mr. Stillson would pay, but his comeuppance was never going to be enough. When his soul returned to the Devil, everything here on this earth would remain the same: Evie would still be dead, and Edith would still miss her every single day.

What Edith hadn't anticipated was there'd come a time after Evie when Edith would experience life in all its sloppy beauty. That Edith would know a time when she spent most of her days and nights wondering how he'd become the man he had and wanting to help pull apart his armor so she could see the man underneath.

And now she did. He was a man who'd hardened himself to keep himself safe from additional pain. He spoke about caring about nothing and no one, but then secretly looked after Edith's entire family.

Since Edward had been born, his family, his friends, the world on the whole hadn't truly cared about him. They'd all been more interested in what Edward brought them, or what he could do for them.

And what did I go and do?

Edith's eyes slid shut.

With her mad obsession, she'd sent Edward, a man she loved more than anyone on this earth, off to war on her family's behalf.

Woodenly and on uneven legs, Evie stumbled toward the bed.

She'd believed there could be no loss greater than that of her sister. Edith now knew different. Were any harm to befall Edward this day, or any, Edith wouldn't recover. She wouldn't want to. There was no world unless he was in it.

Edith's teeth chattered and her legs went weak. With arms that ached, she pulled herself onto the bed still warm from the place she and Edward had lain together. On hands and knees, she crawled, struggling to get herself toward the imprint his body had left.

A movement so easy the smallest babes mastered proved a herculean task for Edith. Each slight movement of her muscles filled her with excruciating agony. Her thoughts also began to move with an infinite slowness.

It was too much.

With a ragged gasp, Edith pitched forward and with her reflexes dulled, she collapsed face first upon the feather tick mattress. A spasm wracked her sore body, and wanting to lessen the agony sluicing through her, Edith attempted to pull her knees into her chest—but failed.

Something is wrong.

Whimpering, Edith used the little strength she had remaining to roll onto her side, and she faced the door.

Edward, come back, please. Edward. I love you.

I need you.

Except, with her throat, raw and tight she couldn't speak all the slow-moving thoughts in her head aloud.

I am dying.

Just like Evie.

I want to live.

Edward.

I want Edward.

It was Edith's last thought before she surrendered to a welcome blackness.

CHAPTER 26

EIGHT HOURS AND FIFTY-SIX MINUTES later, it was done.

As Craven and the team of guards he'd brought with him, dismounted, the blood-red setting sun painted the London sky, and Lucifer's Lair in a courtyard, in a baleful crimson hue befitting a day of savagery.

Except, the fight hadn't ended with the excruciating end his men brought to Stillson, nor the brutal beating they'd doled out to the man's druggist, and all the other thugs whose names Stillson spilled under extreme duress.

Craven tossed his reins over to a waiting guard.

With newly promoted guards, Mollison and Turnbull keeping close at his side, Edward strode to his club.

Bloodlust raged in his veins, more powerful than during any fight he'd fought this day.

Dead. He'd kill him dead.

Craven beat his guards to the inside. Catching both door knobs, he threw the panels wide. The pair of square-built men had guns pointed and immediately lowered them.

"The duchess?" he barked as strode down the hall.

"Ensconced in her rooms," Bullock said, holstering his weapon. "Reports have filtered down every thirty minutes. Aside from…" The two guards exchanged a look.

Craven grabbed Bullock by the front of his shirt and drove him against the wall. "Aside from what?" he seethed.

The man's thick neck moved wildly. "Aside from…" Bullock dropped his voice to a whisper. "some crying when you left the lady this morning, Your Grace, she's been sleeping quiet."

His chest hitching, Craven abruptly released the other man.

The blinding rage which had consumed him after he'd learned of the ultimate betrayal, was suddenly dwarfed by a debilitating image of Edith alone in their rooms. Her musical laughter transformed into tears of grief.

Get your bloody head about you.

There'd be all of forever for Craven to spend making her smile and making love to her. For now, there was one more threat to eliminate.

"Gruffton?" he seethed before they could speak.

Having no doubt been notified of Craven's return, Aveyard, his second in command, as ruthless as he was eager, marched forward.

"Hawley and Cannon are on him," the young, bearded guard called. "They've had him in their sights and can confirm he's not left his place on the casino floors, even once."

I should have bloody suspected as much. Once a betrayer, always a betrayer.

Craven bared his teeth. "Bring him to me."

His loyal crew had already anticipated their employer's request.

Like he was Craven's loyal number one, and not the ultimate betrayer Gruffton came rushing forward. "Haven't left the floors, Your Grace…"

Gruffton's words trailed off. The old guard took in the sight of Craven with his feet planted wide apart and hands folded at his chest. Then, he moved his attention to each forbidding man with weapons pointed.

Gruffton nodded real slow. "All right, oi see what's happening here," he said, the same staid way he might deliver a daily report of the casino floors.

"How long have you been working with Stillson?"

"The minute the lady entered the club. Knew she was going to be trouble just like the other one." Gruffton jabbed a finger at him. "Don't act like ye didn't know it, too."

A pounding filled Craven's ears. He'd sworn to protect Edith; he'd proclaimed her to be safer in his club than anywhere else. All along, whenever she'd been in Craven's club and life, she'd been in danger.

Gruffton smirked; a knowing, mocking, twist of his fat, fleshy lips. "Figured Stillson and I could work together and eliminate the threat."

"The threat?" he whispered. "My *wife*!"

"Bah." Gruffton waved a hand. "She wasn't yer wife at the time," he said, like that detail explained away his treachery. "Stillson wanted to poison the lady, but you and I both know poisoning is a sloppy way to off someone, too much goes wrong when they linger."

His extremities trembling, Craven delivered a swift uppercut that sent his former number-one's head flying back.

"I wasn't going to poison her," Gruffton said defensively, as he rubbed his jaw. "I knew you enjoyed fucking her and I was going to make it *real quick* because of i—"

Craven rammed the top of his skull into the center of Gruffton's face. A dazed Gruffton stumbled backward and fell onto his arse.

His former mentor on dirty fighting gave his head a clearing shake. "Regret teaching you that one, oi do."

"Real quick?" Craven barked over Gruffton.

Getting to his feet on unsteady legs, the guard, in belated recognition of the madness he'd just spoken, lifted both hands. "Oi know. Oi know. Oi should've slit her throat. Made it quick *and* painl—"

With the roar of a rabid beast, Craven reared back and brought a right cross flying. He landed a direct blow with Gruffton's hard jaw. No sooner Craven heard and felt a satisfying crack, he delivered a swift jab that sent the bastard sailing five feet away.

Craven was already on him.

Snarling, he leaned down and caught Gruffton by the front of his wool jacket. Again and again, Craven buried his right fist into the grotesque face of the last man he'd allowed himself to trust. His breath came in harsh, ragged spurts as he beat the guard to a pulp. Drops of blood sprayed his face and still he continued the merciless beating.

Only when Craven's lungs threatened to explode from the force of his exertions, did he let up.

He flexed his fingers and let the mangled bastard go. Between his shattered bulbous nose, eyes swollen shut, and face saturated in blood, the beating Craven doled out left the guard unrecognizable.

From where he lay in a supine position, an odd gurgling formed in Gruffton's throat.

Collecting the towel handed him by Aveyard, Craven wiped the remnants of his attack from his face. He couldn't return to Edith with bruised and bloodied hands, wearing his enemy's blood like a sanguine mask.

Craven scraped a hate-filled gaze over the last and only person he'd brought from Forbidden Pleasures. "Lock him up below until I decide his fate, Aveyard."

Gruffton's fate had been decided long before this moment. All that remained was determining which ruthless way he'd go.

In a changing of the guard, with Craven's last connection to Forbidden Pleasures severed, Hawley and Cannon caught the beaten man under his arms and dragged him to his feet.

Edith.

With two wars won, Craven now had to see the only person he'd wanted and needed to see this day and every day.

Gruffton, in his last display of a fight, struggled against his younger captors. "Fuck you, Craven," he bellowed.

The old guard dead to him, Craven stepped away from his past and made for his future.

"Ye acting all high and mighty," Gruffton shouted after him. "Coming for me like ye didn't do the same thing with DuMond's woman."

All Craven's muscles coiled under that charge.

He turned. "What you and I did are not at all the same!" In a bid to save his former club, Craven paid a bribe to keep rumors from getting out that Lady Rutherford, DuMond's then-new bride, who lived *inside* Forbidden Pleasures, leaked information about their clients' peccadillos.

"Bah, in the end, you and I both did something that was bound to get a lady hurt. Ye know I'm right," Gruffton taunted.

Craven flashed a feral smile. "There's one, significant difference—you put my wife in danger." And now the bastard would pay the ultimate price.

As he reached for the door leading to the private suites,

Gruffton howled with laughter so maniacal it froze Craven in his tracks.

"I said, I *wasn't* going to poison her, Craven."

A queer tingling filled his chest.

Edith.

No. No. With a hoarse shout, Craven barreled through the door.

Gruffton's victorious laughter trailed after him, followed by a wail of misery as Craven's loyal guards finished the beating he hadn't.

All of them forgotten, everything forgotten, Craven took the steps two and three at a time. His breath came in sharp spurts.

"Edith!" he thundered. "Doctor," he rasped, as he passed one of his men.

The guard set off running in the opposite direction.

When his feet hit the main landing, Craven caught the corner of the wall, propelling himself forward, and took off sprinting.

"*Edith. Edith. Ediiiith,*" he roared.

When he reached their room, Craven threw the door open with a force that sent it crashing into the wall. Before it could fly back and hit him, he kicked the panel and stormed inside.

He located his wife in an instant. "Oh, my God," he whispered.

Naked and lying face down on the mattress, it could have been hours earlier, just moments after they'd made love. But it wasn't.

And Craven, man of ice and absent a heart, feeler of nothing, and uncaring of anyone but himself found fate, let out a piercing, tortured cry.

"Edith," he rasped.

Finding his feet, he flew across the bedchambers. Scrambling to get to her, Craven crawled quickly across the bed to get to his still wife. *"No. No. No. No."* All the while that desperate litany fell over and over from his lips.

His hands shaking, he gently took Edith in his arms and guided her inert form over, so she lay upon her back.

"Help me," he cried. "Help me. Someone bloody *help* me!"

Aveyard's answering voice sounded over Craven's shoulder. "I had five doctors summoned. The first is arriving now."

With his entire body shaking, Craven struggled to get his

fingers around the coverlet. When he did, he drew the article up to shield Edith from those waiting outside.

He distantly registered the guard pulling the door shut. The moment the panel closed, a small whimper, like that of a wounded animal, filled Craven's ears and whispered around his tortured mind.

Me. It is me. I am that wounded animal.

And he didn't care. Nothing mattered but her. There was no life without her. There was no purpose without her. There was nothing, but the monotony of existing, as he'd done for the whole of his lonely life until Edith stepped into it.

With cheeks a shade of white to match the white satin sheets, her chest unmoving, Edith lay as still as death.

Fighting the wave of madness threatening to suck him under, Craven lay his chest upon her breast and strained to hear anything.

Bile climbed his throat, and he frantically swallowed it back.

No. No. No. She cannot die. I cannot lose her. I only just found her.

At last, he knew—it had never been about wanting her or claiming her. Craven *needed* her more than he did his beating heart or air to breathe.

And then, he heard it—the slow, weak, thump of hers.

Craven's eyes slid shut. That beautiful, tender-hearted organ still beat. Even as it sustained Edith, it fed him life, too.

He opened his eyes and glared at his unnaturally still wife.

"You will not leave me, Edith De Vesy; this day, or any other," he ordered, harshly. "I bloody forbid it."

"Doctor is here," Aveyard shouted from outside the room. Not waiting for Craven's call, the exemplary guard, who'd proven his efficaciousness this day, let the surgeon in.

Renewed by a sense of determination and resolve, Craven stood and narrowed his eyes on the old, greying doctor who rushed over.

"Save her," Craven seethed. "And I can promise you, that is not a request, it is a bloody command."

As the hours came and went, so too, did doctor after doctor. Keeping vigil at his wife's bedside in the wee morning hours, Craven, discovered an unwelcome truth—a man couldn't just order death away.

Death decided who it came for, when it arrived, and not a goddamned thing Craven did, could hold that unconquerable foe at bay.

With his wife now fighting for her life, his money, title, power, or connections were all as useless as a knife without a blade. Though, in actuality, it wasn't so much as a fight. It wasn't even a fight, at all. Edith may as well have waved a white flag before even stepping onto the battlefield.

Seated on the same chair he'd dragged to Edith's bedside when the first doctor arrived, and his elbows atop his knees, Craven cupped his hands around his mouth and nose.

"I'll have you know, I'm disappointed in you, Edith," he said tersely. "I believed you stronger than this."

He peered at her long, beguiling eyelashes for even the slightest hint of a flutter, but found none.

Panic and anger built in his chest.

Standing, Craven folded his arms at his chest. "You who *dared* to enter my club, lied to me all to get what you wanted and needed, and went to bloody St. Giles alone, would just bow down to death?" he sneered.

Only, the blistering rage that'd served him these recent years, proved utterly useless.

Through his chastisement, Edith remained eerily still. With her arms arranged outside the coverlet, and her hands clasped upon her stomach, she had the look of a person who'd passed and whose body now lay for family to view.

Tendrils of ice wrapped around his heart. In the throes of misery, Craven's angry façade slipped. The spirit drained out of him, and he sank down hard onto his knees.

Gently, he took her hands in his; clammy and cool like the poison was nearly finished snuffing all the life from her.

"Edith," he pleaded. "Wife, you are a fighter, and you were so long before you became a deVesy. I'm going to need you to fight because I cannot," His voice broke. "I cannot fight for you." He buried a kiss on the tops of her joined hands. "It is bloody killing me, love, it is tearing me up inside that you're facing a battle I *cannot* fight for you."

The irony wasn't lost on him. He, who'd prided himself on his might, found himself powerless to fix the only thing that mattered.

Knock-Knock-Knock

The earlier relief and eagerness to welcome a new doctor to evaluate Edith had long since dimmed.

As usual, the dutiful Aveyard let himself inside. "The doctor is here."

Another doctor. What the other man meant was that another bloody sawbones had come to tell Craven the same bloody thing all the six others to come before.

Behind the closing of the door, came a soft, delicate tread that stopped beside Craven.

"If you bleed her, I'll kill you," he said, by way of steely greeting.

"For killing a person with such a process, I would deserve it, too."

Surprise brought his head snapping up.

Caught somewhere between a sprite and child, the petite girl with eerily pale blonde hair fastened at her nape, and serene features, couldn't be more than fifteen or sixteen.

This is who they'd send him?

A growl rumbled in his chest. "Is this a bloody joke?"

"I would never jest about something as serious as bloodletting, Your Grace."

He narrowed his eyes. "*You're* a doctor."

The girl inclined her narrow chin. "My name is Miss Bledoe. I am an herbalist."

"An herbalist," he repeated dumbly.

Then, without a curtsy, without awaiting or asking permission, the latest *sawbones* brought him by Aveyard, moved closer to Edith.

Positioning himself between the two women, Craven hissed. "Do not."

Miss Bledoe remained proudly stoic through Craven's rejection.

"Tell me, Your Grace," she murmured, without recrimination. "You've had how many male doctors evaluate Her Grace today? How many treatments, aside from bloodletting and 'just wait and pray' have you been left with?"

Frantic, Craven looked from the somber herbalist to his deadly-still wife and dragged a hand through his hair.

He gave a reluctant nod and stepped aside.

Miss Bledoe immediately took Edith's left wrist and pressed her middle and index fingers. Through the herbalist's examination, Craven besieged by a profound hopelessness, stood sentry over Edith.

After Miss Bledoe concluded, she faced Craven. The somber set to her features threatened to push him to the point of madness.

"The rate of her heart and slow cadence of her breathing tell me Her Grace is very ill. Based on that and the tightness in her intestines and rapid decline, it's clear she's been given arsenic." Her mouth moved steadily and yet, through the loud humming in his ears, her words came as if she and Craven were corridors apart. "You do not need me to tell you, the usual outcome of that particular poison, Your Grace."

His mind balked and bucked away from the outcome Craven knew she'd predict.

Rage and fear contorted his features. "If you say she will not survive, I will—"

"I am not saying she will succumb to the arsenic, Your Grace."

The first spark of hope kindled in his heart.

"However, I cannot promise you Her Grace will live," she said with a blunt honesty.

"She lives," he hissed.

"But you have my assurance," she continued in that calming way, "I have skills and remedies I can employ and will do everything within my power to help Her Grace recover. However, you must allow me to do my work."

She looked past Craven's shoulder. "I'll require a number of provisions." At some point, Aveyard reentered and stood back by the door like he'd anticipated his services.

While she fired off a catalogue of the items she'd need, and the guard took inventory, Craven remained rooted to the floor and stared sightlessly at his wife.

She cannot die. She cannot die.

The memory of Edith's sorrowful voice punished him for his transgressions against this woman.

"…If I had died today, I couldn't say either way if you were glad I'd gotten my comeuppance or whether a small part of you might somehow miss me…"

And what assurances of his affection had he given his new wife? Craven squeezed his eyes shut.

…I don't dislike you, Edith…

A plaintive moan escaped him. That piteous drawn-out sorrowful sound continued when Craven's stopped.

Edith.

She gave her head a fitful shake.

All around him, Craven's bedchambers came alive in a flurry of movement with servants streaming in and out.

A sweat broke out all over his body.

She cannot die. She cannot die.

As the last servant took their leave of Edith's rooms, Miss Bledoe rolled her sleeves up, and looked to him. "Generally, husbands do not remain in the room while—"

He leveled her with a silencing glare. "I stay."

The herbalist contemplated him. Craven knew the moment she accepted he wasn't just any husband, and even were Satan and God to team efforts, they still could not pull him from Edith's side.

Miss Bledoe inclined her head. "Very well. Let's begin."

CHAPTER 27

FOR MORE THAN A DAY, Craven didn't leave Edith's side. His club, his fortunes, the very world itself could have burned to the ground, and he would neither notice nor care.

In the time since Miss Bledoe arrived and took charge, Edith suffered through new agonizing symptom after symptom. When Miss Bledoe spilled lemon juice down her throat, Craven cradled Edith in his arms like she was no more than a babe. And when she'd retched and heaved up the contents of her stomach afterward because she'd been unable to keep all that tonic down, he'd held her damp curls back and guided her head over a chamber pot. Then, he'd resumed hydrating her with the lemon juice.

Craven had been the one to clean his wife, change her garments, and plait her hair.

When Miss Bledoe stepped away, Craven remained at Edith's side and fed her the smallest droplets of rosehip. Now, perched on the edge of the same chair, he'd kept vigil in, an eerie still hung over the darkened room.

Craven pressed his hands together and stared at her through tired, bloodshot eyes. "I'm afraid if I look away from you, Edith," he said, raggedly. "You will leave me."

She the slight, but spirited, resolute woman who'd knocked him upside his heels, remained unmoving.

He scraped a hand over his unshaven cheeks. "And…" His voice broke. "I won't survive if you do."

His humbling admission was met only with more of his wife's silence.

Something between a laugh and cry gurgled in his throat.

"Does that make you happy, love, knowing you have become the sole reason for my existence?"

The fact remained—he wouldn't survive unless she did. This kingdom he'd built was nothing if there wasn't Edith.

He knew that now when it was too late.

No.

Craven shook his head hard as a welcome fury filled him.

"By God," he growled. "I will not lose you, Edith de Vesy."

Then, as if she'd heard that vow, in the flickering light cast by the hearth, Edith's lashes fluttered.

He scrambled to the edge of his seat. "I saw that, love."

Catching the underside of his chair, Craven dragged it nearer so his legs kissed the bed. "Edith," he said firmly. "Love, look at me. I need you to wake up."

Please, wake up. Please, stay with me.

He peered at his wife and willed her to open her eyes, but that slight movement of her eyelashes may as well have been a trick of the light.

"…*I'm asking if you ever watched a person die…?*"

Heart hammering, Craven jumped up. He scoured the dark bedchambers for the one who'd uttered those words as clearly as Edith had that distant day.

Realizing only quiet lived in this room with he and Edith, Craven retook his chair and sat with the kind of silence and still only a winter's day brought.

Craven dragged a weary hand through his unkempt hair. The day Edith put that grave question to him, he'd been resentful that she was privy to that which he hadn't. Only to discover the Lord was real and vengeful and took delight in throwing that twisted resentment in his Craven's face.

"…*There's pain…Sorrow so deep it's as great as the affliction that left your loved one confined to a bed…*"

He took in a juddering breath, and a smell he'd never before known turned his belly.

"*The air… It has a specific scent; one a person has never before smelled, but so distinct that there's an inherent knowledge of what that stench is—death…*"

Clamping his hands over his ears, Craven jumped up. A cramp

hit his right calf muscle and made his gait unsteady as he limped to the window. Unfastening the latches, Craven threw the crystal panels wide, and let that fresh, night breeze flood the room and drown out the stench left by the reaper.

Craven curled his fingers into the gilded windowsill and ducking his head outside, he closed his eyes and sucked great big gasps of cleansing air into his lungs.

The forlorn wail of a stray dog brought his eyes flying open.

Craven bolted back to Edith's side. "I'm sorry. I'm so bloody sorry," he rasped, falling to his knees beside her. He lifted her hands and brought them to his lips. Ever so tenderly he kissed one and then the other. "I won't leave you, Edith. Please, don't leave me."

She'd robbed him of all pride, and Craven didn't care. She could have that and anything and everything else she wanted if she'd just return to him.

"…But death comes anyway…And when it happens, it comes not with a scream or a cry or tears, but a whisper of breath and then… nothing…

A peculiar moisture filled his eyes and he frantically blinked to rid himself of the blur those drops caused.

Then the truth hit him—that liquid? They were his tears.

I am crying.

Craven did not bother to fight. Burying his head next to Edith's thigh, he broke down. "I-I want to start over, Edith," he pleaded, between heaving, gasping breaths.

He wanted to do it all over; begin again. In that new beginning, he'd not be the rotted bastard he'd been to her. Instead, he'd show her the reverence, respect, and adoration reserved for queens.

"All those things you want, E-Edith," he got out between tears. "I c-can do them. I didn't lie. I-I promised you there'd b-be no lies, b-but at the time, I didn't realize it was a lie."

He bowed over Edith's hands and let his tears flow in penance upon them.

"I can see the w-world through your eyes, but I can only do it, Edith, if you are here with me," he entreated. "I cannot do it alone."

Until her, he'd not realized just how lonely he'd been. His

former friends had looked after him, but they'd been as guarded as Craven himself.

Craven had never shared his life and opened his heart to anyone. "Until you, Edith. Until you."

Emotionally replete, Craven's tears ceased; he fought the bone-weary exhaustion that pulled him toward sleep. "I love you, Edith."

I love you…

Edith had died.

It was a peculiar thing given every part of her from her hair down to her toes ached, and Evie once promised there wouldn't be pain after death.

But Edith like Evie, passed on to the hereafter. For only in her private, perfect heaven did Edward lay beside her and profess his love.

"I love you so bloody much it hurts," Edward whispered, sounding positively angry, bewildered, and exhausted all at the same time.

And it was how she knew…

I am alive.

If every muscle in her body, including her face and mouth didn't hurt, she would have smiled. With great effort, she struggled to open her eyes. An inky blackness greeted her, and she made herself blink through the pain to try and accustom her vision.

Her husband emitted a bleating snore, the sound of which caused her head to throb all the more.

Desperate to see him, Edith turned her head, and her heart cinched. Worn as she'd never seen him, Edward, on his knees, and with his head buried near Edith's leg, slept.

He is here with me.

He could have had any number of servants or doctors or anyone tend to her. Even with that, he'd set a vigil up beside her.

Her throat tightened with a pain that had nothing to do with her recent illness.

Weakly, Edith drew her fingers through Edward's unkempt blond hair. As she lovingly stroked those strands, her husband snored.

A whisper of light flickered in the window, calling Edith's focus away from his beloved face.

Reflected either in her mind or memory, Evie stood smiling, staring back.

"You were right, Evie." With Edith's tongue heavy and her throat thick, her acknowledgment emerged as little more than a guttural rasp.

She'd needed to live and now she would, with this man who owned her heart.

Edward snored himself awake. Her palm resting upon his head, Edith knew the moment he registered that she'd awakened.

Slowly, Edward lifted his head and froze. "Edith?" he croaked. "You are awake."

"Or dead." She attempted a smile.

Her husband struggled to get himself onto his feet. "I have to fetch the doctor. The herbalist. Miss Bledoe," he rambled on, all those names and words rolling together.

Edith caught his hand before he could go. "I don't want you to go." Not lifting her palm from the mattress, Edith patted the spot beside her.

Edward swung a flustered gaze between Edith and the door.

"I am a selfish bastard," he said hoarsely, as he joined her on the bed. "Because I should gather Miss Bledoe, but I cannot bring myself to leave you."

"Or," she murmured, "it may be that you're a devoted husband."

He grunted. "A devoted, *loving* husband."

Her heart quickened.

They lay, face to face, staring at one another.

"Stillson intended to kill you," he confessed. "You found out too much about him."

Edward collected one of her hands and raised it to his heart. "You needn't worry about him any further, Edith. He is gone."

"Gone," she repeated.

The man who'd murdered Evie and attempted to kill Edith was no longer a shadow looming over the Caldecotts. Her husband had erased that threat from the earth.

"I'm sorry," she said, her voice choked with tears. "I didn't want you to—"

"You are apologizing to *me,* love?"

His features tightened.

"I promised you and our future children will always be safe in my care." Edward's throat worked wildly. "I failed you. Gruffton, perceived you as a threat to the club and sought to kill you. You almost died because of me." His breathing grew harsh. "I shouldn't have left you. I—"

Edith touched her lips in a light kiss to his and stayed the rest.

"I am alive," she murmured.

"I love you so much it bloody hurts, Edith," he said hoarsely. "I suspect I always did, as far back as when you were at one of those damned balls, looking so sad, and in need of a dance. I should have whirled you around the room, that night and held onto you and never let go."

Her brain, cloudy from however long it was she'd been ill, sought to make out what he'd just said.

"You didn't remember me," she whispered. "You said—"

Edward pressed a fingertip against her lips, silencing her, and then used that digit to caress the seam of her mouth. "I said a whole number of caddish things I shouldn't have, Edith. You're left with but one recourse."

"And what recourse would that be, Your Grace?"

He touched his forehead to hers. "Grant me forever so I can love you and attempt to make myself worthy of you. I don't know everything there is to know about you, Edith. But God, how I want to. And I don't want to learn because you tell me," he whispered, raggedly. "I want to discover for myself all your peccadillos and the meaning behind each of your smiles. I want babes who look like you and have your spirit."

A breathy sigh escaped her. "I fear I've died, after all."

Edward growled. "You're not allowed to die. I forbade it, and I will continue to do so."

"Of course, you did." This time, the tired muscles of her mouth managed to tip up in a smile.

Edith inched her mouth closer to his. "In which case," she whispered, "the only thing left to be done is for me to live happily ever after with you, husband."

Emotion blazed from his eyes. "Forever," he vowed.

As Edward claimed her mouth in a tender kiss, Edith closed her eyes.
Forever.

EPILOGUE

Kent, England
Six Months Later
The Duke and Duchess of Craven's Hanover House.

HIDING BEHIND AN ENORMOUS, KNOTTED pine tree, and her heart racing, Edith knew her fate was inevitable—he'd find her.

He always did.

He knew where she'd hide before she herself, even knew the places she'd go.

Powerful hands fell over her shoulders.

Edith gasped.

"Caught," he whispered, drawing her back against his broad chest.

Her sweet captor kissed Edith's neck, then alternately bit her, licked her, and suckled.

A little moan spilled past her lips, and she angled her head to better open herself to his skilled ministrations. "I daresay I've never been happier to lose at hide and seek, husband."

He chuckled; a low rumbling laugh that lightly shook their bodies.

"If this delights you, wife, what are your feelings on this?" Edward brought his arms around and with an agonizing slowness, lowered Edith's bodice so her breasts were bare. He filled his palms with the flesh.

Her breath caught on a noisy intake, earning another of Edward's boastful laughs. As he ran his thumbs in tiny circles over her swollen nipples, Edith's eyes slid shut.

When she'd begun her recovery five months earlier, Edward refused to make love to Edith until she'd fully healed and pledged he would be faithful no matter how many months it took until she was her spirited self again.

Not that she'd ever had reason to doubt. He'd remained at her side throughout her convalescence. He'd even had a bed installed in his office so she could recover while he worked.

That long overdue loving had come a fortnight ago, and Edward remained just as insatiable as he'd been since that morning she'd awakened to discover her amorous husband with his head buried between her legs. He'd rung two climaxes from Edith before seeking any pleasure for himself.

Edward tweaked and tugged the sensitive tips of her breasts. The ragged cadence of his breaths bespoke a like longing. He drifted one hand lower and cupped Edith between her legs.

Biting her lip, Edith tamped down a moan. "Making love was not at the top of my list," she chided.

He grunted. "Making love should be at the top of every one of your lists, wife." He tugged her skirts up.

"That is, not for *todayyyy*," she said, her voice fading to a sigh.

"It should be at the top of *every* list and *every* day, love," Edward scolded. "Or I'm doing something wrong."

He softened that rebuke by sliding a finger through her damp curls and found that pearl which drove Edith mad with desire.

Her breath hitched and of their own volition, her hips undulated.

"Right," she rasped. "You do everything right, always."

"Like this?" Edward slipped a finger inside her channel.

Edith cried out, startling the birds in the branches above, into flight.

"I shall take that as a yes, love."

Edith felt the smug masculine smile in his voice.

"You're insufferable," she said breathlessly and continued to rock her hips into his hand.

"Yes." Edward angled her so he could hold her gaze with his fiercer one. Lust and love glinted in his eyes. "But you love it."

"I do," she panted. "I love you. I love—"

He buried his mouth in hers. They engaged in a raw mating

with their tongues. All the while Edward continued to stroke Edith, gliding his fingers in and out.

Edith's breath came in noisy spurts. It was too much. She'd spent too many months without knowing Edward this way.

Crying out, she came in an explosive climax.

Her husband continued stroking her until he'd rung every last bit of pleasure from her body and then caught her against him as she collapsed.

Edward nibbled her earlobe. "Good?" he teased, lowering her skirts into place.

"Exquisite." Edith turned and framed his face with her hands. "It was my number two if that is any consolation."

"It isn't," he said dryly. "But now that we've gotten that out of the way—"

Edith's laugh cut him off. "Stop," she said, giving his arm a playful slap.

Following her late sister's advice, Edith and Edward had taken to beginning each morning with a list of all they wished to do that day.

Edith fished her list out of her pocket and waved it at him.

"Very well." Edward snatched the sheet from her fingers and read. "Ah," he drawled, his gaze going to the blue waters behind her. "Thus our trip to Stonebridge Pond."

Edith nodded and began tugging off her slippers. While Edward divested himself of his boots, Edith moved on to her stockings. The moment her legs were bare, she hitched up her skirts and giggling, she raced for the pond.

Edward came charging in just behind her, swept Edith into his arms, and swung her in a wide, dizzying circle until her breathless laughter melded with his.

He let her down slowly so that her body ran down the length of his. His levity faded, and he ran a tender gaze over her face. "I love you, Edith de Vesy."

"And I love you, husband," she said huskily.

Then, catching Edward's hand, Edith tugged him ahead, and together they ran barefoot through the water.

THE END

Be sure and check out the next installment from Christi Caldwell's Seven Deadly Sins series, coming Early Summer 2024!

USA TODAY BESTSELLING AUTHOR

CHRISTI CALDWELL

Lust
The Bad Earl

BIOGRAPHY

Christi Caldwell is the *USA Today* bestselling author of the Sinful Brides series and the Heart of a Duke series. She blames novelist Judith McNaught for luring her into the world of historical romance. When Christi was at the University of Connecticut, she began writing her own tales of love—ones where even the most perfect heroes and heroines had imperfections. She learned to enjoy torturing her couples before they earned their well-deserved happily ever after. Christi lives in Charlotte, North Carolina where she spends her time writing, baking, and being a mommy to the most inspiring little boy and empathetic, spirited girls who, with their mischievous twin antics, offer an endless source of story ideas!

Visit www.christicaldwellauthor.com to learn more about what Christi is working on, or join her on Facebook at Christi Caldwell Author, and Twitter @ChristiCaldwell!

Printed in Great Britain
by Amazon